SEVEN STARS

[signatures]

For Zui Simon-Scherer,
May this inspire
some adventures
of your own.

For Donna and Doris

First Edition
Published in the United States by Epidemic Books

Epidemic Books
Seattle, WA USA

ISBN 978-0-9844417-4-7

For more information and online forums, visit us at:
http://www.epidemicbooks.com

Manufactured in the United States of America

SARA AND THE CHIMERA

BOOK 2

SEVEN STARS

by Greg Dent and Todd Morasch

PROLOGUE

A hot wind blew hard across the endless red plain. From horizon to horizon, the flat terrain lay blasted and broken under the sunless, crimson sky. Woven like veins throughout the arid crust of earth that made up the desert floor, rivulets of a blood-red liquid seethed, occasionally bursting forth in boiling geysers that rained down in great clouds of ash upon the smoldering ground. Few things larger than a pebble withstood the raw elements here. Even the diamond bones of the ancient dragons that once ruled this vast domain now lay scattered and buried, pock-marked and faded from the biting sands.

The only living inhabitants of the blood plains were the back thorn tumbleweeds—or at least it was surmised. No one had ever seen one of these foul plants when it was alive; the weeds simply seemed to appear spontaneously in a dry and dead state, tearing haphazardly across the landscape, bowling over and slicing to bits anything unfortunate enough to get in their way. Nothing else managed to find a way to live here, or more accurately, nothing else managed to get this far out before it died. Except for one thing.

In this unlikely place, at the hottest part of the never-ending day, a small figure sauntered jauntily along. It was impossible to say from whence it had come; it may just as well have materialized right out of the tumbling ash and sweltering haze. Its four-legged frame was small and its gait was unhurried, yet its approach was not without purpose.

Though seemingly unprepared for the endless desert, the little creature did not appear to notice any discomfort as it walked. It trotted with an unusual impishness, its quick back legs occasionally exceeding the rate of its front legs, causing its rear to swing out sideways as the creature capered on in a diagonal direction. Oddly enough though, the little animal's thick, black fur did not pick up any of the red dust that clung to everything as far as the eye could see—its dark sheen remained unsullied and absolute.

In the distance, not far ahead of the curious interloper, the mouth of a great crevasse split the desert floor in twain. The chasm cut deep into the red rock, its massive scale partially shrouded by a blur of heat. Boiling blood ran in cascades over the sides, draining away far beneath to depths unfathomable.

Halfway down the crevasse, nestled under a sharp outcropping of stone, sat a dismal heap of rusted sheet metal and scavenged bones. If it were not for the complete lack of life anywhere, one might have thought this building the work of some kind of gigantic desert beaver—a dam built in a frenzy of heatstroke against a hysterically imagined flood. Pieces obviously found lying scattered about the wastes had been cobbled together with rust and some kind of leather cord into a pile the size of a small saloon. The deep canyon was all that kept this shack safe from the scouring winds—its construction surely could not have stood for long out in the open.

At what looked to be the front of this collection of junk, a rickety pair of swinging half doors had been hung. Splintered and wooden, these weathered contraptions creaked and flapped aimlessly in the warm and listless breezes that filtered down from the wastes. As the small, black creature approached, the mingled sounds of dark voices, eerie music, and shouting emitted from the scrap heap, rising above the roar of the winds. A somewhat darker hue of red light seeped out from the dim and smoky interior, and a palpable stench wafted out of the many gaps in the construction—registering somewhere between roasted flesh, neglect, body odor, and dry rot. The little animal slowed its pace slightly as it surveyed the tavern, then it shook itself off to fluff up its fur and headed right for the doors without further pause, as if with no trepidation of what lay inside. Skittering easily beneath the doors, it trotted quietly inside.

Half asleep on his stool, the scaly doorman failed to notice the little tailless dog that had just scampered into his place of employment, but the many patrons of the shady establishment took a marked heed of the visitor. As the little dog scanned the smoky room, a sudden silence fell upon the saloon, waking the doorman with a start. After a confused look around, the sinewy, horned creature eventually thought to chance a glance downward. Finally noticing the newcomer, the doorman rocked forward off his stool and moved to block the dog's forward progress. "Hey, watch yourself, meat!" the lizardy creature snarled as he stepped forward. "You've come to the inn on the edge of Dis. What's your business here?"

Nonplussed by the bouncer's line of questioning, the dog merely stepped around him and trotted onward towards the back rooms. Flustered, the doorman reached to stretch out a long arm to catch the dog, but another creature immediately intercepted him from behind.

"Oh, please do forgive us sir," this new creature pleaded at the little hound, grasping sharply the wrist of the doorman and pushing him aside, "it is so hard to find good help out here these days. I want you to know that you are quite welcome here. In fact, all of your services are on us today, and if there is anything you may need, simply ask any of our staff, and it will be provided. As for our doorman, do not worry; he will be beaten severely. In fact, your purchases will be taken out of his pay... and if you care to spend enough, his future children's pay."

With a flourish, the white-faced speaker bowed deeply and removed his silken top hat in a gesture of reverence, revealing a hard, chitinous, yellow pate like that of a locust. For a prolonged moment, the bug creature remained motionless, bowed as low as possible, its red-painted mandibles twitching slightly with apprehension. The dog, however, showed no concern to the gesture, and simply continued on towards the back without a word.

The look of confusion on the doorman's scaly face turned to fear with a single whisper from the maitre d'. "But... but," he stammered as he was thrashed back to his stool by the maitre d's cane, "he can't be. Shouldn't he be... well, bigger?"

Maybe it was a trick of the light, or maybe the inn was built back into the desert bedrock, but the inside of the place seemed to take up quite a bit more space than the outside. The back rooms of the tavern were a veritable maze of booths, niches, and tables, some built right on top of or under others, with small ladders to navigate between. Some booths were even built straight down—black holes from which roguish conversation wafted like the plague. Tiny imps in tailored vests scurried from booth to booth, carrying plates and glasses and occasionally mopping up various kinds of suspect fluids. Though the imps seemed to make a constant effort to clean the place, the dust of the desert still clung to everything, and a stale, hot, earthy scent permeated the air.

Though the booths were innumerable, all of them appeared to be full of patrons of one unsavory type or another. These were not mere terrorists, serial killers, or securities traders—no mortal creatures ever made this journey. Horned devils fresh from torturing doomed souls relaxed here after their decade-long shifts, their scorched pitchforks forgotten in their drink and leaning lazily up against the wall. Long-tailed succubi conspired with one another to hone the words of fear they whispered into the ears of their nocturnal victims as they smothered them. Even a single fallen angel drank alone in a remote corner, contemplating past thoughts and deeds with a regret that would have taken a thousand human souls to hold. Incomprehensible monsters huddled in closets and under tables, practicing for their appearances in nightmares. Vile shades sipped bitter blood-beer. Skeletal kings played cards and smoked thick, acrid cigars, betting as their commodities the decanted souls of their former subjects. None of these things seemed to react with anything other than nervousness to the dog's presence, and they made no objections as he sauntered into their midst and sniffed around. An arch-lord of the nine, glittering and gold, as beautiful as he was terrible, who had come here to "slum it" with the lower classes, turned a blind corner and almost dropped his drink moving aside out of the black critter's path. When the dog had passed, he made a quick line for the exit.

Along the very back wall of the tavern, a crack ran, and from it seeped a darkness, much like light might filter out from a bright room into a dim one. The dog seemed to sense it before it even came into his field of view, and the fur on the back of its neck stood up as it approached. At the base of the old wall, one of the wooden planks had been kicked out at floor level and a small gap gaped into the blackness beyond. The dog slipped inside, and instantly its eyes glowed black, snuffing out the darkness and allowing the light of the hall to cast a thin dusk into the chamber beyond. The intruding light seemed to upset the room's only inhabitant, if one could call it that. The palpable darkness congealed and retreated into the far corner as the dog entered. It showed no shape or features, but when one looked away, there was left the distinct impression that something terrible had been lurking within it. But the sound of the blackness' voice was even worse.

"I expected you sooner."

The dog's jaws parted just a bit, and a different kind of blackness ebbed out, not merely the absence of light, but the absence of anything. As the emptiness touched up against the darkness, the shadow recoiled, pushing itself further and further into the corner. Where the emptiness had touched it, gaps appeared in its form, and the dim light slowly found its way inside.

"Stop! You owe me!" the blackness bellowed, "If it were not for my actions, you would still be rotting away in my master's prison!"

The dog shut its mouth and sniffed around the room. The little hidden space had the look of an abandoned cabin or a hunting shelter. The worn wooden walls and low ceiling were dry and splintered, and the earthen floor was scattered with bones and broken pottery. At the center of the room, the remains of a campfire still smoked, giving off heat but no light. Next to the coals, a small bone bowl lay, as if carved from the top of a tiny skull. In the bowl, a few fingers of a thin, clear liquid still remained.

"The tears of unloved children." The shadow replied without being asked. "A bittersweet symphony on the palate. Go ahead, try some."

The dog circled the room once, then pawed at the ground and flopped down near the coals. With a puff, he blew at the coals and they flared up again, bathing the room in a faint, orange light and causing the shadow to shudder with what appeared to be physical pain. Looking up, the dog nodded at a little imp that waited just outside, beckoning it in to take his order.

"Fresh water in a steel bowl," bayed the dog, its voice sounding like flames consuming a priceless cathedral. The imp's face, showing surprise at the order, nodded and scurried away.

"What exactly is it I owe you, fiend?" remarked the dog after a quiet refreshment. "I'm not sure that I'm feeling particularly generous today, especially given the fact that I more or less freed myself from the Fish Man's prison."

"Nothing too much," leaked the blackness, which had now come out of its corner, and seemed to be occupying the bulk of the far half of the nook. "Information. My master wishes retribution on the Seventh Star of Twilight. I exist to fulfill that destiny. But the Seventh Star does not appear to want to cooperate with this vision of the future. He has vanished completely from all creation."

"You think I care of these matters between Elders?" the dog snorted. "Their days of control are all lost in the past. Creation spirals outward faster than they can even record, and they can do little about it. They need me far more than I need them. No, I'm not interested—particularly in helping the Mongrel. And besides, do you really think your master still cares to carry out the orders of the Octachoron now that he has freed himself from them? Perhaps you should check with him before coming to me."

"My master has no knowledge of my existence." the darkness crackled. "I exist to carry out his subconscious desires. In this way I know him better than he does himself." The shadow waited a pause, but his visitor said nothing. "So, you do not know of the whereabouts of the Seventh Star then? I thought that perhaps from one avatar of darkness to another you might consent to help."

At this, the dog stood up, and though the change was imperceptible, he suddenly seemed to fill the tiny room with his bulk. His eyes dimmed and burned the shadow, which again retreated to the farthest corner of the broken room. "I will take that as a stunted attempt at humor," he replied, "but the next time I can only assume a slight. Do you follow me? There is nothing alike between us, and I feel no camaraderie or pain for you. You seek the Seventh Star? Well, I smelled his stench on the daughter. Follow her and he can't be far behind. But beware, I will not be joining you on your journey. The Seventh Star has powerful allies. In particular, the one called the Starsailor watches over his affairs. Do not underestimate this one; he is ancient and clever beyond even your imagining. The warmth of your companionship is not nearly enough to persuade me to risk everything I have in such a venture. Slink back to your master and tell him I am coming for him soon enough. His triumph will be short lived. His prize will be my prize, and so will the daughter's and all the others'. And then my hunger will be unstoppable."

*****

An hour later, the little dog again appeared alone in the main room of the inn and shuffled to halt. The doorman was busily dragging an unconscious troll out through the front doors as the well-dressed, clown-faced insect rifled through its pockets looking for anything of value. Looking up, the maitre d' realized with a start that the little dog's path of egress was impeded. Without hesitation, the bug clambered over the body of massive troll and doffed his top hat. "It will just be a moment. Hazards of the business, I'm afraid. I trust your stay with us was satisfactory, sir? If there is anything we can do... anything at all, just let us know. We are only here to support our patrons." Again, he bowed deeply.

The dog gave no reply, but simply shuffled out under the doors as the way become clear. The maitre d' clutched his hat and mopped his hard brow as he pushed through the doors and watched the dog pick its way back up the steep slope of the crevasse. The bug sighed audibly and called out to his doorman as he watched the little black dog grow smaller and smaller and then finally disappear into the haze. "Well, that could have gone much worse for us, Tony. I would question the wisdom of playing host to a being such as the Fenris were it not a much larger question to ponder the wisdom of attempting to turn him away. By the way, you know I didn't mean all that about beatings and fines and so on; it's all for show. You must understand the risks we were taking. I know you don't have any hard feelings now, do you Tony? Tony... Tony?"

Taking his gaze off the horizon, the locust-creature turned and looked about him. Beside the great drag marks from the heavy troll, a single set of webbed footprints marked their way across the dusty rock. As they reached the still body of the stony patron, they abruptly stopped, with no evidence of return. Noise could be heard from the inn behind, but out front, only the wind spoke. No evidence of the whereabouts of the doorman could be seen. As the maitre d' stared blankly at the snoring troll, a thorny tumbleweed rolled lazily by.

1

~

A SORT OF HOMECOMING

It was the kind of alleyway that could easily have been found
in any large city, lined on one side by a block-long factory and
on the other by several poorly-maintained apartment buildings. A low web of telephone and electrical wires crisscrossed
overhead, cutting the dark, heavy clouds into irregular sections,
visible in the night only via the reflected lights of the city. At
either end of the alley, a harsh streetlight shone, allowing some
usable light to bleed in and mix with the dim haze that ran all
along the rough-paved stretch. This low, ambient glow filtered
in from back doors and access entrances, dotting the surface of
the pavement and exposing various potholes, storm grates, and
the few broken places where the old brick road still showed
through. The chill, midnight air did not stir on this evening.
The dried leaves of fall from the nearby park stayed where they
had fallen, as did the carelessly laid trash that lingered close to
the many graffiti-marked dumpsters and garbage cans.

All in all, this was a place that demanded no unusual attention—all, that is, but for one small detail. At roughly the
halfway point down the alley, wedged directly between the
windowless backsides of two brick apartment buildings, a three-
foot-high, white picket fence stood firm against the progress of

the city. Beyond it lay a small yard, overgrown and neglected, and just past that stood a narrow, two-story house, blue with white trim, the paint chipped from disrepair. The home was small and, even in its current state, still held the charm of days gone by. The property clashed bizarrely with its surroundings, almost as if it had just erupted up out of the ground and sundered the urban climate in twain. Surely whoever owned it must have passed up multiple offers from developers and real estate investors, and likely had even fought big corporate lawyers to keep hold of the little house while the city sprang up around it. Still, in its novelty, the house held an even deeper value; this was a place that had some luck, some magic on its side—a place where wondrous things could still spring forth.

The little white gate with its broken latch was the first thing to come to life. The owner had often meant to fix the latch, but like so many things over the last year or so, it had continually fallen from memory—recalled only while passing through the gate to take out the trash and then forgotten the moment the stairs leading back to the garden door were ascended. The gate rattled and then crept slowly open, as if some unseen visitor pushed carefully against its hinges, trying not to let them creak. A little maple leaf from the park was the next thing to awaken. It scampered across the pavement, starting with a jolt. Its dance was much less discreet than the gate's, twirling and rising up and down at intervals along the lane until it reached a spot just outside the fence where the old brick of the road was exposed in a shallow pothole. Here the leaf paused briefly before beginning a brisk, winding path upwards, circling the divot. Shortly, the leaf was joined by another leaf and then another. More and more scattered leaves soon came to life, quickly forming a vortex that began to pull in increasingly larger chunks of paper and trash. The violence of this small tornado built at a frightening rate. Within seconds, the small gate was crashing back and forth on its worn hinges and the white fence was rocking furiously, in danger of snapping. Then, through the leaves and debris, swirling a few feet above the pothole, a dim light began to grow. It thrust the spinning rubbish into sharp silhouettes as it intensified, mounting to a blinding white and then abruptly back to darkness. The collected leaves and trash flung outwards in every direction; door lights shattered, and a few nearby garbage cans toppled over, rolling away from the disturbance and scattering their undesirable contents along the alley. Somewhere, a dog barked.

Four small, black paws touched down on the old bricks all at the same time, but instantly, the dark, furry creature that they were attached to leaped from the landing place. Its long, black tail sliced the air frantically as it sprang, as if some yet unseen danger was soon to follow. A moment later, two huge, clawed feet hit the exact same spot, and above them, a dark, hulking creature crouched and balanced for a moment, gaining its bearings. Soon its head rose up, and four, diamond-like eyes caught the dim alley light. Its four large ears shot straight up, scanning for other, non-visual forms of stimulus. This tall, lanky creature smiled at the house, showing a great maw of teeth that not only zippered across its face horizontally, but also divided its chin vertically, running down past the length of its neck. A forked tongue darted swiftly from between the shark-like teeth and tasted the night air.

Once the large beast was sure that nothing stirred, it turned its attention to the small shadow that had proceeded it. The black cat had taken up residence next to the white gate and was currently in the process of cleaning itself, without the slightest concern for the massive monster that now looked down towards it. The tall creature let out a snort that sounded a bit disgusted, and then without warning, it arched its head upwards and threw its shoulders back. The center of its armor-plated chest, from its collar to its abdomen, opened with a jolt, and a small girl, dressed head to foot in black, save for a worn leather satchel strapped diagonally across her back, slid out and landed on all fours in front of the creature. She paused, coughed slightly, and then scrambled to regain her footing. She shook her head back and forth as she stood, loosening her bag and freeing her long, blonde hair from a cap that seemed to melt into her form-fitting body suit.

"Well, is this it?" the tall creature asked, its head quickly righting itself. To anyone listening, the creature's voice would have sounded eerily human—oddly resembling the phrasings of a boy mixed with the low scratch of alien vocal cords.

The girl, who could not have been more than thirteen, looked around and then closed her eyes for a moment before happily confirming, "Yes this is it. We are finally here, Jonathan."

"Well, we were here before, and to be honest, your house looked better there," Jonathan replied. "'Is this the right version?' is what I meant, Sara."

"Yes, it's the right one—the real one," Sara smiled, "or at least, the non-animated version."

"That's too bad. I rather liked the welcome home song the cartoon squirrels and birds sang to you," Jonathan said, lowering his great head with its many teeth so that it was at the same level as Sara's. He peered over her shoulder at the house. "Though I won't miss the cartoon pies; they all tasted like you were eating paint."

"That's cause they were," she said, crossing her arms. "Although it seemed to all the creatures of that world that they were the best-tasting pies ever. See, if you are animated yourself, animated food tastes like it's real."

The big creature's face twisted for a moment as he tried to catch up. Sara was always talking like this, trying to reconcile the craziness of the different creations they passed through with her own scientific nature. Jonathan didn't give much thought to other creatures' perceptions; his many eyes, noses, ears, and even taste buds filled him with plenty of ways to measure the world without bothering with others. Still, he liked to try and keep up with these philosophical conversations if he could.

"You keep referring to things from their world as not real. It felt real to me; it just did not taste good," Jonathan said.

"Well, sure. Things are real there under the laws of that creation," Sara grumbled, "but compared to here... well, there are levels to realities. You can even categorize them—there are cultures that do. Reality is generally measured on a complicated scale of belief mixed with age, not to mention current relevance. This and about twenty other factors determine the standing of one existence to another. I could go on explaining it, but you would get lost, trust me."

Of course Sara was right, not because she thought Jonathan was dumb, but because halfway through starting to explain, she had used her gift to see if there was any point in finishing and had determined that he simply would not get it. This had been happening more and more of late, and Jonathan found it deeply frustrating when she just trailed off rather than at least try. He also suspected she liked to pull this stunt when she just wanted to silence him, like now when she was obviously avoiding something.

"You're nervous." It was a statement not a question, and Jonathan raised one of his giant, double-thumbed hands and placed it on her back, careful to keep his claws retracted.

"It's been almost two years since I was taken from her," Sara sighed. "I can't help but wish there was a way to save her from all the pain and worry she has endured, all because of the stupid Fish Man."

The big creature's face turned into a snarl at the mention of the Fish Man. The fierce look held strong until he caught the scent of doubt coming from his companion. He might not have known everything, like she did, but he had gotten very good at reading her. This was the moment she had been waiting for, and now that it was here she was too scared to move on.

"We could always try time travel, like I suggested before," Jonathan smiled.

"No. I have already told you that all my vast explorations of that have only taught me one thing—it destroys any and all who try. Time, like knowledge and light, has a price to its use, and that price is utter destruction for those foolish enough to attempt break its rules." Sara looked very stern upon finishing, but Jonathan noticed that she still had not yet taken even a step towards the gate.

"She is going to be so happy to see you! She won't care about the last year and a half, she will only care that you're back and she can hold you again," he said softly. Then he turned to the cat, "Tell her I am right, El Gato."

The cat only paused from cleaning itself long enough to blurt out a short meow.

"I thought he was going to be able to talk longer when we got here because of that cartoon world we ported from," Jonathan griped.

"No, the residue of that world seems to have faded the moment we stepped into this one," Sara sighed. "This Earth seems to have that effect. It likes to conceal magic and strangeness when it can. Well... I guess you're right, the sooner the better." She took a few tentative steps towards the gate.

"Your clothing, Sara," Jonathan said. She always forgets the little things, he thought.

"Oh, right." Sara closed her eyes and concentrated. Her black, form-fitting outfit was made of semi-intelligent organic fibers that could shift their composition, shape, and color according to the wearer's thoughts. She had acquired it on an advanced world where she and Jonathan had helped to free some trapped alien miners. The current black bodysuit look was the best for when she rode inside of Jonathan; it delayed her being consumed by his body, and the slime that coated his living cockpit did not cling to it much. As Sara concentrated, the body suit shimmered and formed into jeans, tennis shoes, and a replica of the rainbow sweater she had been wearing the day she was taken. It also formed small, butterfly barrettes that held her waist-long hair back off her face. It was then that her hand touched the small, blue star tattoo on her right cheek. That was not so easy to disguise, but then she realized no matter what that there was a lot to explain. After all, she had been missing for a year and a half. It's not like she had simply gone to a tattoo parlor and was coming home afraid of her mother's wrath. "You had better conceal yourself while we are concerning ourselves with appearances," she said over her shoulder to Jonathan.

Jonathan stood very still and let his skin, armor, and hair spikes take on the colors and shapes of the alley around him. He had gained this adaptation while they had been on the run from a group of interstellar bounty hunters hired by a genetic engineer who had wanted a sample of his spinal fluid. As long as he didn't make any sudden movements, he was effectively invisible.

"Good," Sara approved, looking where she knew he was, but seeing only a slightly warped version of the alley. "You come with me, El Gato," she ordered, turning her attention to the cat. "My mother always liked animals; you will be welcome."

The black cat with the white star on its chest gave an odd look and seemed to hesitate, pacing about in a circle.

"Well, go on, go with her," Jonathan snarled. "Can't you see she's nervous and could use the support?"

El Gato trailed after Sara, but the cat still hung back with some unknown reservation. "Hmm," Sara grumbled, staring at the timid cat, "you would think it was your mother that you had left to worry for over a year that we were going to see." Sara opened the gate and followed the stone path through the overgrown yard and up to the stairs. When she had ascended the four worn, familiar steps, she paused and looked back, beckoning for the cat to join her on the porch. Then, with her heart aflutter and sweat starting to form on her palms, she reached up, made a fist, and knocked on the weathered wood of the screen door.

At first there was nothing. Until now, Sara had avoided using her powers to do anything more than confirm that her mother was home, but when the knock brought no change, she considered looking within and seeing with her gift just where her mother was. It was then that a light beyond the screen and the interior door came on. A moment later, she heard the chain latch being fixed before the door lock was undone. Her mother's face, filled with sleep and hung with the stress of the last year and a half, peeked through the small crack that was as far as the door would open with the chain on. It was the dearest sight Sara could ever remember seeing.

"Mom," she whispered, "it's me."

Her mother turned down to meet her gaze, and recognition washed over her, followed by a panicked attempt to open the still-chained door. After a short, but epic, fight with the link, she flung open the screen so fast it sent El Gato scattering.

"Sara!" she cried, her hands coming to her daughter's arms. "Sara, it's you, it's really you, not another dream, it is you!"

"Yes it's me." Sara smiled even as tears entered her eyes. Her mother flung her arms around her, burying her face in Sara's hair, holding her so tight that it hurt, and taking in a deep breath through her nose. Then she covered her daughter in kisses—on the cheeks, the lips, the forehead, and the eyebrows, and though it was all so much, Sara could not stop herself from breaking into laughter.

"My girl... my dear, dear girl—returned to me after all this time, beyond hope, beyond fear," her mother cried, brushing Sara's hair away from her face where she had disheveled it during their affectionate reunion. "Are you hurt? Are you ok, my baby? Tell me you're alright!"

"I am perfectly healthy, unharmed, and good," Sara reassured, "in fact, even better for seeing you at last."

Her mother's fingers paused for a moment on the blue star brand on her cheek before she finally stood and pulled her clothing straight, stepping back. "Let me have a look at you," her mother exclaimed, her voice beginning to regain its composure. "You're taller."

"Yes, I grew 2 inches and four millimeters exactly," Sara said. "Well, rounded to the nearest millimeter, of course."

"That's my smart girl," and tears streamed down her mother's face with a rush of nostalgia upon hearing her lost daughter spout facts. It was only then that she seemed to notice the small dark shape that had taken up residence behind Sara. Her face was blank at first, but then, as she happened upon the white star pattern in the fur at the center of the black cat's chest, her expression turned all at once to anger. "You!!" Faster than Sara had ever seen her mother move, she had El Gato in her grasp. "You! I might have known; all of this had your foul stink to it." Sara's mother was now violently shaking the cat as she screamed into its face. "Not a word! Not even a warning! You just let me worry that my poor daughter was dead, or worse yet, a prisoner to some foul, extra-dimensional villain!"

Sara was in shock. She couldn't even form the words to tell her mother that El Gato was her friend and had saved her many times. Her mother obviously knew the cat and knew about extra-dimensional beings, yet nowhere in the Font of Knowledge was this fact recorded. The cat kicked its legs weakly, its face filled with fear as Sara's mother continued to scream. "Well, if you're here, then he cannot be far off, so he might as well show himself. Where is he?" She dropped El Gato and looked into the back yard, right to where Jonathan was standing camouflaged. She set her arms akimbo and narrowed her eyes. "Well, show yourself," she demanded.

Timidly, Jonathan returned to his default colors and, with a frightened look, pointed at himself. "You mean me?" he gulped, standing stiffly.

Sara's mother gave a briefly surprised glace at him and then waved a hand. "No, not you, whatever you are... him. Where is he?"

"Who?" Sara asked, finally finding her voice.

Her mother made her way down the steps past the gate and, pushing Jonathan aside, surveyed the alleyway. "Who else would I be looking for? Your father, of course."

"My father?" And, at once, Sara's mind was off. So... her mother knew El Gato. She knew about other dimensions, and she had to then know at least some of the truth about her father, but Sara's gift could see none of this. Sara had of course searched her mother's mind in the past. She had often watched memories of her dad in her mother's head and wondered about what he might have been like. In her mother's mind, Sara's father was a simple dockworker who had loved her and cared for her and died shortly after Sara's birth, crushed in a gruesome industrial accident. Oddly enough, this was still what she read from her mother even now; yet her mother somehow knew the truth. Sara dared not look for her father directly; that was a question she had been very clearly warned against asking. Instead, she looked for a hole in her mother's memory, but there wasn't one. This dilemma went well beyond missing knowledge; this was a contradiction—but the false story held as much truth as anything else when she examined it. Maybe Sara didn't need special powers to resolve this. Her mother was right here; why not just talk to her? "You know about my father?" she finally asked.

Sara's mother had passed into the alley now. She continued to look about, and slowly but surely she began to realize that there was no one else with them. She turned back to the gate, and only then did she stop and take a long look at Jonathan. "Well, you're something, aren't you?" she said. "You actually look scared—which is ridiculous, considering how scary you look."

"I am scared," Jonathan said, his boy-like voice betraying his trepidation.

"And you're just a kid, too, or you're doing a good impression of one."

"Yes ma'am. I am a year younger than Sara."

"Ma'am?" Sara's mother smiled. "I am not old enough to be called that yet. But where are my manners? I am Tessa, but if you're a friend to my daughter, you can call me 'mom' if you like."

"I am her friend," he smiled, rising up proud. "I am Jonathan the chimera."

"Well, Jonathan the chimera, we had best get you out of sight before one of the neighbors sees you. Come along." Tessa waved him through the gate.

Sara's head was still spinning. She was still trying to look for cracks in the false memories of her mother, following different knowledge trails to discern some flaw or blank spot that would account for her being able to know the truth. She repeated her earlier question as her mother ascended the stairs to the back porch, "You know about my father?"

"I know a great many things, Sara," she said, placing a hand on her daughter's shoulder and guiding her towards the door. "And stop wracking your head to find any record or trace of it; your father held that Font longer than you have been alive and he learned its ins and outs. He knew how to trick and hide things from it better than you could imagine. Heck, when I had access to it while you were growing inside of me, I couldn't use it to see the things he and I had done together, and I could remember them. Trust me, that still messes with my head."

"Access? But... you?" Sara would have walked into the screen door if her mother had not opened it for her. Tessa ushered her through and then stood back as Jonathan crouched and twisted to pass through the narrow doorway. Tessa started to enter herself, and then turned back to the star-chested cat. Her look slowly softened.

"Are you even house-broken yet?" she said, her mind obviously wandering back to another day. Finally, she pushed open the screen. "Well, it looks like it could rain, so you might as well come in. Chances are you have saved my daughter from as many tight spots as you put her in, and let's face it, you must have had at least a paw in guiding her back to me."

El Gato passed through the door, but moved very quickly as he came within Tessa's reach. She followed after and shut the door, latching it tightly and throwing the chain. A moment later, the drapes were pulled shut tightly.

The house was in a shambles. Cups and dishes were strewn all over the kitchen, mixed with newspapers and magazines, torn-out articles, and notes scribbled atop junk mail envelopes. The refrigerator was almost buried, covered with flyers and leaflets with Sara's picture on them. With a sweep of her arm, Tessa cleared the table, and real pie with milk and cookies was soon being served in the kitchen.

As the food worked its magic, stories began flowing back and forth from both parties. Sara told her mother about the world-ship, the prison, and the escape. She talked about her and Jonathan's adventures across other worlds and plains. She even produced a variety of souvenirs from her satchel to aid in the telling, passing them to her mother to hold as she explained their significance. Sometimes the chimera would interject, acting out the more exiting parts, waving his arms and pincers about and showing his teeth and claws. He broke a lamp with one of his tails when talking about fighting with the newly-living creatures in the land of the dead, but Tessa only begged him to continue as she swept it up, listening intently all the while.

Sara tried to avoid the parts of the story where she herself was in danger, but it was hard at times, and the worst was when she got to the end and had to tell her mother how they had been fooled by the Fish Man. Her mother listened to it all, her face reacting to each part with the very expressive looks that Sara had so missed. When their story ended, Tessa suggested they retire to the living room.

Like the kitchen, the living room was also poorly kept, with clothes and books strewn all about, but it had a homey feel to it nonetheless. There were lots of plants and art, and even a few actual record albums scattered about by a dusty, old player. Pictures of Sara at various ages were positioned everywhere, tucked into every nook and cranny. A small piano in the corner caught Jonathan's eye, and he sped over to it, running his hands over the keys. After vainly trying to plunk out a few notes with his massive fingers, he shut the lid. "Hey," he said, excitedly, lifting a painting off the top of the piano, "I used to have this in my room. It's a Picasso, I think."

Tessa smiled, "Yes, that's right. Sara painted that."

"Really? The chimera seemed impressed. "I didn't know you could paint."

Sara turned red. "I don't really; it's just something I tried for a while," she said, pulling the painting out of the chimera's hand and setting it face down on the piano. "I just wanted to try to do something that was only me, that didn't involve just reciting someone else's knowledge from my head. It's not important."

Tessa laughed, "You should see her room upstairs. I kept it the way you left it, Sara. It's like the Sistine Chapel in there, every surface covered in some image she had in her head that needed to get out. Some of the older stuff is pretty rudimentary, but you'd be surprised. I think you were actually starting to get pretty good before you left, honey."

"I don't know, mom," Sara mumbled. "But it's been a long night. I really need to find out what you know about dad before my brain explodes." And before she slipped and asked questions about him herself.

Tessa nodded and sat down. Sara settled down on the couch, curled up next to her mother, while Jonathan and El Gato took up positions on the carpeted floor with pillows and blankets provided by Sara's mom. Sara was about to experience something that she was not at all used to—someone telling her a story that she had no knowledge of.

Fifteen years ago, it turned out, her mother had been on some adventures of her own. It had all started innocently enough—meeting a nice young man in her college acting class. However, after a brief romance, it seemed this young man was not what he appeared to be, and he soon confided in his new friend that he was in big trouble for stealing something important. Tessa had been young, foolish, and curious then, and soon got sucked into the man's story. He told her strange things and took her odd places—things and places that no ordinary person should have any knowledge of. At first it all was wild, yet still within the realm of the possible, until one day, strange, dark soldiers appeared, and the young friends had been forced to go on the run. It was the young man's cat, of all things, that had helped them escape their attackers by opening a mystical portal. After landing dead center in a landscape formed entirely of colored glass, everything Tessa knew had been shattered, and it would take her almost a year to finally get back home. In that time, however, Sara's mother fell in love with her father, who as it turned out, was not human at all, but an extraordinary being from a distant dimension. The two of them, along with the cat, shared an exhilarating, dimension-hopping journey that was not entirely unlike Sara and the chimera's own tale. Sara got the impression that her mother had left out certain details, both violent and romantic, but in the end, her mother and father were married, and then Sara was conceived.

"Knowing now what happened to you, my dearest girl," her mother told her after long hours of sharing stories, "I would never have let him place that thing within you. But he was convinced you would be safe, that he had hidden all things that could trace it to you, and that with it you would be gifted in ways that far outweighed any dangers."

"He was right," Sara said, looking up to her mother and pulling her arm out from behind Tessa's back. They had been holding each other so tight that her arm had fallen asleep, but she had not wanted to interrupt her mother's story until it was done. "With all that he gave me, I was able to save myself and help

Jonathan. See, they might have come for me anyway as a means to blackmail father, and without this gift, I would have been unable to do anything about it."

"I suppose that's true," her mother said, kissing her forehead. "Still, I can't help but feel responsible. Sara, if I had made other choices, you could have had a normal life."

"I never understand that," Jonathan grumbled, interrupting.

"What?" Tessa asked.

"That whole 'wishing for a normal life' stuff they always put in movies or books. Give me this any day!" He flexed his claws in front of him. "You won't find me or Sara wanting to give up our superpowers to be like everyone else—and forget any hero, mutant, or wizard who wishes for that; just a waste of a talent."

"Is that how you feel?" Tessa turned her eyes to her daughter, measuring her response with care.

"Sure is," Sara smiled. "Jonathan knows me well." And she hoped that she was utterly convincing. It was not a total lie; Sara did love her gift, but the being chased around creation by otherworldly forces and the dark plans of the Fish Man—that she could live without. Even now, if she tried to use her power to look upon the Fish Man and see what he was up to, all she could perceive was blinding white light; she knew that he was still using the word he had stolen to confound her.

"Well, you're safe here now," Tessa said. "No more adventures for you two for a long, long time. I don't know exactly what I am going to tell the authorities about your return, but we will figure something out. As for you Jonathan, you are welcome for as long as you like. My daughter's protector will always have a place under my roof. Of course we will have to keep you out of sight, but we can figure something out. My parents have a cabin way up in the woods. Maybe we can get you there somehow."

It was then that Tessa noticed the looks on Jonathan and Sara's faces, something like guilt. "What?" she barked.

"Mom," Sara said, "you're not going to like this, but we can't stay."

"What?!" Her mother's tone was sharp and filled with the promise of the anger they had seen earlier.

"We came here as soon as we could. I did not want you to worry any more, but now that you know the truth... well, we have to get back out there," explained Sara. "There are friends out there that need our help, and there's a big mess that we caused that we have to try and undo."

"No," and Sara's mother was standing, waving her arms in front of her, "you are still a child. You cannot hope to contend with what is out there. You have done enough—more than enough—and you're home safe, and this is where you are going to stay."

"Mom, you don't understand," Sara started.

"I don't want to understand," Tessa cried. She lowered herself down and embraced Sara where she sat. "You know what it's been like for me here, worried about you; your gift can show you that. I can't go through more of that, I just can't. You have to promise me you'll stay here safe with me."

The chimera watched the pair holding each other and he suddenly knew what love between a mother and child should look like. Yet at the same time, he knew he would never have a reunion like this, never have a mother love him like Tessa loved Sara. However, he also knew the harsh truth, a truth even now that Sara was too afraid to say—nowhere is safe for us.

2

~

ALONG FOR THE RIDE

Sara lay warm and well-tucked-in amongst the pillows and blankets of her bed. She felt up at the real silk ribbons she had in her hair—her favorite ones. So long had she dreamt of exactly this that she hardly could believe it to be true. In her many travels, she had slept on hard stone floors, dusty desert plains, and amongst brambles and weeds. True, she had also rested in bigger, softer, more-lavish beds than this, but none of them compared to the familiar smell, feel, and touch of her own bed.

Sara had hung her satchel on the head post of the bed. Something about that felt right. It represented all her travels, and she had come to depend on the comforts it contained. There were practical things in there, like her multi-tool that could be a knife or a screwdriver or any handheld device that the wielder desired—another gift from the miners, along with her organic suit. Also quite useful was the near-empty jar of alien peas; one a day held all the nutrition of eating three well-made meals. The bag also held the numerous little knickknacks she had collected on her journeys—like the rainbow stone that shifted colors constantly, or the scarf that always gave off the smell of flowers, keeping the bag fresh. Finally, there were the relics, like the true mirror she had received from the Queen of the Dead. It had proven useful several times, like when she had showed to Jonathan that a monster he was fighting was only an illusion, or when they had shown the vampire known as the Princess of Blades her refection for the first time in a thousand years and, in gratitude, she had given them their freedom. Having all these things that she had gathered on her travels close to the comforts of home gave Sara a warm, safe feeling that she had not had for a good long time. Still, even as she felt the joy and pleasure of it all, for some reason, she could not let her mind go quiet or find a way to sleep.

The revelation that her mother had known her father for more than what he appeared to be kept spinning through her head, and it took all of the careful training she had received from the angel Rithrial to stop herself from searching for her dad and compiling together everything about him that she could glean from any second-hand observations and accounts. Her father may have known ways to conceal certain things from the Font of all knowledge he had placed in her, but she was sure if she searched hard enough that she could find out more about him—and maybe even discern where he currently hid. Sara tensed at that thought. She knew well the danger that bringing such knowledge to light could call down upon her and those around her, and even upon her father.

Sara had encountered holes in the Font before, but once the right key bit of information was brought to her attention, the knowledge about these secrets would normally flower slowly into being, filling itself out elegantly in the great eternal archive. That had been the case when she entered Haven for the first time, and that same flowering would likely also have occurred the first time she was made aware of her father's true nature if not for the warning of the angel. However, the secrets of her mother's adventures with her dad were very different. Throughout Tessa's tale, Sara had attempted to cause knowledge of the details to bloom in the Font, but to no avail. She studied this now, curious to discover its secrets. It took some rather non-linear thinking and interpretation to eventually arrive at the answer. The problem was not that the knowledge had been removed from the Font, but that it had been deliberately obscured, presumably by her father. Only a very specific question would remove the lock on the information and allow Sara to comprehend it. What was he hiding? Sara asked herself what the question was she needed to ask to unlock everything, but there was no reply. She pondered her many options. Maybe if she knew what her dad was thinking now....

Sara stopped her thoughts here for the thousandth time since returning home; it was becoming increasingly more challenging. To distract herself, she focused instead on her mother, how sweet and understanding she had been, and how kind she had been to Jonathan. After sharing tales, she had brought them both to Sara's room, made up a bed of pillows and extra blankets for Jonathan on the floor, and then proceeded to tuck Sara in over and over. She brought out the blue lace ribbons and tied them in Sara's hair like she used to, ever delaying leaving her daughter's side. She would have slept there with them, but Sara knew her mother needed a long-awaited good night's sleep, and her own bed would serve that cause better. Tessa had left them, kissing Jonathan on the forehead and telling him to watch over her daughter. Her mother had drunk a little tea and then checked back in on the two of them no less than six times before finally heading off to her bed, where she fell asleep petting El Gato.

After having heard the whole of their story, Tessa seemed to have mostly reconciled herself with the cat. It was inevitable; Sara understood from her own mother's account that she and El Gato were old friends and had a relationship that went far beyond the rage that had taken her mother when she first saw him earlier that night.

At the foot of Sara's bed, Jonathan lay motionless and seemingly asleep, but Sara knew better. Her trusty companion did not require sleep. Even now he listened to the sound of her breath, ensuring the steadiness of it to measure if she was sleeping well. Sara had become used to this, and often faked the proper rhythm when she was struck with insomnia in order to put him at ease. Jonathan was a creature of instinct. He had grown used to setting his brain on certain tasks like this while his true mind wandered elsewhere. Currently he was enjoying listening to the sounds of the city deep into its night. This was as close as the chimera came to sleep. When he watched over Sara while she rested, he typically fell back into his most animal-like state, surrendering to a zen-like meditation where he simply enjoyed the sounds and smells his many senses brought to him. His mind would slowly explore the world around him, pondering the buzz of distant insects or embracing the sweetness of the scent of freshly fallen rain. Yet despite his apparent lack of focus, Sara knew that the chimera was also constantly aware of anything that might pose some potential danger. His instinct had been sharply honed to warn of all sensations out of the ordinary.

Sara now found herself, as she often did, envying her companion—his ability to be at peace internally, to forget the woes and troubles of the day, and to simply surrender to the sensations of being alive. She wondered if sleep would ever find her and, in wondering, remembered all the things that gave her pause to worry. In thinking of these, her mind tried again to lead her back to her father. She at once diverted herself again. How was Adam doing? Hmm. He was in pain right now, but he was alive, if still in chains. And he had thought about her exactly twice since she had last checked! If only there was some way to get to him. Wait... this wasn't helping. Sara could already feel her heart beating faster, not settling down.

Sara began to think about the room she was in and the house that held it—a distraction she had often used when unable to sleep as a little kid. She thought about the people who had built the house in the late 1920's, part of a massive project to build family homes for the slowly industrializing port city. She viewed the life of the first man who had lived here like an old friend whom she had never met. He had used her room for a study; here he smoked his pipe and read books by classical writers. She knew that there was no way the scent molecules from that smoke could in any way still linger here, but she

could swear that whenever she thought of him she could smell
the leathery, cherry wood of the tobacco wafting through the
room, almost sweet in its aroma. The man had been engaged
to be married when he had bought the house, and his lovely,
pleasantly plump wife had moved in shortly after, filling the
home with the equally delightful aromas of her baking. The
man loved his wife dearly, and secretly wrote her love poems
when sequestered in his study. The man, in fact, wrote poems
about all sorts of things—small objects, details he noticed while
walking to work, cats, aging, and so on. Sara could spend
hours just rereading his works in her head—they were some
of her favorite poems of all time—but on this night she found
herself moving forward quickly along the timeline of the house.
The man with the pipe had gone to war in the late 40's, feeling
it was his duty. When he returned, he found that his wife had
left him for another, and this tragic event, added to his wartime
traumas, changed him. He burnt all his poems shortly thereaf-
ter without ever sharing a single one with another person, and
then he sold the home to a young couple. Sara never followed
too far forward to see what became of him, though he was
long-dead now, choosing to recall him as the pipe-smoking
poet, hopelessly in love with his happy wife.

Sara's room had been next transformed from a study to a
baby's room, replete with hand-painted elephants and giraffes
on the walls. Some of these Sara had actually later repainted
from memory in their original locations amongst her other
works. The young couple never did have a baby, though they
held out hope for many years. Finally they turned the nursery
into a workroom where the two of them wrote and illustrated
the first of many very successful children's books. When the
money started to come in, they soon moved out into a larger
place. The neighborhood had been rezoned in the late 70's,
and in doing so, the address was altered by a few numbers.
Thus, years later, when fans of the couple's children's books
searched for the home they had written their first book in, they
mistakenly thought it had been torn down. After the writer
couple, the house was rented for a time, until at last Sara's
great-grandparents bought it to retire in. Sara's room was then
a guest room where her mother often stayed as a child when

she came to visit. In the mid 90's, the retirees had passed away within a year of each other, and the house was left to Sara's mother, who had lived there ever since.

Sara found that it was often the lost knowledge, like the man's poems or the truth about the children's authors' residence, that she fixated on when she did these dives into her consciousness. For everything that was written down, passed on, or recorded in this world, there was so much more about life that was simply forgotten or lost. Only Sara held these things now; they were her treasures and her curse. She often felt she should spend her spare time, if she got any, writing these things down or recording them, but she knew that even if she did there would always be more and more to do. Sara had once started to write one of the pipe man's poems for a school project, but she had stopped herself about halfway through. It had seemed wrong, not only because it wasn't her work, but because he had deliberately chosen not to share his works with anyone. So these lost moments would be hers alone, and when she moved on, well... perhaps they would be lost forever.

This exercise, focusing elsewhere, had served its function and finally placed Sara at ease. She could feel sleep coming now, and she relished in the last few moments of awareness, her mind slowly doing one last check on her surroundings before surrendering to the world of dreams. Her mother was fast asleep, as was El Gato. Jonathan was lost in his animal nature. Outside, the rain had come and gone, and the calm of deep night had yet to be disrupted by the early-morning commuters. Garbage trucks were just beginning their routes in distant parts of the city. They and the few police on duty were the only ones really stirring, well... them and the highly-trained government swat team.

Wait! Sara bolted straight up in bed. Yes they were there all right, less than a mile away, and en route to her address. Three armored vehicles full of highly trained government soldiers armed to the teeth sped along the empty streets of Tacoma, ready to respond to a terrorist bio-threat. Huh? Sara shook herself, chasing the sleep away from her head. There was no bio-organism made by terrorists hiding in her home. She followed the knowledge thread of the armed response backwards for but a split-second before it struck her—Jonathan. They think he is this organism.

"What is it, Sara?" She could see his four gemstone eyes glowing from the end of the bed. He had detected the change in her breathing the moment she had sat up.

"Trouble," she said. "Big trouble heading our way. We have fewer than ten minutes to get out of here!" Sara was up, her organic clothing shifting rapidly from pajamas to her jeans and sweater. Her satchel was retrieved from the bedpost and quickly secured on her back with its single strap across her chest. The chimera was also in motion. Though his highly-tuned senses could not yet detect any threat, he knew all too well to heed any warnings from Sara.

"What are we up against?" he asked, crouching and moving swiftly to hit the light switch by the door so that Sara could see her way from the room. Jonathan knew that even though her gift let her see in pitch blackness, she always liked to see with her eyes if at all possible.

"Armed federal agents under a false order to contain a bio-organic terrorist threat!" Sara launched through the door and into the hall. Jonathan followed, crouching low and keeping all his limbs in close so as not to knock any of the pictures off the hall wall.

"Bio what?" he stammered.

"You! They have been tricked into hunting you," she returned, not pausing in her stride.

"Well, don't worry—I can just hide. Then they can look, but they'll never find me."

"Thanks for the offer, but they have also been fed false information about my mother." Sara paused at Tessa's door. "They have been monitoring the house. I should have looked for something like that! Their file says she was raised in some sort of cult and brainwashed to build genetically-engineered weapons to destroy the US government."

Sara knocked on the door and then entered, not waiting for a response. "Mom, you have to get up right now!"

"What is it dear?" her mother mumbled, fighting to become fully awake.

"Well, remember when we said danger tends to follow us?" Sara replied. "Well, it has found us; we have to go."

"Go?" Her mother swung her legs off the bed. She was still dressed, having fallen asleep in her clothing. "Go where?"

"Anywhere but here! Hurry!"

"Why? What's wrong?"

"There is a military swat team on its way here to kill Jonathan and to lock you away in a secret prison for the rest of your life," Sara stammered. She leapt to the side of the bed, picking up El Gato under one arm while pulling her mother to her feet with the other. "Hurry!"

Tessa stumbled after her daughter, following her out of the room. She could see the chimera ahead of them already making his way down the stairs to the living room. A rudely awakened El Gato wriggled from Sara's grip, landed on the floor in front of her, and without missing a beat, fell in place behind Jonathan. Tessa tried to wrap her head around what was happening, but the adrenaline was just starting to kick in. By the time she had reached the first floor she was fully awake and was attempting to form a plan.

"Are you sure they cannot be reasoned with or tricked in some way?" Tessa asked her daughter.

"'Fraid not, mom." Sara was held up waiting behind Jonathan, who was having trouble getting through the small arch to the kitchen. "If you saw the fake file they have been fed on you—well, let's just say it makes you look like public enemy number one."

The chimera almost knocked down the kitchen table speeding on his way to the back door. Sara knew Jonathan wanted to be out in the open where he could move if he was going to be forced to fight. She dragged her mother by one arm after him, watching with her gift as the first truck turned down the street in the front of the house.

"Wait." Her mother pulled free from Sara's grasp.

"There's no time, mom!"

"Just a few seconds!" Tessa grabbed her backpack from beside the door. She unceremoniously dumped its contents onto the table and then ran to the pantry.

"Mom, they're almost at the front door! What are you doing?" Sara could see in her mind's eye the armored vehicle stopping in the middle of the street, its doors flying open, and armed troops dressed in black and wearing night-vision visors exiting its back. The second truck was moving to the north end of the alley, and the third was taking a route around the block to cover the south end. If they did not hurry, they would be boxed in, and Sara did not like the idea of them having to fight their way out.

Tessa shoved some canned soup, a bag of cookies, some granola bars, and a first aid kit into the bag, then crossed the kitchen for an open jar of peanut butter. All useful, Sara had to admit—there were plenty of times she had gone hungry while jumping around the universe with Jonathan, and a first aid kit was always handy. Still, her mother was now digging for something else in a drawer.

"Hurry, mom!" she urged.

Her mother produced a flashlight and a can opener from the drawer before finally grabbing the largest butcher knife in the kitchen and throwing everything into the backpack and heading to follow Sara out the back door. All pretty handy items, Sara had to agree.

"They're here! I can smell the gun oil." Jonathan was standing at his full height, his ears and snout raised in the air. "Twelve in the front of the house closing in, and a truck of some sort blocking the far north end of the alley."

"There will be another truck at the south end if we do not hurry," Sara informed. They moved to the picket fence and beyond into the alley. Jonathan placed himself between the armored carrier at the north of the alley and the rest of them.

"I can take out all the street lights," he stated, flexing his head spikes and preparing to fire.

"No point, they have night vision," Sara called out. "And don't use any lethal attack methods; they are just following orders."

"Orders to attack a mother and her daughter? Jerks," Jonathan grumbled, but nodded to the command. "Where are we headed?"

Sara could already see El Gato halfway down the alleyway heading south, and she knew what his destination was. "The park."

Behind them, the house exploded with noise and light as tear gas canisters went off, shattering windows and filling the house with smoke. The armored vehicle at the north end of the alley came alive, its doors flying open and troops spilling out. Sara now ran after the black cat, her mother right behind her. Jonathan followed, but kept his senses focused on the troops at the far end of the alley. His instincts did not fail him. A split-second later the dull sound of gunfire erupted from behind him. Tessa.

Jonathan flung himself to his right, spreading his arms wide and extending his pincers to make himself as large as possible. With a familiar, dull patter, the depleted-uranium rounds bounced off the bony plating on his back. And then there was a sting.

"Jonathan!" Sara cried.

The chimera hit the ground and rolled sickeningly, careening into a clump of garbage cans and leaving an inky maroon streak on the concrete wall. The tear gas rolled into the alleyway, obscuring further gunfire.

Sara hesitated. She took a step towards Jonathan, but then realized there was nothing she could do and quickly turned away and ran. Sara saw El Gato slip around the corner at the south end of the alley, but even as she did, she knew they had moved too slowly. The final armored transport swung out and blocked their escape. Sara was out of ideas. "Hands up! Now!" she hollered to her mother.

Tessa stopped and began to raise her hands above her head. However, as the doors of the armored car began to open, she heard a low fearsome growl come from behind her that sent chills up her spine. With speed unmatched by anything she had ever seen, a dark blur whizzed by her shoulder. The chimera leapt over Tessa and Sara, striking the armored truck with such force that he sent it toppling up onto its side, pinning the occupants inside. An instant later, he was back with the two of them, and he lifted them off the ground, gripping them both tightly, each in one of his hands.

"Hold on, Sara's mom!" he called out. Tessa could swear there was a giant, toothy smile covering his monstrous face.

"Are you enjoying this?" she cried as Jonathan carried the two of them over the top of the toppled truck and across the street, bounding over parked cars and slipping into the dark park at the far side of the road.

"He loves it," Sara answered, her voice betraying her own

excitement.

"Well, I for one am not having fun," Tessa squealed as the chimera dashed through the trees and finally came to an abrupt halt by a large old oak. "I didn't mean you should stop!" she cried.

"We're here," Sara said. As Jonathan put them both down, Sara motioned to a large root of the oak, where the little black cat with the star chest was now sitting.

"And where is here?" Tessa snapped, as much to the cat as to anyone.

"A portal," Sara replied, "but one that should only be used only during twilight, and dawn is still too far off."

"Sara, we don't have time to wait," Jonathan said, his ears perched high on his head. "Those troops have reached the edge of the park, and I can hear helicopters in the distance,"

He was right; she had not noticed the helicopters until he had said it, but there were four black copters armed with machine guns headed their way.

"If we do it now, it'll be a one-way trip; the path will be forever destroyed." Sara looked to El Gato. The cat seemed to shrug and then began to sing. The roots of the tree started to flower, and a small door large enough for a cat opened in them. Sara needed only to glance at Jonathan for him to get the hint. He matched the cat's song, only louder, and the door split open upwards along the trunk of the tree, growing large enough to accommodate them all.

"I am so sorry, mom," Sara said. The lights from the first helicopters could be seen in the distance, combing through the trees. "I never meant to drag you into all of this. I should never have come here."

"Don't be silly, my dear girl," Tessa smiled. "If there is danger to face, I plan to be by your side the whole time." She placed a firm hand on her daughter's shoulder. "I just wish I had grabbed the photo album."

El Gato was the first through the door in the oak. Sara followed after, giving her mother a worried smile. Tessa hesitated and looked up at Jonathan.

"This is it then. I am off on an adventure with my daughter and her pet monster."

"Looks that way." Jonathan tried to give a reassuring look back.

Tessa looked back at the searchlights closing in on them, and then threw up her hands. "Oh, what the heck. I'm sick of both my jobs, the roof is starting to leak, and since Ethan departed, I haven't had any love life to speak of. Let's see what the rest of creation has to offer." With that, she passed through the magical door, followed quickly by the chimera.

3

~

THE TWILIGHT KINGDOM

A vast forest had swallowed the four companions. As the spinning sensation came slowly to a halt, Sara began to make out what appeared to be great oaks looming above them in every direction. It took a moment for her eyes to adjust to the dim light in this new place. This was a land of twilight, and the great, sweeping trees added a crisscross of shadow to what few rays filtered down from the silver sky. Though the trees themselves were elegant and shapely, the darkness between them held sinister secrets, and odd sounds scraped and hummed in the forest beyond.

A sad, sighing creak came from behind them, and Sara turned with an instinctive whirl. Here was the same exact tree that they had entered in the park back on Earth. The tree had stood out in the park, but here in this forest it seemed at home, surrounded by its many brethren. The doorway they had come through could still be seen as a window back to Earth, lit up by flashlights and helicopter searchlights. The portal was swiftly disappearing though as the trunk of the tree twisted, squeezing shut the gap the cat had opened and Jonathan had widened. Sara could just make out a man in armored black clothing raising a heavy modern weapon to the tree as the light winked out. Sara's warning had not been misguided; the trunk did not stop warping after the portal sealed, but continued to corkscrew, and the tree withered and shriveled before her eyes. Its green leaves turned brown and brittle, crumbling away from the force of the tree's motion. A pale amber sap oozed from the twisted seam where the portal had just snapped shut. The tree was dead.

"So sorry," Sara uttered to the tree so softly that only Jonathan heard her. "We could not wait for twilight to come, and we have cost you your life."

A sudden gust of wind whipped through the surrounding trees, accompanied by the roar and rattle of leaves in the wind. The dark wood they had stepped into seemed to grow more ominous. The chimera could not detect any large predators nearby, but all his senses cried out that they were in danger here. He ushered the others forward, his arms outstretched to guard against unseen danger. The wind continued to hound them as they passed from the grove.

Sara knew the menace they had courted by slaying an ancient tree in this realm, and the guilt of it cut at her. She knew the tree was thousands of years old, wise and full of tales of sights it had experienced. This portal had served as a gateway of inspiration for so many artists and dreamers over the centuries. It had been one of the first of its kind in the Americas, and unfortunately one of the last. Sara knew well how rare a tree that took roots in two worlds was, and even rarer one that linked Earth to this place. The wrath of the grove did not frighten her so much as seem deeply deserved. Thankfully, Jonathan had the wits to move them on.

Tessa, on the other hand, knew little of trees and portals and histories. She only knew that this twilight world was not her own. Even in this dim light, the leaves on the trees twinkled with silver, and she was certain there were colors here she had never seen before, or at least that didn't have a name on Earth. Something else was strange as well—the trees were out of proportion, too large and extremely robust. At the base of many of them sprouted large mushrooms that grew almost to her waist. Sparkles of luminous sap ran up and down deep veins in the trees, ending in a burning glow at the tips of the leaves. The wind that seemed to follow them did not dislodge any leaves or cause any branches to break, and Tessa got the odd feeling that it was the trees that drove the air rather than the other way around.

The way was easier than moving through any forest the four had known on Earth; the underbrush was light and did not impede the path in any direction, almost as if it had been carefully maintained by some kind of invisible gardener. Oddly-shaped mushrooms poked out here and there from the larger ones. The caps sat right at the edges of the faint light and appeared to drop down into shadow as the four companions moved, giving the illusion of little people's hats bobbing up for a glance at them. There was no apparent end to the trees as they walked along, and several times they passed under great root archways. "What is this place?" Tessa uttered, almost unconsciously, not even certain who she was asking.

"Ah, well we have come to the Twilight Kingdoms, milady." the star-bellied cat responded without hesitation. "Not a bad place to be at all, but you'd better keep your wits and manners about you at all times if you want to ever leave."

Tessa stared at the cat. "Excuse me?" she exclaimed.

"Yes, exactly," replied the cat. "Use your manners. Just like that. And while I do feel that your tone of voice could use some polishing, still, you are excused."

"Wait, did you say something?" Tessa seemed confused.

"Pffft," El Gato hissed. "You have no problem with portals and worldships and Sara's gift, but you have a problem with talking cats?"

"No." Tessa looked annoyed. "My problem is not with talking cats, but with talking cats that don't talk when it could help save our lives."

El Gato took an uneasy step back from Tessa. "Well," the cat began, "you see, it's like this—not all worlds are conducive to the sort of energies needed to manifest...."

"He talks when he wants to," the chimera grumbled, butting in

"Yes, that much is quickly coming back to me," Tessa scowled, "and if I recall correctly, his lapses in speech always manage to arrive just when you could use his help the most."

"That sounds about right," Jonathan agreed.

El Gato opened his mouth, obviously preparing to fire off some sort of cutting retort, but upon reflection, he shut it again, then simply shrugged and trotted off between the trees. The others followed, the cat subtly leading the way. "The Twilight Kingdoms," he announced, moving on, "are the realms of the fair people. You may know them as elves, sprites, fairies, nymphs, boggarts, etcetera. Their world and Earth shared many places in the days of old; they were almost one and the same in certain regions, but time and the influx of religion and science and the overgrowth of the human race have burnt away many of those bridges."

"Not to mention the one we just destroyed," Sara sighed.

"Best not to," El Gato whispered, "the trees are angry enough with us as it is." He hurried them along, "You can understand why the fair folk move less and less between worlds these days. You try traveling to a place where they don't even believe you exist. Frustrating if you ask me. Trust me though, whether you believe in them or not, they believe in you. If I can give you one piece of advice on the fair lands, it's this—don't put anything into your mouth thoughtlessly, and that goes for words too." The cat was obviously in his element.

Jonathan the chimera began to tune out on the sound of the

cat's voice. El Gato often played the tour guide part too well, offering hundreds of little tips and points of interest, but Jonathan knew that when it came time to deal with the locals, the cat was just as likely to offend someone as he was. Jonathan focused on keeping himself attuned to the present and was relieved to find that both the wind and sense of menace faded as they went further into the forest. As he looked over at Sara, he noticed that she was hanging back, almost forgotten, lost in her thoughts. He slowed his pace, allowing her to catch up to him. "Hi," he offered, feeling slightly lost for words.

Sara took some time in responding. Finally, she noticed her companion at her side. "Oh… hi." She looked down at her feet.

"What are you thinking about?"

"They tore down that tree, you know. I mean, it was dying anyway, but they bulldozed it. All because of us. They cut it into pieces trying to find out where we went."

"Oh." The chimera wasn't quite sure how to fix this.

"Yeah."

"Who is they exactly?" Something was bugging Jonathan about all this.

"The police, stupid. Or the NSA, more accurately. Who do you think?" Sara shot her friend a frustrated glance.

"Well, I don't know," the chimera replied, unfazed. "Why would the police be after us? I mean, they don't know anything about the Fish Man. He doesn't even exist on that world."

"They have us on a terrorist watch list. They had listening devices planted in my mom's house. A computer in Seattle scans the recordings for key words and voice matches. It alerted the agents about five minutes after we arrived. They would have come sooner, but we are listed as 'extremely dangerous', and it was the middle of the night, so it took a little while to assemble the team."

"Right," Jonathan mumbled, thinking. "But why are we on a terrorist watch list? And what were they going to do if they caught us anyway? You think ol' fish face was going to waltz right into the police station and pick us up? Say, 'Thanks for capturing the extradimensional criminals for me boys, keep up the good work!' Besides, how's he getting around anyway without his ship? Something isn't adding up here."

Sara started to make a quick dismissal of the chimera's naive assessment. "Don't be preposterous, it's not the Fish Man who tipped them off." Wait... what had she just said? The words that had come out of her mouth weren't what she was expecting.

"Hunh?" Jonathan seemed surprised.

Sara's brain started to spin. She rattled out the loose thoughts as they came at her, the chimera listening intently as she narrated. "Well, let's see. Our information was entered into the government database by an agent in a highly secretive program. His information comes from a contact he has never seen, but it is a trusted source because it can predict the future and knows how to manipulate people's minds. The government doesn't realize it, but this is not a human source. The watchers... that's what they are called, or at least that's the translation. Superstitious folk call them moth-men, though the term isn't really accurate. There are millions of them, and they have their claws into every universe, watching and waiting. Strange, why have I not seen them before? Oh, right. They are masters of deception and distraction. They are motivated by... aagh!" Sara winced suddenly as if in pain. She had seen something that had upset her.

Tessa found her daughter's side, placing her arms around Sara's shoulders to support her.

"They are motivated by what?" The chimera's many eyes had opened wider. He didn't seem to concern himself with Sara's trepidation.

"Leave it," El Gato butted in. "Can't you see you are upsetting her? Besides, we need her right now to figure out where we are going. I seem to have lost the scent of this trail."

"No," Sara waved the cat off. "This is important." She took in a deep breath and squared her shoulders. "The watchers are dark creatures of control. They are the servants of a race known as the Elders, the people of the first world, the one called Prime. The Fish Man is one of these Elders, but he is no longer pursuing us. We gave him the power he sought; there is no need for him to punish us. In fact, the watchers pursue him too, as he has betrayed his masters. See, these elders, as masters of Prime, are the progenitors of all realities, and they believe that they can and should control everything that has spawned from their creations. The watchers are their army, though they weren't created as such. They were once something that even the Elders feared, but the leaders of Prime harnessed their energies for their own purposes. Now these watchers twist the minds of mortals in order to blind them from the truth of their own power—the realization that they too have the limitless power to create. The watchers crush the spirits of mortals; they smother them with fear and corruption, stifle cooperation, and pit them against one another in a great distraction that they accept as the true thread of their lives."

Sara swallowed hard and continued, eyes flashing with terror. "The Fish Man is their greatest adversary at this point because of the raw power that he wields, but we must be careful. We are second on their list. We have drawn their attention by destroying their worldship. Such an act cuts at the very core of their control, and it has made them rageful. They are timeless, and they will not stop in their pursuit of us. We pose an unimaginable threat to their control, and they want us undone. They want us crushed. We cannot rest here; they will drive us ever forward! And... oww!!!"

El Gato retracted his claws and went back to all fours. "That's enough Sara," the cat interrupted. "You're scaring us all, especially your mom." It was true, Tessa had become increasingly disturbed throughout the rant. "Give it a rest," the cat continued, "for now we have given them the slip. Besides, this realm is as safe from their control as it gets. And we need your help right now in getting us out of these woods."

Tessa hugged her daughter. "Gato is right, honey," she murmured. "Don't forget I know how you get. Don't you remember when you were a little girl and you'd wear yourself out in endless mental spirals? You'd forget to eat even. When you were a baby the doctors tried to tell me you had epilepsy. Your gift is a great tool, but you can't let it consume you. There's still a girl here behind all this data. And she has all the same needs any other girl has. What does your knowledge tell you will happen if we don't find shelter before night falls? It's been twilight for a quite a while now, we can't have much time left."

Sara nodded, drawing in a deep breath.

"And you," Tessa turned to Jonathan.

"Me?" The chimera looked ready to jump out of his skin.

"Yes you, you big galoot. Let's see that shoulder of yours. Don't think I missed what happened back there. I don't know whether you're incredibly brave or just clueless, but you saved all our lives just now."

"Oh, that? That was nothing. No need to dwell on that. You know, it is getting dark; we should really find this shelter you were talking about."

"Oh, don't be a baby." Tessa reached out and grabbed the chimera by the arm, lifting up the first aid kit she had grabbed from the house. Jonathan shrank back in embarrassment. "What's this?" she announced, befuddled. She scratched at the chimera's thick hide, but there was no more than a slight discoloration around where the bullet had entered. "Hm." She handed him one of the cookies from her pack and patted him on the shoulder. "Well, be careful anyway."

As Tessa returned her attention to the cat, who was busily scouting about for a new path, Jonathan poked Sara in the arm. "You know," he mused, between crumbs, "It's kinda nice to have a mom around. We should have done this sooner."

Sara finally looked around them with her mind's eye. "The best shelter is about a ten minute walk from here. There is a dry hollow under a tree that traveling pooka sometimes use as a resting place. Head up this way, to the left here."

As Sara led the group forward, their path soon merged with what appeared to be animal tracks. Jonathan lowered his head and examined them; they looked and smelled like rabbit tracks, but a few feet further they seemed to change to deer prints both in appearance and scent. Still, he could tell they were made by the same creature.

Sara seemed to be regaining confidence after her spiraling outburst. "There are no predators about now, so we should be able to take it easy. We have more time than you might think though. You see, it's still twilight, even though we've been here for thirty four minutes already. It'll be twilight for another eighty seven minutes too. This is the land of the Fair, don't forget. Twilight and dawn last here just as long as day and night. Think of each day as having four seasons. We're about at the end of November in that way. Not a bad way to look at things though really, as a lot of the fair folk perceive time very differently than we do."

"Do you hear something?" the chimera interrupted. The path made a sharp turn around a bush, and right smack in front of them was an enormous brown bear, browsing for berries. The bear looked up at Sara and growled threateningly, then suddenly its face went pale and it scurried backwards, panicked. The next moment, it was speeding off through the trees, yelping like a puppy. Sara giggled. "I thought you said there were no predators here?" Jonathan said, suspiciously.

"Nothing that would consider hunting in the same forest as you," Sara laughed. "Your face could scare off a nearsighted dragon spider!"

"Hmm..., well, if that's true then what's up with this bird?" Jonathan pointed subtly behind him with one ear. "Don't look now!" The chimera's voice dropped to a whisper. "He's been following us for the last ten minutes."

"The blue jay?" Sara replied without turning around. "Why don't you ask him?" She held out her left hand and whistled a quick tune. The little bird shook off from its branch and flapped down to land in Sara's outstretched palm.

"You know the songs of the elves?" The bird's voice was shrill, but melodic, like the twinkling at the high end of a piano. It was almost imperceptible as speech; certainly any talking bird skeptics about would have simply dismissed it as birdsong.

"Yes, little Chopin," Sara replied. "And I know what would look lovely in your nest as well." Sara reached up and pulled a silken blue ribbon out of her hair, one of the two real ones her mother had placed there. The bird looked excited, but hesitated, just shy of taking the ribbon.

"You trying to gift me?" he asked, and Sara at once understood what he was asking. It is one of the most ancient and powerful laws of Fairy that if one accepts a gift from someone and does not have something of equal or greater value in return to repay them with, one belongs to the giver, bound body and soul.

"No," Sara smiled, "It is freely given with no recourse or return required. Though any advice would be very welcome."

The blue jay grabbed the ribbon and deposited it in a hidden place somewhere beneath his wing.

"Are you headed to the city of the fair folk?" the bird asked.

"There's a better road just to the south."

"We are headed that way in the morning," Sara answered, smiling. "We have traveled far though, and are headed to the pooka hollow for the night. There's another ribbon in it for you if you can watch over us tonight. We haven't slept in many worlds now."

The bird flew back over and settled on Sara's shoulder. It looked about at the four companions, then spent a long moment studying the chimera. "I think I can help," it finally chirped. "Just promise that you'll keep that cat away from me."

"Don't worry," Tessa assured, "El Gato was just lecturing us on being polite to the locals."

As night finally descended, the small group came to rest in a cozy hollow beneath the roots of a giant tree. Broad leaves had been packed down into the hollow, providing a natural pad over the hard earth. Shrubs above hid the hole from view, and the watchful blue jay above contributed greatly to a much needed sense of relief. Sara gathered some edible mushrooms, but no one even bothered to eat them or to talk about the day that had just passed. Within a few moments, the light sounds of snoring filled the hollow.

For Sara, sleep had finally come, but still, she did not know peace. Her dreams were filled with visions of black wings and burning red eyes. She awoke with a start after only a few hours of rest. She felt tired, but was used to going on less sleep than most, and something important was nagging at her.

"Jonathan," she whispered into the dark.

A deep, growling, rasping snore came back as a reply.

"Jonathan, don't be an idiot. I know you are awake; you don't ever sleep."

The next reply was silent, but the voice came to Sara in her head. "What?"

"I couldn't just let it go, you know."

There was a brief pause. "Yeah, I knew you wouldn't. So, what did you learn?"

"Well, I decided that the most important thing to ask was how we can stop these 'watchers' from pursuing us, and I got a very interesting answer—the Seventh Star of Twilight."

4

THE QUESTION

"Huh?" Jonathan's voice sounded ghostly in Sara's brain without the added snarl that the chimera's vocal cords added. "Am I sup... wait, why does that sound familiar for some reason?"

"Don't you remember what I told you about your gap of missing time?" Sara returned through the link. "You know about the Seventh Star of Twilight and how he is my father."

"Oh yeah, right," Jonathan seemed slightly worried, "Sara, are you sure this is a good idea? You told me it was dangerous for you to ask questions about him?"

"Yes, and it's been driving me crazy ever since. Still, that was over a year ago; I'm not all that sure that the warning still applies. If he can actually help us, at some point aren't we in danger by not looking for him?"

Jonathan sat up in excitement. "Oh, come on," he cried aloud, forgetting to use the mental link, "that's... oops." He laid back down gingerly. As if in response, the sleeping cat snorted audibly. Though Sara's insight couldn't penetrate far into the little creature's head, the hint was obvious. "This is getting to be a serious conversation," Jonathan sent to Sara, "we need to go somewhere we can talk. Meet me outside in five minutes."

*****

"There's a clearing just a hundred feet north of here," Sara whispered. "That should be far enough away to let them sleep in peace." Jonathan crept off to scout out the area. Sara watched him in her mind and waited for him to give the all clear. Then she turned and looked up at the little bluebird nestled discreetly under a sprig of leaves. "We're leaving them in your hands now, little bird. Take good care of them." Sara brushed the bird's feathers gently and then turned back to catch up with the chimera.

"Whoa, how'd you get here so fast?" Jonathan was lying on his back on the soft grass and looking up at the stars. A little circle of red mushrooms marked the border of the small clearing, one of the very few places in the great forest where one could see the sky. "Anyway, check it out, Sara. They have totally different constellations here," he announced as she joined him. "There's even one that looks like me. Over there. Can you picture the primitive fairies chanting up at it?" The chimera flexed his claws, hamming in his deepest voice, "Jah-nah-thon, the hunter!"

"That one?" Sara replied, looking up. "Actually, the fair folk call it 'Dorka Majoris', or 'The Big Dork'."

"Hm." Jonathan didn't feel like asking for the real answer. A quiet moment passed. "You think these are the same stars they see on Earth, just from a different point of view?"

"Well," Sara began, clearing her throat, "the term star is really a misnomer of sorts. What you are seeing is actually..."

"Forget it," Jonathan interrupted. "I don't really want you to spoil the mystery. Let's stick to the task at hand so we can get back to the others. So you really think we should look for your father, or are you just dying to ask that forbidden question?

The one you claim was brought to your attention by someone in a place I still can't remember we visited." Jonathan always got grumpy when Sara talked about this supposed hole in his memory and missing time. His body had a flawless internal time clock, and he could register no such missing time. Plus, Sara was always dodgy about where they had been or who had talked to them, claiming it was too dangerous to discuss. He sometimes wondered if she made the whole thing up just to drive him batty, but he knew that it was not the case. Sara had plenty of other ways to drive him mental.

"No, it's not that, though I would be lying if I didn't say the curiosity was driving me crazy," Sara said, sitting down next to her friend. "It's more like what other choice do we have? With all the powerful beings that are after us, don't you think we'd fare better if we had one of them on our side. My mother's only human. I mean, she's great and all, but she's just putting herself in danger by helping us. And the cat is useful, but... well, he's not much of a leader. Half the time I don't think he has any plan at all, just makes it all up as he goes along. And who else can we confide in? Half the people out there are already on their side, and the other half would probably just think we were crazy. Not many beings really stray that much outside of their own realities. How long do you think we can keep this up, jumping from place to place, not sleeping, not eating..."

"Or worse, eating paint pies," Jonathan interjected. "I wish there was a place where we could go and fit in. Somewhere where all the other impossible misfits of creation hang out."

She almost had to laugh. Jonathan had just described Haven to a tee, a place he had been completely at home in, yet could not remember the moment he left. Sara wouldn't mind returning there, and for that matter taking her mother to the safety of the Angel Rithrial's realm, but she could not risk it. The beings that now pursued them would notice if they disappeared off the grid absolutely for any long period of time. Drawing attention to Haven could bring about a disastrous series of events, and she had sworn to do her best to keep its secrets. Besides,

Sara just couldn't quite imagine living her whole life out in such a hidden place without any other people around. It seemed sort of lonely in some way.

Sara resigned herself to the truth. "We need someone who knows what they are doing and who understands our enemy. Don't forget that my father is one of the Primal Elders, or was, at least. As unimaginable as that seems, especially given that the Fish Man is also one of them, it's the truth. If anyone understands how they think, it's him."

"Ok," Jonathan stammered, "now there's something I've never understood. If this Seventh Star dude is some primal old fart or a goody two-shoes version of the Fish Man, how exactly can he be your father?"

"Well, he can change form from reality to reality, but that's just it, see," Sara's voice went up in pitch, "he knows how to manipulate the power of creation. That's why we need him."

"But Sara," Jonathan countered, "this could all just be a huge trick to find him. I mean, they could never have believed that they were really going to be able to take us prisoner with that swat team. Maybe we are playing into their hands. Maybe they just wanted to scare you and make you aware of them so you would then expose your father. These watchers may be just using us like the Fish Man did. After all, didn't they use to work for him? These other Elders can't be much different."

"I do see your point, " Sara argued, "but I don't think the watchers have much of an interest in my father. Look at it this way; it was the Fish Man that was looking for him. The Fish Man wanted to find my father because the Seventh Star was the only Elder that had ever successfully rebelled from the council. The Fish Man wanted to find out how he had done it, but my father didn't want to be found because he felt the Fish Man was doing it for the wrong reasons. But the Fish Man got what he wanted; so what use is my father to him now? And yes, the watchers may have him on their list, but he's far less a priority than we are. In some ways, they actually fear him, and probably prefer that he stay hidden. We need my father to help us defend ourselves from these watchers. Even I find them difficult to understand. You can't just look at their actions; they do not do things directly; they prefer to pull strings. The swat team, for example, was just their best recourse at the time. I'm sure they knew it wouldn't work. They just want to keep us afraid and to drive us forward to them. They have their hooks in nearly everywhere, and can control when and where they tighten the screws. Time is on their side. As outer realities like Earth become unsafe for us, we will be forced to leave them, and we will be slowly herded inwards towards Prime. But if you think the terrorist list and the swat team were bad, it'll get even worse soon enough. Their control is tightest over the inner realities that we are moving into. The closer we are to them, the more power they will have."

"So can't we just find further outer realities? I mean, if they don't have their hooks in them so far, won't it be easier to fight them there?"

"I thought about that. First of all, most of the outer realities are unstable, or unlivable. That cartoon world was a good example. How long do you think we could live on paint? And that's one of the better ones. Some are still in the fragile process of creation, and can wink out at any moment if their creator dies or loses interest. I don't know that we can survive another universe collapsing on itself. Besides, they have controls in place out there too, just weaker. But that's where they will fight us the hardest. When we see that we can't win the fight, we'll be forced to port out and move one step further towards Prime. And then it will start all over again."

"What about this place?" the chimera suggested. "This place isn't so bad. The cat said they didn't have that much control over it. Food seems to taste ok here, at least your mother's cookies did. I haven't eaten anything else because of El Gato's warning. How long can we stay here?"

"Not as long as you'd think. There's no way around it. We need him."

"Ok, ok," Jonathan finally sighed, "you win. So what do we need to do anyway? What is it you've been avoiding doing all this time?"

"Simple," Sara smiled, "I just need to ask myself the question, 'Where is my father?'"

Jonathan sighed audibly. "So do it then."

Sara closed her eyes and focused herself for a moment. A second later she opened them again and looked at the chimera, pursing her lips. "That's odd," she mumbled.

"What? Did it not work?"

"I think it worked," Sara said, quietly. "But I didn't get one clear answer... I got seven."

"Seven?" the chimera's ears pointed upwards. "Well, where are they?"

"Well, one of them is me," Sara laughed. "See if you can make sense of that one."

"Hmm... I don't know. Is that like that old song about being your own grandpa? Now how did that go again..."

"No, dork, I think he's hiding in me somewhere. But only partially. There's two others really close by. One's just a few meters away—my mom it seems—and one's not far from here in the city of the fair folk. And then number four is more of a stretch. It's on the realm of primeval flame. Adam! We already know the Neverknight ended up there. And then there's one more on one of the middle realities—no place we've ever been. The other two, I can't say—all I see is darkness."

"That's funny," the chimera replied, "because I just stopped seeing darkness about five seconds ago."

Sara opened her eyes. The night had indeed ended, and

twilight had returned again in the form of dawn. "That's odd," she muttered aloud, "it's morning already, but that only seemed like an hour at most." She concentrated. "Well, the time is correct, we just must have lost track of it somehow."

"Why are the clouds moving so fast like that? Is there a storm coming?" The chimera was still looking up at the sky, though sitting up now.

Before Sara could answer, a strange squeal broke the silence of the forest; something like a buzzing, high-pitched whine. It stopped and started a few times, and then trailed off. "That's my mother calling to us!" Sara exclaimed, "But why does it sound like that?"

"Well, why does it? Don't ask me." Jonathan looked confused.

"Oh no." Sara looked about her. "The mushrooms!"

"What?" Jonathan threw his hands up in a gesture of protested innocence. "I didn't eat any."

"This is a fairy circle!" Sara cried. "Time works differently in here. We have to get out! The longer we stay in here, the faster time moves! My mother sounded like a squeak because her voice was sped up like a record."

"Um... what?" The chimera tried to comprehend the situation, but almost instantly he was bathed in light. "Oh wow, look, it's daytime now."

"Get out!" Sara ran to the edge of the clearing and took a flying leap over the rim of the mushrooms, which seemed to have grown subtly taller since they had entered. Jonathan goggled as she winked out of sight.

"Hey, wait for me!" The chimera looked up at the sky again and saw it darkening. With a single leap, he cleared the circle and landed back in the dim forest. Sara was nowhere in sight. Instantly he went down on all fours, hunting for tracks. Footprints did not show well in the mossy undergrowth, but there was a scent. It was definitely Sara's, but it was over four hours old. He balked at the thought of it; she had left the circle just seconds before him, yet four whole hours had already passed. He locked onto the scent and moved as fast as he could.

This was not an easy trail to follow. There were many un-usual scents in the fair lands, and the chaotic mix distracted the chimera's senses. After a few minutes of scouting, Jonathan finally managed to track Sara's scent out of the meadow. The scent trail crossed briefly through some overgrowth and then started down along a narrow footpath. This rough animal track twisted and turned, moving slowly deeper into the forest. After about the third bend, Jonathan lost Sara's scent com-pletely. Frantically, he sniffed rapidly at the ground, trying to recover her trail. The scents didn't make sense; it was as if Sara has just disappeared. The only odor that seemed familiar at all was the slight smell of blue jay in the air. Jonathan wondered if somehow Sara had found another path. With her gift, she could easily find portals and shortcuts that he would never be able to detect, even with his highly attuned senses.

Jonathan froze up, at a complete loss. Shortcuts and portals were all well and good for Sara, but how was he supposed to keep up and help if she left him no clues? He stepped towards the edge of the pathway, weighing the merits of searching the nearby woods. Suddenly, and by chance, he caught wind of another odor. The chimera could recognize the smell of that cat anywhere, and maybe, just possibly, he could make out the scent of a human along with it—a scent that was already nearly a day old.

5

~

Left Behind

"It just doesn't make sense. Why would they leave us?" Tessa moaned. The question was not so much directed at the cat as at the universe in general. The universe did not answer. Tessa turned Sara's little satchel over in her hands nervously as if in search of clues. It offered none.

Tessa and El Gato picked their way halfheartedly along the rutted dirt and stone road that led through the forest, slowly progressing towards the supposed town that the blue jay Chopin had spoken of. Tessa was sweating and short of breath, having to bear Sara's bag strapped across her chest in addition to her own pack on her back. Tessa's only hope was that they might find Sara and Jonathan with the fair folk; but that hope was a slim one. El Gato could feel the hesitation in every one of Tessa's steps. She was still very much struggling with the decision of leaving the little pooka cove and heading out for the town.

At first, when they had awoken to find Sara and Jonathan

gone, they had thought that they might have been out scouting or off foraging for supplies, but as time passed, it had become more and more clear that something had gone awry. The two had searched the area all around the pooka cove for hours, calling out for Sara and Jonathan, but eventually they had started to feel that they might be begging for the wrong kind of attention from Fairy. El Gato had tried to track the youngsters by scent, but he was a cat, not a bloodhound, and it got them nowhere. The blue jay had not been much help either.

"Shortly after you two fell asleep, they walked into the forest, sort of in the direction of the town," Chopin had told them.

"Why didn't you wake us?" Tessa had snapped back.

"I had the feeling that they were only going a short distance to talk." The blue jay had replied. "Besides, it is bad luck to wake one from the dream world. You might interrupt one of their dream lives, causing terrible harm to the world you are tearing them from."

Tessa was angry with the blue jay, and it had showed on her face, but El Gato knew that anyone who dwelt in Fairy was hard-pressed to wake a sleeper unless it was of the utmost importance. From the bird's point of view, Sara and the chimera had given him no reason for concern.

Tessa and the cat had continued to search around the cove all through the long twilight. When at last day had broken in the morning sky, El Gato had convinced Tessa that they should move out. "Waiting any longer will only leave us low on food and supplies and get us stranded," he had explained to her. "It is quite possible that the two of them got it in their heads that you would be safer left behind with me. Heading out alone would definitely have taken anyone that might be hunting them off our tail. If they are indeed headed in the direction of the city, then perhaps if we hurry, we can catch up with them there."

"I don't think Sara would just leave me here," Tessa had protested. "There is no way she would have left her bag behind if she was going very far. I am sure she will come back here for us."

"I would be an ill guardian if I did not tend to your needs," El Gato countered. "I do not relish the idea of having to eat the food here in Fairy. Remember that we only have that one backpack full of food, and it will only last so long. We need to find a town anyway and get some real shelter for you." With that, he had compelled Tessa to take to the road with him. The two had left word with the blue jay to tell Sara or Jonathan, if either returned to the pooka cove, that they had headed out for the town. The bird had given his word as a valiant and honorable friend and knight of Fairy to deliver the message if their companions should return. El Gato wondered how a blue jay might be a knight, but then again, many might ask the same about his own qualifications. The two had then gathered their few things and were off.

In the first hour, the two companions had trekked out of the forest through the animal trails, found the old road, and then followed it until they had reached a larger, more well-traveled road, paved intermittently with gray stones. This they had walked all through the day and again into twilight. The trip had not been a monotonous one though; on the way they had crossed several old stone bridges, passed the overgrown ruins of several castles and fortresses, and tiptoed through sacred groves of trees—some so thick and wild that they blocked out the daylight. Here Tessa could not see, and was forced to use the flashlight she had thrown into her backpack. The light of the flashlight had upset the cat though, who swore he could see better without it, and who constantly complained that it caused his eyes to adjust.

What confounded the two companions the most about the journey though was that they passed no one on the road; neither did they see any signs of civilization—only ruins and wilderness. Once in the distance they had heard a great howl, and El Gato, doing his best to act unconcerned, had hurried them along out of the thicket that the road had cut through.

Now, once more, twilight was beginning to dim, and stars twinkled to life in the sky above them. Tessa was less than happy to be left in the hands—or rather paws—of the cat. Though she had only known him for a short time before this, her memories of him all revolved around the chaos that he had brought into her and Sara's father's life. She could not stop feeling that she had left Sara behind, and with each step, she felt more and more like she was going the wrong way. Again and again the thought came to her that Sara would not have left her if she could have at all helped it; she would not have wanted Tessa to worry all over again. It could only mean that something else, something unforeseen, had intervened, and that made her fear greatly for her daughter, giant monster bodyguard or not.

"I think something bad must have happened," Tessa worried aloud. "What if they ate something? You keep saying that we should not eat the food here. What does that do?"

"Sara would not have done that, not while we have supplies, anyway," the cat replied. "She would know better."

"Know better than what?"

"Think about your fairytales," El Gato said, "like Rip Van Winkle. What happened to him?"

"I am not in the mood to play guessing games," Tessa snapped, and she shot the cat a look that only a mother can give—a look that said playtime was over.

"I am not trying to vex you," the cat soothed, "just trying to get you to think in terms of the stories you have read that involve the fair folk. Rip Van Winkle ate and drank with the wee folk, no? And then he slept. When he woke and returned home, decades had passed. See? Fairy runs on its own laws, and one of these is that time here is not as constant as in other places—step into a mushroom circle, drink a thimble of fairy wine, or eat a sweet fairy cake, and you either step deeper into Fairy or let a little bit of it into yourself. Doing so subjects you to the fluid and shifting rules of time in this realm. A day here could be a decade elsewhere; you could return to Earth to find everyone you know long since passed."

"Do you think something like that could have happened to Sara and Jonathan?" Tessa asked, her mind instantly jumping to the gravest of scenarios.

"What?" El Gato pondered. "No. Sara would never. She knows these things, of course; I mean, she knows everything. She would not make such an amateur mistake. You have to bear in mind that we have been to countless worlds and dimensions together, and she is well aware to steer clear of local pitfalls."

Tessa nodded, El Gato was right of course. Her daughter was better equipped than anyone to avoid such traps and pitfalls, but the nagging voice inside her would not give up so easily. She countered the cat, "True, but Sara is prone to distraction. She might have missed something or been deep in thought about something else."

El Gato had already considered the many grim possibilities of misbegotten fates that may have befallen Sara and Jonathan, but he had kept them to himself, not wanting to distress Tessa further. Whatever part of him it was that understood humans knew that Sara would want her mother to be out of danger. It was obvious that if Sara had directly attempted to be honest about her and Jonathan going on by themselves that Tessa would never have allowed it. To El Gato, it seemed reasonable that Sara had taken it upon herself to run off with Jonathan, knowing that her mother would be safe with the cat. After all, she could always check in on them with her gift to ensure they were alright. What dug at El Gato though was that his instinct did not seem to think that it all quite panned out. At the very least, Sara would have told him or the bird that they were going, if for no other reason than to allay the fear that some awful fate had befallen her and the chimera.

The star-chested cat stopped walking and hopped up onto a fallen tree at the side of the road, quickly plopping down into a sitting position. He and Tessa had been moving without a break for a good while, and walking upright always made his back paws ache. Tessa joined him on the log and took off her packs. She pulled out a granola bar from her own bag and then thought the better of it, remembering El Gato's warning about food and drink in Fairy. If this was all they had, it would be better to save it; their meager rations might have to last quite a while. El Gato took note of the action and interjected.

"No, you should eat it," he said. "You starving yourself will not help us."

"But we may well be stuck here for a while," Tessa countered, "and I have no wish to be affected by this realm's freaky time. I can just see us being forced to eat here and then decades passing and Sara becoming an old woman, or worse, having needed us and we were not there."

"Well, it's too bad we don't have any cold-forged iron or stale, bland bread," El Gato said.

"Why is that?" Tessa asked.

"Well, cold forged iron is a neutral sink," El Gato explained. "It is proof against magic, and especially proof against Fairy. It is a symbol of an industrial age and a move away from nature. It sort of acts as a grounding element, keeping you from slipping into the loopholes of time that exist here. Iron also is the only element that you cannot get energy from, either though fusion or the reverse, fission. It takes more energy to break it apart than it gives off, and more energy to combine it than it releases. Did you know that iron is not only the central element on Earth's periodic table but also in one of the largest account of elements in the principal library of the great archive? Now that's worth seeing; it's a chart so large that it is written on a wall several miles long and at least...."

"Wait," Tessa interrupted, "forget about the iron. What about the stale bread?"

"Well, bread is similar to a lesser degree. No one would make a weapon out of bread, but it still grounds certain Fairy magic. I suppose it's also something produced in a more industrial society... but then primitive natural beings bake too, and fairies love pastries. No, I think bread is more tied to home and hearth. It binds a person to his home, offering him some protection. The stale part just makes it less attractive to fairies; they are ageless and do not like things that fade to dust in time. Maybe that's why cakes and sweets are ok with all that sugar they...."

"Yes, yes. Very interesting," Tessa cut in again, "but if we had bread, what would we do with it?"

"Oh," El Gato looked at Tessa, who was digging now through her backpack. "Well we would both need to carry a small amount on our person and, at the very least, it should allow us to eat here without being subject to Fairy time. It should ground us to Earth's time, as long as the bread was made there."

Tessa's head was buried in her backpack. She had not taken any bread from her kitchen in the heat of their escape, but she had used this backpack a week ago when she had volunteered at the youth shelter, and she had packed a tuna fish sandwich on rye bread. She had eaten it, but not all the crust; the ends she had placed back in the plastic bag and then stuffed into the backpack. She could not recall if she had removed the sandwich bag. The old Tessa would never have forgotten to do so, but since Sara's disappearance, she had become far more distracted and disorganized.

"You think you have bread in there?" El Gato asked, a little surprised. He recalled her commenting that she had peanut butter but no bread.

"If I did, would it matter that it was not homemade?" she asked, now beginning to lose hope that the bag was still in her pack.

"No, if it is stale and made on Earth that's all that should matter," the cat replied. "Heck, if it was made in a factory, that might make it even more effective against the natural nature of this realm."

Tessa was about to give up—fearing that the crusts may have been dumped out with the rest of the bag in her haste to escape—when she recalled the small, inside pocket and remembered that she often stuffed her garbage in there to keep it separate from the rest of the bag's contents. She opened it without looking and felt inside.

"Here!" she cried. "Here. I have a crust of rye bread over a week old right here.

"Well, I'll be," El Gato grinned. "If we both keep some of that on us, we should be more than able to eat and drink in moderation here in Fairy without fear of the years passing elsewhere."

The two smiled at each other, and Tessa passed him some crust. It was a small victory, and in no way allayed her fears for her daughter, but still, it felt good.

"Maybe our luck is changing for the better," the cat grinned, his eye teeth shining.

As if in answer, there came a snort and a squeal from the direction they had just passed. The sound startled them both. They looked up to see a great boar heading down the road towards them, but before that could alarm them, they realized that it was tied to a harness and that it pulled a wagon behind it.

The two sat startled. El Gato started to pull Tessa off the log into the woods, but then thought the better of that. Going off the path in Fairy was never smart. Besides, by the time the idea had occurred to him, the single occupant of the wagon had already spotted them.

A haggard and weathered old woman looked down on them from her perch atop the wagon. She reined her boar in with a quick word and considered the two of them. The woman was aged beyond measure; her face was deeply webbed in wrinkles and warts, with a long, twisted nose that hooked at the end. Her large ears came to distinct points, one facing up, the other down. She was garbed in a brown, faded dress that looked patched together, and her bushy, white hair was held down with a bright red cap. For all her weathered and worn appearance, she smiled in a bright and inviting way that gave her a warm affect in sharp contrast to her general look.

"Oh! I hope the two of you are not brash highwaymen set upon robbing me," she whistled, her voice filled with false fear. A wink shot down at Tessa and El Gato.

"No, no," El Gato bowed, leaping off the log. "Dear lady, we are nothing of the sort, I assure you. May we introduce ourselves? I am El Gato, the brave and forthright servant of the lady Tessa here."

"Oh, are you?" the old woman grinned. "Charmed." She nodded her head to Tessa and then to the cat; her boar let out a great snort. "I am no lady though," she laughed, "just an old mother. You may call me Gran."

"Nice to meet you, Gran," Tessa smiled.

"Tell me, are you two heading for the town?"

"Indeed we are, old mother," El Gato purred.

"Well, it is a long way off still from here, and you are on one of the seldom-used roads," Gran said, rubbing her hand on her chin. "I would be deeply remiss in my duties if I was to pass on and leave you stranded here. Would you care for a ride?"

Tessa smiled widely and was about to accept, but El Gato interjected before she could speak.

"Oh, we could not dream of accepting such a gracious offer without arranging some way of paying you back for your trouble."

"Oh no, I could not ask anything of two such wayward and fellow vagabonds." Old Gran grinned even wider. "No, I offer you a ride free of all obligation and payment, and along with that gift, freely given, I would love to include some of my sweet cakes."

"Fair enough." El Gato smiled and waved Tessa toward the wagon. He did take note that the old mother had not made her first offer clear and free of obligation. He wondered if there might be a hidden danger to this, but he was getting rather tired of walking. Don't look a gift boar in the mouth, he told himself.

Tessa and El Gato rode in the back of the wagon on top of some old flour sacks, and they chatted with Gran briefly as they each pretended to eat a small sweet cake. El Gato signaled to Tessa how to pinch off little bites and toss them over the side. Though they were safe in the knowledge that they were protected from the effects of fairy food, something just wasn't quite right here; the two still felt more comfortable sticking to their own food while it lasted. Besides, stale bread certainly wouldn't protect them against any poison or potions that might lurk hidden in the cakes.

After a while, El Gato found that he was more tired than he expected, and noticed that Tessa could hardly keep her eyes open either. Something about the sway of the wagon coupled with the strong floral scent there in the back seemed to lull him.

"What is it you keep in these flour sacks?" Tessa asked, noticing how soft they were.

"Why, flowers, my dear." Old Gran smiled, and Tessa thought that her mouth seemed unusually wide. Tessa pulled back some of the coarse cloth, and was greeted by a colorful pile of poppies. The scent they gave off was captivating. Tessa breathed it in and smiled, reminded of her childhood. She was quite tired herself, and looking over at the cat for guidance, she saw he was already fast asleep. The flower sacks were so soft.

"I apologize for being bad company," Tessa murmured, "but we have been walking for quite a while. Do you mind if we sleep for a bit?"

"Mind? Oh, quite the contrary," old Gran replied, "I insist you do." As Tessa sprawled herself out beside the snoring cat, she thought she detected just a hint of something wicked in old Gran's tone, but maybe that was just the fatigue getting to her.

6

~

THE BLACK WOOD

Sara burst through fairy ring and hit the ground rolling. Behind her, the mushroom circle looked just the same as it had before she and Jonathan had wandered into it—unassuming and even hard to see in places where the grass grew long. There appeared to be no one inside of it, but Sara knew Jonathan was there, hidden by the ever-quickening time distortion. He was moving to follow her, but she could tell he would not jump free until well after dark that night, and she could not wait; time was of the essence. Sara could just smack herself for falling into such a trap, but she had no time now to dwell on could-have-beens. She shot off in the direction her mother and El Gato had taken, running at her fastest clip. She was a half day behind them. In her mind's eye, she could see that they had reached a well-traveled road and were heading towards the nearby town. As far as she could tell, the two were all right, but she could sense her mother's worry, and it dug at her to know that once more she was causing her mother anguish.

Sara found the trail the others had taken and jumped down onto it from a ledge above. She used her gift to land in just the right way and in the right place, avoiding sliding on the loose dirt and twisting her ankle. Using her gift for physical actions was something she had become far better at since meeting Jonathan. When the two of them were linked in his body, she could not help but apply all her knowledge to the almost limitless potential of his adaptations. Now, even in her far more limited form, Sara now readily applied the same technique. She paced herself as she ran, factoring in the distance she needed to close between her and her mother, carefully monitoring the speed they were traveling and the limits of what her body could maintain. The pace was slower than she would have liked, but she knew it would allow her to catch up with the other two by some time the next day if she did not stop— sooner if Tessa and the cat took a rest. This pace was chosen to push Sara to her physical limit—she would collapse from exhaustion shortly after she found them, but she would end her mother's worry that much faster.

There were, of course, other things to factor in. Jonathan would be free sometime after nightfall, and he would pursue her at full speed, never slowing or tiring. That would bring him up to her well before she got to her mom and the cat. However, the chimera could always run into trouble or some other delay, just as she might herself, so the best thing was to keep moving. With a thought, she formed sleek, comfortable running shoes and gear out of the organic suit; she was going to need every advantage she could get.

Sara's breath had reached a steady rhythm and her body had just gotten over the first hump of running when she noticed a small shadow that swept in front of her and then back again.

"Aha, I thought that was you," the blue jay sang.

"No time," Sara panted, "can't talk." Sara had not factored in conversation to her calculations for speed. Any extraneous effort would ultimately slow her down.

"Oh, I know you are after your mother and the cat," Chopin chirped. "I was told to deliver a message if you returned. I have been scouring the area for any sign of you. I must say you are in a hurry. You're already at the edge of my search range. It's lucky I found you."

Sara already knew the message. "I know they're headed for the town."

"Oh, well... good then," the blue bird kept pace with Sara, flying alongside her. "They will be a good way off by now. Do you intend to run the whole way?"

"Yes," Sara was beginning to become a little annoyed. She knew the bird meant well, but she could not afford a protracted conversation at this point.

"I feel a little bad. Your mother was very upset that I did not wake her when you two went off."

Sara was actually happy about that one. If Chopin had awakened them, they still would not have been able to locate her and Jonathan, and they might have set off earlier, giving them even more of a lead.

"Where did you go?" the bird asked.

"Mushroom," Sara panted. "Circle."

"Of course," tweeted Chopin, "terrible nuisance that. I should have warned you all about the local ones; they're only good if you have in-laws coming to stay for a week and you want the week over before it starts."

"Not your fault. Need to keep running."

"Yes, yes of course you do," Chopin said. "You're a good-hearted girl; you don't want to concern your mother any more than you have to. Well, the least I can do is keep you company on the trip—while you run your heart out. Actually, wait... that really is the least I could do. I could do more." And with that, the bird was off, quickly disappearing into the forest.

"Thank goodness," was all Sara thought, and she placed the

full force of her concentration on the trek ahead. She could see a shortcut in her mind's eye. If she turned off the trail and cut through some trees, she could bypass and then rejoin the trail further down. The terrain was rougher there, and she would have to climb over a fallen tree or two, but it would cut a good ten minutes off the journey, even accounting for difficulty. Sara smiled; there were hundreds of such little short cuts that she could take along the way that would make the trip faster and faster. Soon she rounded a corner and jumped over a log, landing a few feet beyond the trail.

The moment her feet touched the ground, Sara recognized the error she had made. "One should never go off the path in a fairy tale," she remembered, a moment too late.

The trail behind her was gone, and the shortcut was now muddled and confused. All around her the dark forest rose up. The great twisted pine trees and wild thickets interwove, creating a maze of underbrush that blotted out the light of day. Sara turned in the direction she had just come from, her own eyes now confirming what her mind already knew—the world around her was in flux. She knew the trail still existed; it just wasn't where it had been before. Its location changed subtly from moment to moment. She was now deep in the dark woods of Fairy.

All around Sara—as far as she could see—oppressive, cracked tree trunks twisted about, their roots forming shapes, their limbs casting shadows. Sara felt like she was being stalked. Others in this predicament might have shrugged off the feeling, convincing themselves it was all in their heads, but Sara knew better. She was a little girl, a stranger to Fairy, and the moment her foot had set down beyond the path, a silent echo had reverberated out through the darkness, and there it had alerted all the creatures that hunted the black wood. Even now, dark, frightening creatures were beginning to stir, their hungry bellies crying out and their mouths beginning to water—all at the idea of tasting the flesh of a little human girl.

An icy chill ran down Sara's back, and she knew fear like she had not known since she had been a small girl staring into the black of her closet at night. Suddenly, as if in answer to her fears, a howl cut the air in two. It was far off, but so loud and deafening that Sara shrank and covered her ears. The terror blinded her, and for a moment she lost touch with all her knowledge; she knew only animal fear—what a deer must feel when a hunter is bearing down on it.

"Stop it, think!" Sara said to herself, biting her own lip. She could outdo this trap and find her way back to the trail. She just had to avoid the creatures of the black wood beyond the path. She started to compute the possibilities, but then something changed. The terrors were now all shrinking back into their dens, holes, and hollow trunks. She had been spared for the moment, but it gave her no comfort. Sara knew why they had retreated; the howl had been more than just a signal that a hunt was about to begin. It had been a warning to all others that this little girl was claimed—a warning from the most terrible and fearsome of creatures: a big, bad wolf.

Sara bit down even harder on her lip and a small drop of blood formed and then fell to the ground. The moment it touched the forest floor, it was soaked away into the ground below. "This whole place is thirsty for my blood," she thought to herself. She shivered, and the cruel trees around her creaked in gleeful response. Her heart was now pounding so hard in her chest that she could hear it thumping in her ears.

"Stop it, Sara!" she snapped at herself out loud. "This place wants you to fear! It wants you to panic. Keep your wits." Sara searched for the path again in her mind. It was still moving, but it seemed more stable now. Was there a pattern to it? Yes, there was. What was the pattern? The answer came immediately. Sara's exit from the black wood moved with the very thing that hunted her. The closer it came, the closer the trail edged in behind it. Before, when so many had started to rise to hunt her, the exit had been in chaos. Now it followed only one creature, the big, bad wolf that stalked steadily closer.

At that thought, a second howl cut the air, and Sara felt an almost overwhelming instinct to run. "No," she told herself, "it wants me to run." If she ran, it could easily keep itself between her and the exit. Like it or not, the best chance she had at escape would come when she was in the most danger—confronting the very creature that now sped towards her. The next howl cut the air again, this one loud enough to crack tree branches, and so close she could almost smell the creature's breath. She did not run; instead she turned towards the sound. She clenched her fist and stood as tall as she could. "If I give into fear, I am as good as dead," she said, trying to convince herself more than anything.

"Ooooh, but that is already inevitable," a low howling voice that turned into a growl issued from beyond the underbrush.

Sara knew what had come to a halt there, and she knew that by standing her ground she had already confused the creature, making it wary.

"Show yourself," she said, for the moment playing her part.

It slid from the underbrush on all fours, utterly silent, moving more like a panther than a wolf. For Sara, seeing something in her mind and seeing something for real was always a little different. The wolf was as large as a horse; its head and mouth alone were almost as big as Sara. Its body was sleek and starved looking, covered in matted black fur. Its thin legs ended in huge paws with foreboding claws as black as its fur. Its tapered head started out wide but ran into a long, thin snout, lined on top and bottom with teeth. The crown of these jewels were four great fangs the size of daggers—two on top and two below. Still, none of the wolf's features were more frightening than its eyes. These two white-blue pools of ice held the knowledge of hundreds of such hunts, and regarded Sara with only a bottomless hunger.

"My, what big eyes you have," Sara said, using all her will to maintain her composure.

"You know your lines," the big, bad wolf snarled, amused with its prey. "Well, if that's how you like it, I will humor you. All the better to see you with, my wayward child."

Sara saw the forest behind the wolf, and there light was beginning to form, filtering down through the trees. "The exit," she thought, "just behind him." She just needed more time.

"My, what big ears you have," she said, slowly.

"All the better to hear the thump, thump of your heart begging to be free of your chest, my sweet." A great line of drool slid down the wolf's fangs and plopped onto the ground. The wolf slowly paced around Sara, inching closer and closer. The exit moved with the wolf, remaining constantly behind it.

Sara saw her chance with her mind's eye. It was slim, but worth the risk. "And such a large nose," she mocked. Sara smiled, keeping up the appearance of composure as she rotated slowly, keeping herself facing the wolf as he leisurely paced around her.

"All the better to smell the fear rising in you, basting your insides, and sweetening the taste of your meat." Sara could now feel the breath of the wolf upon her, hot and moist with a scent like rotten fruit.

Sara's chance would come soon. She just had to delay somehow. "I am not like other girls, you know. I know the truth of this tale. There is no woodsman to save me. I know that when I say the final line, you will eat me and it will be done."

"How refreshing," the wolf snarled. The big, bad wolf then grinned, stooping and bringing his head level with Sara's, his teeth inches from her throat. "So few children these days really do know the truth."

"Yes, all the old tales have been watered down," Sara agreed, "made nice so the good guys always win." Sara continued fighting against every fiber of her being that screamed out to run. "Just a little more time," she screamed in her head.

"How boring," chuckled the big bag wolf. "But we know better, don't we."

"Yes," Sara replied, "the stories were meant to warn children—to teach them the harsh truth."

"Yes," the wolf responded feverishly. The big, bad wolf nodded, more drool running out of his mouth and down to Sara's feet. "And the harsh truth is that the big, bad wolf eats the foolish girl who strayed from the path, leaving her lovely white riding hood covered in the red of her blood. And no woodsman comes to save her, because no one cares about a foolish little girl. For the girl, there is only the belly of the big, bad wolf—no brave saviors, no heroes, no knight in shining silver armor."

"No," Sara smiled, "so I guess I will just have to settle for one in blue."

The big, bad wolf pulled his head back, and for a moment looked confused, but then, all at once, he was drowned in an explosion of blue light.

"You shall not harm her!" Chopin cried, as he and hundreds of his brothers and sisters streamed in from the golden light of the exit. Each, in turn, struck at the wolf with their beaks and claws. One would be nothing to the big, bad wolf, but seven hundred and forty two was another matter all together. Sara had seen the birds in her mind's eye searching for her. Chopin had left her to gather them so that they might, with their combined numbers, lift and fly Sara to her mother. She had stalled the big, bad wolf long enough that they had found the passage between the path and the black wood, and now she had her chance to escape.

Sara bolted to the side, moving around the wolf and the blizzard of blue jays, but through the blur she caught a glimpse of an icy blue eye following her.

"No, no, noooooooo!" the big, bad wolf howled as he crashed

and snapped his way through the feathered onslaught, "You will not free yourself, little lamb. I shall dine tonight on all your tasty bits."

All of Sara's restrained will to run now burst out of her. She did not think she had ever moved so fast, but still the big, bad wolf was faster. His head broke free of the swarm and he snapped his way towards her, gaining ground faster than Sara's feet could take her to the exit. She ran, knowing it was hopeless, and then out of the corner of her eye, she saw Chopin fly past her towards the big, bad wolf, a flash of light reflected off of something held tight in his feet.

"Now foul beast, you will taste silver," the blue jay cried, his little bird voice twittering faster than other animals could speak, "the silver of the sowing needle of the king of grandmothers, gifted to me when I charmed her by telling her the tale of a fairy prince!" With that, Chopin dived forth, zipping past the snapping maw and driving the little needle into the right eye of the big, bad wolf.

The howl that next cut the air was like no other, filled with all the hate and pain and darkness that was soul of the monster. Sara did not look back; she sprang through the exit and onto the path, coming out where her shortcut should have ended in the first place. She was followed by a stream of blue that shot forth from the black woods and up into the sky. The sound of the howling seemed distant now, and Sara knew the big, bad wolf would not pursue them out onto the path. He was retreating to his den one eye maimed—the price for hunting her.

The blue jay flock surrounded Sara, singing songs of victory and odes of courage to those that had fallen in the fight. Sara realized almost at once that not all the blue jays had survived the melee. Of their number, twenty-seven had fallen to the claws and mouth of the wolf. As Chopin descended from the group towards her, she was overcome with guilt and remorse.

"I am so sorry," she said as the little bird landed on her finger, "you lost friends and loved ones in risking your lives for me."

"No, sweet girl, blue jays always fight the creatures of the black wood," Chopin chirped, "it is how we earn our honor and titles. Today, however, we got to save a fair maiden in the process."

Sara could not help but smile as the bird knelt on her finger and kissed her hand. Despite the kind gesture, she would always remember the names of the blue jays that had fallen here, and if she ever found peace, she would write each one's story. "You are brave, sir knight," Sara replied, "you and all your friends have my everlasting gratitude."

A great cheer went up among the birds, and they began to chant, "Lady Sara, Lady Sara!"

Sara blushed and looked down. Only then did she notice how long and low the shadows were. It was twilight, almost night. Time in the black wood was also different, and she had lost too much of it.

"Good knight," she said to Chopin, "does the offer still stand to fly me to my mother?"

"Indeed," the blue jay chirped. "Let us gather some of our string, and with it we will each tie a tether to you."

"I have a better way," Sara smiled. With a thought, Sara made her organic outfit begin to produce small but very strong strings, like thick, sparse fur. There were more than enough strands for each blue jay to take one. Before long, Sara was airborne.

Fairy from above was breathtaking and mystifying. Blue rivers cut up a patchwork of deep forests that all blended haphazardly into haunted hills and fields of colorful flowers. Slender towers topped with long, streaming flags poked up at places amongst the landscape. Some were silver and full of grace, others dark, ruined and foreboding. In the distance, the gathered towers and monuments of the fairy city just barely blotted out the rim of setting sun. Sara laughed and clucked as she rode above the landscape at the base of a sea of blue jays. The breeze was cool and refreshing. It all felt like some beautiful dream. It was not until the night sky washed over the land that she checked in on her mother and El Gato.

"Oh no!" she gasped.

"What is it, my lady?" Chopin inquired, concerned at Sara's sudden paleness.

"It's my mother; she is in terrible danger."

7

~

DINNERTIME

Tessa felt ill as she gradually came to consciousness. Her vision was blurred; all she could make out was a general darkness and one large, flickering light source. She instinctively moved to rub the sleep from her eyes, but her hands were blocked—pinned to her sides by a set of metal bars. This was not right; she shook herself and tried to focus. As the fuzziness of the world began to sharpen, the light in front of her slowly formed into the shape of a campfire. It had been built in a shallow pit, and a great black kettle had been hung above it. This was now in focus, but there were still parts of Tessa's vision that remained indistinct. As she studied the phenomenon, she quickly realized that there were bars between her and the fire. Tessa tried to jump away, jerking her whole body, but only then did she realize that she had been crammed into a tight iron cage. Her knees were bent tight against her chest, and her arms were pressed up against the bars at her sides. The pain had not hit her yet, but she could tell it was coming. She fought the urge to panic. Several deep breaths later, her eyes had better adjusted to the darkness, and the grogginess was fading unpleasantly fast. Her body ached and burned, but she fought through it to take a second look at her surroundings.

Tessa was trapped in one of several dirty cages of all different sizes that occupied this side of the fire. Her cell was shaped like a birdcage, round with a dome top—and though it was one of the largest of the group, it was still far too cramped and small for a full-grown woman. In several of the other cages, she could make out other trapped creatures, as well as a gory collection of bones and litter. Amongst the living, there was a brown rabbit in a dapper waistcoat, a sad little robin, and—in a cage right next to her own—the familiar form of a scruffy black cat. But El Gato was not just simply caged. His forelegs were tied firmly behind his back, and his hind legs were bound together tightly with silver cord. As Tessa gazed in his direction, he looked up and caught her eyes. He motioned with his head in the direction of the fire. That was when Tessa finally saw the old woman on the far side of the steaming pot. She was cutting up a carrot and adding it to the bubbling stew.

"What happened?" Tessa exclaimed in her loudest whisper.

"I know this looks bad," El Gato whispered, "but don't worry. I still got this one." He scrunched up his whiskers in thought and stared at the fire for a moment. Finally, he looked back at Tessa. His face did not show confidence. "How far can you spit?" he offered.

Tessa thought the ubiquitous cockiness in the cat's voice sounded a little less convincing this time. "What?" she said again, noticeably louder this time, forgetting to whisper.

"You awake finally, deary?" the old woman croaked from the other side of the pot. "We trust there'll be no trouble from you like from your little friend. Almost picked the lock with his claws. Had to tie him up, yes we did."

"But I warned you though," the little brown rabbit called out, his voice shaking. "That should buy me a reprieve, right?"

The old woman stopped her chopping and walked towards them, wiping her bony hands on her apron—hands that Tessa now noticed sprouted long, claw-like nails.

"Reprieve?" the crone laughed unpleasantly, fingering the rabbit's cage. "You've only earned yourself an extra day or so, little nugget. But don't get it into your head that I'm being kind. It's just that rabbit and human don't mix well."

"But you said if I kept an eye on them..." the rabbit cried, "warned you if they tried anything, you'd set me free!"

El Gato rolled his eyes. "Hey, just a little tip," he sniped, "she's an old witch, evil heart as black as pitch. She is not going to set you free. Though I would have if you had let me finish picking the lock."

"Oh! Old witch are we?" the crone snarled. Her voice seemed to grow deeper. "You really are a dim-witted cat, can't even see through a dingy disguise. And I thought cats were above being fooled by appearances, yes we did now."

El Gato narrowed his gaze, almost closing one eye as he looked at the old woman. There was no glamour on her, he would have noticed that. But wait... there were faint edges to her face, and when she moved, up her sleeves he could just catch the slightest glimpse of an unpleasant greenish-gray colored flesh. And when she smiled, her teeth were not the teeth of a human, but sharp and sprouting in rows. And worst of all, there was the red hat.

"Oh, hairballs," El Gato moaned. "I must have been tired yesterday not to see it."

"Ha ha haaa! Stupid kitty!" The old woman's voice became maniacally dark and alien. She threw off her dress and peeled back the skin of her face, revealing it to be but a thin mask of rubbery leather. There, beneath the disguise, was the greenish-gray skin, cruel red eyes, and twisted features of a goblin—but not just any goblin, a fearsome redcap, the grim sub-race infamous for soaking their head cloths in the blood of their victims.

"You cretin!" Tessa hollered. She struggled violently in her cage and managed to break through a rusted spot at the bottom. She forced a haphazard foot out through the bars, kicking wildly at their captor. But the preternaturally quick redcap easily stepped over her blind thrust. It laughed again, jumping backwards and twirling about, with the dress held high above its head.

"You can thank me mother," the goblin cackled, "she is the one that loaned me the dress! Nyaa ha ha haaaa!" The redcap clicked its heels and let the dress fly from his fingers and spin away into the darkness. The goblin skipped back over to the cauldron, then leaned over it and grinned at them, all pleasantries falling from its face. "Yes! Now I will be eating like a king of old," it shrieked, "dining on the flesh of humans as my kind once did before your foul race chased us off into the corners of creation!"

"You may want to reconsider your plans," Tessa snapped, "we have very a powerful guardian following behind us. Even now he will be tracking you. You harm us and what he does with you will be even less pleasant."

The redcap stopped in its tracks and covered its mouth, looking frightened. Then slowly it burst into mocking laughter. "Come out!" it hissed. "Come out, powerful guardian!" The goblin paused and looked around, waiting for comic effect. "Hmm... well, I don't see anyone offering to save you," it mocked, returning to the side of the cauldron. "This guardian best hurry, because as soon as I finish spicing the pot, you're going in... in pieces." The redcap produced a rusty knife from his belt and began to cut more vegetables and herbs into the stew."

"You should eat me first," El Gato spoke up. "Cat makes a better first course."

"Enough!" the goblin snarled. "Silence, all of you. The next one to speak gets his tongue added to the pot." The goblin flung its knife against the cat's cage, rattling the bars. Its full fury showed on its face. "No one is coming to save you," it hissed. "No one is out there, and you are all going to be eaten in good time, so wait your turn." It turned its back to them, picked up a worn ladle, and began stirring the pot slowly, savoring in the aroma.

From the shadows beyond the campfire, Sara could see the hurt and terror that swept across her mother's face. Beside her, the blue jay Chopin drew his lance. He moved to hold it up to signal his flock to attack, but Sara stopped him with a hand.

"No," she whispered, keeping her volume to a level that she knew would not reach the ears of the redcap. Fortunately, the crackling fire and the goblin's own hooting and humming worked to her advantage. "It's too dangerous."

"We are not afraid, lady Sara" the bird returned, his own chirps a little too loud for Sara's comfort.

"Quiet," she cautioned, laying a finger to her lips, "I have no wish to see more of your people die. And besides, I also can't risk that creature hurting my mother while she is caged. We have to find a better way, something more stealthy... safer."

"I think I can pick those locks," Chopin replied, his voice almost comically low now. Sara had to tap into the Font to make out his words. "My lance is good for that as well."

"Yes," Sara whispered, her gears turning, "but what if you're seen by the goblin, or the rabbit gives you away?"

"Well, then we need a distraction," the blue jay offered, "something that foul creature would not dare to look away from.

"Almost ready!" the redcap cried as he danced toward the weathered cages, making sure to stay out of reach of Tessa's free leg. The goblin fondled the edge of its unpleasantly stained knife and eyed her hungrily. "Well, now," it mused, poking her through the cage as it talked with the tip of the blade, "should I eat an arm tonight? Or maybe that long, lovely limb you tried to kick me with." Little trickles of blood began to run down Tessa's skin.

To Tessa's horror, she realized that the goblin planned to keep her alive for the next few days, eating her piece by piece—not that being shoved in a pot all at once was any kind of a reward, but still, the idea chilled her. How had this all gone so horribly wrong? "You're a coward," she spat, running out of good ideas, "you haven't the guts to face me in a fair fight."

"Oh, in that you're quite right," the goblin mused, "and thankfully, I do not have to, thanks to me dear, dead mother. She taught her son to hunt so well and cleverly... so well indeed. And I do so miss her, but then these roads aren't traveled as often as they used to be—and even then they never really did provide enough for two." The little creature smiled hungrily.

"What happened to your mother?" Tessa asked, regretting the question the moment it came out of her mouth.

"Oh," the redcap howled, "she was a greedy, mean old thing. Barely ever gave me a table scrap; so one day I hit her over the head with a pan and buried her before she woke. But don't worry, I did dig her up again though... a few days later to get the dress! Hha hhaaa haaa!"

The redcap spun and twisted in front of her, laughing in glee as it prepared to strike its first true cut. As Tessa stared at the flickering blade, something moved. She could have sworn that she had seen something dark and dirty float into the air beyond the fire. Then the smoke shifted, and yes, there it was again. Whatever it was, it was about the size of the goblin, but Tessa could not fully make it out.

The redcap took note that his audience was not paying attention to him and stopped his dance. "What are you looking at?" the goblin spat.

"Bullwog William Messalmush, I have come for you at last!" echoed a cruel voice, reverberating through the night. The name sent a shockwave across the whole body of the redcap. He jerked around to face the voice so fast he almost fell to the ground cowering and covering his head in fear.

Floating in the air beyond the fire hung the gnarled visage of an old goblin, dressed in the very clothing the redcap had just used to impersonate his mother. The air around the figure shimmered with a blue glow, and an unearthly noise accompanied it, like a hundred moths trapped in a lampshade.

"How can it be?" the redcap hollered, peeking impishly through his fingers. "Is it really you, momsy?"

"Yes! Who else but your own dear mother," the figure crowed, its accent strained, "back from the hole in the ground where you put her before stealing her best dress to trick travelers in our family's time-honored tradition."

"Oh momsy, I am so sorry," the goblin screeched, tearing at its hair and crawling on his belly toward the floating figure.

"Keep your head low, you worm," the figure hissed.

The redcap worked his way around the fire, groveling, "Please, momsy! Have mercy on me! Do not drag me down into the land of the dead with you! Forgive, forgive." He finally came to rest under the phantom, wiping his head penitently in the dirt.

"Your momsy is not in the forgiving vein this night, Woggy" the figure cried melodramatically. It made a strange waving motion with its left arm over the head of the prostrate goblin.

"Please forgive! Please." The goblin let out a mournful howl and then cut it short. His face slowly came up to meet the floating phantom's gaze.

"You dare look upon me?" the figure yelled, but the redcap did not turn away.

"Momsy... why do you smell like a little girl?" it hissed.

"Because I ate one only an hour ago," the figure answered.

"Really?" the redcap mused. The goblin rose up slowly onto its feet. "I did not know spirits needed to eat." Quick as a flash, the goblin had a hold of the phantom's leg.

The little creature was far stronger than it looked. The floating figure tried to pull away, but the monster's grip was like steel. It pulled downward, and the figure slowly descended, accompanied by a furious fluttering.

"Well well, it looks like we have another for dinner," the redcap laughed. "Did you think you could trick me, little girl? My mother was a thousand times more frightening than you."

Sara could see the goblin's sharp teeth and knew that he meant to eat her then and there. She shook in fear. What sort of words could defend her from such a single-minded foe? None came to mind, and Sara prepared for the worst. But then a blur of motion caught her eye, moving in rapidly behind the goblin.

"You want a mother to fear?" Tessa said. And as the surprised redcap turned to face her, she smashed an iron skillet full force against its face. The goblin let go of Sara and stumbled, falling to one knee. Tessa did not retreat, but came forward, raising the skillet again. "No one lays a hand on my daughter, you got that Bullwog William Messalmush?" She bashed him again, right on the top of his red cap, knocking the goblin clean out.

"Mom!" Sara gasped.

Tessa stood over the fiend—the pan still held like a weapon—watching to make sure it was truly unconscious and not faking it. When she seemed satisfied, she looked up to Sara, whose face was now exposed as the goblin-mother visage melted back into her organic suit—a face covered in shock.

"What?" Tessa asked. "He deserved it, right?"

"Remind me never to make you mad again," El Gato quipped.

Sara and Tessa looked over at the bound cat. Chopin had decided not to come near enough to free him from his predicament. "You comfy there?" Tessa smirked at the little creature.

"What, me? I'm fine." the cat remarked, defensively. He looked over at the fallen redcap, then gazed at Sara and then up at his bonds. "See," he offered finally, "I told you I had this one."

*****

It was just over an hour later that the chimera, panting and in a panic from having smelled the goblin, came bursting through the underbrush, only to find all of his companions sitting lazily around a fire, sharing vegetable stew with a smartly-dressed rabbit.

"I smelled a goblin!" the chimera breathed.

"Oh, him?" Tessa asked, motioning to the wagon where the redcap sat tied and gagged. "No need to worry; I made short work of him."

"Huh?" Jonathan uttered, confused.

"Looks like Sara has a new bodyguard," El Gato mused, "and if I might say, she is far easier to look at."

And a better kind of laughter filled the little campsite.

8

~

THE ANSWER

Sara's eyes fluttered open to the first silver rays of dawn. The forest that had only yesterday seemed so ominous now seemed pleasant, almost welcoming. One by one, the birds in the forest awoke and began to sing. Woodpeckers added a steady staccato rhythm. Next, cicadas and crickets joined in, and finally frogs croaked out in the mists, adding their deep bass voices to the music of the forest. Sara had been in woods before, but something about this fairy forest was different, There was a unity she had never experienced. The animals all seemed to know what the others were doing, as if they followed some hidden conductor. Or was it hidden?

Sara followed an angle she had never really pursued before, entering the conscious thoughts of the frogs and tapping into their perceptions. Yes, there it was! Sara couldn't exactly hear it, but she could understand what it sounded like. It was not unlike when she used her knowledge to "see" around her, even though she couldn't really see anything. This was "hearing". There was a sound that permeated the forest that was inaudible to human ears. Two sounds actually. They came from the trees. One was high-pitched and was generated by the vibration of the leaves. It sang like a violin, guiding the melody and singing the sweetest song Sara had ever heard. Beneath this pitch was the pulse of the roots, far too low for Sara to hear, but she could feel it just slightly in the ground, or maybe she just thought she could feel it since she knew it was there. It drove the beat of the song like a bass drum, beating out the time. And the beat was not constant, but changed over time. Each animal acted as a single musician in the great orchestra. Sara closed her eyes again and listened to the music, snuggling farther into the warm arms of her mother, who, even if she was not consciously aware of it, could hear the song of the forest as well—for her own light snoring was timed perfectly with the beat.

Sara had not slept like this since she was a little girl—with her mother's arms wrapped tightly around her like a blanket—but it felt wonderful. For so long had she been without someone to care for her that she had almost forgotten what it felt like. She had not been too keen on it the night before, but Tessa had been so emotional over having lost and regained Sara for a second time that she had vowed never to let go of her again. She had cooked Sara and the others a delicious stew and served it to them all, ensuring first that Sara and Jonathan both placed some of the stale Earth bread on their persons. The meal had rejuvenated them, but only enough to feel their bodies again, and the exhaustion had come over them quickly. With Jonathan there to watch over them, the four others had simply headed for the first dry, mossy spot they could find, and had passed out in seconds. There was something in the fairy food as well that had helped their sleep. It wasn't so much the various chemical compounds that formed it, like the familiar nutrients on Earth, it was more of an energy that came from being grown in fairy soil—an energy that Sara's knowledge called, for lack of a better word, "magic". The food transferred this energy to the eater. So unlike with sleep on Earth, where the sleeper often awoke more achy and disoriented than the night before, the fairy magic gave sleepers here a full, true rest. The body felt supple; the mind felt clear.

Sara could sense that Tessa was beginning to stir from her slumber, but she did not hasten to wake her. The fairy magic needed to be left alone to work its benefits. Soon enough, Tessa's eyes opened, and her face instantly beamed at the sight of her precious daughter curled up in her embrace. Her voice was clear, and held no trace of rasp or grogginess. "I dreamed you had turned into a bird in my arms," she murmured, "and I kept holding on to you to keep you from flying away."

Sara blushed. She realized that the last time her mother had really known her she had been almost two years younger. Pretty soon Sara would indeed be flying away, but for now, Sara didn't mind the baby talk. In fact, it felt right. "I dreamed that dad was here too with us," she replied. "That we had a family again."

"Did you?" Tessa shot her a coy look. Her daughter often knew far more than she let on. "You aren't just saying that because you know I felt him too? And yes, I know it was a dream, but he seemed so close, like he was watching over us. Do you think he knows where we are? I'd be shocked to think he left us without any kind of a plan for us. That's not really like him."

"Well," Sara began, "to be honest, I never really got to know him all that much. And it's not like the Font gives me a real clear picture either. If he's really related to the Fish Man, what we see of him isn't really what he is. What do you think? Do you think we can trust him?"

Tessa wrinkled her brow. "You know, we didn't really get to finish our conversation from the other night. I got the impression that there was something you weren't telling me. Let's start with the big questions. He is alive, isn't he? Do you know that much?"

"Mom..." Sara hesitated, "I'm not sure I should..." The look on Tessa's face was too much for Sara. "Um, well. Yes. Yes he is." Sara sat up, facing her mother. "But we need to stop there. He's a dangerous subject to pursue. There's far more to him than even you are aware. He's a being of great power, and I believe he only ever really showed us a single facet of that. And there are powerful foes looking for him, some of the same that are after us. If they know that we know where he is, we could be in even more danger."

Tessa's look hardened. Some of that old love and wistfulness was still there, but the hurt and deprivation overpowered it. "Ok. So where is he?"

"Mom, I just said that's a dangerous subject, didn't you listen? I don't think I should tell you that."

"Sara." Tessa's eyes narrowed. There is a way a mother can say her child's name that says more than words can explain.

"Ok! Ok!" Sara didn't really want to hold back anyway. "But it's complicated. Like I said, there's more to him than you realize. He's not just hiding in a cave somewhere. If I think about where he is, I get seven distinct answers. It's even pretty hard to focus on any one of them, as they all come in at once. It's like a symbol of light bent through a prism. But I can figure it out if I concentrate. I do know one of these places is me, and another is you. So in a way, he is here with us, I guess."

"What's that supposed to mean?" Tessa seemed surprised. "One of his many locations is me? Where in me? Inside me?"

"Well, no, not like that." Sara concentrated to figure out how to explain this to her mother in a way she would understand. "I told you he's more than you realize, and far older. You're thinking of him as a person, with a physical form. But he's beyond that. He's more of a concept than a being. I think the idea of him is within you, since he touched your life. But only a part of him, since you only ever really knew a part of him. Same with me."

"A part?" Tessa protested, "But he's my husband."

"Was," Sara clarified. "'Until death do us part.' Remember that? The part of him you knew really did die, and then it passed into you and became part of you. I do believe that was his final part as well. The rest were already spread out. Since that death he has not existed in any form."

"Hmm." Tessa was a little hurt, but seemed to have gotten something from the explanation. She paused, and Sara could see the conflict in her, but finally reason won out. "Ok. So where are the other locations? Are they all someone your father knew too?"

"Well, the third location is in this realm. It corresponds to a maiden located in the city of the fair folk just ahead, but of course her connection with father, if there is one, would have been erased from the Font. The fourth location corresponds to Adam, the Fish Man's Neverknight. The one that helped us defeat him. I don't know why father would know him, but if the Fish Man is father's kin in a sense, father could have had some hand in the creation of Adam's powers. The fifth is less of a link; it lines up with a great inventor in one of the mortal realms." Sara thought for a bit. "I can tell you that all three of these people have missing time in the Font. Kind of like Jonathan does from when we went to Ha..." Sara could sense the chimera's upper left ear trained on her. "Kind of like Jonathan does," she reiterated.

"But that's only five, Sara," Tessa seemed more fascinated than upset now. "You said there were seven."

"The other two are obscured somehow. One corresponds to a terrible monster, but I can't really see him. All I see is darkness. He seems to eat the knowledge of the people around him. I could go deeper there, but the more I see the more I don't want to see any more. I'm not ready for him. I really don't think he's connected to father though. There's something I'm missing there. As for the last one, well, I don't know. The answer seems to shift every time I focus on it. Sometimes I get the impression it's in this realm too."

"Hmm..." Tessa's mind began to churn. Sara instinctively tuned into it, following its processes and discovering exactly what Tessa was going to say even before she said it.

"I know it's dangerous to look for father," Sara pleaded, "even to think about it, but we're already in danger. I don't know that he could make it any worse."

"But, Sara..."

"No, look. If anyone can help us out of this, it's him. I mean, I know I have all the answers, but the problem is I don't really have the right questions. He understands what we're up against. In fact, he's up against it himself. I'm sure he could use our help as much as we can use his."

Tessa smirked. "You know, Sara, I have my own reasons for wanting to see him again, but if you just want him for information, then you are not only missing the point, but missing the obvious. You want the questions? Just ask the Font what the right questions to ask it are."

"Mom!" Sara rolled her eyes. "If you really had access to this thing at some point, you sure didn't understand it much. I can't do that. It doesn't work that way. That's like the whole predicting the future thing. The Font doesn't know the future, and even if it did, most of the time it'd be wrong. Besides, I do want to see dad again just as much as you do, but right now I just want to get us out of danger. Now, if you have any real questions, I'm open to them. I've run out of lines of knowledge."

Tessa nodded and thought for a bit. Then she raised an eyebrow. "Does each location contain a particular part of your father?" She asked.

"Um, that's kind of silly, but...." Sara closed her eyes briefly. "Yes. Actually, yes they do." She seemed surprised. "Not in a physical sense, though; father's not a physical being. The location you occupy carries his heart and his love. I seem to correspond to his knowledge. The Neverknight exists along with his courage and will. The inventor, of course, seems to have father's creativity. The fairy maiden has his intuition. And the other two are harder to pin down. His sensuality, for lack of a better word, seems to lie within the shadow creature. That's the closest thing he has to a physical presence. The last one is the trickiest, but I think it has something to do with his caution, maybe a form of introspection I'd guess." Sara drew a quick breath from having spoken so quickly. "What all that means exactly, I can't say. The knowledge may be in me, but I don't really have the right link to follow to get to it. Look at it this way—I wouldn't have been able to see any of this if the a... if I hadn't been told father's true name. That name was like a bridge to more knowledge. When I was a kid and thought about my father, all I got was how he was a dockworker who died young. There may be other missing bridge pieces out there. Something simple that can help me put more facts together. What that would be, I don't know. Something that would give me new questions to ask."

Tessa touched her daughter's arm softly. "Don't try to get everything at once, Sara. Besides, I think we have all the knowledge we need right now."

"Huh? What do you mean..." but before Sara even finished the question, she realized she could just look into her mother's mind.

"Sara, your father didn't commit suicide. He wouldn't have broken himself up without a purpose or a plan to return to his true state. You were an infant when he left. Your missing knowledge was erased only to ensure that you didn't try to find him until you were ready. If anyone has the knowledge you need it's the people that knew him. We just need to gather them all together in one place and see what happens. I have no doubt that the way to bring him back is locked in you somewhere. Just think of these people as six keys to your lock. We can do this."

Sara pursed her lips in thought. "But mom, that's just going to be impossible. The seven locations are scatted across all creation, and some of these people I don't think will even want to cooperate with us. And getting from one realm to another isn't just a trivial matter. You think if it were that easy we wouldn't have rescued Adam by now? Even if we weren't being hunted, lining up all seven locations would be a difficult prospect, but with the watchers on our trail, it's just absurd to even consider. There has to be another way."

Tessa smiled and hugged Sara. "Come on now, Sara. Anything's impossible if you don't try. What do we have to lose here? And look, we don't have to do it all at once. You said the third location was just nearby? You think that's a coincidence? Perhaps I'm old-fashioned, but I'd call it fate. We're going there anyway; what harm would it be to follow up on this lead? Just breathe and take it one step at a time. Besides, you are forgetting you are part of a team here. And a pretty good team, I might add." Tessa looked around her. "If anyone can sort out this mess, it's these friends of yours."

Jonathan wasn't even bothering to pretend to not be listening at this point. He grinned in response to Tessa's words. The bird, Chopin, was nested neatly in the chimera's spiky mane. Sara looked over at the cat, the only thing still sleeping in this extended dawn. His tail was slowly sweeping through the air, tapping the ground in time to the rhythm of the trees.

9

~

HEROES' WELCOME

Dawn turned slowly into spectacular day. The warm sunlight seemed to pierce every gloomy corner of the forest, sweeping away the shadows and the lurking dangers. It was as if a cloud of malice had been lifted from the land and Fairy finally fully welcomed the five unlikely travelers. The croaks of the frogs and the drone of the cicadas gradually faded, giving way to the lazy twitter of birds. One by one, songbirds of all stripes began to settle onto the slow-moving wagon, their song sung as if in honor of the travelers' victory.

"I swear, this thing is getting heavier!" Jonathan puffed as he trundled forward, the yoke of the wagon gripped firmly behind him in his bony pincers.

"I swear our chimera is getting lazier," El Gato retorted, "after all, we just dropped the little rabbit off with his family, that should have lightened your load." The cat tugged the reins sharply to the right. A distinct circle of clearance could be seen around El Gato, the only area of the wagon where the birds had not settled.

"Look," the chimera sighed, "I told you, you don't need to do that. I can see where the road goes. Besides, if you need me to stop or go the other way, you can just tell me. Explain to me again why we couldn't get the boar to do this?"

The cat glanced back at the massive boar curled up in the back of the wagon, its stinky bulk wrapped around the firmly bound form of its master. As El Gato turned, the blanket of birds shrank back from him another six inches.

"He refused to budge," Sara interjected. "Besides, if there is any kind of an ambush, you need to be able to fight without having to worry about the wagon full of your friends careening off into the woods full tilt."

El Gato turned back around. The songbirds resettled. "You know, I am getting kind of hungry," the cat hissed under his breath.

"Don't you dare." Sara flicked his ear for the thought. "And not just because they saved me from the wolf. You know better than to eat a songbird in Fairy. You won't be able to speak for a month."

"A month? Oh, come on. You're just making that one up," grumbled the cat.

"Oh am I?" Sara replied, raising an eyebrow. "It's part of the general laws of the forest. It comes right after 'needing to take your hat off when talking to a gnome' in the Codex Sylvanus."

"Codex what?" the cat responded, incredulously.

"OK, here we go again," Tessa interrupted from the top of the wagon, "more of these arbitrary rules. You know, I don't understand how anyone manages to survive here. No eating, no sleeping, no stepping off the path, no giving gifts... I thought Fairy was supposed to be fun."

Sara pursed her lips. "It's a different world, mom. It's got its own rules. They aren't arbitrary; they're natural laws. You can't judge Fairy by Earth standards." Sara paused for a moment. "Look, imagine one of the fair folk were to suddenly port into the middle of New York City. Someone tells it 'Hey, you can't walk in the middle of the street, only on the side.' That would seem pretty arbitrary. And then you're walking along and suddenly everybody stops for no reason, just because some little thing on the other side of the street is red instead of green. Then you see a woman who looks upset and you put your arm around her to comfort her, only to have the cops start running after you. And don't even get me started on the subway. See, just because you don't understand something doesn't mean it doesn't have weight." Sara paused and studied her mother, who was still quite unsatisfied despite the explanation. After a moment, Sara continued, "OK, look, we have another quarter-hour before we reach the city; maybe this is a good time to go over some of these rules with everyone. We need to stick together; the time differences alone could screw up all our plans if we don't know what we're doing."

Tessa shrugged, not entirely convinced by Sara's arguments. "Well, it can't hurt to go over the basics," she stated.

"It's hard to generalize here," Sara began, "the laws can change from place to place, much like on Earth, and there's really a lot of grey area between good manners and making a grave mistake. Let's start with this one. Laughter. If you don't know what to do in a situation, you can always laugh. Unless you are talking to the Queen, but that's a whole different matter. Fairies are a jovial folk who like to live a pleasant life without suffering fools who take everything too seriously. Laugh and you can flatter a fairy who tells a story, laugh and you can break the tension. Open your mouth and speak, and you are bound to say the wrong thing. Laughter is talking without words. Although it probably should sound real. Maybe we should practice." Sara took a small sip of water, then snorted halfway through and spit a broad spray over El Gato.

Chopin twittered and Tessa let out a rollicking belly laugh. "Not bad," said Sara, "almost convincing." Jonathan let out a tremendous off-key bray, like a sick donkey. "How about you just play the strong, silent type," Sara remarked.

"OK," Sara continued, "now let's go over a few ground rules. Always bow or curtsey when meeting someone new. Do not shake hands. Pay attention when crossing water or going over bridges; if possible we should always do this together. Having a pointy appearance will help you blend in better. A pointy hat or pointy shoes are a good start. Don't talk about money. The fair folk abhor money and find it degrading...."

"Wait, what?" Jonathan interrupted.

"Money," Sara reiterated. "Don't talk about money."

"Well how do you buy something here?" Jonathan asked, confused.

"Buy? Like what?" Sara asked.

"I dunno. Like food, or clothes, or a place to stay for the night. You know, anything."

"It's complicated," Sara sighed. "You either trade something else or you get them to give it to you without strings attached. But never let anyone give you something without stating it's a free gift; that is essentially an open-ended trade. You agree to the trade and imply that you are willing to give whatever the other person wants whenever they choose to take it."

"OK," said Jonathan, "oddly enough that makes some sense. But what can you trade? Isn't that just essentially money?"

"No," Sara answered, "money has no value in and of itself, that is the difference. You can't eat money, use it to fix your roof, clothe yourself with it—well, not properly—or entertain yourself with it. All you can do is trade it for something else. So if you give money here, you are essentially trading something of no value for something of value, and then you get stuck in the gifting thing again."

"Right, exactly," the cat interrupted, "but the question was 'what can you trade?'"

"Oh, right," Sara continued. "Anything really. It just needs to be something the other party wants. You can give them food, clothing, art, clean their house, harvest their fields, give herbs from the forest. Whatever you can think of."

"Ok, so what are we planning on doing when we get to this town," Jonathan countered, "we don't have anything to trade. I mean, I'm hardly in the mood to go cleaning someone's house or plow their fields right now."

"Well," Sara said, "knowledge is a commodity in any place, and I have as much as we could ever need. That is our most valuable treasure. But I don't think it's wise to show our true natures so readily." Sara looked around at the wagon. Most of the belongings were junk. Broken lanterns and spoiled ointments. "Well, we have the redcap," Sara pondered, "but you can't really trade people. Or at least we don't want to go down that road."

"Not true," whistled Chopin. "Fair folk offer great reward. Anyone who brings in the bandit that eats travelers. This is a very good trade."

"Hail travelers!" The golden voice rang out gently but loud, catching everyone by surprise. "This is a most unusual craft and steed. What is your business here in the city of Nod?" Twenty feet above and just ahead of them, balanced gracefully on a sturdy branch across the road, stood a radiant knight, slight but fair, with golden leaf armor, almond eyes, and long, pointed ears. He held a staff that looked like a living flower, but Sara knew that its thorny point was as sharp as any spear.

"Good day, sir knight!" Sara stood up on the seat of the wagon and curtseyed; she had formed a simple dress out of the organic suit. "We are travelers. Yes, our mode of travel is strange, but we are training my young dragon here. We seek shelter for a time in your fair city, and wish to partake in your festivals and peruse your markets. And..." Sara paused for dramatic effect, "we come bearing the scourge of the black road, captured alive and ready to be presented to your Lady." She swept her hand back and waved at the redcap, who writhed and did its best to turn invisible, though to no avail. The songbirds parted to give the guard a clear look.

The guardsman's eyes widened. "Indeed," he responded. "Well, this is a pleasure in truth. We have awaited this hour for many a long day." The guard bowed to Sara. "I am afraid we do not welcome dragons in our city, but our Lady is sure to make an exception in your case. He is not ill-tempered, is he?"

"Do not worry," Sara responded, "he is fully ensorcelled to my will. Jonathan," she barked, "dance!"

"What?" Jonathan's voice came only in Sara's mind. Sara took the reins from the cat and gave them a jerk. The chimera broke into a clumsy improvised routine, spinning on his toes like a ballerina, and then kicking his feet out like a Russian folk dancer. He ended with his arms thrown wide.

The elf seemed satisfied. He nodded to a golden eagle hidden nearby in the foliage, and the bird took off, speeding in the direction of the city. The guard raised his spear and waved his hand. "Your way is prepared, milady. Go with our blessing. And know that our Lady will welcome you in person. This is a bold catch, and there is ever a place here for those such as you."

The wagon drove onward, and it became soon quite evident that their coming had been announced. Sprites flew up and gawked at them. A family of rabbits chanted "Hip, hip, hurrah!" as they passed. Even a few brave gnomes came out from the trees and followed behind them. More birds flocked to their side, and dryads began to come out of the woods to curtsey. Within a few minutes, the wagon had become a parade. And finally, the city came into view.

Jonathan had expected a great clearing of flowers with a grand city in the center, but this was not the case. Through the shadows he could see up ahead what looked like a great wall of living silver, nestled amongst the trees of the forest and stretching high into the sky. "It's silver-vein ivy over stone," Sara answered, reading his mind. "The fair folk never kill a plant in order to build. They simply redirect nature itself to do what they want.

Within the city, the tops of ornate palaces could now be seen over the wall, with colorful flags streaming from their pinnacles. From the city, cheering could be heard, and the fair folk spilled out onto the road to greet them. The road up ahead ran across a simple arched bridge over what appeared to be a forest brook and then ended in a massive golden gate. Sara seemed apprehensive. "Do not be afraid, but we must stay together when we cross here," she hissed. "It is not what it appears."

Jonathan inched a bit closer to the wagon as he pulled it over the bridge. It did seem to take longer to cross than he thought it should have, but there were no ill effects, so he put it behind him and headed to the gate. The enormous golden portcullis marked the official entrance to the city of Nod, and it was flanked by two great, lofty oaks, serving as towers in the city wall. The gate itself was over forty feet high and appeared to be made of solid gold bars, reinforced with silver chains. As the travelers approached, a great clanking sound was heard, and the gate began slowly to rise up into the wall above.

Colored streamers passed over their heads as they passed through the gate and into the grand marketplace of Nod. Colorful booths made of silk-draped saplings ringed the town square, each one indicating their wares via the use of painted banners made without words. All manner of goods were on display, from potions to pillows to petit fours. The people of Nod raised glasses in honor of the victorious travelers, and songs began to ring out. Bursts of golden glitter caught the sunlight as they were tossed over the heads of the newcomers.

The people of Nod were tall and slender, with hair the color of flowers and thin, elegant faces that gave no hint of age. Their clothes were ornate and flowing, and their voices smooth and delicate. Though they seemed friendly, they still made Jonathan nervous. "What am I supposed to be doing here?" he asked Sara, speaking directly into her mind.

"Just smile and wave," Sara whispered to him above the din. "You'll see soon enough."

After but a moment, the noise of the crowd began to hush. The people still seemed joyful, but their eyes looked to the sky, where the tallest spire in the city grew—a great white twisted tusk, like that of a continent-sized narwhal. A gasp went over the crowd as a small golden figure appeared from the top. It hovered in place for a moment above the city and then began drifting slowly downwards like a falling blossom. As the figure approached, the travelers could see that it indeed was the great fair Lady of the city herself, gliding towards them on gossamer wings.

Jonathan had never seen such a vision of female beauty. Even Tessa seemed to be enraptured with her presence. The Lady of Nod was slighter than the elves, as if more finely made. Her gossamer gown matched her lace wings and flowed down past her feet, making her appear much larger than she likely was. Her hair seemed to be made of silk, and blossoms bloomed along its length, flowing out of her as if delicate vines from a living plant. When she spoke, her voice soothed all who heard it, filling the square with peace and softness.

"To whom does Nod owe its honor?" the Lady asked, looking clearly now upon the ragged and filthy wagon as the birds scattered away and took up new roosts atop the market stalls.

"I am Sara." Sara replied, her mind racing rapidly through the ties that bound this great Lady to this place. Sara curtseyed. "And this is my mother," she finally added. Sara knew that it was simply an invisible pollen that came off of the great Lady that was so intoxicating, but still, she had trouble resisting its effects.

"And how then, Sara," the Lady remarked, "did you and your mother come to take the blood-road marauder? I understand you command the services of a dragon, but I see naught but a feeble hatchling and a cat." The Lady waved her hand and several guards came forward to take the goblin from the wagon. The boar leaped up and roared at them as they came to take its master, but Sara called to it in the goblin tongue, reassuring it. The guards took the redcap to a small marble stage at the edge of the square where a set of sturdy iron stocks stood empty. The boar took a prominent position at the foot of the stage as its master was placed into the stocks.

"It was mere luck, Lady," Sara responded. "We were simply passing through the wood and ran afoul of this charlatan. My mother and I had been separated, so the goblin did not know that I followed close behind. I distracted the monster, but I must say much of the honor belongs to the brave Chopin here. We could not have done it without him."

"Nonsense," a twittering little voice broke in, "Dame Sara is as skilled as she is humble. It went more like this...." And the little bluebird flew forward and bowed to the Lady of the city in midair. "If I may, my Lady," he tweeted, and then flapped out a dramatic but rather accurate account of the whole affair. Chopin took the part of Sara, and other birds flew in as needed to stand in for the other players. When he came to the part where Tessa clobbered the redcap, the great Lady furrowed her brow.

"A pan? Brilliant. Cold-forged iron to the crown, as effective a remedy as could be devised. But do you mean to tell me, little bird, that our new friends conquered the marauder without even employing the services of her dragon?"

"It is all true, my lady!" the bird chirped.

"Hmm... the great Lady looked over the travelers. These two must be great witches indeed. They obviously have much knowledge but are still able to conceal their true natures from me, presenting only the appearance of weak, foolish, ill-prepared mortals. Such skill is an extraordinary rarity, and so it is with great pleasure that I proclaim Sara and mother Tessa heroes of Nod, along with their bold familiars Jonathan and the cat! Show them your welcome!"

The crowd began again to cheer. As the shout went around, a break formed in the ranks and a small train of robed figures came forward, bearing some small items atop two silken pillows.

"Sara, knight of Nod, step forward," the great Lady announced. Sara stepped toward the monks and paused before the relics. "Since you have shown great clarity of thought and great courage, you are granted the gift of water." The monks presented one of the silken pillows to Sara. On it was nestled a silver flask. "Behold, the flask that never runs dry!" the Lady purred. Sara lifted the object off of the pillow. It was lighter than it looked, no more than a feather in her hand. She removed the top and fresh water began to pour out. She caught it with her hand and tasted it. It was delicious. Pure and essential.

"Thank you, milady," Sara said. She curtseyed to the Lady and to the monks. This was a great honor indeed.

"Tessa, knight of Nod, step forward!" Tessa followed Sara's lead. Though she was older and wiser, she had none of Sara's insight into this drama, and far more trepidation. "Since you have shown great strength and great capacity for action, you are rewarded with the gift of food." Tessa lifted a small leather bag off of the pillow presented to her. It was also light, perhaps as heavy as a roll of bread, and the ancient cord came unknotted easily as she pulled on it with her fingers. Inside the bag was a golden-brown honey seedcake, about the size of a hockey puck. Though the cake weighed about as much as the bag, the bag did not seem to have gotten lighter, and as Tessa put her hand back in, another seed cake came out. She reached in again, and came out with a third. She brought one of the cakes to her mouth, and when she saw Sara nodding she took a bite. It was sweet yet hearty, and considerably more filling than it looked.

"Thank you," Tessa murmured, bowing to the great Lady of the city.

"Your gifts are granted to you freely, having been paid in full by the capture of the murderer of the black wood," the Lady explained. "Use them well. You have come to our rescue, and as we help you, there is no doubt that the circle will bring you around again to help us when fate strikes. But put that behind you; today we celebrate your arrival."

The Lady clapped her hands. "A feast!" she shouted, and the crowd went wild at the suggestion. Wine was spilled, jigs danced, and cheers made as the crowd gathered around the newcomers and pulled them towards the center of the city.

In the confusion of the mob, Sara somehow found herself separated from the others. The streets had become narrow, and seeing the layout of the city in her mind, she slipped away from the revelers and took a shortcut through an alleyway. As she parted from the crowd, she noticed a small, masked, green-cloaked figure moving after her. This person was no bigger than Sara herself and did not seem a threat, but also did not seem to be much interested in dancing or revels. "Lady Sara," the figure whispered in a girl's voice as it caught her wrist. Sara whirled around.

Before Sara could query the stranger, the green mask was taken away and the heavy cloak dropped to the ground. There, before Sara, stood her double—a girl bearing her exact features, only replete with pointed ears and gossamer wings.

10

~~

SISTERS

"Sister," Sara gasped. "You're my half-sister."

"Indeed, your gift does you credit," her sister resounded in a voice that mirrored Sara's almost perfectly. "I had feared that you might think me a doppelganger come to replace you, but no, what I have foreseen is true. You carry the Font of All Knowledge with you. You cannot be deceived; all creation is an open book to you."

Sara almost protested; she knew better than anyone that she could indeed be deceived, tricked, and even surprised. It had never occurred to her that her father, being a creature as old as time, might have other children. She could now see the life of her half-sister starting to unfold, but she held back in taking it all in. She wanted to hear it from her lips.

"We could be twins if not for your fairy features," Sara remarked. She smiled and took her sister's hands. The two of them twirled around, taking each other in.

"I have so waited to meet you since I first learned of your birth."

Sara wondered at that—they looked the same age, but then she knew the answer to the mystery right off. "You're almost three hundred years old," Sara gasped. Fairies did not age like other beings and were virtually immortal—they could be killed by violence or they could fade if they gave into autumn, but they never showed age like humans, remaining eternally young and beautiful. Sara's sister might even be more so, being the half-daughter of a fairy and an ancient being. It suddenly struck Sara that she herself might not age like others due to her father, and at once she knew it to be true to some degree. She would age normally until adulthood and then it would slow. Though how much slower she would age and in what respects involved so many factors. After all, her father had been human when he had been with her mother, yet a genetically perfect human, with no unhealthy traits and with cells that could regenerate far better and more effectively than others. Still, her mother's side had a history of heart disease and cancer—all factors that might affect cellular degradation....

"Where is your amazing mind taking you to right now Sara?" her sister asked, and Sara was pulled back by the question.

"Sorry, I am prone to distraction," Sara blushed, "hazard of the gift."

"I understand. I often lose myself when I use my own talents."

"Talents?" and Sara immediately knew. Her half-sister was a seer, gifted with the power to scan forward though all of the millions of diverging paths and see possible outcomes of the future. "You're a seer."

"Yes, but we jump too far too fast. May I have the honor of telling you my own tale?" her sister asked.

"Of course." Sara smiled and decided to do her best not to let her gift get her ahead of actually getting to know her long-lost sister. "I always wanted a big sister; I used to dream about it all the time."

"Well this is Fairy; perhaps you dreamed me to life." Her sister led her to a nearby bench and the two sat down, still hand in hand. "Tell me, in your dream, what was your sister's name?"

"Aras," and the moment she said it, Sara knew it was indeed her sister's name, both because of her gift and also because of the smile that came to her sister's face. "But I did not dream you to life; you're older than me. The name thing is just my gift working on a subconscious level."

"Is that what your gift tells you?" Aras asked.

"Well, yes."

"But you asked the question from a scientific point of view. A view reflecting where you have come from. You do not even realize the distinction—it is implied because it is your belief system," Aras said, brushing Sara's hair out of her face. "Perhaps it is just as true that you dreamed me into being and so I am, and that, being a fairy, time does not hold sway for me. Or perhaps you simply dreamed of an older sister, so I am."

"What?" Sara's gasped. "No that's not how it works, or at least I don't think that's how my gift works. It gives me the real answers, not ones that assume my internal beliefs or perspective." But suddenly Sara wasn't so sure if all her questions weren't colored by unspoken personal beliefs about how the universe worked. If the Font answered her within the limiting boundaries of her own bias, then she often might not have gotten the whole picture. But no, her scientific understanding had been confirmed over and over in the responses that she got. There was a rhyme and a reason for everything, and she had not just dreamed her sister into existence.

Aras saw the twisted look that came over her sister's face and smiled kindly, "I am not trying to confuse you, only open you to other possibilities. It is in my nature to be a creature of intuition and instinct rather than fact and science. The two are not mutually exclusive; they can in fact work in concert together, creating a rare symmetry that can lead to what many call genius."

"So you're admitting I did not dream you into life," Sara sighed, relieved.

"I am willing to concede that there are other possibilities, such as the story I am about to tell you." Sara could see that Aras was about to tell her the truth about how she was born and how she came to be here to meet her, but why did she call it a "possibility"? Her sister was going to be more challenging to be around than El Gato.

"Our father came here to Fairy over three hundred years ago," Aras began. "He was a refugee of sorts; his worldship had been taken from him and he needed a place far away from those who would seek to rein him in—a place where he could have the time and peace to decide his next move. He was badly hurt when he arrived here, and taking a mortal form brought him almost to the point of death. It was my mother who first found him and sheltered him. She cared for him and hid him while he regained his strength."

Sara let her mind see it all as her sister told her, trying to allow the knowledge to come to her at the same speed in which the story was relayed. It was a great comfort to be hearing something about her father at long last and not have to fear that in asking she might bring danger down upon him.

"Once he was healed, he took up residence here in Fairy, and along with the aid of other friends, he slowly but surely hatched a plan to undo his masters. All the while he courted my mother. She made him wait a decade before she kissed him for the first time. They loved as only immortals dare, but father had a course, a purpose, and after thirty years with my mother, he could no longer delay that destiny further. Before he went, he blessed her with a child—me—and then he was gone."

Sara knew this story, only told through a different set of lives. Briefly she wondered if her father had left a trail of children throughout creation, but the answer was quick in coming; she and her sister were the only offspring. Still, Sara now had a sibling who knew all too well what it was like to grow up without a father.

"Our father thought my mother and me safe here in the free fair lands. He must have, or he would never have done what he did next. He found his worldship—the one he had been stripped of for refusing to do as his master demanded. He broke it with the aid of the Starsailor and then stole the Font of all Knowledge. We did not know what he had done then; we only knew that he had to stay far away from us so as not to involve us in the peril he had invited upon himself. But it was not to be." Aras paused, and Sara saw the pain that flashed across the oddly familiar face. "They came hunting father— dark things with blazing eyes. My mother was a great lady of the twilight kingdoms; she used her powers to conceal me and met them unafraid. For all their power and all their blackness, they were no match for her, and she burnt them and struck them down with her silver blade. Until it came—dark upon dark, teeth and claws and eyes...."

Sara saw it briefly in her mind's eye, and it hurt, like drinking a milkshake too fast, like nails on a chalkboard, like looking into the eyes of the Fish Man. She pushed the image from her mind, unable to bear to consider it.

"It killed my mother before my eyes, and it would have found me and destroyed me had it not been for the arrival of the inventor—a bold friend of our father who, under instruction from the Starsailor, had come to save us. Too late for my mother, he saved only me and fled. I was his ward and daughter for many years, until one night our father came to me in a dream. In it he told me that I had a sister; that she was blessed with all the knowledge he held, and that now he must gift me as well with all of his intuition. When I woke, I could see all the possibilities that lay ahead. I could follow a path of choices to its end. I was a seer. The inventor took this as a sign; he gave me a necklace—this very necklace."

She held it up and Sara saw it was golden and expertly crafted. From the swirling golden chain hung a pendant with seven dull gems that seemed off in comparison to the brilliance of the rest of the necklace.

"The great inventor told me to hold on to the necklace and that one day my sister would know what to do with it. I was to wait for you, but I could not. In too many futures I saw danger come for you and your mother. I could not sit still and just let you suffer the same fate as me. I resolved to come to you and protect you. In looking out for you, I failed to see the danger to myself and I was captured before I could make it to your side."

Sara again felt a rush of the familiar. She knew all too well the pitfalls of powerful gifts and of failing to see all ends of a problem.

Aras continued. "I was taken by the Mongrel, the very creature I had hoped to protect you from." Sara could hear the hatred in her sister's voice, the same as in hers or Jonathan's when the Fish Man was spoken of. "I was too valuable as a seer to be destroyed, so I was put to work on the worldship as one of many prognosticators and prophets they employed to read the future. They had ways of knowing if you lied, but it did not mean that I could not withhold information. I saw that you would be placed next to the chimera, and I saw that you would free each other. I even saw that you would destroy the worldship and set me free. Yet I failed to see that it was all part of a darker plan."

Sara heard the same shame in her sister that she and Jonathan had felt far too many times since falling for the Fish Man's plot.

"Still, all is not lost," Aras smiled widely. "Our father is very wise, and he meant for us to be together one day, and here at last we are."

The two sisters embraced. Sara did not know that she had ever met someone with whom she shared so much. She wanted to pour out her heart to Aras, to tell her everything, to let her know that she understood.

"I know," Aras said before Sara could say anything. And Sara knew that she did know.

They stayed there for a time, silently comforting each other, both with tears in their eyes, and when at last they pulled away, Aras produced a small handkerchief and wiped Sara's eyes.

It was then that Sara turned her focus back to the necklace. She reached out and touched it and was about to ask the Font about it when a sudden burst of noise cut her off.

"There you are!" Jonathan yelled, crashing around the corner. "Your mother is worried sick about you! Where have you been?" As the chimera noticed Aras, he did a double-take, his ears sinking back in confusion. "Why are there two of you?"

"Jonathan," Sara said, standing and motioning towards Aras, "this is my half-sister, Aras."

"Your half what?" exclaimed the chimera.

"Her half-sister." And without hesitation, Aras walked right up and offered her hand, palm down, to Jonathan, who timidly shook it. Then suddenly realizing that this was Fairy, he instead knelt and kissed her hand, blushing a bright shade of red. Hoping to change the subject, he turned to Sara. "Your mother will be worried," he squeaked.

"Let's not keep her waiting," Aras interjected. "I would very much like to meet her." Aras, without waiting, began to walk towards the square. Pipers could now be heard coming from the town center, haunting and enticing, but playing slowly.

Sara knew this was a gathering song. Other formalities would have to wait for later. She rose and fell in behind her sister, contemplating just how her mother might take this news. Jonathan brought up the rear. In Sara's mind she could hear his voice, "Your sister has wings."

"She is half fairy," Sara returned through the link.

By the time they had reached the square, the music had become much more urgent. Other pipers had joined in the harmonies, and some fairies were beating on great copper bowls, filled partly with water to produce different bass notes. The fair folk were gathering, and the great Lady floated in the center of the square, tossing handfuls of glittering dust on the gatherers. Wherever the dust landed, those around it began to dance and laugh.

Sara did not need to worry about where her mother might be; she knew immediately where to find her. Across the square, she could make out the familiar figure pacing furiously back and forth before a stone bench. The star-chested cat sat on the bench licking at a colorful sweet cake. From time to time, he mewed bleakly at Tessa, hoping to calm her down. At the sight of Jonathan approaching and waving, Tessa's face lit up. She ran towards Sara, shouting at her for being foolish enough to separate herself from the group yet again. But it wasn't Sara. Tessa's jaw dropped in confusion and astonishment when she saw the pointed ears and the almond eyes. Then behind this imposter, Tessa finally saw her true daughter. But before she could move to scold her, a glitter of dust fell about Tessa's face and the world fell away.

The dancers moved to the speed of the music, weaving in and out of one another, creating intricate patterns that changed with the harmonies. This was a three-dimensional dance (and maybe more), with winged dancers moving up, down, and across the circle. Though Jonathan was not familiar with the dance, his body seemed to know the pattern. Despite his size, the other dancers did not seem to mind him. They passed him as any other in the dance, twirling and spinning him, touching and embracing him as they went by. The feeling was exhilarating; something in the dance caused his adrenaline to flow, exciting him, accelerating him, and filling him with a wild euphoria. He could feel his place in the dance and his body responded naturally; this was a feeling he had rarely experienced—one of belonging.

Tessa felt the thrill as well, but for her it was more the excitement of terror—of being in a precarious and foreign situation and not being able to stop herself from flinging herself headlong into it. The dance was exhausting, but primal and irresistible. Tessa felt fully engaged in it on all levels, and as her mind relaxed to focus on the patterns and the music and the pleasure, her body slipped away from her. She experienced a sense of painlessness, of being a creature of pure spirit—one joined to a higher consciousness. Soon she had forgotten all about her daughter, their predicament, and the mysterious stranger, and knew only of the dance.

Sara had a harder time fitting in. Her mind was too big to turn off, to drift away, and she found herself tripping and falling, colliding with the other dancers. As the faces flew by her, each identity popped up into her brain, their stories beginning to unfold and then being interrupted by another and then another. Here was tiny Mab, the midwife of the fair folk, and here was Robin Goodfellow, smiling and pinching her as he went by. And now she could see the chimera in the full glory of his physical nature, spinning and twirling through the crowd like an acrobat. She saw her sister blended in with the crowd, completely at home in the proceedings. She even saw the bluebird Chopin, rolling through the air like a stunt pilot. And here was her mother, grinning and sweating, doing her very best to keep up with the fairy dance, and enjoying every moment of it. Only the cat remained an outsider. She could see him crouched under the food table, eyeing the proceedings with caution. Suddenly, an elf slammed into Sara at high speed, leaving a deep gouge in her arm from his ornate jewelry. She could not feel the wound—she felt only a pleasant buzz, but she could see the blood flicking here and there. Something wasn't right.

The dance had been slowly speeding up until it was now a pure frenzy. Her mother was drenched in sweat, and Sara could sense bruises and cuts on her as well. She caught a glimpse of her in the crowd, and her clothes were torn and ripped. Though Sara could no longer feel her own body, she knew that her tendons were straining too hard—these human bodies were not suited to move this speed. Jonathan. Sara saw him go by in the crowd and she flung herself upon him, clinging to his narrow waist. Instantly she was jerked off her feet, and she thought she would spin out of control, but she held on tighter and kept her grip.

"What are you doing?" he sent to her through her mind. He seemed angry with her.

"Stop! Now!" Sara shouted to him on all wavelengths. Despite the odds, Jonathan stepped out of the circle and stopped, if only to pull Sara off of him so that he could rejoin the dance. "Wait," Sara called, frantically, "I need you!"

"What is it with you?" Jonathan shouted above the din, his irritation showing easily. "Can't anyone ever have any fun around you?"

"It's not me," Sara said, trying not to let the chimera's altered tone get to her, "it's my mother. She can't take the strain. We're not built like you."

Jonathan finally saw Tessa twirl by. Her clothes were in tatters and her body was covered in bruises.

"There's no way to get her attention," Sara moaned. "I need you to get her."

Jonathan understood what he had to do. He rejoined the dance, waiting for his pattern to cross with Tessa's. The trick was not to lose himself again until he found her.

Soon enough, Jonathan emerged from the dome-shaped blur of the dance holding a struggling Tessa. He set her down on the stone bench and she leapt back up again, flinging herself towards the dancers. As she ran, she twirled, and her dizziness sent her sprawling onto the cobblestones. She did not move for quite a while after that.

*****

Tessa awoke to the most incredible body aches. Her mouth was parched, and her clothes—or what was left of them—were soaked through with sweat. Sara knelt before her on the bench and bound her cuts with strips of tattered cloth. Behind her again stood the doppelganger, and Tessa's brow furrowed with confusion that blended into the pain.

"It's ok, Mom, Jonathan got you in time. You are going to be sore for a seriously long time though." Sara cleared her throat. "There's someone you need to meet. This is my half-sister, Aras. She's the one we came here to find."

"Sister?" Tessa's eyes burned, and a large vein stood out on her forehead.

"Yes," Sara confirmed, "she is father's daughter. From three hundred years ago. Born long before you were even in the picture." Sara's tone was patronizing, as if to remind her mother whose land they were in.

"Oh." Tessa didn't quite know what to say. She stared at this strange likeness of her daughter, and then it curtseyed before her.

"I apologize for the poor timing," Aras murmured. "I can explain more, but perhaps this is not the most comfortable place. I have a bower in the city; you will be safe there, and there we can better attend to your wounds."

Sara looked back at the swirling mass of dancers. Now even she couldn't tell one from another. "Yes, we should go," she agreed, "as soon as possible." Aras led the group away and Sara followed, talking to her sister in hush tones as they walked. Jonathan scurried back to gather some of the sweet cakes, but then thought better of it and hurried to catch back up with the group.

It was only El Gato who stayed with Tessa. "Well, you took that news surprisingly easily," he mewed, "too easily, I'd say. Are you alright?"

"Yes," she replied flatly.

"You do know he loved you," the cat offered. "Still does, wherever he is. You can't let the past get the better of you. Can't blame people for things that happened before you existed."

"I know." Again Tessa's voice was flat. "It's just everything else that I'm not so sure about. All this may simply be a part of his grand plan. Even Sara."

"It may well be," El Gato purred.

"And I may not be able to forgive him for all the danger he has placed my daughter in," Tessa spat, turning her head away.

11

~

THE PENDANT AND THE STARS

As the twilight again began to fade into darkness, Sara, her newfound sister, and their companions walked slowly through the city, the sounds of the dying celebration drifting away on the breeze. "It's this way," Aras called to the group, "not far." Aras subconsciously touched the metal of her necklace as they walked, feeling its pattern and its weight. Whenever she touched the pendant, the second gem in the setting, a sapphire, began to glow with a dim indigo fire. The light of the gem brought her attention once more to the question at hand.

"Does the pendant actually have a purpose?" Aras asked, her curiosity finally overcoming her trepidation.

"It does," Sara explained. "It is for all of us to use in concert. Look, I'll show you." Sara reached out her hand and Aras unclasped the jewel and handed it over. As Sara touched the necklace, the large amethyst at the top glowed bright purple. "Now you touch it as well." Aras reached out and touched the pendant, and again the deep blue sapphire lit up, yet the amethyst still remained lit from Sara's touch. Both gems now seemed brighter than when lit separately. Aras let go, and her blue stone remained lit for a few seconds—the sapphire's light faded much more slowly this time than before.

"Now mom, you try it." Sara handed the pendant to her mother. As Tessa picked it up, the fourth gem, a bright green emerald at the center, lit up. "See, it's basically a lock," Sara stated. There are seven keys. The three of us are each one of these keys. If we can get all seven of the gems to glow together, I believe we can return my... our father to life. I don't think it's that impossible a task. I really do think it's what he expected of us. I mean, look... we already have three of the seven keys and we just now started looking. We just need to put our minds to this and we can get it done."

As they spoke, their path took them past the main gates and the market there. The stalls were all closed for the night, folded up like new blossoms. Fairy was incredibly clean. There were no paper wrappers or plastic bags to turn into garbage. Everything here was made of leaves and flowers, and when things fell to the ground, they simply decayed and blended into the grass. Still, an unpleasant odor, accompanied by a low whimpering, wafted their way as the group passed through the square.

There bound near the main gate, still locked into the iron stocks, was the redcap. Its boar had been driven out of the city and it stood alone, beyond the bridge, sulking. The redcap stiffened as it saw the companions. "Please!" it called to them. "Please! I have learned my lessons! I won't hurt you again. I can be of great use to you here!"

Tessa was shaken and seemed upset at the sight. "What is to become of him now?" she asked.

Aras put her hand on Tessa's shoulder. "Nothing," she whispered. "His fate is left to nature. He will remain here until he is reclaimed by the wind and the sky."

"At least give me some food," the goblin gasped. "I am so hungry, so weak."

"I don't see what harm that would do," Tessa argued. "After all, we have so much here. It seems wrong not to share some of it." She moved towards the platform.

"No." Aras spoke. She blocked Tessa's path. "It is forbidden to interfere with the prisoner."

"Why?" Tessa responded. "If something is broken, you fix it. How is this creature ever supposed to learn how good people act if good people treat it badly?"

"Mom, we should go," Sara interrupted. "This is out of our hands now."

Tessa looked stern. "I just don't like to see anything suffer," she exclaimed. "Even that thing. Surely there must be some other way, some place for it."

"Not all things that are broken can be fixed," Aras stated, leading the group out of the square.

"Hmm..." Tessa stewed, "see, that's where you fair folk and I differ. All things need love and compassion—especially those who have never felt it. And nothing's fixable if you don't try."

"Fairy law can be harsh, even cruel," Aras agreed, "but the red-cap made its course—one of cruel violence and pain. It delighted in the suffering it brought to others, something no one here will engage in. It will not undergo mockery, nor will those that dwell here take joy in its pain. Instead they see the fate left to the goblin as a foregone conclusion. To us, the creature is already one with the air and soil."

Tessa looked back at the pitiful monster, no longer able to harm and trick others. She knew that it would never hesitate to hurt those that it found in its clutches, but still she could not help but feel for it. "The laws of my world are no better. Still, to let it starve seems so... well, vile."

Aras nodded. "I understand, you are still very young though.

With time, you might come to see the reasoning behind our ways."

"What?" Tessa started to protest, but then recalled that regardless of how Aras appeared, she was in fact centuries old. "Oh, right. Perhaps. Take me away from here."

"Of course." Aras led them away.

The company moved through an arch of flowers and passed into a narrow lane. Behind them, the voice of the goblin rose up, breaking the tranquility of the setting. "Witch!" it called after them "Foul hag! I'll eat your eyeballs and dance on your daughter's grave!" The shouting continued until it had faded from earshot.

Before long, the party came to a slender elm nestled into a grove behind a stone wall. "This is it," Aras murmured. "It's not much, but it's home." Aras stepped forward and circled the tree three times, counterclockwise. She stopped and put her hand on the trunk and closed her eyes. Then suddenly she was gone.

"Whoa," Jonathan stammered, "what's going on?" The cat had been following in Aras' footsteps and now disappeared itself. Tessa looked confused as well.

"We're just getting some rest," Sara calmly stated. "The tree is Aras' house... or bower more accurately. We're just going inside."

Jonathan looked at the tree, then at himself, then again at Sara and her mother. "Um... but we can't fit in there. Am I missing something?"

"Well obviously the tree is a portal," Sara huffed. There was a pause. Sara probed Jonathan's mind and realized he still hadn't gotten it. She shrugged and continued. "Not to another world exactly, but just to another space. Like when you imagine an imaginary place in your head. Do you know that if you focus on the details hard enough and long enough it'll actually form a reality—there will become a place somewhere in creation where it actually exists. See, the trees here aren't like on Earth; they're not just ordinary plants. They dream, and when they dream, they dream of a place. And then we can go there through the tree."

Jonathan looked a little lost. "Ok. So it's a portal?" he asked. "Are you really sure we want to leave this place already? I thought we were pretty safe here."

"Actually, since you mentioned it, the bower is just about the safest place we can go now," Sara countered. "There's only one way in and out, and a tree has a very stable sort of mind. It'll take years for any change to occur in there, if it ever does."

"How do we get out again?" Jonathan asked, looking sideways at the tree.

"Oh, just go inside," Sara gasped, exasperated.

Jonathan stepped forward and circled the tree until Sara told him to stop. He reached out and touched the same knob that Aras had touched. He closed his eyes. Nothing happened. "It doesn't work," he called out.

"You need to know the proper name of the tree," Sara called back. Then she stepped forward and whispered it to him.

"Herbie," Jonathan murmured under his breath. And then he was gone.

*****

Tessa was the last of the group to enter the bower, having insisted that Sara could not be left alone, even for a moment. She hadn't given much thought to what a fairy's home might look like, and was stunned by the change in scenery. The bower was beautiful. A daisy-dotted carpet of moss stretched over a rambling but cozy meadow, walled in on one side by living wood and on the other by a colorful stone grotto. Overhead, glow bugs crawled about on the ceiling, casting a dim but pleasant light over the scene. Vines and leaves and flowers sprouted from every surface, shooting out in pleasant natural arrays of foliage. From the grotto, a stream trickled, crossing the meadow and disappearing into a gap in the far wall. Several rose arbors stood around the room, forming the exits to different chambers. Each arbor bore roses of a different color, perhaps as if to signify the purpose of the rooms. Sara was currently on the far side of the little stream, laughing and rolling about on the soft mossy carpet. Tessa could hear Jonathan's exuberant voice coming from another room. He seemed to be busy in exploration. Tessa turned and looked back from where she had come. There, in the vine-covered wall, was set a round, glass window, and the grove where the tree stood was in plain view. Tessa reached out her hand and saw the glass ripple and flow like the surface of water. It almost seemed like she could just dive back into the outside world like one might jump into a reflecting pool. Well, the outside world could wait.

"Welcome." Aras' voice startled Tessa. The silky moss and the trickle of the stream absorbed all sounds of footfalls. Aras handed Tessa a large white flower. "Picked fresh," she assured Tessa. Aras gestured to a flower-covered wall near the grotto. "Try it. Just turn it over and bite the end."

Tessa did not want to be a poor guest, so she did as she was told. The stem of the flower came off easily and a thin, sweet liquid poured into her mouth. It tasted of rosewater and honey. Though there was little more than a few sips of the clear liquid, it seemed to fully satisfy her thirst. Aras tugged at Tessa's grimy sleeve. "It looks like you could use a bath," she stated, matter-of-factly. "Come, let me show you the grotto."

Aras directed Tessa to a low-roofed chamber down a spiral path from the level she had entered on. The air here was white with steam that rose from a deep pool, nestled snugly in the great roots of the tree. Aras offered Tessa towels and robes before returning to the others, and soon Tessa was settled into the steam of the grotto bath. The light here was a dim turquoise glow, and the warm water felt alive. The bath caused Tessa's skin to tingle all over, and she could feel the stress and strain of the last few days melting away. She lay her head back and the great roots adjusted to fit around her body and spine. This she could get used to.

Sara found Aras as she returned from the lower floor. "You know, sister," Sara exclaimed, "there are rooms in the bower you have not opened yet. Would you like to see them?"

Aras seemed surprised. She began to protest, and then quickly remembered Sara's gift. She flushed. "The bower is new to me, sister. It recently belonged to a family of fair folk that disappeared in the black wood. If there are other chambers here, it is because I have not needed them. The bower responds to the needs and desires of its dwellers. I do not think you will be able to access these rooms."

"Nonsense," Sara smiled. "You are no longer one, but a family. The tree will open the way for us. Come, do you wish to see?"

Sara took her sister's hand and led her through the red arbor. The room beyond was a sleeping chamber with a broad bed of flower petals. Curvatures in the wooden walls of the chamber provided a natural counter, upon which a handful of jeweled boxes and combs sat. A rustic, wooden stool sat on one side of the room before a silver mirror. Sara strode toward the far wall and pushed her hand into the vines and leaves.

"But there's nothing there," Aras protested.

Sara smiled and pulled the vines back like a curtain, revealing a warm chamber beyond covered in colorful silken rugs.

Sara stepped into the room, and the stale smell of dusty clothing surrounded her. Long mirrors stood on some of the walls, and exquisite silken curtains hung between them. This was the bower's master wardrobe, unneeded since Aras had been living here on her own. Aras stepped forward and pushed aside one of the curtains, revealing a deep closet full of unusual costumes.

Sara did the same. Each of the curtains hid different closets meant for different people and different occasions. Most of the clothes were very rich. "The previous occupants were nobles," Aras explained.

Sara needed no explanation. She reached into one of the back closets and pulled out a multicolored court jester's suit, replete with tassels and bells. "This is your size, sister," she laughed, handing it to Aras.

Aras' eyes bulged for a moment, and then she laughed aloud. "Only if you wear this," she countered, reaching into another closet and pulling out a ratty black robe sown out of crows' feathers.

"Eww!" Sara snorted between giggles. Then she thought for a bit. "Wait, I know where to get something more your style," she finally said, and then shot off into another closet where she rummaged around in the back for a bit. "Here!" Sara produced a stunning gown of white silken lace, embroidered and fit for a princess. A silver tiara and glass slippers finished the outfit.

"Wow!" Aras whistled, nearly tripping over herself to run and feel the fabric. "It's beautiful!" she cried. With haste, she began to change into the dress, finishing with a smile and a curtsey. "But who's going to escort me to the ball?"

"Why the dapper prince," Sara laughed, and with a thought, she altered her organic outfit into a leaf-patterned tuxedo.

"Wow! Sister, how did you do that?" Aras exclaimed.

"Oh," Sara smiled impishly, "I have magic clothing. I can make it look like anything." With that, she changed her tuxedo to a fair facsimile of the dress that Aras was wearing—though it did lack some of the detail and bead work.

"Amazing," Aras gasped. "Truly you are full of surprises, yet I can't help but think that using your magic outfit takes some of the fun out of dress up."

Sara considered this and decided that her sister was right. She dived into another closet and returned with a lavish, pink and burgundy gown. Her organic clothes formed into a simple slip, and with Aras's aid, she laced and buttoned the dress about her. It did not fit as well as her organic suit, but it felt so much more extravagant. Plus, it was fun to have her sister there helping to cinch her into the dress.

Sara found a silver crown for Aras and a delicate tiara for herself, and the two did each other's hair up with silver pins. Soon they were decked out and standing before a full-length mirror admiring their handiwork.

"I fear for any princes who cross our paths," Aras laughed. "We will smite their hearts with a glance."

"We should show my mother," Sara exclaimed. She was enjoying the pleasant distraction from her all-too-complicated life.

Back in the central chamber of the bower, Tessa, wrapped in robes, had fallen asleep on a large fluffy day bed with El Gato curled up at her feet. Jonathan was below, taking his own turn in the grotto. He had woven a flower garland for himself, and he sipped at the nectar as he busily switched between the hot and cold pools.

"This has got to be good for my complexion!" he yelled up at the others.

Tessa looked so at ease, fast asleep on the couch. "I don't dare wake her," Sara whispered, a little sad that she could not show off the outfits to her mother.

El Gato raised a sleepy face to the two sisters, his tail wagging slowly. "My, but don't the two of you look fancy," he yawned.

Sara and Aras both bowed and then twirled. "Such fine ladies should not be let out without an escort," the cat continued.

At that, Sara and Aras, in sync, glanced at each other with impish grins, then smiled back at the cat.

Moments later, the two were rushing back to the wardrobe laughing, trying to keep a hold of the wriggling cat that howled and scratched at them. "Please, my lord," Aras giggled, "there is no need to protest! This is all for your own good."

"Yes," Sara agreed. "After all, what's a king without his crown!"

Sara and Aras took turns finding items for the king while the other kept guard of his majesty. Soon enough, the chagrinned cat was plopped in front of a mirror. A pair of oilskin fishing boots covered his hind legs up to the hip. A velvet vest covered his chest, stuffed with a pillow to give him a more regal paunch. A gilded belt was tied around his waist to hold the pillow in place. A white silk ruff circled his neck, and atop his head was a jaunty wide-brimmed hat, crowned with a peacock feather. Draped around his shoulders and hanging down to the floor and trailing out behind him was a splendid red fur robe, with spotted white collar.

El Gato was annoyed, to say the least. He had protested and threatened all through the dressing process, but his cries had fallen on deaf ears as the two girls had gotten caught up in a swirl of playful bliss. Now however, as he caught sight of himself in one of the mirrors, he had to admit he made a striking king.

"Well, I've looked worse," the cat announced, sticking out his tongue, "but don't think you won't pay for this sooner or later. Sooner actually, I'm thinking."

"Hmm," Sara pondered. "I think he looks more like a highwayman than a king."

"Something's definitely missing," Aras agreed.

The cat considered them both with trepidation. "What are you up to now?"

Sara thought for a moment, pondering the cat and various kings past and present. "Jewelry!" she announced abruptly.

"Yes, exactly," Aras said, excitedly. "But I don't see much in here. They must have kept that in a separate chamber."

"You've got the pendant," Sara countered. "That's pretty regal."

"True, that's a start," Aras replied. She unfastened the jeweled pendant from around her neck and clasped it above the cat's ruff, letting it hang down over the silken puffs of fabric. "There."

Aras stepped back and Sara propped the cat up on his hind paws for another look in the mirror. "You know," Sara whistled, "it does seem to help. Now if we could just...." Sara paused, mid-thought. She looked up at Aras and knew that she saw it too. She looked back in the mirror. The pendant hung from the cat's neck, and the fifth gem on the chain, a large topaz, glowed with a warm light.

With a flash, the cat, realizing his error, wriggled free of their grasp and shot towards the exit, oilskin boots a flying. "Not so fast!" Sara shouted, throwing a discarded boot at him. The shoe hit the exit just before El Gato, and his little paws, already hindered by the padded vest, tangled up with the long boot, He skidded off into the door jam and Aras pounced on him, grabbing him by the scruff of the neck.

Sara closed on him and the two looked at the cat with cold suspicion.

"I think it's time you start explaining a few things," Sara growled at the stunned cat. Sara ducked into one of the closets and came out with an old wicker laundry basket. She overturned it and dropped it over the little creature, trapping him like a bird in a cage. Aras sat down on the top of the basket to prevent it from going anywhere. "I know you have knowledge that's not in the Font," Sara continued, "if any of it can help us get my father back, then you'd better spill it now, or you're putting us all in danger."

El Gato looked around his cage, considering his options. Finally, he sighed and settled down into a seated position. "I will say nothing to my captors," he finally spat.

Sara waved for Aras to go guard the door and then lifted off the laundry basket. The cat had lost his boots and hat, but the vest, ruff, and cape still remained in place, albeit somewhat askew. Sara unfastened the belt and removed the pillow, straightening the rest of the outfit as she did so. She left the pendant on his neck; the fifth gem still glowed a pale yellow.

"You have been keeping secrets," Sara prompted.

Finally, the cat regained enough of his dignity to speak. "What secrets do you speak of? You knew I was friend and companion to your father."

"Yes. We did know that, and you have known him longer than maybe any of us," Sara replied back at him. "You have done his bidding in the past, that much I am sure of."

"Well," the cat offered, "I have worked with him, but I don't work for him. And yes, I may have had something to do with the theft of the Font of All Knowledge. You might say I have a way with worldships." El Gato grinned.

Sara processed the new information and then started poking at it in her mind, trying to see what it might lead to. It wasn't really much. Though she remembered quite clearly that the cat had known its way around the Fish Man's worldship. "Who do you work for, then?" she finally asked.

"Nobody," the cat replied. "Or I work for myself, that is. Though I do favors for many, including the master of the library who you met."

Library? Sara was suddenly struck by an odd thought. Just like her, El Gato could recall Haven and its master the angel Rithrial, yet the cat had no Font of All Knowledge within him to protect him from Haven's magical disguise. How exactly did this tiny creature manage it then? Sara pondered the possibilities. A cat's mind was never a simple thing—a maze of riddles and contradictions, false leads, and even out-and-out lies—but for El Gato to be able to recall Haven, that was a feat indeed. Who was she dealing with here really? The cat did not give Sara time to dwell on the thought though, as he continued his explanation.

"I work mostly to ensure my own freedom. And I have made much progress. Your father first employed me to assist him because he realized that, being a cat, the Font of Knowledge could only hold so much sway over me. Well... employed is the wrong term; we worked as a team. Once we realized we had the same goals, we needed no payment from one another; it was a mutually beneficial arrangement."

"And to what end?" Sara shot back, not pausing.

"I told you. Freedom. Not just freedom for me or him, but freedom for all realities, the end of control, suppression. It's all cats desire. I don't know about the Seventh Star. I think he just had the foresight to know it couldn't last and get out early. I must say that my old friend would be quite touched to see those he loved more than life together at last. It was a great dream of his, you know."

"Is that what this is all about?" Sara was annoyed. "He didn't want to be there when his families found out about one another, so he's making us reconcile without him? No need to deal directly with the consequences of his actions, just let us all sort it out on our own? He's just a coward!"

"No, no," the cat interrupted. "That's not it at all. You can't just think of him like some slack-jawed mortal. He wanted to challenge you, to ensure you had the skills you needed to have before the chaos that his return will bring ensued. And he didn't want to rush you. You are free to seek him at your own pace."

"Hrm." Sara bit her lower lip. She looked up at Aras and then at the cat. "Well, I feel rushed anyway, and even a little betrayed. You knew about this necklace and Aras, didn't you?"

"I know a great many things," the cat returned, turning his back on Sara. "That does not mean that you or anyone else is ready to hear them."

Sara was not swayed by the cat's argument. She was not a fan of being manipulated; the Fish Man had made certain of that. El Gato might well have planned their trip here to Fairy and her and Aras's meeting well in advance. He might yet still hold not only the answers to what they needed to do, but also the questions they needed to ask. He was as slippery as a wet fish, and there was a large part of Sara that would have liked to pin him down here and now. But in the end, and with a great sigh, she chose to let it go for the present.

"This changes little," Sara announced, "other than that we have one more of the keys to unlock father's prison. And that didn't take us long at all. I think we can collect the other three soon enough. We just need to work together and stick to the plan."

"Which is?" Aras asked.

"To gather all the keys into one place," Sara replied.

"So, who is next?" El Gato asked, untangling himself slowly from the lace ruff and furry cape.

"Adam." A wave a guilt flooded over Sara as she caught a glimpse of herself in the mirror. How dare she play dress up while Adam was imprisoned and suffering. " We just need a path to get to him," she said. She began to remove the dress.

"I hate to discourage you," the cat interjected, "but I am afraid that pathway is beyond my powers. Although I have no doubt that all the necessary portals are known to the Font."

"Yes, I'm sure they are," Sara agreed. "I just need to find the right route." She pondered for a while. "Arrgh... you know, this portal business is quite a bit easier if you don't really care where you are going to. If you actually want to get from one specific place to another, you have to be at the right place at the right time in several jumps in a row—and the right time for one jump is always the wrong time for another. We take the wrong portal and we could be stuck somewhere for years. Not to mention the fact that in many realms, time can be sped up or slowed down."

"Can't you ask the Font any question?" Aras asked.

"Sure," Sara replied.

"So just ask it where we need to go to get there from here."

"I did," Sara sighed. "That was actually the first thing I asked. But it merely told me that there is no direct way from here to there. Well, at least no simple route exists. It's not just a question of raw knowledge, but of figuring out a pattern. I need to break the problem down into questions that can be answered. That's what I'm working on. I started with all the portals near Adam. Then I looked at ways to get from here to all those realms, or at least the safe ones. No answer again, so then I have to work backwards again from each of those to find a path that works. That's a lot of combinations. So far I've only got one match, but it takes two years of traveling. I'm not sure we can last that long."

"Two years?" Aras asked. "Didn't it take them two hours to flush you out of Earth?"

"Close enough," Sara moaned. "Well, cat, did my father think of this one? Maybe we can't learn the skills we need to find him without him." Sara sat down and slumped back against the far wall, her head buried in her hands.

Aras spoke to fill the awkward silence, "I've been wondering something, sister. What exactly did the cat mean by 'the Font of Knowledge could only hold so much sway over me?'"

"Huh?" Sara hadn't been listening. She started to rewind in her brain to figure out what Aras was saying, but Aras repeated herself first.

"I said, why is the cat not beholden to the Font in the same way as the rest of us?"

"You know, that's a good question," Sara replied, pondering the answer. "I don't know exactly. He just isn't really contained in the information there. I mean, cats are always a bit wonky, but not like this. It's not like dad, where the information has been removed or blocked, it's more like it was never there in the first place. Even the stuff we've done together, it's like he wasn't there. The story gets rewritten without him, as if Jonathan or I did all the important stuff he did." Sara looked at the cat. "Maybe he can tell us."

"Oh, good luck; I'll never tell that," El Gato moaned.

Sara reached for the laundry basket.

"Here's a thought," El Gato spoke quickly. "You are trying to get to your friend, yes, but perhaps you are not asking the right questions. So there are no portals that exist now to where you want to go. Ok. But what if I could take you somewhere where you could make a portal to anywhere you desired?"

"He's bluffing," Aras called out. She noticed the cat was edging slowly towards the door.

"No," Sara countered. "Well... maybe." Sara dropped the basket. Was this possible? She rephrased the cat's question in her head. "No, it's true! Why haven't we thought of this before?" Her own rhetorical question answered itself in her head. "Oh, yeah that makes sense. This is going to be risky."

"What is?" Aras seemed interested.

"The Heart of Music," Sara responded. "It's an ancient place, near the center of creation. It touches all realms—or at least all realms that have music of any kind. But it belongs to the Elders. They use it to send out their watchers. It can connect to anyplace one desires; you just have to know the right song to bridge the gap. If we found our way there, we could then use the Heart to make a portal to anywhere we wanted to go."

"Hmm, I don't know, Sara," Aras looked nervous. "I think we need to stay clear of the watchers. I remember all too well the blaze of their cruel, red eyes when they came for my mother. You think they'd leave their primary means of transport un-guarded for us to just waltz in and use?"

"Oh, there are guards," Sara explained, "but the Heart's not ex-actly the watchers' primary mode of transport anymore. Now that the Font of All Knowledge is lost to them, most of the codes are unknown, so they can't just come and go anywhere they want. Really, the Heart of Music sees little traffic these days. Besides, they are expecting us to be running from them, not running right to them. We might be able to catch them by surprise."

"That's true," Aras said. "Isn't that how you took down the worldship?"

"Sort of," Sara mumbled. "Really, I think we only succeeded because the Fish Man wanted us to. So that he could gain the ship's power for himself."

"You know," Aras pondered, "I think I'm starting to see father's plan in all this. It sounds like stealing the Font has already cost them much of their precious control. And his rebellion showed those they would send after you that it's possible to rebel themselves."

"I also believe he has a plan," Sara said. "That's why we need to find him. But we need to stick together. We need all seven of us in one place. The longer we delay, the greater our risk that one of us will get hurt or lost."

"Such as the cat," Aras asked.

"Yes," Sara replied. "Such as the cat." Sara looked over at the pile of clothes that had been keeping the cat entangled. He was nowhere to be seen. The embroidered vest stood empty, still holding its shape. The pendant had dropped to the carpeted floor. Sara picked up the precious treasure. "Come on," she said, "let's go tell the others."

12

~~

WATCHERS

"Come on! We have just fifty seven more minutes to be in position." Sara sighed and leaned up against the cliff wall. Behind her she could barely make out her mother struggling onwards through the swirl of snow.

Tessa had undergone a much-needed change of clothes, and now wore a basic fair-folk travel outfit, courtesy of Aras' bower. These simple threads—a dun tunic and matching leggings—were of remarkable make. The cloth looked, breathed, and hung like silk, but was actually woven from plant fibers, providing for much greater durability. Over her shoulders, Tessa had wrapped a heavy, elven fur coat, or at least that was what it appeared to be. Her fairy cloak did look like fur, and was indeed quite warm, but it was actually fleeced with down from a eider tree. In any case, Tessa definitely looked less out of place now in Fairy—well, mostly. Unfortunately for Tessa, fairies all had tiny feet.

Sara sighed again, louder this time. She could sympathize with her mother having trouble on the narrow, snowy path with only a pair of sneakers, but heck, Aras could fly. What was her excuse?

"I'm sorry," Aras sighed, "I'm just not used to this pace." Finally catching up, she hovered over to Tessa and held her hand as she crossed the narrow stone bridge. Aras' wings buzzed loudly, and she looked pale. Sara could see that her sister was having trouble simply staying aloft.

"No," Sara called back to her, "that's not it." Sara looked out on the great expanse of the endless forest beneath them. Far, far below she could make out the lights of Nod. "It's the air up here. It's too thin. Your wings weren't designed to fly this high." Sara was beginning to regret not spending one more night in the comfort of the bower. "Jonathan," she called, knowing that if anyone could hear her from this distance through these winds it was the chimera, "we need you back here now!"

A few moments later, the familiar spiky form soon appeared out of the clouds above. The chimera faced downward, clinging to the surface of the cliff with tiny traction pads on his hands and feet. "All clear up there, boss," he grinned. "You were right as usual. A couple of them were getting ready to drop some pretty big cheeses on us."

"Blast these diary fairies," El Gato remarked, peering suspiciously into the fog from out of Tessa's coat.

"Any chance any of that cheese survived?" Tessa huffed, relieved that she was finally able to brace herself against solid stone again. "And how do they keep cows way up here anyway?" she panted.

"Bat milk," Sara interjected flatly.

Tessa looked a little green. She even waved off the cream-colored wedge that the chimera held out to her. "Never mind," she remarked. "I shouldn't eat while I'm exerting myself anyway."

"Ahem!" Sara coughed loudly. "Fifty three minutes," she announced.

"I don't think we're going to make it," the cat responded. His face retracted back into the folds of the coat.

"We'll make it!" Sara replied, flustered. Wait, would they make it? Sara ran a few parameters in her head. Yes they would. "But we have to change the plan. Jonathan, I need you to take us up the cliff one at a time. Take my sister first; she should be safe from their little pranks up there."

"Aye aye, captain," the chimera replied impishly. He reached out an arm and guided Aras onto his back. "You sure I shouldn't take someone else too? She's light as a feather!"

"You can take the cat I guess, but don't let my sister's fairy magic fool you," Sara cautioned, "she can be more of a burden than you think."

Jonathan nodded, feigning agreement. He grabbed El Gato, who Tessa fished out of her coat. The cat scampered up into his thick mane, coming to rest between several of his long, sharp back spikes. Jonathan clambered back up into the clouds. He had no idea what Sara had meant by Aras being a burden. Even now, she was holding her own weight by flying, and was only holding on to him for the sake of speed. He had a feeling the full explanation wouldn't make sense to him anyway.

Sara and Tessa took meager shelter under a little outcropping that kept the snow off the path. Both exhausted, they sat down on the narrow trail and set their backs against the stone of the cliff, their feet dangling out into nothingness. Tessa took off one of her socks and wrung it out. "It's too bad they don't make any of these magical fairy clothes in reasonable sizes," she sighed. "I must look like some kind of clown in these baggy knickers and this puffy shirt."

"True," Sara agreed, "but you also look quite the adventurer. And that coat seems to be keeping you relatively warm. An hour from now we'll be in a completely different world anyway."

Tessa tugged the down coat tighter around her. It felt like tree bark and moss, but it moved and hung like wool and fur. "I'm not entirely convinced that's a good thing," she replied, pensively, "but if you really think we're in danger here...." Tessa slipped her damp sock back on her swollen foot. "I just don't understand why we had to climb all the way up here. Didn't you say that Fairy was the realm of a thousand portals? Certainly there's an easier one we could have opened somewhere closer to the ground."

"I told you that already, mom," Sara whimpered. "We aren't opening the portal, it's being opened from the other side, and we need to be there before it closes. It doesn't open from this side. Actually, it doesn't even really exist on our side, because you can't honestly get to where we need to go. You can only get from there. But that's exactly why we need to get there. It's also why we'll be safer there. Jonathan and I tried this before with the world ship. When they are chasing you all over creation, the last place they expect you to go is where they are."

"Ok, fair enough," Tessa mused, now working on the other sock, "I guess I can just trust you on that. But what I don't get is why we had to make such a rush of it. I mean, we could have scaled this mountain last night and had all the time in the world. Why cut it so close?"

Sara looked upward. The bitter winds shifted and the clouds parted, revealing the edge of a dark battlement perched high above. "There's no way I'd risk getting here in twilight," she murmured. "There are other things here besides sprites."

Tessa shuddered, not even quite knowing why. She hadn't really thought about it until now, but in under two short years, her daughter had grown into just about the bravest person she'd ever known. Sure, maybe Jonathan was a little more bold and carefree, but he was basically indestructible, so what did he really have to worry about? Sara had everything in the world to lose, and not much hope for gain. Of everyone, Sara knew full well what they were up against and how slim their chances were, but she never lost heart. She just looked at each roadblock one puzzle at a time. So much like her father.

A light dusting of snow fell past their faces and into the void below. "Hey, who called for the taxi?" the chimera quipped, his head suddenly poking over the lip of the overhang.

Now there's an approach, Tessa thought to herself. The chimera not only never lost heart with all the danger they faced—he actively enjoyed it.

This was the part that Sara both dreaded and lived for. The chimera would have to carry them both in one trip. He stood before Sara and his head folded back, his jaw opening vertically and splitting the neck apart with it. With little further fanfare, his body cracked open down the middle, revealing a disturbingly fleshy cavity within its center. Before Sara could have any second thoughts, thin, sticky tendrils shot out from the cavity and gripped her, pulling her quickly and firmly into the opening.

As fast as it had split open, the chimera's body now snapped shut, enveloping Sara in a warm, slimy womb. Sara saw darkness only for a moment before their minds joined into one and the chimera's body became Sara's as well. The world looked so different through these eyes. Everything was sharper, more distinct, but there was also simply more to see. Sara could see the heat coming off of her mother, and even the unique signature of her scent. The chimera lifted Tessa onto its back, and Sara could feel the power in its limbs. Lifting a fully-grown woman was no strain at all—it felt to Sara no more than lifting a glass of water or a book. Then they shot up the cliff.

Tessa had of course heard about the two of them joining—Sara wearing the chimera like living armor—but she had never actually seen it happen. It was all she could do not to gasp. It looked as though her daughter had been swallowed whole. Tessa did her best to contain herself. She did not want to offend Jonathan or come across as weak or unaccepting. She did, however, let out a few yelps, and her heart rate quickened as the chimera shot up the mountain with her in its grasp. Tessa doubted that she could ever get used to this.

To Sara, what had seemed a terrifying ascent just moments before now became simply an exhilarating climb. The howling winds felt merely bracing to the chimera's thick skin. Even gravity felt more like a vague guideline than a law. The chimera rushed up the cliff face in great bounds, throwing itself upward in excessive leaps with its legs, free arm, and the two pincers on its back.

Outside of the chimera's body, things felt a bit different. Even in the firm, yet gentle grip of the chimera's free hand, Tessa could not help but feel trepidation and more than a little concern for her own safety. Soon enough, as if reading her thoughts, the chimera turned and looked to her with a childish smile on its face. In a gnarled voice that sounded a little like her daughter's, it spoke, "Don't worry mom, Jonathan knows what he is doing. He would never drop you. Just try to enjoy the ride."

Tessa tried her best to smile back, and began to answer, when from above, a shape appeared. "Look out!" came her reply instead.

The chimera moved like a blur. It pushed off to the left and reached with his free hand towards the trunk of a small, scrubby tree that protruded from the rock face. "No, not there!" Sara sent through the psychic link as a heavy wooden milking stool went plummeting past. Too late. Jonathan grabbed the branch and used it like a pivot to swing himself upward. Halfway through the motion, the rock of the wall crumbled and the roots of the tree pulled away from the cliff. The chimera shot out into empty space.

Jonathan had this. He had done this dozens of time in practice. The only difference here was Tessa. The extra weight was unbalancing. He had to shift his grip. He twisted her about and tossed her downward below him. Now he just had to change his momentum, recatch her, and....

"Mom!" Sara felt her mother's weight disappear; they had lost her! There was no time to argue with Jonathan. He had somehow lost his grip and she had to act now. Sara lunged forward and caught at her mother's ankle. The weight sent them forward, rolling over in an ungainly flop. Sara could hear her mother's heart racing and feel her sharp breaths through the chimera's grip. She never should have taken her mother into danger like this. She had to get her out. Sara's brain raced, calculating the trajectory of the fall.

"Sara, stop," Jonathan's voice pleaded in her head.

Stop? No way. If she didn't do something, her mother was going to die. And it would be all her fault. Sara clutched the screaming Tessa close to her and felt the rush of wind pushing them upward. Sara crunched the numbers of their falling speed—thirty seconds to impact. What could she do? Sara started to take inventory of the chimera's systems.

"Sara!" Jonathan's voice came again, "Let go!"

"Let go? Of my mother?"

"No... of the chimera! I've got this!"

Uh-oh, what had she done? She did need to let Jonathan take over, but something was wrong. Because of the sudden shock, she couldn't disengage. Sara needed to try a different approach. She needed to force her mind to relax into the background. She had to focus on something else—like the Heart of Music, maybe. She had only one shot. Sara concentrated. Yes, there it was. The watcher had just arrived, and Curiosity was now browsing through the archives looking for the right song. It hadn't been played in quite a while....

Finally free from Sara's control, the chimera reached his arms and legs out, flipped over, and flattened himself like a starfish. The rush of air from below buffeted up against his body, slowing the descent. He reached his laden arm down and guided Tessa tight up against his chest, securing her arms in place across his back with his pincers. He tilted his hands and feet like rudders and quickly spun around to face the cliff wall. Then he dipped his head slightly downward and inched toward the wall until it was just a reach away, but still moving too fast to grab onto. Quick as a blink, the chimera leaned his head and shoulders forward, catching the wind and rotating his body vertically, so that he was now standing straight up in mid air. A sudden blast of air from his dorsal jets cut their speed in half. Three more blasts, and the chimera reached out and grabbed at the wall with all four limbs. He skidded against the stone, and the skin on his right palm tore open, sending thick blood spraying against the cliff. He pumped his legs against the wall rapid fire, kicking upward and releasing repeatedly. The brief seconds stretched out into what seemed an interminable length, but in the end, the chimera finally came to a firm halt on the wall, clinging only a few meters above the solid surface of a large jut of stone.

"We've lost precious time, Sara," Jonathan's voice came to her in her head. "Stay back. I can do this."

Sara could hear her mother's heart racing and feel her tears against her chest. Her emotions screamed out for her to do something, anything to help her mother. But anything she could do now could only make things worse. Sara needed to let the chimera do his thing. She wasn't needed here. She needed to get lost in her thoughts.

Sara let the physical world go and retreated into her mind as Jonathan took over their shared body. This was the proper balance now. Jonathan handled all control of bodily needs and concerns. And with no concern for the physical world, Sara could now fly through the Font. In this state she didn't have to ask it questions, it responded as her own thoughts. Here, she was the Font; nothing separated her from the knowledge she sought—well, so to speak. There had to be some difference, right? For some reason the answer to that question seemed slow. That was odd. How well did she really know her own knowledge?

Sara tried a test. She thought about something she knew well herself, like what her middle name was. The answer came in a flash. According to the Font, the answer had actually come a few milliseconds before she had finished asking the question. Now she asked herself something she didn't know. What was her sister's middle name? Lily. Now, how long had that response taken? 12 milliseconds after the question. Interesting. So what had caused the delay? No answer came.

No answer? Wait, why? Was the Font located so far away that some kind of lag occurred over the distance, like with a long-distance phone call? No. Interesting. Sara had always assumed that it simply took the Font a certain amount of time to process her questions, but why would it be any slower than her own head? Unless.... The idea took Sara aback. What if there was another consciousness on the other end—something that filtered or altered all the answers before they came to her? She put the question to the Font, and a shocking response came back: Yes.

So her father really had been with her all along. The Seventh Star, or at least a part of him—the piece that resided in Sara— acted as her filter, holding back the flood of information, but also holding back some of her answers. This shook Sara deeply for some reason, but before she could consider the ramifications, she was snapped back into reality.

"Heads up!" The chimera swung to the left as a heavy chunk of stone whistled past. Tessa lurched uncomfortably, but remained firmly in Jonathan's grasp. A burst of chittering laughter came from above.

"Dang, sorry," the chimera said aloud to no one in particular, "I thought I'd scared them all off." They had reached the top of the cliff, and the last twenty feet of the journey consisted of an ominous stone wall, black with soot and age. The crenellations at the top of the wall were worn and broken. Above the wall could be seen the pointed spires of an ancient black castle. Dark clouds blocked out the sun, and the air around the spire was thick with the dark shapes of bats. The constant shrill of their shrieking dulled all other sounds.

"To your left!" Tessa yelled, and the chimera put up a quick palm to block a small radish that had been launched from a tiny slingshot. A second later the chimera was over the wall and on the battlements.

The little sprites scattered at his approach. They kept up their attacks from a distance, but ineffectually. Without gravity on their side, their little missiles lacked any real sting. The chimera fired a few spikes just wide of them to scare them off, but he seemed to lack the heart to injure the little creatures.

"We can't just let them run," Sara injected into the chimera's thoughts, "when the watcher arrives, they will give our presence away."

"Well, I'm open to ideas," Jonathan thought back. "Trying to round them up is like nailing water to a wall."

"Don't let them distract you," Sara replied, "we just need to catch one. And then we need my sister."

"Go get her then." The chimera cracked open and spit Sara out onto the stone walkway. Sara shook off and then scrambled down a ruined stairway. She was none too glad for the brevity of her stay within the chimera; she knew the danger of remaining too long joined.

Jonathan took stock of the three or four little sprites in his immediate view. The one with the slingshot was the most annoying, though the spitters and the one that kept insulting him were little better. The spitters... limited range on those little guys. Jonathan caught sight of a small shadow across the courtyard near a broke carriage and got an idea. He crouched and fired a quill just in front of the nearest spitter—it spooked and scattered to the left and then back at him, angered. The little spit ball hit the chimera right in the knee, and he put on a fair show of being disgusted. "That's it, just stop! I can't take it anymore!" he yelled, jumping off the battlement into the rubble-strewn courtyard below. Laughing mercilessly, the sprites pursued. Jonathan lumbered through the rough tangle of thorn vines that had filled the vacant space of the castle bailey, feigning entanglement. A glob of guano whizzed by his ear, and then more spittle hit him on the back. "Arrgh!" he yelled, ripping out of the vines and heading for the shelter of the toppled carriage. He approached it with a few bounds and then leaped over it. A little sprite buzzed in after him, spitting away. Where Jonathan had leapt over the carriage, the sprite moved to pass under. As it neared the underside of the carriage, a small, dark form suddenly appeared out of the shadows, and with a pounce, it was upon the little sprite.

El Gato held the tiny fairy down with one claw, his other paw raised in warning, claws out. The sprite was thin and pale, almost insect-like. Its limbs were long and slender, with little barbs along their length. Its wings were thin and gossamer, like those of a dragonfly. The little face that had appeared human from a distance seemed quite alien up close. Its hard, chitinous head was almost featureless but for a sharp, round mouth and a set of multi-faceted eyes. The thing's overall appearance was difficult to grasp. From one angle it appeared to be a tiny human, but from another, it looked like a mantis. The sprite thrashed about and tore at the cat, but another paw came down and pinned it. Sara walked up and grabbed the pinned creature, slipping it into a long stocking that she had taken from her sister. The other little sprites looked on in horror at the scene.

"Fairy silk, that should hold you for long enough," Sara grumbled at the little trapped creature. Then she turned to the others. "Crawl back to your holes," she cried, the language shrill and foreign to Tessa and Jonathan. "Your friend will remain with us for one hour, after which time we will let him go. If any of you shows yourself or makes as much as a sound during that time...." Sara picked up a stone and made a motion to smash it against the writhing stocking. The little creatures gasped and backed away. "And that goes for you too," Sara snapped, poking the captured sprite. "Not a motion, or you get it." The stocking went limp.

Sara moved on to the task at hand. "Now, everyone! You must hide yourself as I say," she called out, starting to point out locations to her friends.

Six minutes later, the courtyard was empty. Howling winds swept overhead, and the shrieks of bats filled the air. The thorny vines occasionally shook from a strong gust, but other than this, nothing stirred. But then, almost imperceptibly, the sounds of the winds and the bats began to gradually diminish. Soon enough, they had blended into a low hum, like the roar of a distant beach. Though the sun was still out, darkness now began to seep out of the grim well at the center of the castle bailey. It began dimly at first, but then it spread, forming into an intense shadow radiating out of the well like some kind of reverse floodlight. Then something blocked the darkness.

At first there was just a hand on the edge of the well—though to call it a hand was generous at best. While humanoid in basic shape, the hand was clawed and covered in dark feathers, and the palm and fingers were unusually long. Wherever the hand touched the stone, it left a little dusting of grey powder behind. Soon, another hand joined it on the rim, and then something terrible raised up out the well.

It was black, and where it caught the fading light, it revealed a feathery texture. Great, shimmering wings adorned its back and shrouded its hunched form. Though its shape was indiscernible, it gave the impression of being coiled, waiting to strike. Two jagged claws hung low from arms pulled tight against its hollow chest. Above them, a thin, wolf-like snout protruded from the wings and sniffed the air. The head was dark, and blended jarringly the features of wolf, raven, and insect, with a beaky mouth filled with jagged teeth and two massive, bulbous red, featureless eyes almost entirely concealed behind black lids. What at first appeared to be long bat ears jutting from its forehead were actually antennae, fishbone shaped, with frills running their entire length. A dim red glow seeped from the creature's eyes and bathed everything it gazed upon in a pale, bloody hue.

The creature seemed uncomfortable in the daylight. It walked on its hind legs, though it did not appear suited for such mobility, and it lurched uncomfortably—or rather popped—as it moved along, snapping suddenly from one place to another a few inches forward. Its wings spread out behind it as it stepped forward away from the well. They were scaled and moth-like, waxy and spotted from behind, black on black. The wings fluttered briefly, humming for a moment and kicking up a foul smell.

The watcher walked forward a few more paces on legs like those of a great raptor. It paused in the courtyard for a moment, sniffing the air again. Its prodigious eyes never came fully open, but rather remained crimson slits. Eventually deciding that it had nothing to concern itself with, it loped up the broken stairway with speed and grace that defied its awkward appearance. It stood on the edge of the wall and leaned forward. Its four-sectioned wings spread wide, and as they reached their full span, what appeared as a great pair of cold green eyes flashed into life in their markings. The creature rose up on the winds and then dipped down out of sight, disappearing behind the walls of the broken fortress.

"Hurry, we have only seconds!" Sara's voice broke the eerie silence. The carriage door burst open and Sara and her mother spilled out. Across the courtyard, an overturned water trough righted itself, and a slightly dusty Aras and El Gato struggled out from underneath. The thicket of thorns parted, and the large form of the chimera tore out of the gap. All of them made for the well.

The cat arrived first, and leapt headlong into the radiating blackness, disappearing. Next, Aras glided swiftly down into the cold depths. The chimera followed soon after, hurtling over the side and downward. Tessa ran up to the edge and froze, staring down nervously at the black hole. The flood of darkness that shone out of the well was receding quickly. It had raised up to the sky when the creature had burst forth, but now it barely rose up ten feet.

"Jump!" Sara cried, shaking the little sprite out of its silken prison. "Don't think, just jump! Trust me, mom, it's the only way!" Sara swung her legs over the little stone wall and slipped down into the void. Tessa followed after her, and then a split second later, the beam of darkness was gone. Once again, the wind howled over the black castle and the cries of bats filled the air.

13

~

THE HEART OF MUSIC

The darkness of the portal remained, though the air and the sound had changed. What had seconds ago registered on the senses as an intensely natural, outdoor place suddenly felt claustrophobic and controlled. The air no longer moved and the wind no longer howled. At first, this new place seemed silent, but as ears adjusted, hundreds of distant sounds could be heard, each different and distinct. But before the sounds could be identified, the darkness began to fade. What was black now turned to grey, and as eyes adjusted, gradually to a pale red.

The world itself had turned to colored crystal. The portal had closed, leaving only the shallow engraving of a circle upon the ceiling above. The five travelers were most definitely indoors, but it wasn't clear if there was actually an outdoors to this place. Walls, floor, ceiling, doorways—everything was made of some kind of translucent glass-like material. Where passages passed near the portal chamber, they could be seen ghostlike through the walls. Where nothing abutted, the translucent glass just faded away into opaque light. Beyond the walls, the passageways appeared to shift, moving from one place to another in a series of fluid, graceful motions.

As if in juxtaposition to the graceful architecture, a variety of clutter had been piled in every corner of the small room and stacked against many of the walls. Consisting of old crates, boxes, and all sorts of odd, archaic-looking items and relics, these knickknacks appeared to have been set about the room at random, though not without care.

"We made it," Sara intoned breathlessly. "Welcome to the Heart of Music!"

"Why do they call it that?" Tessa asked, without bothering to pause and hazard a guess. Sara did not reply, but simply closed her eyes and held out her hands from her sides. The distant sounds that had initially seemed random now began to blend together. Most hummed softly like a warm vibrato, while others were creaks, bells, wails, taps, or crashes. Together they formed a symphony of sorts, and flutes and strings could be heard in places providing harmony. Though it had been quiet at first, the music seemed to be picking up volume. There was a definite ebb and flow to its tones. Tessa got a vague impression that the sounds might have coincided with the movements of the passageways, but it was impossible to be sure. Whatever this place was, it was big.

"This is the enemy's stronghold?" Jonathan asked. "Looks more like a museum." He lifted a dusty statue off a crate. "And where are the bad guys?"

"No, don't worry, it's not a stronghold," Sara replied, "it's more like a train station. El Gato, maybe you should explain this place."

The little cat looked up at the group and mewed, rubbing himself up against the archway leading out.

"Seriously?" Sara sighed. "Fine. Well then I guess it's up to me. But we should get moving first. This chamber could dead-end at any moment." Sara stepped out of the chamber and the others followed silently, each looking around suspiciously in a combination of confusion and awe.

They had stepped out into a long, smooth, crystal passage-way—tubular, like the inside of an organ pipe. It did not move constantly, but in little timed jumps, turning and twisting to its own tune. Though the section where the five travelers walked did not lurch, they could feel the floor vibrate as changes occurred farther off down the tunnel. At times, other passageways touched up against the sides of this one, producing a haunting sound like a tubular bell ringing. When a collision was particularly forceful, a crash like a cymbal was heard, and an archway opened up between the two tunnels. These links could be seen forming and disappearing far off down the tube in a distant show of light and shadow. After they had walked what seemed an impossible distance to measure, an archway eventually opened to their left and Sara led them through.

This new passage was wider and darker, appearing almost red instead of a pale pink. Along the walls, little dark bumps occurred at random intervals, and these almost looked to be part of the passageway until they too began to move about. Aras moved over towards one and gasped, jumping back. Each little bump was a little creature—no bigger than a dinner place—flat like a crab and supported on ten spindly little legs.

"Don't be scared," Sara interjected, "the hermites just clean the place. They are pretty much harmless. I mean, well... just leave them be."

Jonathan moved over and looked at another of the little creatures that appeared to be scratching itself with one of its back legs. From closer up he could see that it was in fact rubbing one leg across another like the bow of a violin. He suddenly realized that a musical buzz that was echoing about that he had attributed to background ambience was actually coming from the little spider-thing. He glanced over at another nearby hermite that looked to be chewing on its front legs. Upon inspection it was actually blowing into tiny hollows in the shells of its legs, creating different little piping tones. The hermites followed the group from a curious distance as they made their way down the tunnel, their numbers slowly growing as they covered more territory.

"I didn't feel comfortable talking and navigating at the same time," Sara griped, "but we're in a vein now, so there should be more stability here. It's also much easier now to keep track of where we are going."

"Where are we going?" Jonathan asked, unconsciously leaning away from the spidery pipers that skittered along the tunnel wall.

"We are headed to the heart," Sara replied.

"Huh?" Tessa butted in. "I thought you said we were there."

"Right," Sara explained. "We are now in the Heart of Music. But we need to get to the heart of the Heart of Music."

"Okay..." Jonathan mocked, before finally deciding not to waste time dwelling on the obvious, "and why is that exactly? Not that I'm so keen on staying here with these bugs."

"Well," Sara answered, "travelers normally arrive at the center of the Heart in the great portal room, but we waited quite a while before jumping into the well, and the branch that held the gate to Fairy was already moving off. See, each of the various...."

"Yeah, yeah, yeah," Jonathan interrupted, "the heart of the heart, moving hallways, branching gates, and all that stuff. That's all great to know, but what's at the heart that we need to get to?"

Sara cleared her throat. Jonathan immediately went on high alert, knowing that this was a sign that Sara was about to launch into a big speech. When Sara talked, she tended to neglect their safety.

"The Heart of Music was discovered long before the worldships were built," Sara began. "It was long the way that the Elders of Prime interacted with other realities. Think of it as a primitive worldship. Instead of a big, comfortable, controlled space that can travel quickly through the space between realities, it's a tangled web that lives in that space all the time. It touches upon thousands of realities as once, and can legitimately touch any reality at any place, although it only forms portals when directed to from the inside. Listen to the music around us. What do you hear? Long, long ago the Elders realized that the music of the Heart reflected the realities that it currently touched upon. If the heart were to touch upon Earth for example, somewhere in central Europe say, the music it would play might sound something like Bach. But here's the key. The two phenomena are not cause and effect, they are appositionally integrated— so therefore it follows that if one can change the tune of the Heart, one can direct where it touches upon."

From where they were heading, the tunnel ahead forked into two, or more accurately, the wider tunnel ahead of them forked into two and they were presently moving backwards up one of the forks towards the junction. As they passed into the larger tunnel, the walls again grew a darker red, indicating a closer proximity to the center. Jonathan noted with some trepidation that the hermites here grew larger as well. He wondered what they might possibly eat.

Despite the change in scenery, Sara continued uninterrupted. "There was one Elder in particular that dedicated his life to studying the songs of the Heart. He eventually learned how to control them. He was a tinkerer, and had a love for puzzles and patterns. He is called 'The Sower of Visions', although few know him by that name anymore. For thousands of years now he has been referred to only as 'Curiosity'. For long, he was the boatman of the Elders, taking them where they needed to go and picking them up when they needed to leave. With the acquisition of the Font of All Knowledge, Curiosity no longer had to discover the tunes by trial and error. His job became considerably easier, and he reverted his attention to his other passion, collecting."

"Wait, this guy doesn't sound all that evil," Jonathan interrupted again. "Why is he working with the bad guys?"

"Evil is a matter of perspective reality," Sara answered. "Curiosity is an Elder. The Heart is used for control. In fact, the Heart was the chief instrument responsible for the Elders' initial control over all other realities. Though the Elders themselves used the Heart in the older days, with the advent of the worldships, it was no longer needed for this purpose and the Heart became relegated to transporting the watchers... that thing we saw. The heart was once their primary means of spreading chaos and misinformation, but my father dealt them a grave blow when he stole the Font of All Knowledge. Now that the Font is no longer in their possession, they can only use the Heart to go to known locations. See, one must know the song that corresponds to one's destination in order to go there. That's why the watcher that came after us had to appear high up on the mountain instead of right where he wanted to go. If my father hadn't stolen the Font, they would likely have caught us long ago."

"If your father hadn't stolen the Font," Tessa added, sarcastically, "they wouldn't be after us in the first place."

"Right," Sara replied, "and you'd still be paying taxes and commuting to work every day... or at least until your society began to achieve something meaningful and the watchers brought it down from the inside." Tessa opened her mouth to argue, but then thought better of it.

"Anyway," Sara continued, "Curiosity dwells at the heart of the Heart. His formal position is to create the portals that allow the watchers to pass through realities at will. However, there are so many watchers and so many places to be watched now that the Heart has become a major bottleneck, and the watchers have mostly resorted to using existing portals between worlds—much like we have been doing. Twenty years ago, this place would have been crawling with watchers, but now it sees relatively little use. That's why as important as it is, it has few defenses. And also, the main defense is that no one can get in without Curiosity opening a portal from the inside. Now, as Elders go, Curiosity is not one that would be considered evil, but still, I would not wish to run afoul of his attention. Currently, he is in meditation. If we move quickly, we can avoid him altogether. With the help of the Font, we should be able to bypass his expertise in using the Heart. Ah... it seems we have come to the atrium."

The tunnel ended quickly ahead, running into a number of other tubes and forming a massive hallway that ran to a giant red doorway at the end. Jonathan noted that the hermites here were as large as garbage pail lids. He kept on his toes.

The door before them was round and shaped like a flower, the crystal petals all coming together to form a tight diaphragm. At the center, a golden circle was mounted, and a ring of little holes was set around its edge. Sara walked up and placed her fingers in the holes, spinning the circle a certain distance each time in a series of measured movements. With each turn, the wheel produced a different sounding note, as if air was being forced through the lock. After seven turns of the dial, the disk tilted back and the flower began to open, revealing a dimly lit room behind.

Row upon row of objects and treasures stood arrayed and piled into the dark chamber. Masterful statues stood watch over the collection, and complex tapestries lay scattered about, half unrolled, and leaning up against the ruby walls. These were clearly the choice objects and artifacts. As the flower again closed up behind them, the dissonant and conflicting music that had played in the tunnels now formed into a single, harmonious tune, haunting and beautiful. It changed character and style over time, perhaps conforming to the tastes of the realities the Heart touched upon. The translucent light that lit the tubes did not seem to penetrate the walls of the heart here. Instead, the place was lit by braziers of blue everfire that descended from the ceiling on iron chains. The room was roughly circular in shape, and numerous open archways led to what appeared to be similarly appointed rooms.

"Come on," Sara warned, "we should get to the center before Curiosity wakes."

None of the others budged. "What is this place?" gasped Tessa, looking around her at the strange relics, each seeming to come from a different world.

"I told you," Sara sighed, "he's a collector. Where do you think he keeps everything? Now come on, we need to get a move on."

"I don't know," Jonathan mused, "I mean this hardly looks like junk. Don't you think there's something in here we can use? Like what's this?" Jonathan picked up a strange-looking compass that had no marking on it, only a crystal face, an etched gold body, and a single, red needle in the center.

"Hmm," Sara thought for a moment, "I guess you can take that. Now come on."

"But what is it?" Jonathan reiterated.

"It's a lost compass. If you lose something, that will point you to it. It was commissioned by a great and powerful king. He lost his daughter and could not bear to live without her, so he collected all the great mystics and magicians in the land. All of the kingdom's resources and monies were poured into that little needle. The kingdom collapsed and fell to ruin. In a few years it was overrun by another power. Still, the king did find his daughter."

"Really?" Jonathan seemed a little nervous holding the little object. "Where was she?"

"The needle directed the king off the edge of a cliff."

"Oh." Jonathan put the little compass back down in its original place. "How did it end up here?"

"Well, it was a greatly treasured relic for generations, and it was much loved, but then someone eventually lost it."

"Sara, what's this?" Aras had picked up what looked like a

small, simple, delicate flower encased in glass.

"It's the first flower," Sara huffed, impatiently, "ever. Now come on, we need to get a move on."

Aras stared at the little object in awe. Her eyes widened, and then suddenly she hurled it to the floor. It landed with a thud, undamaged. "It's beautiful," Aras murmured, visibly upset.

"Mom," Sara tugged at her mother's sleeve, "tell them that we need to get going. We're in danger here."

Tessa shook off her daughter's hold. "We're in danger everywhere we go. I don't know about this plan. Maybe Jonathan is right. Maybe something in here really can help us." Tessa picked up an old, cracked, wooden cup. "You know," she said, "if I didn't know any better, I'd say this looked like the holy grail."

Sara shrugged. "It's all just stuff," she grumbled. "Don't forget, the most important things in life aren't things." But no one was listening. Sara looked around for the cat, but he seemed to have wandered off. Sara walked over to a table and picked up a thin chain with a platinum sunburst hanging from it. She approached Jonathan, holding it hidden in her hand. "Ok, Jonathan," she began, "you're probably right, but we do have to go, and most of this stuff is just as dangerous as useful. If I just give you the best thing for you here, will you come with me?"

"What?" The chimera looked up startled from a shelf covered in little bottles full of wispy, white smoke.

"Don't touch those," Sara warned. "Here, take this and come on." She held out the amulet.

Jonathan picked up the small chain and looked at it briefly, then followed after Sara, who had acquired a bright little lantern to help them navigate the gloom. Tessa and Aras seemed hopelessly lost in the collection, and did not even notice the two of them leave. "What's it do?" the chimera asked after they had left the room.

"It enhances your telepathy," Sara replied. "At the very least it'll increase your range. But you may notice yourself occasionally hearing the thoughts of others."

After navigating several more wings of the collection, the two friends eventually passed into the room at the center of the Heart. It had only a single, open entrance, save for a tall, ornate set of iron doors at the far side, which appeared stoutly locked. The room itself was smaller than Jonathan had expected, and unusually cramped. What space there was was filled with all manner of keyboards, pedals, stops, and switches. Organic looking tubes and wires ran from the controls into the walls, floor and ceiling. The music that washed over the Heart seemed more clear here, more focused and intense. At the very center of the room sat a plain, worn stool, wooden with three stubby legs. Sara wandered over and touched it pensively. It appeared to have been made for a rather large creature. "I think a chimera would fit here rather nicely," she said, looking up and grinning.

"What is all this stuff?" Jonathan asked, stunned by the sheer quantity of devices packed into the small chamber.

"What does it look like?" Sara asked. "It's a pipe organ. Actually this entire reality is a pipe organ. This is just the control room. You can get to anywhere in all creation from here. You just have to know the right song to play."

Jonathan looked around again. "This whole place? Look, I don't know who you think I am. I can't play this. I have trouble enough just keeping track of one keyboard. This is just ridiculous. Does it even come with a training manual?"

"Don't worry," Sara replied, confidently, "you know I plan father ahead than that. I can direct you. I just need your skill and dexterity to pull this off. We'll need to join again, but I promise I'll be better this time. We were made for this machine, me the conductor and you the musician."

Jonathan stepped over to the chair and ran his fingers over the massive keys of the central board. They looked ancient, carved of bone and ebony. Each key had a different visage etched into it, like a portrait gallery of ancient kings. "Ok," he spoke, quietly, we can do this. But where are we going?"

Before Sara could answer, a shadow passed over the two friends, and they looked up to see an imposing figure looming in the open archway.

"Curious, most curious," it spoke, "but I don't think you'll be able to accomplish much here without my permission."

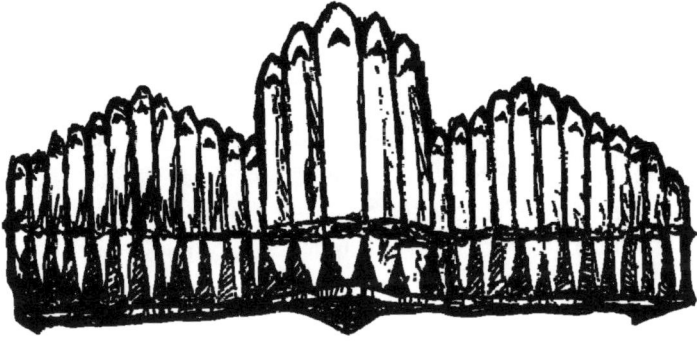

14

~~~

CURIOSITY

The dark form of the Primal Elder filled the single archway of the control room, his long shadow falling over Sara and Jonathan. The Elder's feline face betrayed no emotion. Like all his kin, his appearance was unique. He was tall and sleek, with a panther-like head. Black fur covered his body, with the exception of a white, star-shaped patch that stretched over his left eye, oddly reminiscent of El Gato's mark. A third eye stared out lidlessly, directly in the center of his forehead, and though he was indeed cat-like, he bore no visible ears, but only a smooth, fur-covered brow. He was dressed in mismatched and patched clothing, his robes adorned all over with baubles, jewels, and small, sculpted pieces of bone and ivory. Sara heard the chimera rise and move to place himself between her and the Elder, but before he could fall into place, Curiosity spoke.

"It's a very nice instrument don't you think?" and a clawed hand with eight fingers—somewhere in form between a human hand and a paw—motioned in a fluid gesture to the organ. Sara watched as the chimera turned back to the keyboard and seemed suddenly and utterly enchanted by it. Jonathan sat back down and, as if in a trace, stared forward at all the many keys.

"Try it, my boy," the Elder whispered, his voice soothing and filled with hidden power. "See what happens. What do you like to play? The Moonlight Sonata? Chopsticks? No one's ever tried those before. You might find somewhere completely new."

Curiosity, ignoring Sara, passed forward around her and laid one of his large hands on the chimera's shoulder, placing the other on the organ. The instrument vibrated with the touch, humming to life. Various parts of it flowered open, and the pedals, keys, and buttons all moved to position themselves to the reach of Jonathan's limbs. Utterly enthralled, the chimera began to play.

"Wait, Jonathan!" Sara snapped, her fears of where a random song might open a portal to overcoming her fear of the Elder. "You should not play with that, it's no toy!" But the chimera was lost in the layers of the organ.

"It is no toy indeed," hissed the elder, turning his attention now to Sara and baring his long, pointed canines as he did so. "Now what have we here? The little girl that all the old ones have half of creation in an uproar looking for. And she comes strolling into our den, with not so much as a 'by your leave'." One of the Elder's hands shot out and gripped Sara's arm in an iron clutch.

"Jonathan!" Sara cried.

"You will no doubt see that he is lost to you for now, little Seventh Star... as are the rest of your so called friends, taken in by my power and chained in loops of thought and wonder."

Sara suddenly realized what had befallen the rest of her companions—all seduced by Curiosity, trapped and unable to move beyond their excitement at discovering so many interesting and new objects. Only Sara herself had remained untouched by the Elder's power. The fact that she already knew what everything was before she touched or held it guarded her against Curiosity's spell.

"All right, Sower of Visions," Sara trembled, "you've got me. What do you plan to do with me?" As fast as the question came, so did the answer, and Sara was surprised that the Elder had no clear idea as to his next move.

"Now there is an old name." The Elder laughed and threw back his head before leaning forward and bringing his third eye up to Sara's face. "You do pose a stimulating problem, don't you." His voice was low and full of menace. "What my masters would not give to have you in their possession again— or rather to have that which you carry." The Elder brought the point of his foreclaw down to the center of Sara's forehead, right where his third eye was focused. He pressed slowly until he broke the skin, then released and watched as a drop of blood ran down—first onto her nose and then off to the side, flowing below an eye and continuing across her cheek, giving the impression that Sara might have been crying bloody tears.

"You are a cruel one, just like the Mongrel," Sara spat.

"No," Curiosity purred, "you mistake me. It is not cruelty that you inspire in me, but rather envy. You who within the limited recesses of your fragile, temporary form hold the key to all knowledge—the answers to the unanswerable, the secrets of the far gone ages, the rhythm and songs to unlock all worlds."

Sara was suddenly struck by the understanding that for a being who had been named Curiosity, the Font would be the greatest prize of all. She could see now that he had never been allowed direct access to the Font before—his dark masters had only fed him the knowledge and songs that suited their own purposes. Now, in his very grip, he finally held the key to all the answers he could ever ask.

"We could make a deal," Sara said. To her surprise, the Elder released his grip on her arm and stepped back. Of course, this did not mean that she was safe; Sara knew that Curiosity could move far faster than she could ever hope to, and even if she could outrun him, he held her mother, Jonathan, Aras, and El Gato in his power.

"It would be madness to betray my masters and agree to aid you."

"Not madness, just curiosity," Sara tempted. "You know that they will never let you have access to what I carry. Through me, all the answers you seek can be yours at last. And if you help me and my friends, we may be able to offer you the protection of one more... one who has defied your masters on more than one occasion."

"You mean the Seventh Star of Twilight?" the Elder snorted. "I would be in even more trouble if I involved myself with him. Besides, do you know the prize I would win if I were to deliver you to my masters?"

"I know it would not be free and full access to the Font of All Knowledge," Sara said. She folded her arms and turned her nose up at Curiosity in a look of defiance. "There is no prize in all creation that could serve your desires better than having me as a friend—I know it and so do you."

"Such risk would require a great reward." The big cat smiled.

"Indeed. Well, any question you wish answered, you need never look further than me. And do not forget, you are the one true master of this realm. You know all its ins and outs. You could easily deceive your masters and keep them from finding out you worked with us."

"Easy? To deceive my masters?" Curiosity chuckled. "We both know that's not true."

"Together we could do it." Sara could tell Curiosity was coming around to the idea, she just had to push him over the edge.

"I know the answers to the three most pressing questions on your mind—the three that you think about more than any other questions."

"Answer them and I will help you." Sara could hear a hint of desperation in the Elder's voice.

"No. I will answer one of them now and then the other two later, each in exchange for passage to and from one location we need to visit."

"Deal." Curiosity put his paw out to shake. "But beyond that, we will have to renegotiate our arrangement, understood?"

"Agreed," Sara nodded, and the two shook hands, "So which of the three do you want to start with?"

"You know them already—the cruel triad that plagues my mind and keeps me from my other exploits," Curiosity stated rather than asked. Sara could see that it amused him that she already knew the answers—after all, he had written volumes on the questions and spent untold hours in meditation and exploration.

"I wonder," the Elder continued, "of the three, which do you think is the hardest to answer? Wait, no. You would find none of them hard. Rather, which would be the most difficult to find the source knowledge to... that is, for someone other than you?"

Sara considered the question. It was less about the facts and more about her own opinion, as arguments could be and had been made for each of the choices. Sara liked questions that factored in her thoughts; it allowed for her to be more than just a parrot. However, as she contemplated the dilemma, she found that she was distracted by Jonathan's ever-present music. It had changed from a simple tune to a more and more complex series of notes, and was slowly, yet steadily, increasing in speed. She looked at Jonathan and already his hands were a blur, moving so swiftly that they were beginning to test the limits of his chimera muscles.

"What's going on?" Sara asked, pointing to Jonathan.

"Oh my," the Elder spat, "in all my excitement, I forgot what I did to him!"

"And just what is that?" But even as Sara asked the question, she had the answer. Curiosity knew that physically he was no match for the chimera. He also knew that Sara might have a way to counter his influence. So he had set Jonathan on a course to play a song that would wear him to ashes.

"Easy, easy," Curiosity soothed, placing a hand on the chimera's shoulder. But to Sara's dismay, Jonathan did not slow his pace, but only pressed on even faster. He rose up now to his full height, his feet dancing across the pedals. "I fear we may be too late!" the Elder warned. "He is headed towards the crescendo! To hear it is all his mind and body care for."

"No!" Sara's heart lurched. If Jonathan played through to that moment, his body would melt and fall to nothing. "Jonathan," she thought, reaching him through their psychic link, "please, Jonathan, you have to stop playing." She got nothing back. How could he be such a fool? Sara began to feel anger towards her friend, but then quickly remembered a moment from only hours before. She had been in control and Jonathan had tried relentlessly to get her to release so he could save her mother. No, Sara knew how hard it was to let go in that finely-tuned body. This was not Jonathan's fault—he simply could not hear her, or could not comprehend her speech through the blur of his concentration.

"He isn't responding to our mental link; I can't reach him," Sara exclaimed, knowing that there was so little time remaining. Already, smoke could be seen on the surface of the chimera's skin, and he was beginning to radiate heat. "If he dies, our deal is utterly off! You hear me, Sower of Visions?"

"You are linked to him psychically?" The Elder spun around,

intrigued.

"Yes." Sara did not want to waste time in speech.

"If only we had time." The Elder sighed, "I have a pendant that, if activated, could increase your link in both distance and intensity."

"Yes you do." Sara smiled. And that pendant was currently hanging askew on the chimera's neck, hidden from view in the spines of his back. Sara did not ask the Elder more, but immediately acted to bring it to life. "Awake, Manas, and open the true eye of my friend."

The charm buzzed and glowed, hovering out of the spines in which it was hidden. Sara focused her thoughts to link with Jonathan, but the effort was unnecessary—she already was connected. She could see what he saw, and all the world slowed as she adjusted to the chimera's perspective.

Under Sara's influence, the keys of the organ changed, becoming the flames of the chimera's doom in their shared vision. They moved their hands away, and looking up, they saw now the Elder. Emanating from him they could see a primal light—a white-green hue that sang of creation at its dawn, when all was new and angels set about in the creation of all things, real and conceptual. Then, through the chimera's eyes, they saw Sara. As if suspended in time, she shone blue, and the star on her cheek was not a simple tattoo, but a living vibrant thing of beauty. They looked deeply into their own face, and from the top of Sara's head, a great library filled with books of every shape and description sprung, stretching out into creation and touching every living thing. They saw the Elder reaching for the necklace—he moved so slowly, even though Sara knew it was with superhuman speed. They considered moving to block him, but before the chimera could raise his arm, the necklace was snatched away. Sara was back in her own body.

Jonathan dropped to the ground. He was still smoking, and he looked more weakened than Sara had ever seen him. She wanted to run to him and touch him, but she knew his skin was currently near boiling—193 degrees Fahrenheit to be exact. Instead, Sara turned to the Elder and shot him a very cross look. "Are there any other traps that you are currently too distracted to have undone? My mother and sister are still under your spell, not to mention my cat. Curiosity killed the cat after all, right?"

The Elder was indeed distracted. He was staring at the scorched necklace in his paw. "What was that?" he murmured. He seemed to slowly come back to reality, noticing finally that Sara was speaking to him. "No," he replied, "the others are safe, unharmed. Distracted, yes, but as safe as babes reading a children's tale." Then he leveled his three eyes on Sara. "How did you do that?" He held the pendant out before him. "This necklace has an incantation to increase physic abilities, but I have never seen it do that... and what language was that?"

It had not even occurred to Sara that she had spoken in a different tongue. Also, she had not even thought about it at the time, but she had not spoken the command that the Elder knew of, but instead the one that could make the item function at its full power, granting the wearer true vision. She looked at the necklace now and realized that the Elder had also been there with them, seeing through Jonathan's eyes. Curiosity was shaken. Sara could sense a touch of fear in his complex mind. After an eternity of living, it was only now that he had finally seen himself as he truly was. But it was a once-in-a-lifetime occurrence. Sara also knew that the power of the enchanted jewel was fully spent; it would never work again.

"Sara, you saved me," she heard in her head as Jonathan regained his feet, "again. Like you always do."

"Like we do for each other," she returned, and she was aware that their link had been made stronger by the experience.

The Elder was looking strangely at the two of them, and for a moment Sara feared he might still be linked to them, but she knew with another breath that it was not so.

"You two are indeed impressive," he spoke. A great warm smile spread across his feline face. "I can only imagine the mischief you must have caused the Mongrel when he came to have dealings with you."

"Well, if we caused him any pain, he deserved it," Jonathan spat.

"Here, here young lad," the Elder piped, and Sara could see a new respect for them growing in Curiosity. "Throwing in with you and yours may not be such an ill-advised idea after all." He paused for a moment, and Sara could see he was bracing himself for something important. Then he spoke. "I am ready for my first question to be answered."

"Ok," Sara announced, a little apprehensively, "which one do you want the answer to?"

The Elder rubbed his chin with one of his eight-fingered paws. "What the starshine," he mused, "I'll go for the most common, yet hardest, 'Which came first, the chicken or the egg?'"

15

~

INTO THE FRAY ONCE MORE

"Come on, just a few more gallons," Sara pestered. "You need to drink as much water as you can retain without slowing yourself down with bloating." Sara was standing on the far side of the well, her hands on her hips and a stern look on her face that warned against any protest or disobedience.

"I am trying," the chimera winced. He bore a sickly look on his face, which was literally tinted green. "This is worse than any torture the Fish Man ever did to me."

"Well, if you don't like it, we can always have you grow a few camel humps," Sara countered.

"What? Oh, come on! Those would look so stupid. I am supposed to be the most fearsome monster in creation but, 'oh, I have camel humps'. 'Eeew, run away, the camel hunchback is coming to get you!'"

Sara wrinkled her nose in a look of utter confusion and then rolled her eyes. How an eight-foot tall monster with clawed arms and giant pinchers, covered in armor plates and spikes could still manage to hold on to some vanity about the way he looked was beyond her, but that was Jonathan for you.

Sara thought better of deriding her companion and returned back to the situation at hand. "What about the cooling pores I asked you to evolve along your back spikes?" she asked. "You will need them if you are going to be able to dissipate enough heat off of your body. I don't want to cook in there any more than I want you to burn up."

"Yes, I know. Between the fifty times you have taken over my form and the two hundred times you have explained to me the evolutions I will need to survive, I think I get it—you are turning me into a giant air conditioner. I just don't see why I have to drink all this water now, when you have the fairy flask to supply me with an unending supply."

"Trust me," Sara assured, "to keep you cool enough for me and to prevent your insides from turning to pudding, we are going to need to keep you fully hydrated at all times. I promise you, the moment we set foot on that plane you will thank me. If we are going to have a chance to save Adam, you being a giant air conditioner is exactly what we will need. Now no more talking—you are letting valuable moisture evaporate every time you open your big mouth." Sara could not help but feel a twinge of sympathy for Jonathan. He really did look miserable, but she knew they would need every drop of liquid to survive where they were going, and by her calculations, the chimera's body could still absorb another three gallons at least. "Drink!" she commanded, pointing to the well.

"How goes the hydration?" Tessa asked, rounding one of the glass halls of the Heart of Music and entering the well room. She was no longer dressed in her borrowed fairy clothes, but now wore an outfit provided by Curiosity—and one far more befitting an extra-dimensional explorer. She had replaced her tennis shoes with sturdy, dark brown, leather boots that came all the way to her knees and that buckled all down the outside with inlaid gold fittings. On her legs, she sported thick canvas pants with matching leather patches sewn along the sides. Multiple interlocking belts hugged her waist, and above these sprung a loose-fitting white shirt, topped off with a sharp, leather waistcoat and form-fitting gloves. She had replaced her backpack with numerous pouches that attached to her belts and with plenty of hidden pockets sewn within the vest and the pants. Sara could read that these pockets were all fully outfitted with equipment of all sorts that her mother had determined might come in handy, including such items as a spyglass, a sewing kit, various medical devices, and even a magical compass that could point to portals between worlds, all courtesy of their host.

Tessa had also done her hair up in a tight bun on top of her head. This, on top of everything else, gave off an air that she was ready for anything. Sara, for the first time on their journey, now saw her mother in a very different light. It wasn't as if her mom had been a burden before—quite the opposite in fact—it was just that up until this moment Sara had taken her for granted. Now, looking at her mother in her full regalia, Sara realized that she was far more than the housewife and caregiver Sara had always known her as. She might not have visions or super powers, but she was anything but ordinary.

"Mom! You look ready to take on anything," Sara said, joining her mother and motioning for her to spin around.

"Thanks! I found most of this in a trunk," her mother smiled. "Not sure these clothes were meant for a woman—and the boots are a little large, though they should do better than my ratty old tennis shoes. I do have to admit I feel kind of tough."

"Well, I pity anyone who tries to mess with you. And that compass should come in handy too."

"Oh yeah," agreed Tessa, "Curiosity gave it to me. It's supposed to work in..." She trailed off, realizing that Sara already knew what the compass could do and most likely understood exactly how it worked and how to repair it if it malfunctioned. "I am still not sold on all of this, you know."

"I know mom, but time is of the essence. There is only so long that we can hope to remain hidden from the Elders and there is just too much to do to keep the whole crew together."

"Yes, but you going to the plane of primal fire." Tessa wrinkled her nose in the same way Sara would when she disapproved of something. "It sounds like you are stepping into an oven."

Sara placed a hand on her mother's shoulder, "Don't worry, we are not going to the heart of that plane. In fact, we are going to be far on the outskirts, and though temperatures can be extremely hot there, I am going to use my gifts to guide Jonathan through relatively cooler areas."

"I know it has to be you two, but I just wish there was a way I could be going to the fire world and you were the one heading out to talk to some old inventor."

"I owe it to Adam to save him personally," Sara sighed. Her mother could tell that Sara was very upset with herself that she had taken this long to attend to helping her friend. "If not for him, we would all be scattered throughout creation, lost with no hope of finding our way back, and he is suffering even now."

"You care for this boy," Tessa stated rather than asked. She had had a brief moment of recognition and wondered if her daughter had her first crush.

"What?" Sara was befuddled. "No... I mean yes... well, I don't even know him. Up until an hour before he sacrificed himself for us, he was an unreadable assassin who was hunting us down."

That would certainly draw her daughter's attention, Tessa realized—a boy who she could not simply know everything about with a thought.

"Are you sure you can get to him?"

"Yes, I have it all worked out," Sara assured. But that wasn't true at all. Sara was sure that she and the chimera could survive for a brief time on the outskirts of primal flame, and she was almost certain they could navigate to the citadel where Adam was being held, but there were many other factors and dangers that she could not predict the outcome of. She kept these from her mother, knowing that she would never be able to convince her to let her go if Tessa knew the whole truth. "I assure you we can make it through safely if whiny-boy over there can just ingest one more gallon... and maybe an extra just in case."

"I am going to throw up," the chimera hissed.

"No talking," Sara reminded.

"Maybe you should give him a break; he looks fairly sick." Tessa walked over and patted Jonathan's hunched over form on the shoulder. He looked at her and did his best to smile without looking sickly.

"You remember everything I went over with you?" Sara asked her mother as Jonathan lowered his head once more into the well.

"Yes, I have it all memorized," Tessa replied, feeling less like the mom and more like the child here.

"Good, then it's time," Sara said. The chimera let out a sigh and stood. Sara walked up to him, and barked out her orders, "Divert all the water from my chamber and open up."

With a groan, Jonathan stood and, closing his eyes, seemed to concentrate for a moment. Then he arched his head back and his midsection split open down the center. Little rivulets of liquid ran down onto the floor.

Sara shifted her organic outfit from jeans and her rainbow sweater to a full bodysuit—one designed to hold off as much heat as possible. She removed her leather satchel and placed it on the ground near the well, realizing that it would only slow her down and take up precious room. It was hard to leave it behind, but she would be back for it. She then turned her back to the chimera, clutching the fairy water flask close to her chest.

Three tentacles shot out and began to pull her into the chimera's torso. She looked to her mother, speaking even as her suit formed around her face. "Do not underestimate the inventor; he is more than he seems." And then Sara was inside the chimera, his chest armor closing around her. She finished her warning through the chimera's mouth, in growly snarls that sounded more like her intonations than Jonathan's voice, "He will tell you his secrets if he wishes. I dare not blow his cover; we need him on our good side if we ever hope to get dad back."

"I will do my best," Tessa assured, then patted the big monster before her on the arm. "You take care of my girl, you hear me?"

"I will," Jonathan said with the same mouth Sara had just used.

Tessa was amazed how easily she could discern which one was talking through the chimera's body. She watched as they turned and headed towards the organ chamber. Her heart was aflutter with anxiety, and she had to fight not to chase after them and demand that they remain safely there with her.

"They are better at this than you think," a familiar voice spoke. Tessa looked down to see that she had been joined by El Gato. He appeared to have forgotten all about his earlier muteness— though to be fair, he had only begun to speak once Curiosity had touched the star on his chest and commanded that he state his name.

"What kind of mother lets her child go rushing off into danger?" Tessa asked the cat.

"Running to find it or waiting here for it to find them, your child was born to danger," the cat purred. "At least this way they are doing something about it."

Tessa tried to tell herself that she agreed; she just was not sure she believed it.

"We should head that way too. After all, we also have some-where to be." El Gato led the way.

The chimera entered the organ chamber. There, Curiosity awaited their arrival, kept company by Sara's sister.

Aras walked up to the chimera. "You in there, sister?" she asked. Sara nodded with the chimera's head. "I am not sure I will ever stop finding the two of you joined amazing," Aras continued. "Have no fear that your way back will be open when you need it. Curiosity is under my watchful eye now, and I have warded myself against his tricks."

A look of hurt came over Curiosity's feline face. "No need for all that. I will keep my word, just as Sara has kept hers. Be-sides, I have two more questions I am dying to get the answers to."

"And you shall have them just as soon as I return along with my mother, El Gato, and Jonathan," Sara assured, talking through the chimera.

"Come close," Aras beckoned to the chimera with her hand. She leaned in and whispered into his ear, "When you see the stallion tile with the green aura of flame, you must act alone."

Sara momentarily thought she had misheard her sister, but then remembered that Aras had a gift to see into the future, "We will, sister," Sara guaranteed.

"I was not talking to you, sister, but to your gallant protector," Aras corrected.

The chimera rose up, and Sara could feel him blushing. "Did you hear that?" Jonathan thought to her. "She called me 'gal-lant'. You never pay me compliments like that."

"Well, you are very brave," Sara thought back.

"I suppose I am," he returned through the mental bond.

"Or just too dumb to run away from danger," Sara returned. She was starting to feel the water log of the chimera's body, and it was not entirely comfortable. The sooner they were on their way the better. Once they were in the plane of fire, that water would be used up all too soon. Out loud, through the chimera's body, she spoke, "We are ready to depart."

Curiosity nodded, and from a string around his wrist he took what looked to be a tiny key. "Do not lose this," he spoke as he slipped its tether around the chimera's neck, "it is your ticket back here when you are done."

"What is it?" the chimera asked, using Jonathan's inflection. He lifted the tiny object in his hands and peered at it.

"It's a reed," the chimera replied to itself using Sara's mannerisms. "It's a piece of the mystical organ. If we blow it, it will sound here, no matter where in creation we stand. When Curiosity hears this note, he will know to play the song to open the portal to our prearranged exit point."

"Ok," Jonathan replied to himself, "but what if we're not at the exit point?"

"Then we don't blow it," Sara again replied. "Or maybe you could say 'we've blown it'." The chimera smiled at her own joke.

"Oh," Jonathan's voice replied, and the chimera's face turned to a look of nervousness. "Well, whatever, let's just do this. Heck, we've never had one of these before. I don't see how it can hurt."

Curiosity stepped forward and took a heavy key from beneath his robes. He unlocked the bolts of the great iron doors and slid them apart. With the lightest of touches, he pushed on the surface of the doors and they swung open, revealing a massive, hemispherical room beyond. This rotunda lay at the true center of the heart, and its great, domed ceiling gave a breathtaking view of the colors and pathways of the sprawling Heart of Music. The chamber was sparse, but decorated with elegant statuary and low marble benches. Curiosity bowed deeply and then turned to his organ and began to play.

The chimera shuffled gingerly into the rotunda. From the vantage point of the great, circular room, a fantastic show was now beginning. Throughout the halls of music, the tones flowed and echoed, and then soon, far off in a distant chamber, a small pinpoint of light flickered into life. It danced briefly to the organ's tune and then proceeded to shoot upward and diffuse into the glass of the ceiling of its tiny chamber. Then the glass of the distant chamber itself began to come alive. The light crept along the walls of the room, enveloping them and leaking out into the small hallway that led into it. Soon, the glass of this capillary also came alight, and the shining glow began to flow all along it, flowering out to fill various veins and chambers throughout the Heart. As the music played on, the many halls and corridors of the Heart twisted and began to move in time. When these passageways touched, the light shot off along the new branches, eventually forming one great swirling pattern, spiraling out from the rotunda. Then suddenly, as if drawn by a magnet, the chamber containing the original point of light rose upward, curling about on its branch so as to just lightly touch the far wall of the rotunda. At the point of contact, the surface of the great dome melted away, providing an archway into the small, curio-filled room where the light had first ignited. In the far wall of this chamber stood a large door, from which red light, deep and hot, smoldered.

Sara and Jonathan approached the portal just as Tessa and El Gato entered the round antechamber. The chimera looked back at them and gave a nod. Then mist whistled from spikes that stood up on his back, and his skin seemed to harden. Within him, Sara twisted open the water flask and let it begin to flow, replenishing that which was being expunged from the spikes. She breathed now via the organic tube that always encased her mouth within the chimera and that fed her directly from the chimera's lungs.

"We are ready," Sara thought to Jonathan. She could feel just the slightest chill through her insulated suit, but knew that would not last. Jonathan moved them forward and, without any further ado, leaped into the opening. The moment they were past the threshold, Curiosity ceased his playing. The light patterns began to quickly dim, and the portal chamber pulled away from the wall of the dome, its branch twisting and twirling away off into the darkness, back to wherever it had come from.

"They will return," Aras said, as if stating a fact.

Tessa could not, however, shake the feeling that separating from her daughter was not only dangerous, but irresponsible. "I don't feel like a very good mother right now."

"I don't know much about good mothering," El Gato shrugged, "but I bet a common thread is that good mothers often feel like they are not doing enough. But I have been with those two through thick and thin, and I would not be surprised if they were having the time of their lives right about now."

Aras approached Tessa, speaking, "You have naught to fear. They will return, and you will see her again very soon. I have seen it."

"Oh right," Tessa thought to herself, "the future sight that this mysterious fairy clone of my daughter can use."

"Remember what I told you of the Inventor?" Aras continued. "I was his ward for a time after all. He is a great man, but he can be extremely stubborn and set in his current course. I have already foreseen that if I tried to retrieve him, he would not come, but you... you will bring him back with you, I am sure of that, no matter what it takes."

Tessa tried to take comfort in the assurances offered by Aras, but Sara had already said that no future was set in stone. There could be many outcomes that Aras might not see. Still, Tessa thanked her by mustering a confident smile; she could not help but feel motherly to Aras as well, due in part no doubt to how much she resembled her own daughter. Tessa had to remind herself that Aras was actually far older than her, just as she had to remind herself that her daughter was far smarter than herself. She lost heart for a moment. What exactly was her place in all of this? What could she hope to offer?

As if the cat had read her mind, he chimed in. "Time to prove we have something to offer to this quest," he purred. Then, bowing to Curiosity, he announced, "Maestro, if you please."

"Indeed." The elder handed Tessa her reed for returning. After a grand bow back to the to the cat, he then turned to his organ and began to play. Before them, the lights and song in accordance with each other began to weave their own door. As their portal slowly formed, Tessa went over the instructions Sara had given to her in her head. Once the door was ready, El Gato waved his paw for her to follow and then passed the threshold. Tessa started to step after him, and then paused and turned back to Aras and Curiosity.

"You take care of yourself as well," she smiled at the fairy girl. "Don't spend all your time looking out for our futures."

"I will try," Aras smiled back.

Then Tessa was gone. The organ stopped, and the portal melted away behind them. Silence slowly came again to the Heart of Music.

"You should eat something and be at peace," Curiosity said. "I will wait for their request to return and send for you as soon as it comes in."

"Yes, that is agreeable," Aras nodded.

A key on the organ played a single note on its own. "Oh that was fast," Curiosity mused, placing his full attention on the organ. "Oh no. No, this is not good."

"What is it?" Aras asked, detecting the concern in his voice.

"This request is not from your companions, but from one of my masters' servants." He gave her a grave look. "We must conceal you from them."

Aras was suddenly struck by just how poignant Tessa's concern for her truly was. As she looked into her own future, all she saw was darkness.

16

~~~

PRIMAL FLAME

The heat hit in a wave of blasting wind, almost knocking the chimera off of his feet. Jonathan crouched low, his claws digging into the hot rock beneath them. The ash that ripped about them forced him to close all his eyes save for his four insect-like gems that measured the heat. Sara had not been kidding; it was hot here, hotter than he had imagined. His body responded instantly by hardening, forming armor around his more exposed areas of skin—a natural defense that unfortunately threatened to decrease his mobility.

"Let the water flow and carry the heat out through your spikes," Sara sent to him through their psychic bond. "And we need to move; this rock is sinking into the lava below."

Jonathan focused, and the water that saturated his body passed along through his system. It sweated out from his skin, turning almost at once to steam. It found its way to his spikes, where it hissed out in a buzz, whistling as if from hundreds of tiny smokestacks. But just like Sara had told him, the heat did dissipate. The sensation was still intense now, but not as unbearable as it had been moments before. Jonathan stood, shaking his whole body like a wet dog, fighting back the extra layers of armor that had started to form around him. As he shook, he surveyed their location. They were currently perched high on a rocky crag. The wind and ash crashing around the summit lowered his visibility, but he could make out other similar rocks nearby. Below, the hot glow of a molten river appeared to be growing ever wider.

"Hello, we need to move!" Sara ordered. "This rock we are standing on is melting, and it will soon be sinking downwards towards the lava. If you think it's hot here, you don't want to find out what it is like down there."

"Right. Got ya," Jonathan thought back. "Which way?"

Sara pointed with one of the chimera's arms. "That formation there is in the process of rising. Leap to it. We need to make our way further to the right to get to the iron citadel, but there is no point in trying to go in a straight line if we end up cooking."

Jonathan ran forward on all fours, even momentarily using his back pincers to make the leap. Sara could never have done that. She understood all the physical requirements of the jump and the mechanics of the chimera's body, but unlike Jonathan, she lacked the instinct to execute such amazing feats on the fly. Of course, she was not completely at one with the body of the chimera monster like Jonathan was. She was a passenger and hoped to remain so. She held no desire to ever join as one with the chimera, although Jonathan and this journey might well place her in danger of just that. They had a good distance to go here, and she would not be free to disconnect from him until they were inside the relatively cooler citadel.

"Sara," Jonathan thought as he landed, legs and arms spread-eagled and clinging to the side of the rock, "I am losing water. I can tell the cooling is slowing down."

Sara inwardly cursed herself. She had been so busy considering the dangers of staying in the chimera for too long and in plotting the best course to the citadel that she had forgotten about the fairy water flask, which had gotten jostled in the action, narrowing its stream to a trickle. It was serendipitous indeed that they had ended up with the flask; Sara found it hard to believe the fair lady did not have the gift of future sight. Though it supposedly poured a magical and unending supply of water, this was not entirely true. In truth, the flask was simply a tiny hole into the realm of primal water. It was unending only in that primal water had an effectively unending supply to offer.

"Water?"

"Sorry." Sara focused, twisting the stopper of the flask fully open.

"Oh thanks, that's much better," Jonathan thought, and he began to swiftly traverse the face of the large rock.

Sara checked herself. This was one of those moments where, if the roles had been reversed, she would have chastised Jonathan. He had simply thanked her and kept on his way. "I need to be nicer to him," she thought, "after all, he is the most loyal and caring friend anyone could hope for."

"Where to now, boss?" Jonathan asked.

"Wait, rather than thinking words to you, let me try pictures." Sara opened up a map in her mind of the current layout of the area they were in. It was a massive lake of fire, nestled in the crater of a great volcano, with immense rock formations constantly rising and sinking out of it. Just above them was the border with the realm of primal air, and that was the only reason they were even able to breathe here. Sara showed Jonathan the place where, high up and somewhat away from the heart of the crater, a sharp iron peak thrusted—and at its base stood a fortified citadel, cast out of the iron of the mountain itself. Though grim and blackened with soot, the cold look of the towers was utterly deceiving.

"That's where we need to make it to, and fast," Sara said.

Jonathan had not stopped moving all through the sharing of images. He continued up over the top of the next rock and down its far side.

"But take care," she warned, "if we go lower than this line, we will not last long." Over her mental image, she superimposed a line that showed where the heat would become unbearable. Next, she indicated to Jonathan which rock formations were in the process of rising and which were sinking. A series of directional lines zigzagged across the image. "I have charted the best course based on current information. Just think of it like a video game."

"Actually, I never really played video games," Jonathan informed, "but that's ok, I have a feeling I would have been great at them." He took a flying leap forward, expelling steam from the air jets on his back to propel him further. Sara gasped—the jump was ill-timed and they would never make it to the next large rock. But to her surprise, Jonathan suddenly bounced upwards off of a car-sized chunk that been spit up from below. He rode the rock up until it lost momentum, and then he sprang forward, twisting about and landing on the next large formation. Sara had not shown him the smaller rocks in her mental map—not wanting to confuse him—but she could tell that he was navigating only partially from her map, choosing instead to employ all of the chimera's natural senses. He had detected the smaller rock shooting up with his sensitive ears—all the sound and wind giving him almost a 3D view of the world, not unlike a bat's echolocation. The chimera moved along the course now with all the speed and raw power of his amazing form—the boy and the monster one and the same.

As they shot across ravines and up sheer cliffs, Sara got the strong suspicion that Jonathan would indeed have been extremely good at video games. She could not help but feel the rush of speed and physical prowess that the chimera's body offered. However, she also feared that deeper connection, for it meant that she was creeping ever closer to becoming one with the chimera—or to put it bluntly, from having her mind join with Jonathan's and her own body digested. Sara did not relish the possibility.

"Once inside the citadel, I will be able to survive outside the chimera," she thought to Jonathan, "my own organic suit will offer me enough protection. The temperatures are far less there, mostly because the being holding Adam wants to keep him alive."

"To draw us there, right?"

"Not us, me," Sara sighed. "After all, I had a hand in killing her sister."

"I am still not sure how you hope to fight this creature."

"I don't," Sara thought. "I plan on getting in, freeing Adam, and then fleeing back to the Heart of Music. To be honest, I did want to get us a little closer, but it's one thing to know the right song and another to play it perfectly. We can make it from here, so this will have to do. It would have been a cinch if we could have just had Curiosity open a portal directly into the citadel, but that would have set off the traps of Adam's jailor. The place is heavily warded. This is a mission that requires stealth and speed."

"Well, it's a good thing you have me then, isn't it?" And as if to make his point, Jonathan ricocheted back and forth between two rock faces, moving one step closer to their goal and further from the heat of the molten lake.

"If I forget to say it sometimes, let me be clear," Sara replied, "I could not do any of this without you."

"I am glad to hear that," Jonathan thought to her, "I was beginning to wonder if you really needed me any more at all, what with your sister and your mother, El Gato, and well... your father, once he is returned to you. I guess I just didn't know if there would be a place for me in your life anymore."

"Jonathan," Sara spoke sincerely, her heart in the throat, "you

are my best friend, and let's not forget why we are doing this—
it's so we can be free, no longer hunted or used as pawns in
some cosmic game."

"Yeah, that's what worries me."

"How so?"

"Well, Sara, if we do succeed... if we do finally get free from
being hunted and pursued, messed with and abused... if we do
get the happy ending, what will you need me for?"

Sara's chest constricted. She understood his fear. After all,
what place would a killing machine have in Tacoma with her
and her family if all of this ended well. Then again, what real
chance was there that any of this would actually end well.

"Jonathan, I am not sure there will ever be a happy ending. In
fact, with our gifts, it's likely we will spend the rest of our lives
running."

"Yeah, good point." Just then, they sprang out into the open,
reaching the top of the canyon the chimera had been scram-
bling up through. They were high enough now that they were
clear above the ash storm. As they gazed out above them, they
caught sight of two massive phoenixes dancing across the raw
red sky, their blazing tails interweaving as they twirled about
each other. The great creatures' course took them forward
toward the iron mountain that was now clearly visible. They
shimmered as they went, as if mirroring the fire storm below.
Slowly but surely, the blazing trail of the passing phoenixes
cut a line of fire across a golden sky filled with alien stars and
strange constellations.

The vista was breathtaking, and even as the rock they rested on
began to skink back into the ash storm, the two friends stood
frozen in awe. "Wow," Jonathan sighed out loud, then continued through their psychic link, "the things we have seen...."

"Yeah, who would have thought?"

"Sara?"

"Yes?"

"Just promise me if we get that happy ending, that you will always be in my life, always."

"I promise," Sara thought back. However, at that moment, she was happy that their thoughts were still separate—because there was a part of her that wondered if she had just lied to her best friend. Jonathan was very young, and though Sara was near the same age, her wealth of knowledge offered her insights he would not have until he was far older. One of these was the fact that relationships had a way of changing and even ending, but more than all that, it was that Sara could not see Jonathan happy in the same ending she had in mind for herself. He was happiest here now in the heart of danger. He was at his best not just in the frying pan but in the fire itself. Where would he fit in a normal, calm life?

The ash storm rose up again around them, shaking them both from their moment of contemplation. Jonathan propelled them forward. He scampered down across a charred rock field, over a canyon, and then up another cliff face. Sara could tell that Jonathan, having now seen their goal, was relying less on her aid and more on instinct, though it seemed to serve him well. The chimera was designed to survive, and on some level, it knew instinctively not to allow itself to descend too far into the heat. Only once did Sara correct Jonathan's course—when he had headed for one of the rocks that Sara realized was only a thin coat of crust covering a huge molten bubble of magma. They were making record time now, and Sara was beginning to detect only the first warnings of the chimera beginning to digest her. The constant flow of water from the fairy flask kept the acid from concentrating, giving them time to reach the iron citadel. In fact, Sara was almost certain that they would make it there with time to spare. That was, until she chanced upon the creature that stalked them.

She had been so focused on their path forward that she had

not spared a thought for what laid behind them. And it was not until the beast was just within striking range that she had detected it. "Jonathan!" she cried aloud through their shared mouth.

Jonathan sensed the heat just as the warning came, and expelling a cloud of steam from his back jets, he changed direction with jaw-wrenching speed and dove sideways.

The giant lava serpent ended up with a mouthful of rock rather than the organic morsel it had been stalking. It reared back in rage, and its thermal vision again found the tasty cold spot, now off to the side of where it had struck. Its prey was crouched and looking ready to counter. The serpent hissed. Its rage that its patient hunt had not paid off now fueled its choice to strike at its prey in the open.

Jonathan stood utterly still as he watched the great serpent composed of lava coil and prepare to strike again. Sara remained silent within him, knowing that he would judge the moment the attack would come better than she could. They both held their breath. The only sounds were their hearts beating in unison and the pumping of the water from the flask.

The creature struck with blinding speed, but the chimera countered even quicker, swirling up through the blazing snake's coils and out the other side. Jonathan launched several of his back spikes at the beast as he passed it. Each hit its mark flawlessly, one to each eye and four more to the creature's throat, but to Jonathan's dismay, all the spikes disintegrated on contact.

"Flesh thing, you will burn well," the serpent hissed at them. The language was that of primal fire, and Sara, without even thinking, translated it for Jonathan. The beast followed its lunge with several quick strikes, each dancing closer than the last.

Sara could sense the land mass they were on descending into the heat below. If Jonathan turned his back to run, the snake would have them, but if they could not finish this fight quickly, they would cook. "We need to hurry," she relayed.

"Hurry and do what?" Jonathan sniped back. With the next strike that came at them, Jonathan tried a different tack. As the serpent's head came in at them, he somersaulted over it and expelled as much water as he could at it from his back jets. From the spray, parts of the snake's molten skin hardened briefly to rock, but moments later, it reheated and became molten again.

"You cannot harm me, flesh creature," it hissed.

"I need more water," Jonathan thought to Sara as he hopped back and forth, moving left and then right. The molten jaws of the serpent snapped at them over and over, giving him no time to pause or think, only to react.

"I am pouring it as fast as I can!" Sara thought, her own body jarring about rapidly within the living armor the chimera provided her.

"Not fast enough," Jonathan replied as he moved one of the connecting tentacles that joined him to Sara to the mouth of the flask. He drank deeply from it, the water coming as fast as he could ingest it. He opened the jets on his back and opened all of his pores, allowing the water to rush over him. On his next jump, Jonathan stumbled. But instead of getting up, he crouched and grabbed at his knee as if in pain. Sara watched the serpent's mouth widen as it moved to swallow them.

"What are you planning?" Sara cried in the chimera's head, but he was silent, focused, ready. The answer came to her. She felt the sword blades on his forearms flex, and then they were swallowed whole.

The serpent rose up in triumph, but even as it did, in a place just below its head, its body began to harden. It seemed to chuckle for a moment. "You think turning me to rock will harm me? I will simply reheat and be fine," it snarled. Steam poured from the serpent's mouth. Already the creature could tell that the water coming from its recently-swallowed prey was evaporating. But suddenly there was a loud crack, and then another. Two long blades now protruded from either side of its neck, shattering through the stone. In a snap, the blades moved counter-clockwise, slashing in a great circle around the snake's neck.

With a great crash, the serpent's head rolled forward, coming clean from its body. With a final look of surprise, it crashed to the lava below, melting away into the molten river. The rest of the body toppled back, and at the place where the cuts had been made, steam filled the air. From out of the steam hurtled the chimera, singed black from head to foot. As he turned and looked at the melted body of the snake, he let out a terrible roar. "I may not be able to hurt lava," he sent to Sara, "but rock, no problem."

"Not bad, flesh thing," Sara joked, caught in the thrill of Jonathan's reckless plan, "but if we do not move now, we are going to be a little too well done."

Jonathan took her point and once more launched upwards, catching at a rock formation that was rising nearby. He proceeded to climb upwards, moving away from the heat of the molten rock below until the temperature became tolerable. He then darted from one formation to the next, cutting the shortest of paths that he could to the iron citadel. At last, they came against the crater wall, the sheer bluff face fading away both above and below into the smoke and ash. A lava fall ran down from above, its final end feeding the lake below.

"It's up there." Sara thought. "Follow the lava; its source comes out from just beneath the citadel."

Jonathan leapt to the wall and began to climb, finding that the surface of the solid unmoving rock of the cliff was far easier to transverse than the ever-shifting landscape they had left behind them. Even though he now clung close to the lava fall, the heat became less and less as they ascended, something that Sara also became aware of within the chimera. But even as one danger relented, another began to rise. Sara knew that she had pushed her stay within the chimera to its limits. The acid of his chest cavity was beginning to intensify, and she was starting to notice that the walls between her and Jonathan's thoughts were breaking down. Their psychic bond had been intensified by Sara's awakening of the necklace, but this now worked against her being able to resist joining with his mind completely. She knew they needed to hurry.

As they ascended above the ash and smoke, Jonathan adjusted the chimera's skin color to match the iron rock face with metallic hues and textures. Sara had not even had to consciously warn him about the fire imps that lined the cliff top above. He had just known, because she knew. Next, he adjusted his course, moving parallel to the cliff's top and sliding under the lip of the lava flow. Here was the cylindrical tunnel that served as the trash chute for the citadel. Sara had planned this as their secret entrance, but she had never briefed Jonathan on its existence. It was a tight squeeze, but the chimera shimmied inside. As Jonathan tightened their body and constricted their limbs to propel them upwards, Sara had the uneasy feeling that she was now more chimera than she was the girl whose body rode in the creature's chest plate.

17

~

THE DOUBLE

The narrow cobblestone alleyway had an unmistakable charm.
Its worn and uneven surface set one at a natural swagger,
providing an immediate connection with the countless proud
generations who had built this city. Every few feet a niche or
alcove shot off into the shadows. Carven archways led into the
little fountained courtyards where children had once played,
lovers had once waited, and no doubt assassins had once hidden. Today, however, the alley was still. The fountains had
been shut off, the windows shuttered, and a heavy dusting
of snow covered over everything... well, almost everything.
Though the snow masked the dirt and the age of the place,
it was clear to Tessa that the city of Arcadia had seen better
days... yesterday even.

The numerous pieces of heavy broken stone that littered the
alleyway told the story well. Though they cut deeply into the
snow of the path, they themselves bore no more than a trace
of powder. Tessa didn't need Sara's powers to know that the
nearby sounds of thunder were not just the effects of some

gathering storm. Tessa eyed the heavy stonework nervously, looking up and coming to terms with the fact that there was still much more left to come down. "Think we may have come at a bad time?" she whispered, though her companion did not appear to be listening. He had climbed up on one of the larger blocks and was busily licking the snow out of his paws. A moment later, he hopped down and rubbed pleasantly against Tessa's boot, purring.

"Oh for Pete's sake!" Tessa rolled her eyes and put her hand to her forehead. "Do you ever talk when it might be of use!" She turned and began to storm off down the alley. "Well, whatever," she snapped to nobody in particular. "At least we have a plan this time." Tessa stopped at the end of the alleyway and peered out into the street. The distant stampede of running feet could be heard in all directions, but the space ahead was empty. Smoke drifted in from the right, obscuring the view, but through it Tessa could make out faint figures in what appeared to be metal armor struggling loudly with buckets of water. To the left, a six-legged animal about the size of a horse whinnied and reared, straining to break the tether that kept it in its pen. The echo of small-arms fire rang out somewhere on the next block.

"Well, I don't think your owner needs you now," Tessa murmured. She grabbed a hold of the horse creature's tether and cut it in two with a small knife. The beast bucked and fought; Tessa soothed it with a calming hum and stroked its neck. Tessa had spent time with horses all through her teen years working out on a farm in Puyallup on her summer breaks. She had always been good with animals, and soon she had calmed the beast and was beginning to climb atop it, cat tucked under one arm. "I guess all those years of wanting a pony of my own finally did amount for something," she commented aloud to herself. "Well, let's get going!" She shook the reins. The beast strode forward into the street. Tessa tested its response to her and felt ready to kick it into high gear.

With little warning , a strange roaring shattered the calm. The sound of a mighty engine blasted open the air, and a slim, dark shape screamed by just above. Something heavy fell from the craft, and before Tessa could even think to ponder it, it struck the corner of the building that bordered the little alleyway and burst into an all-consuming flash of pure heat. A sound accompanied the flash, but it was so loud Tessa could not hear it. The air just pulsed once, and everything went white.

*****

To Tessa, it seemed like a small piece of time had simply disappeared. She was distinctly certain that a second ago she had been mounted on a creature, but now she was lying sprawled against a wall, her ears hurt, and there was a cat licking her face. In her mind, there was nothing in between, but time had obviously passed. First of all, there was nothing resembling a horse anywhere in sight. And second of all, the alleyway they had just come from was no longer there. There was just a big pile of rubble squeezed between two shattered buildings. Uh-oh… the alleyway.

Tessa ran back to the entrance to the alleyway. Heavy pieces of masonry filled the little space. What had moments ago been defined by an absence of stone was now very much defined by a surfeit. And that surfeit was definitely in Tessa's way. "The mural!" Tessa cried. "We need to be back there when we blow the key to get out." Tessa pulled at the heavy stones, but they did not desire to budge. Without thinking, she clambered up the pile of rubble and attempted to make her way back between the fallen buildings.

Five minutes later, Tessa had gotten nowhere. Her boot was lodged deep in a hole, and her arm was bruised and hurt from where a rock had rolled down upon her. She needed help.

"Help! Help us, it's an emergency!" Tessa cried as she headed into the smoke, arms waving. Ahead of her was a strong-looking figure emerging from a building with an empty bucket. She grabbed his arm. "Please, can you help me?" she pleaded. "We are trapped here."

"Laka daela fim?" the man replied confusedly, backing away from her. Tessa was taken slightly aback when she realized that the head she was looking at was more like that of a lizard than a human. In kind, the being eyed Tessa strangely, then pushed her away, returning to its work. Behind her, the cat let out a poignant meow.

"Oh." Tessa stood dumb for a moment. Of course this would happen, wouldn't it? This wasn't Fairy, and Tessa was not Sara. Without access to Sara's powers, Tessa could neither speak to or understand any of these people. Maybe being an interdimensional explorer wasn't such an exciting prospect after all. Tessa turned and looked one last time at the blocked alleyway. "Well, there's no going back out that way. I guess we are going to just have to follow the plan and hope for the best."

*****

Ten minutes later, Tessa slipped out of a stone archway and came into first sight of the palace of Arcadia. It was not quite what Sara had led her to believe. True, there were golden towers and rugged battlements and exquisite ornamentation, but the shimmering dome of energy covering the whole thing was decidedly out of place. Sara had explained that there was an energy field which prevented them from porting her directly into the palace, making her current journey necessary, but Tessa hadn't expected it to be so distinctly visible. Not far above the palace, a battalion of wicked-looking crafts hovered, barraging the shield with some sort of energy weapons. With each hit, the dome shook, but it seemed to be holding fast for the moment. Tessa found her motivation to enter the palace to be wavering.

To her left, Tessa could see the main gate of the castle, and things there didn't seem to be going much better. Behind the energy barrier, a crowd of archers worked, firing blue flame arrows out of the shield and trying futilely to drive off a squadron of heavily armored vehicles. These sleek, advanced crafts had the look of futuristic tanks equipped with battering rams. They had gathered like vultures about the entrance, waiting for the shield to fall. Along with the archers, a number of catapults and trebuchets were engaged in flinging heavy stones at the dark vehicles, but were having little more luck. A single one of the ebony crafts had taken a lucky strike from a catapult and lay smoking in the middle of the city square.

In front of the archers, a troop of mounted knights had formed, lances pointed at the sky, and looked to be preparing their final stand. All about in the heart of the city, foot soldiers had gathered, just outside of arrow range, waiting for the gate to fall. Tessa wasn't at all certain the archers would be able to tell her from the soldiers at this distance, but she had to go in.

An ancient road circled this part of the palace, dotted with squares and monuments. Tessa only needed a moment to cross it, and then the outer wall of the palace would shield her the rest of the way. She had to pick the right moment though. Time was wasting. Suddenly, a gasp went up from the troops. Across the square, the soldiers in black were pulling down the largest monument in the city—a great dragon-winged woman with sword held high—and it began to topple forward with a massive crash.

With all eyes on the massive statue, Tessa ran for the far wall. She closed her own eyes as she darted out across the open street, not wanting any circumstances to dissuade her from her goal. She counted to five before opening them again. The old stone wall was just ten feet in front of her. She dove against it with a gasp.

Tessa pressed herself up against the outer wall of the castle. Keeping her hand against the wall, she ran to the right, away from the main gate. To her relief, the sounds of battle receded somewhat into the distance. She passed two large iron doors— both firmly sealed—before she came upon her goal, a fair-sized alcove set into the wall. This semi-circular indentation was about twelve feet across, with cold, stone benches lining the curved sides. At the focus of the semi-circle, a statue stood, a young man flinging himself into open air, arms and face raised to the heavens in supplication. On the far side of the circle, at the point where the benches met, a fountain was set into the wall, sculpted to appear as the beast pursuing him.

"Heh," Tessa laughed, "he kind of looks like you." She looked over at the cat and smirked. El Gato did not respond, but only tucked himself into the shadows under one of the stone benches. Tessa grumbled to herself, then reached up and felt around behind the head of the open-mouthed stone cat from which liquid water still poured, even in the winter air. Seven gems studded the panther's collar (one missing), and Tessa touched three of them in a strange and deliberate order. Next, she reached into the open mouth of the stone figure and pulled forward on a hidden catch. Sara had said this part would not go well if she hadn't gotten the order right on the collar. Tessa held her breath.

With much less sound than Tessa expected, the fountain clicked and spun back into the wall a few inches. She put her hand on the stone cat's head and pushed, and the fountain turned completely to one side, revealing about a two-foot gap leading into the darkness. From one of her belt packs, Tessa fished out the flashlight that she had brought from her own kitchen and switched it on. A warm glow spread out from it into the dark passageway. The way was dusty, and Tessa had to stoop to enter. El Gato fell in behind her and Tessa pushed the fountain shut with a click. She realized as she turned back to the darkness that she had neglected to ask Sara how to open the door from this side.

The narrow passage quickly opened into a small chamber, a guardroom from the looks of it. There was just enough space to squeeze past the contents of the room—a wooden chair and a dusty spear. On the opposite side of the chamber, stone stairs spiraled downward. They were narrow and old, and Tessa's boots rang out on the hard stone as she tried to navigate them; she prayed that nothing was there to hear. Perhaps twenty feet down, the stairs opened into a series of dank passageways. Unfortunately, Tessa had spiraled around so many times that she had no longer any idea which way was which.

"Wait, we need to take the east passage," Tessa hissed to the cat. Which way is that? El Gato sat down at the crossroads and peered about down the three tunnels. After a moment or so, he shrugged and looked back at Tessa sheepishly. "Great! Just great," Tessa fumed. "You know, I'd think with all the tricks you have up your sleeve that you'd have some kind of sense. How exactly is it that you manage to always seem to get through all the difficult situations you end up in? Or are you just doing this to torture me?"

Maybe it was the light, but the cat appeared to smile, just a bit.

Tessa directed her light down the passages. They were narrow and dirty, though dry. Dusty webs stretched across the archways, and various dugouts along the way looked to contain old caskets or urns. "Catacombs," Tessa mumbled to herself, "they could go on forever." As the light moved, Tessa could just make out small forms scurrying out of its range as it passed over them. From somewhere nearby, the unsettling sound of something being gnawed echoed. Tessa was without her safety net here; losing her direction wasn't in Sara's plan.

Tessa bit at her fingers. "Wait! Didn't Curiosity give us some sort of compass?" She fumbled about in her pouches and pulled out a thin, golden dial. She opened it and held it out in front of her. The needle spun slowly around in circles, never seeming to settle on any one direction. "Arrgh," Tessa cried, smashing it against a wall, "what a piece of junk. Ok cat, we're going this way." Tessa stormed off down the center hallway. "Not as many cobwebs here... good enough for me."

About five minutes later, the two companions came to a dead end. If this was the place Sara had described, there would be a ladder hidden in the ceiling, concealed in the cobwebs. Tessa winced as she reached up into the webs, but soon enough her hand struck something solid. She sighed in relief; she was back on track now. She pulled on the ladder and it creaked down. Tessa scooped up the cat and climbed upward through a rather tight passage, eventually finding herself in another empty guardroom with another empty chair. However, the sounds of battle could be heard distinctly here, and every few seconds, the walls shook and the floor lurched sickeningly. She was running out of time.

Tessa looked around. One of the walls was made of wood, and had a little plate mounted into it that looked like it could be slid back and forth on a track. The sounds of commotion came from just beyond. Tessa slid open the plate, revealing two small holes in the woodwork. Light came streaming through them. She put her eyes to the holes.

The next room was some kind of laboratory. Long tables held beakers and vials full of strange liquids. Narrow glass tubes snaked about the room as if part of some great distillery. A forge was set at the center of the room, and the coals had been neglected and were now dying down. Complex machinery lay about the room in various states of disassembly. Several large vats filled with blue liquid stood at the edges of the room, some with what appeared to be odd creatures floating in them. The high stone ceiling of the vaulted room stretched away into darkness, and ornate paintings circled the room, obviously far older than the current accoutrements. Scurrying about from table to table were three rather haggard looking lizard men, quickly yet carefully pushing various items into sacks. The three men appeared to be following orders barked at them by someone Tessa couldn't see, but who obviously was some sort of officer. "I think we've come to the right place," she whispered to the cat.

Just as Sara had described, a loose brick pulled away to reveal a hollow behind, and Tessa reached in and fumbled around looking for the catch. Soon enough, a click sounded, and a large section of the wooden wall swung open, carrying with it the ornate gilded picture frame that had obviously disguised it from the other side. Tessa discovered that she was standing about six feet above the floor of the room, but her entrance had been apparently unnoticed in the commotion. She jumped down.

Now that Tessa had entered the room, she could see the commander. He was turned away from her and was gathering books off of a shelf above one of the lab tables. From what she could make out, he looked to be human. He wore embroidered, blue, woolen pants tucked neatly into knee-high boots. A white cotton shirt with rolled-up sleeves served as laboratory smock. His platinum hair was quite long, running past his shoulder blades, and was drawn back in a silver ribbon. His belt was heavy with pouches, and a leather bag hung from a strap at his side. A large knapsack lay on the table in front of him, and as he finished stuffing it with books, he hefted it up and spun around.

Sara had warned Tessa to be expecting something out of the ordinary, but she wasn't prepared for this. Tessa staggered backward. "Ethan!" she cried, and then fell forward in a heap.

Tessa awoke a moment later as two lizard men grabbed her wrists and dragged her to her feet. What had she just seen? What was going on? "No, you have to let me go," she shouted, "that's my husband!"

"Pel ani feit," one of the lizard men remarked as he wrestled with Tessa. "Gol naxx," the other seemed to agree. Soon enough, they had tied her hands together and fastened her to a marble pillar. After a few more orders from their commander, they turned back to their bags and started to flee the room.

"What? You can't just leave me here!" Tessa shouted. "I need your help! Ethan, tell them to let me go!"

The long-haired officer picked up a sack of laboratory equipment and headed out of the room. Just as he reached the archway, he stopped, turned, and looked at Tessa one last time. Tessa could now see her mistake. His features were all familiar, but his face was smooth as marble. There were no flaws in his skin, only pale, cold silk—a perfection that her husband had never possessed. The lack of faults caused a chill to ride down her back. No glimmer of recognition appeared on the man's face, and he shook his head and turned again to go.

"Mrrrrowwr!" The scientist nearly collided with the slim black cat that had sat itself down right in the center of the archway. At first the startle turned to annoyance, but as the cat stretched his front paws upwards and the stranger noticed the white star on its chest, his eyes widened in shock. The scientist stepped back for a moment, obviously weighing his decision heavily. His assistants had already fled down the hall. Finally, he dropped his bags and pulled out a long knife from his boot. He strolled quickly towards where Tessa sat tied against the pillar. Circling about her, he cut the rope, and then hauled her up, spinning her about to face him. He studied her face for a moment. Up close, his eyes were like nothing Tessa had ever seen—like fierce balls of smoky glass lit from behind with a deep blue flame. Finally, he spoke. "You seem to have an interesting companion," he intoned, speaking flawless English. "Please explain yourself."

"You..." Tessa stammered, unsure of anything anymore. "I know you. But you can't be... my husband died a decade ago. We have a daughter."

"I assure you, I have no offspring."

"No?" Tessa was actually not sure that this was not Ethan. "Well, I do. She's in trouble... we are all in trouble. I was sent to find the Inventor. She... my daughter... sent me here to find him."

"I have worn that name before." The man who mirrored her husband drew closer, his interest piquing.

Of course this was who she sought, Tessa realized. It would be far too unlikely for some random person to wear this form. Her head was still spinning as she tried to understand why her husband and this inventor looked so alike, but quickly she realized she was missing too many pieces. Now was her one chance to speak.

"My daughter, Sara, said you would know her father. To me, he is Ethan, but to you... she said you would know him as the Seventh Star of Twilight. He needs your help."

At the mention of the Seventh Star, the fire in the scientist's eyes flared up, but then just as quickly subsided again. The inventor's demeanor changed, and he dropped the ropes that held Tessa, leaving her once again to her own power. "Aye," ne nodded, his tone quite serious, "I know well the Seventh Star, milady, but no, I am not him." He laughed, still somehow keeping a serious manner. "I see how it would be fitting to his sense of humor though to take my form amongst humans. And you are wedded to him?" The stranger's eyebrows rose in surprise. "Odd," he spoke, "I am usually quite adept at spotting those that are more than they seem."

The palace shook again, even harder than before, and Tessa nearly lost her footing, falling forward into the arms of the stranger, who seemed oddly unconcerned by the upheaval. Tessa quickly pulled away, but not before she caught his scent— it was not the familiar musk of her late husband, but welcoming nonetheless, like fresh fallen rain and wild grass. The sounds of battle rang closer now, and hard and frantic footfalls echoed nearby. A crack formed in one of the walls, and some of the liquid-filled tubes tipped over and smashed onto the floor. "Our defenses have fallen," the stranger announced somberly. "I must go, but..." The stranger's brow furrowed for a moment as he studied this interloping woman like an oddity. He reached out a hand to touch the fur of the cat, who had jumped up to a nearby table, and who seemed to be engaged silently in the conversation. "No," the inventor finally spoke, shaking his head, "I cannot help you now. I am afraid you have come at a bad time. I have worked with these people for over twenty seasons, and their situation is now as grave as it has ever been. I cannot abandon them when they need me most. But I cannot leave you here. We must flee. Come. I believe you already know the way."

The inventor thrust his knapsack into Tessa's arms and then heaved the cat up into the hollow in the wall opened by the secret door. He then hastily shoved a table in front of the hole and hurried across the room to pick up a sack that the lizard men had left behind. Tessa began to climb up onto the table. There was little time to argue.

Suddenly, from the darkness in the wall came a great yowl, like the roar of a miniature tiger. The crunch of boots and the muted clunking of armor accompanied the sound. Instinctively, Tessa flattened her back to the wall, hiding herself behind the great painting that had hinged open to reveal the secret door. A split second later, two armored men burst forth from the spy chamber and trampled across the table and down into the room, firing some sort of heavy energy rifles as they ran. The inventor was just standing and turning around with his bag as they bore down on him, and he fell, struck by multiple bolts of searing crimson light. Tessa could not help but notice as he fell that his expression seemed more surprised at the fact that he was falling than at the men rushing in.

18

THE IRON CITADEL

"This will bring us out in the..." Sara started to analyze the map in her head.

"...underbelly of the main tower, the servants quarters," Jonathan finished for her. While currently useful, this synchronicity was not a healthy phenomenon. Sara realized that her organic outfit was now beginning to weaken from the acid in the chimera's chest cavity. On an entirely different level, she could feel the limbs of the chimera working to propel their body up the chute, and the chimera's senses slowly becoming her senses. She could feel Jonathan's excitement and trepidation mingling with her cool resolve and planning. Though this all felt quite natural, even right, she willfully resisted the merging. She did not want to become the chimera. Didn't she?

Ahead, a dim light grew slowly larger, marking the exit from the garbage chute—salvation was only moments away. Sara knew that the temperature within the citadel was cool enough that she could survive without being encased in the body of the chimera. But was it really worth fighting? Once Sara was fully at one with the chimera, she and Jonathan would become a being of unrivaled power, all knowing and all functional, able at a moment's notice to adjust their physical form to match any situation. They could take their enemies head on and confront directly whatever challenges came their way—and they would never be alone again. Wait... that last part wasn't Sara's idea, that was a Jonathan thought. Sara pulled upwards with her two long clawed arms and pushed down with her back pinchers to reach the grate faster. She gave no consideration as to whether or not the dim room ahead was occupied, but simply shoved her way up out of the grate and then forced her chest open to set her body free.

It had never worked like this before. Her mind did not all at once depart with the ejection of her body. Instead, a single tentacle remained attached to the back of her neck, and for a few fleeting seconds, Sara saw her own body from the eyes of the chimera. Then, her consciousness passed from her, and she felt for a moment lost, as a piece of her stripped itself away. Slowly though, she came to realize that the piece that had faded was not her but Jonathan. She gradually found the walls of her personality rising up once more, and she opened her eyes and drew in a gasping breath. The oxygen filled her lungs and rose to her brain in a riot, as with a diver who had lingered too long underwater. She focused her vision and was happy to discover the chimera sprawled across from her, its chest plate slowly zipping back up as the last tentacle retreated inside.

"I am me again," she murmured. Then, noticing all at once that her organic outfit was literally smoking, she scrambled for the water flask which had fallen out of the chimera and now lay a few feet from her. She hastily drenched herself in water from head to toe, diluting the acid and washing it away. As Sara washed herself, she paid no attention to the chimera who was now staggering back to his feet. Jonathan too had been stunned by their separation. His mind, however, was slower to recover.

"Are we two again?" he stammered in the growling, yet boyish, tones of the chimera's voice.

"Yes, and just barely," Sara replied. She was standing bent forward now, one hand on her knee as she used the other to pour water over her head and hair where the organic suit had now peeled back.

"What just happened?" Jonathan murmured.

"What do you think just happened?"

"We were almost one," Jonathan said, and his tone seemed at once amazed and saddened.

"Yes, along with my body almost being devoured and you and I spending forever trapped together as a monster." Sara almost at once regretted the harshness of her reply; after all, it was not Jonathan's fault he had tried to eat her. But before she could even start feeling bad, she saw that the slight had just bounced off him. Jonathan's simple good nature was a powerful force indeed.

"Hey, you never know; it might have been fun. Though I think I was likely to have gotten lost in all that knowledge you carry around." The chimera made a yuck face, sticking out his tongue. "How you can stand to have all that in you?"

That was almost funny to Sara. As much as she feared becoming a chimera, Jonathan feared having to be tied to the Font of All Knowledge. "Well," she smiled, "we cannot push it like that again."

"Agreed."

Sara stood up straight and began to wring her hair out, and then finally noticed there were others in the room with them—fire imps. Two of them were crouched along the railless iron stairway that led up out of the dim room. The imps were slick and scaly little creatures, each about half Sara's size. They had tiny wings, twisted horns, and cruel faces that mocked those of human infants. The moment she saw them, they knew. Both turned to run up the stairs, climbing over each other, shoving and pushing to be the first to escape.

"Jonathan!" Sara pointed, and the chimera whirled around. "Get them before they can warn anyone we are here!"

Jonathan cleared the first set of stairs in a single bound, coming within inches of the little critters. They scrambled and squealed at his looming presence, and one shoved the other back towards the chimera. He caught the little creature in one hand and continued in his pursuit of the other. Up they went, around a switchback and through an archway. He had the second imp almost in his grasp when a sharp pain in his palm suddenly distracted him. The little imp in his hand had heated its own scales to a white hot temperature, causing the chimera to yelp and fling the creature to the side. Jonathan brought his burnt palm up to his mouth and began to lick it and blow on it. The imp regained his footing and, with an evil laugh, was off after its friend.

"So, it's going to be like that," the chimera snarled. He forgot his injury and shot off on all fours after the imps. He fired two of his back spikes, but was shocked when the imps evaded them, laughing at him and mocking him in a language he did not understand. Jonathan crashed around a corner, sliding uncontrollably on the smooth surface of the iron floor. This cost him all the ground he had gained in the hall before. He grumbled under his breath and adjusted his footpads, allowing him to cling to the ground much in the same way he could cling to walls, increasing his speed and agility. Still, the two little imps avoided more volleys of spikes, and then, part running, part gliding, led him up another twisting flight of stairs.

So focused was he on his pursuit, Jonathan failed to notice any of the tiny nooks or alcoves where the small imps could have easily escaped him. He did briefly feel Sara trying to convey something through their telepathic link, but he ignored the interruption. Whatever the message was, he was too centered on the task at hand to take any heed of it. He gained ground, edging ever closer to the two imps, and each almost fell into his grasp at different times, but both managed last minute escapes that brought forth cruel taunts and laughter. Finally, they all came hurtling through a tall set of doors just as the chimera pounced on one of the imps. Before it could super heat, he sprayed it with a jet of water from his mouth. The creature cried out, then hardening, cracked apart.

"That will teach you," Jonathan declared in triumph. "Now where did your friend get to?"

It was only then that the chimera took in the surroundings of the room he had burst into. It was a large open chamber—circular, but instead of bearing a roof, the great shaft rose to the sky, lined on all sides with spiraling stairwells, like the threads of a great screw. Sitting on those caged stairwells, and positioned all around the chimera, were fire imps. And if that wasn't enough, scattered amongst them were a number of squat, bright-burning lizards, all staring coldly at Jonathan. He could not have hoped to count them all, and though they were all small, their numbers dumbfounded him.

Suddenly, a shadow, or rather a light, passed over Jonathan, and he looked upwards into the expanse of the shaft above him. A great firebird, almost twice his size, was circling above him. It looked on him with blazing eyes and a recognition he could not place.

"So... at last you have come," the bird cawed, in English of all things. "It seems the lady of the Iron Citadel has spoken true, and I shall at last have my revenge."

"Revenge?" Jonathan did not know why, but he felt he should know this flaming bird.

"Yes, revenge, against the one who shamed me and then stole away the life-giving clock," the fire hawk screeched.

"I stole what now?" Jonathan was at a loss.

"Do not mock me, creature," the bird cried. "You are the one who came from the land of the dead at the request of the black queen and took the watch that made life where there was no life. And then when I was sent to hunt you, you shamed my companions, and my victory over you was stolen by the compassion of a weak pale paladin."

"Oh, I remember you now," the chimera nodded, and the whole episode from the land of the dead came rushing back to him. "Sorry, it's just that we have been through so much since then, I kinda forgot. How have you been?"

"How have I been...?" The fire hawk was torn between confusion and rage. "Waiting all this time to have my revenge! And now I shall; you will mock me no further." Ablaze with fire and wrath, the hawk descended on the chimera.

*****

Sara shook the rest of the water off as best she could, briefly turning the organic suit's surface to one that was nearly frictionless, allowing excess water to drain away. Almost at once, she wondered why she was even bothering to dry off. The heat of the inner citadel would dry her fast enough, and the wetter she was here the better. She began to climb the stairs in a casual pursuit of Jonathan, and as she did, she rewet her hair and transformed her suit to a textured surface that would help better to dissipate the heat.

Where was he anyway? In her mind's eye, she could see Jonathan still chasing the imps and moving further into the citadel. It should not be taking him so long just to grab a few imps. She hurried her pace, deciding the sooner she caught up with him the better. Where exactly where the imps leading him anyway? The answer came just a quick as the question, and Sara's heart leapt. She tore at once into a run. Through their psychic link she attempted to warn Jonathan of the trap that lay ahead. The thought did not seem to reach him. Their link generally worked best if they were in line of sight, but Sara had hoped that due to the deepening of the bond that she would have been able to reach him. However, it seemed that Jonathan was so fixated on his course that he was blocking her out.

She needed to be closer if she was going to force her voice to be heard. She ran as hard as she could, fully aware that the heat of the citadel would limit the amount of time she could keep up such a pace.

With her gift, Sara monitored the unfolding scene in the central shaft where Jonathan was now being threatened by the fire hawk. She had of course known that a giant bird of fire was one of the guardians of the citadel, but she had not looked deep enough to realize that this hawk had a personal grudge against Jonathan. She had long ago decided to avoid the central open shaft, instead planning to take a secret inner stairwell straight to the top. Now there seemed little choice but to enter the fray and attempt to help Jonathan defeat the creature— though in doing so she would most likely need to remerge with the chimera and link the fairy flask to his system. That thought alone was disquieting enough, but combined with the knowledge that they were running out of time before the mistress of the citadel returned, the whole plan was now in danger.

Sara was no fool. She had chosen the time for their assault carefully to ensure that it coincided with the absence of the tower's ruler. Now that they had been exposed, it was only a matter of time before she came for them, and with her here, the chance of success was close to none.

*****

Jonathan evaded the fire hawk with all the speed and skill that his body afforded him. This area was an ill-chosen one for the hawk. Though the room was very large in its circumference, it still restricted the hawk's movements. In the open, the hawk could choose carefully his moment of attack. Here, it was forced to maintain a circular pattern and could only attack when it looped in towards Jonathan, when it could finally pull in tighter and take a dive. This made its moments of attack utterly predictable. Still, the chimera could not keep this up forever, and the hawk showed no sign of fatigue. Did a creature of fire even get tired, Jonathan wondered.

Jonathan surveyed the room, determining the best routes of escape. There was the door he had entered through, but he did not like the idea of confronting the hawk in an even tighter environment like the halls, where it might corner him and fry him to a crisp. The other egress was up, and in that direction he could see several possibilities, as the shaft above was dotted with scaffoldings and other makeshift outcroppings. Dropping one of these onto the hawk might do the trick.

It was then that he caught Sara's scent; she was near. He reached out through their bond. "Sara, stay out of this room. I have run across an old friend who is not too happy to see me."

Sara reached the door to the central shaft and quickly scanned the room beyond in her mind to get a look at the fight. The hawk might have been totally focused on striking the chimera, but there were far too many imps and fire lizards looking on. One might easily spot her if she was not careful.

"Jonathan," she sent, focusing hard, "can you hear me?"

"Hear? No. But yeah, you're in my head."

"We have to get to Adam and use the whistle to get out of here, and fast."

"Tell me something I don't know. I am a little busy here at the moment."

"Come to me," Sara relayed, "we can join together and use the flask to cool that bird off."

"No."

"What do you mean, no?"

"There is a green flame horse tiled into the floor in here," Jonathan replied. In fact, he had been moving towards Sara's position when he noticed it for the first time. "Aras said that I must refuse you when I see the green horse. If we join we now, we will not succeed. You have to go on without me, that is if you know some way to proceed."

"I do." Sara felt uneasy about leaving him, and not just because she was worried for his safety. He was her protector. With him near, she didn't have to fear anything. Moments before, all she had dreaded was joining with the chimera again. Now she could not get her legs to move to leave him. "Well, at least let me throw the flask out there. You can use it to drown that crazy bird."

Jonathan dodged another assault from the hawk and came tumbling to his feet right on top of the green tile horse. He took it as a sign. "No, you need it more than me. Now get going, I will meet you at the top. If you get Adam free, you use the whistle that moment; no waiting for me. After all, once you are back with Curiosity, you can teach him the song to open a portal to me anywhere."

That was true as long as Jonathan was still alive. Sara hesitated. "Go!" Jonathan snapped in her head. Sara followed him in her mind as he leapt off the ground, bounced off of the roof of one stairwell, and then jumped to another. He was five stories up before she finally moved. The top of the shaft was open to the tower above, forming the center of the queen's throne room. If Jonathan moved like that the whole way, he would easily beat her there.

Sara doubled back, skirting the outer wall of the shaft until she found the tile mosaic depicting dragons devouring a phoenix. She pressed the eye of the largest of the dragons, whose head was bent low, and then she stood back. All the tiles of the mosaic trembled for a moment, and then they peeled back, rearranging themselves into an archway with a reborn phoenix tiled about its threshold. Sara did not delay to admire the craftsmanship of the door, but passed through it onto the hidden stairwell that spiraled upwards, carved directly into the walls of the shaft. Sara chose her best pace and began her ascent. There was no light source within the tunnel; Sara used her gift to maneuver. It was hard going. The stairs were not made for a human, and each was about three feet high. So steep were the steps that Sara more crawled than ran. The organic suit covered her from foot to neck, including her hands, so she was thankfully able to use her arms to help pull herself along, not having to concern herself with the heat of the iron. The heat of the air was another matter. The air was more confined within this stairwell, and the temperature was stifling. Several times she was forced to pause to drink out of the flask and to douse herself with the cold water. It was the danger of the queen's return and her fear for Jonathan that drove her to push herself ever faster, or at least that's what she tried to tell herself.

In truth, now that Sara was so close, she could almost not contain her excitement. She had been so good at not letting herself think about Him too much. He had been so distant, but soon she would see him again. Soon she would free him, ease his suffering, hear him, smell him. She shook her head violently.

"Come on Sara, you're not some silly schoolgirl," she spat out loud. "You barely know him and, trust me, he does not know you even exist. Well, not like...." she trailed off. She turned her thoughts to the task at hand. She scrambled up the steps, her legs and arms straining from the workout. That's it, she thought, keep moving. Still, her heart pounded, not just from the exercise, but also the anticipation.

Sara was almost to the top of the shaft when a sudden explosion shattered the darkness and light burst into the stairwell. Dust and stone filled the air before her. She covered her eyes and turned away, afraid they had found her. Then in her mind's eye, she saw who had burst through the wall. Thrown was a better term. The chimera was gaining his feet, tossing aside rubble. He was burnt black in many areas. One of the pincers that extended from his back lay broken and charred. Sara could see that he was in an utter rage, and before she could even attempt to communicate with him, he snarled and flung himself back out into the fray. A blast of fire briefly engulfed the hole, and then the sounds of the conflict faded away into the distance.

There was so little time. Jonathan could not hope to hold out against the firebird much longer, and Sara could feel the approach of the mistress of this house. Sara hurried forward. She climbed cautiously over the rubble and past the opening in the wall, experiencing a moment of vertigo as she caught sight of the fall that awaited her should she slip. Then she was off again. It was only moments later that she breached the far side of the secret tunnel, coming out through a grate in the throne room.

She found him at once with her eyes, lying broken, ragged, and in chains at the foot of the alien throne. His body had burns and scars all over. His dark hair had grown now almost to his waist, and his metal wings were wrapped in barbed chains and held in a mockery of flight over his head.

"Adam," Sara breathed, frozen in horror at the sight of him.

The prisoner's head slowly raised up, and through the disheveled locks of his hair, Sara made eye contact with him. At first, he did not seem to know her, and then he spoke in a raspy voice.

"Is it really you?"

"Yes." And she ran to him. She could not help herself; she wrapped her arms around him. At once she regretted it, as she felt him stiffen in pain. "Sorry!" she gasped. She fell back, kneeling to the floor in front of him.

"No... no," the broken knight coughed, and Sara saw his face alight with a smile. She smiled back, and the two stared at each other. Sara felt at once unsure, overwhelmed and yet impossibly happy. How ridiculous was this? Here she was, trapped in the heart of an enemy fort, her best friend in danger of being roasted, the odds of escape becoming ever more unlikely, and yet she was happy.

"I am going to get you out of here," Sara whispered, regaining her wits and moving forward. She produced a set of lock picks that she had taken from Curiosity's collection, and she set about the locks on his chains. She freed his wrists first, then went to work on his leg shackles. He wrapped himself in a cloth that Sara had carried over to him.

"How are you here?" he rasped, his voice a mere whisper.

"Oh come on now, you know us," Sara said, freeing his legs and standing up to undo the first of two locks that held his wings, "after all, you chased us all over creation and never even came close to catching us. There is nowhere or no one safe from us if we put our skills together."

"The chimera is here too?"

"Yeah… he is the one causing all that commotion down the shaft over there."

"I never thought to see you again."

Sara paused with one lock remaining and knelt down to Adam's level. "I have watched over you every day. It is my greatest regret that we were not here sooner to free you."

Adam's smile turned thoughtful and his bright blue eyes filled with tears. "You should never have risked it. You should not have come here."

"Indeed," a voice like coal crackling on a fire came from behind Sara, "you should never have come here."

19

~~~

BATTLEGROUND

One of the armored soldiers turned the inventor over, and the second peered down at him. Their helmets were carved with horrific visages that made Tessa wonder what might be under them. "Tek hamm," one of the fully-armored warriors announced. The two soldiers clumsily shoved all of the equipment off of one of the lab tables and hefted up the limp scientist, laying him out and binding his feet and hands with what looked like black rope, but which constricted of its own accord once attached. The men began to search the helpless inventor's pockets.

"Hey!" Tessa knew the soldiers could not understand her language, but for this they didn't need to. Startled, the men whirled around, spotting Tessa and rushing toward her where she stood crouched on top of the table by the secret exit. Tessa could see that she had only once chance. Tessa grabbed the edge of the large glass medical tank mounted against the wall to her left and pushed with all her strength. Her muscles strained, but the thought of never seeing Sara again pulled her through the pain. With a loud pop, the tank came away from the wall and went toppling forward onto the soldiers, shattering and knocking them sprawling. Glass shards flew everywhere, and a heavy wave of viscous, blue liquid crashed across the floor of the laboratory. Several strange, dead alien shapes lurched out with it, spilling chaotically across the room. Live wiring that had come loose from the back of the tank now danced about in the madness, sending white arcs of electricity through the rushing mass of liquid. The soldiers convulsed in sudden shock and then collapsed to the floor, still.

Unsure about trying the floor, Tessa hopped from table to table to reach the inventor. "Oh please, don't be dead," she hissed under her breath, awash with fear over what would happen to the Seventh Star if any of the seven were to be killed. Tessa felt sick. This mission might have ended before it even got off the ground. But mission aside, having now seen this inventor who looked so like her ex-husband, Tessa could not escape the fact that she wanted to see Ethan again, despite all her anger towards him.

She put her hand to the inventor's neck. He was breathing, but oddly cool to the touch. His skin was supple, yet smooth like polished stone. Where the bolts from the soldiers' weapons had struck him, his clothing had burned away, but his flesh was unscathed. Tessa fumbled around in her belt pouches and eventually came up with a small vial. She uncorked it and waved it under the stranger's nose, and he awoke with a cough.

The inventor's eyes widened at seeing Tessa crouched before him. "What..." he stammered, "What happened?" Then, realizing he was bound, he began to fight against his restraints.

Tessa tried her knife on the strange black cord that bound the stranger's wrists, but not only did it not cut the black cords, they moved of their own accord to avoid the blade, putting her at risk of cutting the inventor. "You got shot," she fumed, "what do you think?"

"No," the inventor barked, sitting up and pulling against his bonds, "of course I got shot." He flexed his arms and legs, and Tessa could see the muscles under his clothing strain, but the cords only bit harder into his flesh. A hint of fear started to spread across the scientist's face, but Tessa spared him any further anguish. Thinking quickly, she picked up the device, still lying on the table, that the soldiers had used to extrude the black rope. On the back end there was a hooked blade. She pulled at the cords with it and they snapped at once, shredding and then evaporating into the air.

The inventor shook the blood back into his hands and then finally took a pause and noticed the mess of the laboratory. He looked at Tessa again with some amount of wonder. "Who did you say you were again?"

"I didn't." Tessa looked angry.

The inventor was on the floor now, unhurt—the live current appeared to have shorted out somewhere. He stooped over the soldiers and examined them. He lifted one of their ornate-looking rifles. "Demon forged," he whispered, "it can't be." He looked up at the open hollow in the wall, where a small, black cat was now sitting, watching them. "We can't go that way," he announced. "They are waiting for me. Come on, we are going to have to leave out the front door."

The inventor waved Tessa down towards him and began stripping the dead soldiers of their armor. Tessa balked at seeing their faces. "They are human," she gasped.

The inventor seemed puzzled by her comment. "Of course they are," he replied. "Who fights the wars on your world?" In a few moments, Tessa and the scientist had stripped the soldiers of their uniforms and then hastily began to pull them on over their clothes. "Forget the heavy armor," the stranger warned, "we don't have time. Just grab a helmet and a vest." He tossed Tessa a rifle and retrieved the damp knapsack from under a table. "Let's go."

The inventor and Tessa, El Gato in their wake, rushed out of the laboratory without a moment to spare. As they entered into the ancient maze of halls that made up the interior of the palace, they caught sight of another platoon of black-armored soldiers moving straight towards them. "Kalt," the inventor shouted, pointing down a side passage, "del var tel dana!" The platoon leader nodded and led his troops down the side hall. The inventor continued forward in the direction from which the other soldiers had come. "That should only keep them busy for a few moments," he said, looking back towards Tessa as he ran. "We have to keep moving!"

The vest was heavier than it looked, and the helmet fit poorly; Tessa had to hike it up on her face so the eye slits met with her line of vision. She had not been used to this kind of exercise in years; this was not a treadmill or a yoga class at the gym. Her legs were cramping up and her breath was shallow, but her fear drove her onward. This situation was growing more surreal by the minute. The halls that she was now sprinting through were alabaster, expertly cared for and all laid out like a grand museum. Ornate paintings of a foreign history lined all the walls and even many of the ceilings. Alcoves and intersections were marked with grand statues of long-dead kings and statesmen, all quite unlike any she had ever seen back home. But for all their beauty, there was no time to stop and drink them in. She had to move.

Soon enough, they came to the central hall of the palace. Rubble and bodies lay scattered about the grand mosaic floor, and the ancient, gold-inlayed wooden entry doors had been split open by a blow of massive force. Fires were smoldering everywhere, and all about, the wounded were moaning in misery. Tessa froze up, completely lost for a course of action, but the inventor did not hesitate. He ran over to one of the fallen soldiers in black and hefted him up, dragging him to a sitting position, then he waved Tessa over. Bewildered, Tessa came, and was directed to grab one of the fallen soldier's shoulders. Together, the pair hauled the wounded soldier to his feet. He was alive, but barely conscious. "What are we doing?" Tessa hissed.

"Saving this man's life," the inventor replied. "Now just keep your mouth shut and move." Together, they dragged the wounded man out of the palace and past the flurry of soldiers that was now pouring in and out of the great hall. A few men who seemed to be of higher rank called out to them and the inventor replied to them in the same strange tongue. The officers waved them out towards a small frigate that had landed just beyond the main square in front of the palace. Soon enough, Tessa and the stranger had handed the wounded man off to medical personnel, who whisked him up into the dark ship. Their mission completed, they headed back towards the fray, but then quickly turned off down a side street leading away from the main square. "Just keep moving," the inventor whispered, "this is still a battlefield, they will assume we are on patrol."

No one seemed to take any note of the sleek, black blur that shadowed the pair, clinging to walls and slinking under the bellies of the war machines. The star-chested cat seemed to have an uncanny gift for moving when and where no one was looking. He progressed undeterred through the chaos around him, constantly keeping Tessa and the inventor in his view.

A few minutes later, the companions had escaped the crowd and were holed up in the shell of a bombed house to catch their breath. Tessa and the inventor sat on the floor, their backs to a thick stone wall, while El Gato crouched near the entrance, his ears up and alert. "I don't suppose you brought anything to eat in that bag?" Tessa moaned.

"Eat?" the inventor replied. "No. Can't say I considered that."

"Well, it's a good thing you have someone sensible around then," Tessa smiled. She reached into a pouch and pulled out what looked like hard bread. "It's elven. There's a lot more to it than it looks."

The inventor reached out and took a piece. "That seems to be the theme of the day," he remarked. He took a few bites and a few deep breaths. The color began to creep back into his cheeks. He held out his hand to Tessa. "I'm Michael, by the way."

"Tessa." She wasn't sure whether he intended to shake her hand or kiss it. She kept her hand to herself.

"I have to thank you for saving me back there," Michael spoke. "Because of you, Arcadia may live to see another day."

Tessa furrowed her brow for a moment. "How do you figure that?" she finally replied.

"I have knowledge of how their warplanes function," Michael explained excitedly. "With your help, I believe I can commandeer one and take them by surprise."

"With my help?" Tessa was taken aback.

"Well, I can do it on my own, but it would be easier if you wanted to lend a hand."

"Are you insane?" Tessa cried.

"No, look." Michael flipped open his backpack and pulled out a small black box fitted with buttons and wires. "This is a control module we took off of one of their downed ships. I've been working on it, and I think I've figured out how to send an override command with this to any other circuit in their system."

"No." Tessa was all for scientific discovery and geeking out over engineering designs, but this really didn't seem like a good time. "I think you are missing the point. Have you no sense? There's nobody left to save. Your city is a bombed out, burning shell, the palace is overrun with the enemy, and whatever leadership runs this place is surely captured or killed. You may live to fight another day if you can keep your head, but Arcadia is done. I mean, did you even think you had a chance? Fighting a technologically advanced army with horses, pointed sticks, and rocks? Who does that?"

"A fool, milady", Michael nodded, "but there is no honor in only fighting battles you know you can win. But I think you have missed the point here as well. Our weapons are not sticks and rocks, but heart and truth. Every one of us that lives in peace and dies with his head held high drives a wedge into the soul of the enemy. Do not forget that all who oppose you are only people as well. All societies are made up of individuals. We may be losing now, but when the battle is over and the Lorn return to their sterile, loveless homes, they will wonder why they too cannot live like us."

"The Lorn?" Tessa replied? "Who is that?"

Michael laughed. "You came here that blind? You are braver than I thought. The Lorn are those we fought today... those you killed." He narrowed his eyes as if in judgment at Tessa. "They are united in their narrow vision of the world, their culture twisted by the golden tongue of a traitor—a false prophet, who has convinced them that god is a being who must only be feared. They suffer and toil endlessly to appease their god's supposed wrath. They worship him with "progress" as they call it. Imbalance is more like it—the need to constantly build for the sake of building and grow for the sake of growing. While Arcadia has its music, its art, its freedoms, and its passion, they have their progress. That's why I'm here. Without my help, what chance does the peaceful and happy savage stand against the industrious invader?"

"And what do you bring, exactly?" Tessa began to realize that this stranger did not belong here. These were not his people, and this was not his fight. He was a world hopper, like her.

"Knowledge," Michael smiled. "The forbidden fruit. I keep the enemy at bay, and they keep their innocence."

"You mean you keep it all to yourself?" Tessa exclaimed. "If you want to help these people, why not share it with them?"

"Oh, I do," Michael nodded, "but few of them find it of interest. They say that they do not want to learn of any technologies that they will become enslaved to. If it weren't for the Lorn, they would be right too."

"But there is the Lorn."

Michael nodded pensively. "Yes, so there is."

"Look," Tessa explained, "I have an idea. You want to help these people, but you can't do it today. Don't throw your life away. You need allies. I need your help. My daughter needs your help. My husband needs your help. And if what they say is true, he can be a great ally to your cause when he is free. And Sara has gifts too—far more knowledge than you might ever hope to possess. Come with me and leave this place behind for a while. Surely they are seeking for you, even now."

Tessa could see that her words hit home on the inventor, and his face went tense for a moment as he weighed the situation. In the end though, her words could not balance out decades of work and ambitions. "No," he replied, looking up at her with firmness. "I have given my word here, and that is a bond beyond all reason. I must stay. The Seventh Star is old, milady. He can wait, and he will be there when this is done. However, you have done me a service, and I will escort you to safety."

*****

Night had fallen over the city of Arcadia, and except for the fires that still burned, there was no light. Bombs fell in the distance, occasionally lighting up the night like a flash bulb. It appeared that the city was being methodically destroyed. The three companions trudged silently through the snow, ignoring the blasts, Tessa and Michael still dressed in black, and El Gato creeping behind through the shadows. Tessa and Michael kept their heads turned away from one another, as if each was trying to pretend the other did not exist. Finally, as they reached a crossroads, the silence was broken.

"I must leave you here, milady," Michael hushed. "It will not be safe beyond the next checkpoint. If you continue on to the left, you will soon find yourself in the forest. I do not think the Lorn will pursue you into there at this time."

"And what of your people?" Tessa responded. "Do I need to fear them dressed as an enemy like this?"

"If my people arrest you, tell them, 'Michael soll fait.' They will leave you be."

"Fair enough," Tessa replied, tossing off her helmet and shaking out her hair. "Still, I'd feel better if you could explain to me how this thing works." She lifted the heavy black rifle that hung at her side.

"Yes, I can do that," Michael nodded. "This, of course, is the trigger, and this knob sets the power level. One notch just causes pain for riot control, two notches can knock a man out. Above that, you are into lethal territory. This lever here opens the energy chamber—in case you run out of power. Oh, and this is the safety. You will need to switch this off to fire at all, though hopefully you won't have to."

Tessa thanked him and nodded. She couldn't help but notice the rifle had been set all the way up to six when she had picked it up. Michael turned and walked away. At twenty paces, Tessa lifted the rifle to her shoulder and peered down the sight. It seemed Aras had been right about her after all. "Sorry," she whispered as she pulled the trigger, "but my daughter and I need you too much." Two shots, and Michael went down in the snow.

Tessa put down her rifle and ran over to the fallen form. Like before, the rifle had burned holes in his clothing, but Michael himself was still breathing. The star-bellied cat approached, looking startled. Tessa grasped Michael by the strap of his backpack and dragged him towards the cat. "I don't care where it leads," she snarled to her tiny companion, "find us a way out of here now."

20

STEAM

"Go!" Jonathan snapped at Sara through their telepathic link. Why wasn't she moving? He could still smell her in the hallway. For her safety, he decided it would be best if he put some distance between himself and the doorway. If just one of the fire imps happened to notice Sara, he was uncertain he could protect her—at least not without taking her inside the chimera's body, and that could prove disastrous on its own. Besides, there was Aras' warning. Jonathan had dealt with future readers before. He did not like the idea that any future was set in stone, but far too many times he had witnessed the power of those that looked down the webbed roads of possibility, and he did not want to tempt fate.

Jonathan bounded up off one ring of the great stairwell and then another, gaining height and speed. This sudden shift in tactics caused a ruckus, as imps and lizards scattered and the fire hawk was forced to adjust its swoops. In the confusion, the chimera managed to ascend some distance up the shaft, but the gain was short lived. The flame imps and burning lizards all pursued him, moving up the iron stairs with remarkable quickness. Others watching from high above started to hurl loose bricks, rubbish, and even tiny fireballs at Jonathan.

The flame hawk swung in a loop, and then, shooting fire out brightly from its tail, it spurred after him, crying out, "You think to take me on in the air? This is my domain." The taunt was followed with a hail of cruel laughter that the imps gleefully echoed.

High above, Jonathan could still make out several sections of construction scaffolding near the top of the shaft. With few choices available and little time to think, he marked them as his current destination. However, before he could get more than a few jumps in, an iron harpoon shot out from the stairwell and hooked into his calf with a cruel barb. The attack was followed by three more that Jonathan avoided—two by twirling in mid-air and the last by deflection with his arm blades. Each missed harpoon fell limp and then began to retract back into small, decorative holes in the iron cages through which they had been fired. As if on cue, Jonathan felt the pull of the chain that had snared his leg. He extended the blade on his right arm and moved to cut through it, but before he could, a sudden light approached. The flames of the fire hawk engulfed him.

With no other way out, the chimera dived downward through the fire, heading in the direction the chain was already dragging him. He was blind and burning, and for a brief moment, in pain everywhere. Finally, he plummeted out the other side of the hawk's flames. Jonathan landed hard against the roof of the stairwell, just above the slit where the chain that held him was being retracted. On the stairs below, he saw the four imps working the crank winch that was steadily threatening to pin him to the spot. His own anger and the animal rage of the chimera overtook any other concern. He fired a barrage of spikes from his forehead. All had been tempered and hardened in the heat of this realm, and each hit its target, scattering off the imps. The final spike struck the release for the chain crank. Jonathan braced his feet against the iron cage of the stairwell and pulled hard on the chain with his hands, spinning the winch freely and granting himself a good deal of slack.

In the meantime, the hawk had maneuvered around for another attack and was now diving down towards Jonathan's position. Jonathan waited until the last possible moment, and then bounded up the wall and sprung backwards, flipping over the oncoming fire raptor, chain still in tow. The hawk rebounded empty-handed off the wall, scouring with its scorching claws the surface where Jonathan had been moments before. Instantly, the hawk rotated and pounced after the chimera. And that was just what Jonathan had been hoping for. He scrambled upward, dodging the hawk's thrust, and then leapt outward, off the wall again, holding the chain tight in his right hand. Again, he dove downward, this time wrapping the iron chain taunt around the hawk. The startled bird, entangled, plummeted violently downwards as the winch now spun wildly, releasing the capstan.

As the chain finally reached its end, the bird swung down in an arc and crashed hard into the wall, while Jonathan grasped desperately at the rim of the stairwell below. Bellowing angrily to scatter the imps, he crouched down on the railing and reached down with his left hand while firmly pulling downward on the chain to keep the hawk in place with his right arm and pincer limbs. He pushed the harpoon forward through his leg, lodging it in the filigree of the ironwork of the cage. He then reached down with his sword blade and sliced through the armor and some of the muscle of the back of his calf, cutting open his leg and finally freeing it from the hot iron barb. Above him, the fire hawk still struggled, twisting and writhing in the tangle of the chain. He cursed Jonathan, and his rage stoked the flames of his form. Jonathan did not hesitate, but instead continued to move, leaping and bounding up the shaft to find Sara. He paused just long enough to stick his tongue out the imps, who in seeing their master undone had lost bravado and now scurried to avoid him.

The chimera had just about reached the scaffolding that he had originally intended to drop onto the hawk when the whole of the shaft shook with a terrible roar. Below him, the fire was billowing everywhere, filling the lower shaft and licking its way rapidly higher. Then, from its center, the fire hawk burst upward. The chains, now molten white around its body, were melting away in the heat. The bird exploded up the shaft like a missile. Jonathan tried to avoid its onslaught, but was struck mid-leap with a powerful blast from one of the wings. Burnt and off balance, the chimera smashed into the old stone wall near where the scaffolding had been assembled for repair. The wall gave way.

Jonathan found himself sprawled onto a hidden inner stair. Any amount of thought would have directed him sprinting upwards in safety, but as he freed himself from the dust and rubble, his animal fury took hold. He roared forth a challenge and then sprang back out of the hole and into the shaft. He fired his spikes and lashed out with his tails. Soaring in midair, he danced against the hawk, whose own fury had easily increased its size by a factor of three. The chimera's spikes burnt away before they hit their mark, and his tails and claws were only painfully singed for their trouble. With another slap of its blazing wing, the hawk sent Jonathan spiraling downwards, smoking, burnt, and wounded. With a great caw, it dived after him.

*****

Sara turned slowly. She knew what to expect, but still dreaded seeing it with her own eyes. The bright mistress of the Iron Citadel crackled and blazed only a few yards from her and Adam. The goddess was the mirror image of her sister, only formed of molten rock and fire rather than ice and cold. The face was the same—a skull with deep eyeless sockets, long flame-tipped fangs, and a mass of horns in the mockery of a crown. The upper body was hard and sunken—a tangle of ribs from which sprouted six arms ending in razor-sharp, burning-clawed hands. The goddess' lower body evoked that of a giant, flaming scorpion, with eight legs and a long stinger-tipped tail that flicked and flexed, hungry for a victim.

"How long I have waited," the goddess sizzled in the primal tongue of old that was both forgotten yet universal, "held my favorite plaything in torment, knowing you would come for him. And at last you are here, though I must admit I am rather underwhelmed. I expected something more from the sorceress who helped to end my sister."

Sara swallowed hard and stood up slowly. She used everything in her mental arsenal to remain outwardly calm. "Appearances can be deceiving," she said. Sara was proud that her voice did not crack or show signs of fear. Behind her, she heard Adam stir. He would try to protect her, but in his state they did not stand a chance in a fight. No, Sara had to use her head and figure a way out of this. "Stay still, servant," she barked at Adam, and saw that it had the desired effect on the flame goddess.

The goddess was suddenly unsure of Sara. After all, this was the girl that had slain her sister, and though she appeared to be no more than a mortal child, she commanded both monster and knights. Was there some hidden danger in this girl that the goddess did not perceive? What was this girl? How had she known to come here when the goddess was far off, treating with her brother of wind. How had she destroyed her sister? What knowledge the goddess did have of this young sorceress had come to her from a source darker than most she treated with, but none the less reliable. The goddess' minds raced. There were too many questions, but ultimately, they did not matter. This was her abode of influence, her trap; this little girl could not hope to undo her here within the seat of all her power.

"You think yourself a match for me?" The crackle of the goddess' voice betrayed her apprehension.

Sara had to be careful. Boast too violently and this creature would attack; seem too weak and the same might happen. "Your sister saw no threat in me either."

That had the desired effect. Sara knew that the sister of ice had possessed powers of perception beyond that of the monster she now faced. Adding doubt would give the goddess pause. If Sara could stall long enough, buy enough time, then perhaps Jonathan would make it to them, or she might chance on a way to best this creature.

Flame burst forth from the cracks in the goddess' molten skin, and for a moment she seemed ready to attack. Adam was now to his feet, and he ripped away the final chain that held him, but Sara's raised hand held him at bay.

"Surely you do not hope to avoid conflict with me?" the goddess jeered, "there can be no pardoning what you have done."

"None?" Sara questioned. "Why couple my crime against your family by adding another death?" Sara was now feverishly considering routes of escape. If she blew the whistle to call for the portal, the goddess would surely strike her. And Jonathan was still below, locked in a battle for his own life. But maybe she could convince this creature to allow them to leave out of a sense of self-preservation. "Your sister was cold and vain," Sara stole the words right out of the fire goddess' own opinions of her sister. The two had never really gotten along, and for reasons that went well beyond their elemental differences. "I never intended her ill will, but she would not relent. In the end my hand was forced."

That produced an odd look of introspection on the eyeless face. "Really?" the goddess croaked, "that's not what I was told. I heard that you used my sister for your own end and then destroyed her through trickery when you no longer had need of her.

Told? Told by whom? Sara wondered, and to her own shock, no answer came, yet neither did the blinding light that guarded the Fish Man. No, this knowledge was hidden in a different way, more like it had been with the Neverknight before she had freed him. This was something old, erased and concealed in dark and teeth and hate. A shudder ran over Sara's body. Immediately she scolded the error of letting the fire goddess see weakness in her, but the reaction to her shudder was not what she would have expected.

"Yes... that one," was all the goddess said, and she shuddered too. "So, you have lied to me; now speak truth to white flame." Suddenly, the goddess' empty sockets blazed with white fire and she locked Sara in her gaze.

Despite all her powers, Sara found herself bound to the eyes
of fire, unable to blink or look away. She also knew what this
was. She was unable to lie, and she could feel her lips start to
move. The words she spoke were the truth, but the phrasings
were not quite her own. "I needed a way aboard the Mongrel's worldship," she began. "I saw that they were planning
to take your sister prisoner, so I journeyed there. When they
attacked, I stole aboard the ship. Once there I sought out the
Neverknight on the advice of a future seer. The knight took
me captive, and I freed your sister to battle him so that I might
escape. I then helped the Neverknight defeat her, and I freed
him from the Mongrel's grasp. At no time was your sister ever
a concern of mine. She was merely collateral. It did not matter to me if she lived or died."

The spell that had held Sara broke and she was in control again.
She fell back and Adam caught her in his arms. Sara could not
help but notice that the truth seemed a lot like what the fire
goddess had already been told by her dark informant.

"Of no concern? So then, you are a killer without conscience."
The goddess' legs clicked up and down with rage and she
seemed ready to charge. "Well, whatever you are, I will not
falter in my course. Fate has bought you to me, and I will do
my part. Now, you die."

*****

Jonathan struck the ground with a sickening thud. He had never ached like this, not for a long time, not since before he and
the chimera had been made one. Still, he had to keep moving.
He knew that if he did not, he would fall into the clutches of
the firebird. He strained to act. He needed water. His body
was fast dehydrating, and without water his cells could not
regenerate and would not continue to heal him at the pace he
was taking damage. And he needed something else even more
than that. He needed to be able to fly so he could outmatch
this monster.

Still, he needed to move, and despite all the pain and all the hurt of the chimera's body, it was built to endure, and reflexively, it leapt out of the way of the oncoming attack. Moving always felt right to Jonathan. In his past, he had been unable to move for so long that no amount of pain, no amount of hurt could stop him now, as long as movement was still physically possible.

"You are slowing down," the fire hawk cawed. By this time, it was over six times as large as it had been when the fight had first begun. Its anger and frustration towards Jonathan fueled its flames ever higher. "You won't be able to avoid me much longer."

It was true. Jonathan knew it even as his body attempted to adapt to the conflict. He could feel himself losing ground. Water, water was what he needed. The chimera could draw water from the air though its skin, but here in this shaft, enclosed with an ever-expanding fire beast, there was no water to draw from anywhere. The chimera's body was remarkable, capable of any adaptation, but it was also organic. Unless he was willing to turn himself to stone and live out creation as a statue, Jonathan could not see a way out of this mess for himself.

"You really have bested me," Jonathan sputtered. "You win. Really. No hard feelings."

"Fool!" the bird wailed. "You act like you don't even know me, then you don't remember our great rivalry, and now you try to placate me with kind words. You think I will let you go? You, who sought me out here? We are each other's ultimate nemesis."

"I didn't even know you were here," Jonathan said. He slumped down to rest at the bottom of the shaft. He could move no more. His cut leg gave out on him and he slid to the floor, his back against the wall. "Really. I am sorry you wasted so much time hating me. To be honest I don't even think you made the top ten list of my enemies."

"You dare... you dare continue to mock me!" The fire hawk's voice was like thunder. His body burned brighter, stronger, larger. His wings filled the whole of the upper shaft, and the entire iron citadel shook with his rage. "Now it ends in fire and death. I will leave nothing but ash for you to be remembered by."

So brightly did the hawk burn now. It dived, with all its flame and fury focused towards Jonathan. The chimera strained to rise. His wounded leg would not move, and he knew this was the end. He thought about Sara. He thought about Tessa, El Gato, and Aras. And for some reason, he thought about an angel he had once met in a dream.

As the fire hawk bore down, all the shaft in flames around it, there was a strange and sudden glitch. As he neared Jonathan, there came a brief moment when, for a split second, the fire was gone. Then almost immediately, there followed another such moment, then another, and then suddenly there was no fire in the air at all. The shaft was dim again.

Jonathan thought he had witnessed a miracle until he caught sight of the small object falling toward him. He strained himself to reach up, and caught it in his hand. It was warm, and light, and no bigger than a kitten. Nestled in his palm sat a small, black hawk. It seemed injured, and it looked up at him with fear and wonder.

"You the same hawk?" the chimera asked.

"I am," it said, in a small voice.

"What happened?" Jonathan inquired. "I thought you were going to kill me."

"I burnt out."

"Huh?"

"All my rage, all my hate," the hawk explained sheepishly,

"it burnt away all my magic and my firepower." The hawk paused for a tense moment. "Are you going to kill me now?"

"No," Jonathan said, setting the hawk down next to him and gently patting him on the head. "Let's just call it a draw."

"Really?" the hawk was visibly surprised. "I would kill me if I were you. Don't you hate me?"

"No," Jonathan replied, closing his eyes. "You made me mad a few times today, but like I have been trying to tell you, I never have hated you."

"Wow. I guess I hate enough for both of us."

Jonathan gave a smile at that, but still he slouched a little lower. All over he could feel his body freezing up—weak, dehydrated, done. "Water", he thought, "I need water... and wings would be nice too." From every side, Jonathan could see the imps and lizards creeping closer.

*****

The fire goddess was done talking. She lurched forward, driving herself towards Sara. Just then, the whole of the citadel shook with such violence that it gave even the goddess pause. In that moment, Sara was given the freedom to act. In an instant, she had the fairy flask out and she twisted it open, spraying water in a stream that struck the goddess' lower body. It was a weak attempt, but Sara had no other tricks up her sleeve.

The goddess let out a laugh as she remounted her attack. "Do you really think you can harm me with such a feeble amount of water," she cackled. "It would take a torrent, like ripping a hole in the bottom of an ocean, to harm me."

Sara saw her doom before her now, as the goddess' claws struck forward, but just before the first strike, a shimmering shield appeared before her, and the claws crashed into its wavering surface. Before Sara could react, she felt strong arms wrap around her from behind, and she was lifted up, rising over the goddess into the air.

"I have you, Sara," Adam proclaimed, but Sara already knew that. However, this flight would not last long. Adam's wings were far too injured to allow him to carry them both any real distance. They came crashing down on the far side of the great shaft, where below, Sara caught a glimpse of the great bird of fire, huge and burning, headed downward to consume her best friend. She wanted to aid Jonathan, to at least see how he was doing, but she dared not take the focus off her own enemy.

"I cannot carry you and remain aloft, but I will not let this monster harm you, brave girl," Adam spoke, setting her down on the far side of the pit. With a leap, he flew back into the air, and like a hero, dived straight for the goddess. "You found me unconscious and weak and chained me!" he proclaimed as he struck one of her horns from her head with the blades of his wing. "You tortured and used me as bait for a trap! Now you will face me in open combat!"

It was a brave boast, but Sara knew he was too weak to keep up the pace with which he currently assaulted the fire goddess. But then again, maybe he wouldn't have to. Sara found the whistle around her neck, and bringing it to her lips, blew with all her might. The portal could get them out and free them. Besides, if they had to, they would open another right on top of Jonathan to get him. Sara sat breathless, waiting for the first signs of their escape route.

Beyond the pit, Adam fought with all of his might against the mistress of the Iron Citadel, but his long imprisonment and weakened state were already showing, and the goddess knew it. His telekinetic powers were quickly fizzling out, and he pressed the fight only on sheer adrenaline.

"You are brave, knight. And you have changed my mind. I will not kill you or the girl quickly," she taunted. "I will cripple you both, then lead you to suffering." The taunt only empowered Adam, who gave no reply, but only concentrated on the

battle. He drove forward, cutting the tip off of one of the goddess' spindly legs.

Where was the portal? Sara could not understand what was
taking Curiosity so long. She looked now, and fear gripped her
chest; he was not in the organ chamber. They were trapped.
Sara watched as the goddess struck back, her arms and limbs
driving Adam backwards, her tail coming closer to a strike
against him with each attempt. Below, Sara could sense the
chimera alive but utterly spent. Off on another world, her
mother and El Gato were also trapped and in danger. Even her
fairy sister now hid away in a darkened corner.

Come on, Sara thought, you know everything. Think. Only
one path now—defeat the goddess first then escape, she
thought. But how? For some reason, she recalled the goddess'
cruel taunt, "It would take a torrent, like ripping a hole in the
bottom of an ocean, to harm me."

A hole in the bottom of an ocean? Yeah, good luck, Sara
thought. But then she was struck with an idea, one that could
lead them to both freedom from fire and the end of the goddess.

Sara stood up. She grasped the fairy flask in her hands. This
was a tiny portal. A gate to the primordial world of water.
A small hole, but a hole nonetheless. Sara bent back the silver inlays on the mouth of the flask, reshaping the wards that
protected against the water pouring out at full blast. She bent
them into the shapes of their counterpart symbols, and water
began to strain against the valve, trickling out in streams.

"Adam," she cried. He chanced a look at her. "Cut it in half!"
Sara threw the flask with all her might in the direction of the
goddess. Adam danced back and jumped into the air, then
pushed forward. He did not know what he was doing, but
he knew Sara was smarter and wiser, and he trusted her. The
flask spun towards him, but as he moved to strike, the goddess
turned and caught the flask in one of her six hands.

"No more tricks, little one" she hissed at Sara, but she took her gaze away from Adam. In that instant he struck, his good wing cutting through the goddess' fingers and severing the fairy flask. The goddess howled, but her cry was immediately drowned out by a sound like metal ripping. In the air above the goddess, where Adam had cut the flask, a great hole tore open, and water gushed out in torrents, as if from the bottom of an ocean. A massive wave swept the goddess off her feet and sent her spiraling down into the great shaft that made up the center of the throne room. From up the shaft, a heavy steam began to rise, rapidly heating the air.

Adam took flight and came to rest next to Sara. Water continued to inundate the chamber, slowly flooding in a wide, curved fall into the great shaft at the center of the throne room.

"You did it!" Adam said, patting her on the back. "You saved me again!"

"We did it!" Sara smiled, then grimaced. "Oh no! Jonathan!" she cried, remembering he was down the shaft.

As if in answer to her distress, a great humming sound came out of the steam, accompanied by what could only be the chimera hollering a triumphant, "Wooooohoooo!"

Jonathan exploded up out of the shaft, his body already beginning to heal itself. He hovered in the air before them, propelled by four giant dragonfly wings that buzzed loudly, keeping him aloft even though they seemed far too small to do so.

"Sara," he exclaimed, "I ask for water and you give me an ocean! I love it!"

Sara could not help but laugh, and Adam joined her.

"So let's get out of this place," the chimera said, coming to land next to them, "blow the whistle."

"No. Change of plans," Sara returned, "Curiosity has been

waylaid by his official duties. We must wait here until he has freed himself from his masters' call."

"Fair enough," Jonathan shrugged. "Is is safe here?"

"Well," Sara pondered, "it should take some time before the inhabitants of the citadel regroup to come after us. But...."

"I don't mean to spoil your reunion," Adam interrupted, "but has anyone noticed it's getting kind of hot in here?" Sweat was beginning to bead up on Adam's skin.

Sara whirled around. From the great pit and from all around them, hot steam continued to pour as primal water and primal fire battled out this new boundary with one another. They could not remain here. In another five minutes, she and Adam would both be cooked alive. And only she could get inside the chimera. They needed another way out.

"Yes. And getting hotter," Sara remarked. "Even if we take to the air, the portal will soon be inaccessible." She scanned their choices in her head. "I don't like this, but there is another way out—but we have to go now."

"If you say so, then let's go," Jonathan replied, dropping to the floor, "but can I bring him?" Jonathan held up his palm. A small, black hawk lay injured within.

Sara of course knew exactly who this was. She had to smile broadly again. Only Jonathan would think to save someone who only moments before had been trying to destroy him. "You can," Sara laughed, "but don't worry; Hyax cannot be harmed by heat. Why don't we just agree to fetch him later? Besides, I don't think he'd do very well where we are going."

"And where is that?" Jonathan responded.

"We are going through there." Sara pointed at the ever-widening source of the water.

21

~~~

THE DARK AT THE DOOR

"Oh my, has it been a day in Fairy already?" Curiosity gulped, looking towards Aras. "I am being summoned to reopen the portal to the realms of the fair."

Aras remained still and calm.

"I do not think you are grasping what I am trying to tell you," continued Curiosity, nervously stroking his whiskers. "The watcher for whom I opened a portal to that place, the portal you used to trick your way into here, he is returning. He is signaling now for a door."

"I imagine so," Aras answered, still composed and relaxed. "This is the hub of their comings and goings after all."

"Well, yes, but they use many paths and gates to make their rounds. I see them frequently enough—though to be honest, they use this place mostly to transition from the prime reality to the outer ones, and they seldom take notice of me—a habit for which I am utterly grateful."

"Why? What do you, a Primal Elder, have to fear from one of their kind?"

"Can a parent not fear his children?" Curiosity looked pale and ashen. But there was more. A torn look flashed across his face, as if he was weighing whether to share something. Finally, he looked up at Aras, half in terror, and whispered, "They take things."

Aras was unsure what he meant, "Things? What things?"

"Well, not things... feelings mostly, but they can take memories, knowledge, even beliefs," The catlike Elder shook with a chill. "In their place they leave holes—places inside that are empty and lost, places that will itch at your feelings. You may not even truly know that they are there, these vacant spaces, but you will feel them. They will haunt you, like the dream of a lover that you have never met yet you feel for as if you had been together the whole of your lives. Like a promise you want to keep but cannot recall to whom it was made. Like a terrible premonition that you've done something that will cause horrible harm, but are blocked from correcting it. Only fear, pain, and hate can filter into these hollowed-out voids. The empty spaces draw these emotions to them wherever they manifest in one's existence. Once full of those dark tidings, they then bleed them outward, coloring everything in hurt, everything you do and everything you touch."

Aras suppressed a shiver of her own. "This one will not simply pass through," she spoke. It was her gift speaking.

"No. This watcher was sent to Fairy to find your sister and her creature, and now it is returning with nothing. It will speak with me at the very least, and it may know that your sister has been here. These things see creation from different angles than everyone else. This is why they were created by my masters. Time, space, and distance matters less to them than pain, fear, and control—these wavelengths are how they perceive the cosmos. A watcher can move in between moments, passing from one dark thought to the next. They can hide in the corner of your vision just beyond seeing, or burn you with the full force of the harsh reality from which they are sewn."

Curiosity sank, deflated, into the organ chair. "I may not be able to hide what I know from this thing. What if it discerns that I have spoken with you? What if it knows that I have betrayed the Primal masters? What if...."

"What ifs are my specialty," Aras interrupted. She had heard enough. Dark and strange this thing might be, and even slightly outside of time, but it was still beholden to the future that was fast approaching, and Aras could see the angles and paths that would dissuade its attention. "Do exactly what I say, and I promise the watcher will come and go without forming undo suspicion."

Aras judiciously controlled her tone and affect as she informed Curiosity of the correct course of action for him to take, but there was something unspoken that itched at her as she looked forward. This was not unlike one of the holes that Curiosity had described, only this was not a hole in a single person but in the ever-weaving fabric of the near future. Aras had detected holes before—forever warriors employed by the Mongrel caused rifts that made her prognostications difficult—but this hole was more. It had a feel more like the rifts that the Neverknight had created before being freed, only darker. This void was not made by the watcher, but it followed close in its wake, and it made the black of the watcher seem utterly dull by comparison. Aras tried to focus on the task at hand, but she could not fully lose sight of this anomaly in doing so.

Aras finished briefing Curiosity, and as he began to play to open the portal, she sprang into action. Two rooms over she found, hidden behind the crate, the large perfume kit she had seen in her future sight. This was one of those paradoxes that could only occur when looking into the future. Aras needed a way to cover the scents of herself and the others so as to escape detection. In a possible future, she saw herself using this kit—a kit that she did not even know was there until she saw herself using it. These sorts of logic wheels could confound and even disturb others who thought about them too long, but they were almost second nature to Aras.

Aras sprayed a variety of raw scents with abandon everywhere, starting first with the great rotunda where already the portal to Fairy was opening. She then worked her way back into the organ chamber. From there, she moved about the main arteries of the Heart and the chambers that belonged to Curiosity, leaving a trail of sneezing hermites in her wake. She did not have time to spray everywhere they had been, but then she didn't need to; rather, she sprayed only were where she foresaw that the watcher's path might cross theirs. Finally, she returned back to the organ chamber, where she deposited the perfume kit on a small table next to Curiosity, who was just finishing his song.

"It's done. It's here," he murmured.

"Remember what I told you," Aras said as she placed a comforting hand briefly on his shoulder. "You'll do fine." She was then off, down the hall at the rear of the room to hide. It was hard for her to imagine that the Mongrel and Curiosity were of the same race, primal beings of creation, but then the Mongrel had not spent his entire existence under the tight leash of the Elders. These more empowered beings, like the Mongrel and her own father, were something else—in some ways less sterile and stagnate, in others, far, far more dangerous and powerful—their effects on possible futures were utterly impossible for Aras to predict.

Aras had just about reached the small chamber in which she intended to hide when she felt the difference in the coming air. The future where she hid while Curiosity put the watcher off their trail was gone, and with it had vanished her reunification with Sara, Jonathan, Tessa, and El Gato. Aras looked for other roads she could take, other paths that might prevent or circumvent this disturbance, but there were none. It was here where that dark hole that hid from creation so well now presented itself, and though Aras could see none of its future actions, she could see the ultimate outcome of its course: disaster. Again and again she read forward, but in the end she decided to turn away from the safety of her hiding space. She had promised Curiosity that he would not be exposed, and she could still deliver that future, even if it met her own fall.

*****

The watcher Bal-Hazaran stepped into the circular, translucent chamber at the center of the Heart of Music. Its great, powdery wings cloaked the remainder of its form, concealing all but the dim red glow of its eyes beneath. The click of its claws and the soft shuffle of dragging feathers were the only sounds it made as it passed deliberately towards the ancient doors, leaving the fading light of the portal behind it. Its breath was irregular and gave a slight rise and fall to the wings that shrouded it. Every so often, and just for an instant, the creature seemed to skip a beat in time. When it did, it suddenly shifted a few paces forward—one moment one place, the next somewhere else—like a film missing a few frames. Where it passed, the air became both hotter and cooler in patches, its wake disturbing the calmness of the atmosphere.

The watcher knew where it was going, but did not seem in a hurry to reach its destination. As it arrived at the great doors at the far end of the chamber, it raised its snout out from its wings just enough to scent the air. Almost at once, it snorted the perfume back out and the feathers on its body ruffled. It then twitched instantly back towards the way it had come, opening both its wings wide and filling the chamber with the red light of its eyes. It was the sort of motion someone made when they thought they were being followed—turning quickly to catch their pursuer—but the rotunda behind the watcher was vacant, still, devoid of any mystery tracker.

The creature's wings gradually descended back to their original positions, masking the room from the red glow. The watcher turned back and rapped sharply with the iron knockers of the heavy doors, leaving all in shadow behind him.

The shadows of the rotunda were not idle as one might expect. Once the watcher had moved on, they slipped from where they should have been confined and then tangled sickeningly together into a mass, advancing to follow in the watcher's wake.

*****

Curiosity felt the watcher's approach and fought back the urge to turn and face the doors to the portal chamber. Instead, he stayed on task, focusing on the perfume kit just as Aras had told him to. He delayed looking up until the click of claws came to a halt directly behind him and he could feel the cold heat of the watcher's eyes on his neck. "Salutations friend," he chimed, trying to sound as casual as possible, "to what do I owe the honor of this visit?"

"Why lie, shy eye?" The creature's voice came haltingly, like the dark, whispered sounds out of an open closet at night. "Wrong is right, honor spite. Do not hide; you do not like… to have us nigh, within your sight." A watcher always spoke in broken, twisted rhythms that as often as not did not seem to make any sense.

Curiosity knew better than to read too much into the watcher's words; this was part of how they worked their way into a person, striking subconscious chords deep within one's heart, dislodging old fears and unnerving even the strongest-willed adversaries. "Well, that may be, but here you are anyway," he countered, before turning back to the perfume set and beginning to tinker away. "You must forgive me. I have been very preoccupied of late trying to produce a new primary scent that no one has ever smelled before."

"Snivel, drivel, stink and sniffle," the watcher whispered.

Whatever that meant, who could say. Curiosity had not found it wise to engage the watchers too deeply. He had gotten "stink" out of that sentence, so he went with it. "Ah, yes. Sorry for the odd smells. I forget you have such a sensitive… well, senses. But come, you have not yet called for a new destination. Is there anything out of the ordinary I can do for you?"

At once the watcher shifted instantly in space, materializing directly in front of Curiosity. It did not change its pose, and still stood shrouded, eerily calm in outward appearance. Curiosity tried not to jump; he was used to their popping about, but his nerves were shot, and he jerked in spite of himself.

"Itchy, twitchy, hue and cry. Something missing where I fly."

"Oh yes?"

"Empty forest, empty wood. Empty tree where once it stood. Empty hearts up to no good."

"You don't say."

"Stinky, smelly, acrid air, stench of Fairy follows near. Linger children, do you dare? Chill the bone to enter here."

That came across clearly enough, maybe. "Who do you mean?" Curiosity replied.

"Thinking, leaking everywhere, pages falling from her hair." The watcher began to survey the room as it talked, the red of its eyes tinting everything as it exposed its face and neck above the shield of its wings. "Knowing, touching, life's great chain, fountain filling up her brain, running fast with one so dear, little boy or monster feared. Hiding, sliding, biding time, until our Indred stills their thrill."

"Sorry, I don't know whom you speak of," Curiosity answered, "but then I have been rather distracted since last I saw you."

The watcher turned the full force of its gaze upon the organ master. If Curiosity had been anything other than a Primal Elder, he would surely have suffered actual physical harm from the glare, whether merely burst blood vessels or even harsh, burnt scars. Being what he was made the experience no more enjoyable though. These things had been made by the Elders to employ against all manner of creatures in creation, even their own kind. The old one who had made and forged them had dipped deep into places and forces even the other Elders were barred from, and his success had cost him everything. Now, in the light of those red eyes, Curiosity wished that that achievement had not left these things in its wake, free and unleashed upon creation. The Primal Five claimed that the watchers were their servants and remained under the control of their unbreakable will, but Curiosity wondered, could monstrosities as these really be subjugated, or did they merely play a waiting game, searching for the right moment to dethrone their masters.

The scrutiny lasted only a few moments, but to Curiosity it felt like hours. Finally, it was done, and just as Aras had predicted, the watcher seemed to lose interest. It moved off again, back towards the great hall, giving only a passing order as it departed the room, "Play the one true song."

Curiosity knew what the order meant. It was time for him to open the portal to the Prime reality. He breathed a sigh of relief as the organ room became once more his. Then he closed his eyes, tilted his ears back, and let the notes flow, passing from him to his fingers to the organ and back again.

*****

Aras stopped, with just a single hallway between her and the organ room. She could hear the watcher's whispers, but could not make out what it was saying. She had forsaken her hiding place for more information, running full-speed down the colored halls, circumventing the arrival room to arrive at the far side of the organ chamber. Unable to glean anything new though, her fear soon overcame her. She turned away from the voices and retraced her path in reverse. After passing through a long hall, she came to a hub room filled with many of the oddities collected by Curiosity that cluttered the Heart of Music. This chamber was darker now than she remembered, and though she knew it was not possible, she felt as if the shadows in the room constricted when she entered.

Again she ran into the blind spot in her foresight. She could not even see what would happen in the next few seconds, but she could see that if she did not intervene now that Curiosity would be exposed and all would fall to ruin. So she chased back her fear and spoke, "I know you are here."

There was a ruffle in the dark corners of the cluttered chamber. "Know? What do you know?" a sharp voice crackled back like a thousand nails on a chalkboard.

Aras did not give into the image. "Why are you here?"

"The why is never so important as the when," the voice returned, "you should know that better than anyone, little prophet." The shadows of the room rose and fell with each word, and Aras thought she could make out mouths, even teeth, there among them. What was this thing, and how was it concealed from her visions?

"Fair enough," Aras decided to play along, "so why now?"

"Oh, because now is the moment that I can do the most harm." With that, the shadows bubbled forward and came to life, forming up in the center of the chamber before Aras. They rose up dark and slick, leaving the burned in impression of teeth and claws and eyes, all black within black. Aras felt her resolve melt away as the thing became clearer. It was sick, twisted, as if made of torn intestines and demon bones. And it was all black—an awful black, like blood from the deepest of wounds.

Aras could not stand it. She turned away, her fairy wings wrapping around her body as she shrunk to the floor, face buried in her hands and her own fingernails digging into her skin. She wanted to undo this moment, to go back and take a different route no matter the outcome. She wanted to unsee the thing that now breathed foul breath upon her neck. Could her sister see her now? Could her sister see this creature? Aras almost screamed, but just in time she moved a hand from her eye to her mouth. She dare not alert the watcher and run the risk of exposing Curiosity's betrayal. That was why she was here, to stop this thing from doing just that, even if it meant....

Aras could not stand to think of this thing touching her, let alone what its teeth, claws and dark fingers would do to her if it unleashed itself upon her, but now that it was here, now that she had seen it, she could foresee only one course of action. She readied herself, braced her courage, and found a little of her will, but all of that faded when next the creature spoke.

"I consumed your mother." The voice was flat, mocking, and utterly honest.

Aras knew the statement was true the moment she heard the words. She felt hot tears enter her eyes. Her fairy heart began to pound in her chest with a horrible rhythm.

"The process is not quick," the darkness screeched, its many mouths now inches from her back. All the hair on her neck stood on end. "It will not be quick for you either once I am certain that you are of no more use to me."

Aras heard the thing move around her, yet also felt it pass by, as the creature gave off a resonance that vibrated in the air. It was moving away now, and Aras felt her breath return to her, but she could not let the monster escape. She knew the outcome; this thing would leave a sign for the watcher somewhere that would alert it to the fact that they had been here, and that would lead to ruin for them all. "Wait," she gasped in an effort of sheer will. She felt the shadow's eyes on her again. "What are you after here?"

"Pain," the dark thing chuckled.

"Yes, but there is something more you wish to achieve." This was an educated guess based on the many possible and horrible futures in which this darkness got its way.

"I want to finish what I started with your mother," it creaked, far more concerned with causing as much harm to Aras than it was with hiding any absolute truth, "I want to kill both your parents."

The Seventh Star, yes, Aras realized. That is what is missing in all of the futures where this darkness achieved its success. Aras knew what she had to do, and she knew that if she was going to fully convince this creature, she was going to have to look upon it again. Mother give me strength, she thought. Father, if a piece of you is in me, I need it to shine now. She opened her eyes and took in completely the nightmare before her. She could feel its blackness seeping into her heart. She spoke.

"If you carry out your current plan and expose our presence to the watcher, you will fail." Aras had to lower her head at the end, closing her eyes so tight it hurt. She now wished she was a blind prophet. The first part was a lie; if he exposed them they would all be destroyed. But now it was time for the truth that the creature would not be able to resist. "Your only chance to encounter the Seventh Star directly and exact your vengeance is to hold me prisoner and wait for Sara and the chimera to come and save me." Aras knew this to be true, because if she were taken by the watcher, the pieces of the Seventh Star would never be together and he would not be able to form.

"You are not to be trusted," the shadow squawked, "but you are right in one thing, you do make an excellent bargaining chip. You see, nothing that I devour ever truly escapes me; it's time you rejoined your mother. I promise you will regret this."

As the darkness enclosed around her, Aras already did.

22

WITHOUT A PADDLE

The force of the water rushed hard against them, steadily increasing as they pushed forward. It wasn't just the current that fought them, but the total chaos of the flood. The crashing of the water drove out all other sounds, and the enveloping spray and foam made vision useless. They could only keep going forwards. "Push!" Sara urged through the chimera's psychic link. "Use your jets! You don't need any of that stored-up water anymore. Push it all out!"

Jonathan focused and fired all of his jets at once. Clutching the Neverknight tightly to his chest with one arm, he stroked forward with the other and kicked hard with his legs. Even Adam feebly kicked forward for whatever good that did. Still, the force of the water only grew stronger and stronger as they pushed in. Yet just when it seemed they could move forward no longer, the resistance began to fade... or rather it was gradually being replaced with something else, a force pressing in from all around them—pressure. They could swim freely here now, but everything felt tight, constricted. The feeling was not unlike floating in zero gravity, only it hurt everywhere. Sara realized that if it hurt this much in the chimera's body, then to Adam it had to be truly torture.

It took Sara a moment to notice, but the sound and the chaos had stopped too, replaced now by an eerie silence. Not far behind them they could see the rift between the worlds—it looked like a blazing sun floating in the darkness of space. Actually, that was about all that could be seen; blackness faded off in every direction. Here and there a luminescent jellyfish floated, filling the darkness like distant stars in the night sky. Sara marveled at the illusion, instantly mapping the constellations in her head.

"Sara!" Jonathan's voice broke into her thoughts. "Sara!"

"What?" Sara sent back. "Relax, there is no one after us here, and there are no predators nearby. We really could use a break. Besides, look around us for a moment, it's so beautiful here."

"Adam can't breathe!" Jonathan sent back. "We need to get to the surface fast!"

"Wha...?" Before Sara could even finish the question, she immediately knew that the bubble of air Adam had formed around his head was gone. His exertions had depleted it of oxygen, and when he lost consciousness, the pressure had swept it away. How could she be so stupid? She had been so lost in her thoughts that she had nearly killed the very knight she had come all this way to save. The surface... that was not really an option. Sara crunched the alternatives in her brain. "It's too far," Sara sent back, "we'd never make it in time! But swim this direction, fast!" Sara pointed with one of the chimera's own arms to indicate the direction he needed to swim in. The powerful legs kicked, and the great beast shot away in the darkness, still clutching its now-limp cargo.

"Down a bit, and to the left! Right here!" The chimera bumped up against something soft but solid in its path. Reaching out, it grasped at the object and then lifted the limp knight to face it. The chimera shoved the knight's face up against the bottom of the object and then simultaneously pushed Adam upward and dug into the surface of the object with its claws.

A second later, the Neverknight's head popped into the round object and a cascade of bubbles spewed out with a flatulent report.

"What are you doing?" Jonathan sent out to his internal companion.

"Kelp," Sara responded, "well, sort of. This is a giant variety we don't have back on Earth. But it's got floating bulbs full of air, just like the ordinary kind. There's enough air in here to keep Adam breathing for five minutes maybe. We should be able to get to the surface eventually by jumping from bulb to bulb. I'm plotting out route now. We're just on the edge of a kelp forest here. That should give us plenty of time. We don't want to go too fast anyway because of the pressure. I'm sure you are fine, but Adam could get the bends pretty easily."

"Well duh, I know about the bends," Jonathan replied. Sara knew he was lying, but this was no time to challenge him. They had to get Adam operational.

Sara scanned Adam's condition with her mind. No water in his lungs, luckily enough. They had managed to get him here before he totally lost consciousness, but he was weak and in a great deal of pain. Using the chimera's hands, Sara reached out and dug her fingers into a few key places on the knight's body. Pressure points. That would dull the pain for a few moments, enough to allow him to swim about and hold onto the kelp on his own. There were also some plants nearby that could be used to dull the knight's aches and pains; but that was secondary to their survival. They needed to focus on just one kelp bulb at a time.

Sara pointed, and Jonathan could see the next bulb through the chimera's gem-like thermal eyes. "Adam is totally blind here," she messaged to him, "it's too dark. We need to guide him."

Jonathan tapped Adam on the shoulder and tugged up. Sara scanned through the knight's surface thoughts until she determined that he understood and was ready. She told Jonathan to go. The chimera wrapped a hand around the knight's shoulder and kicked hard with his feet. They shot up about forty feet, and the chimera was forced to use the sword blade on his free arm to cut through the kelp leaves that grew across their path.

"OK, stop," Sara commanded. Jonathan grabbed the stalk of a large plant just below the bulb and pushed the knight up to grasp it as well. Adam put his mouth against the base of the rubbery bulb and the chimera slid in a finger and pierced it to release the air. As the air escaped, Adam gripped it with his mind and formed it into a telekinetic bubble around his mouth.

"You're doing good!" Sara burbled through the chimera's mouth, but with the distortion from the water, she doubted that Adam understood her.

"Ok," Jonathan asked, "so how far is it to the surface now, Sara?"

"Not so far we can't make it," Sara responded, "another five hundred feet or so."

"What? This is ridiculous! That's another dozen kelp bulbs. One slip up on any of them and Adam's a goner."

"You got any better ideas?"

"I don't know. Can't we feed him air somehow. We could probably grow a tube or something. Besides, is there even oxygen in these things?"

"Not very much," Sara replied, "but that's actually a good thing. At this pressure, normal air can kill you. And we don't have time to grow a tube. Besides, how do you know it won't be like an elephant trunk? Actually, that's not a bad idea... nobody would even notice your camel humps with that thing."

"Eww, ick! Don't you even think about it. I can't wait to get you out of me." Jonathan braced himself, tapping Adam again to signal it was time to move on. Adam nodded, focusing to keep the air bubble in place, and they shot up through another tangle of kelp.

Omniscience isn't always all it's cracked up to be, Sara had often said. Ask the right questions and you can make anything happen. But ask the wrong ones, or just leave one little detail out, and you could end up kidnapped by aliens, lost in a fairy tale, or in this case... swimming blindly into a school of ravenous sharks. Big sharks.

"Shark!" Jonathan screamed through the psychic link as they tore through a giant kelp leaf and slammed into the rough underside of the great beast.

"No," Sara added, "sharks... as in more than one! And giant primal sharks, at that." There were at least six of the great fish all around them, and they didn't look like they wanted to chat. The blood from Adam's wounds had drawn them in, and now they were closing on the scent.

The first of the huge fish thrashed about and lunged straight for Adam, who the chimera had been holding out in front of him, almost resembling bait. There wasn't time to think. Jonathan threw Adam upward as hard as he could. The shark shot past and slammed into the chimera with its side and tail. The sandpaper-like skin burned against the chimera's armored hide.

A second beast torpedoed itself at the chimera, and Jonathan kicked upwards, gliding just above it in the water. Now it was on. The sharks lunged at the chimera, and it was all Jonathan could do to avoid their blows. Adam was nowhere to be seen, and Jonathan did not have time to look for him.

"I don't want to hurt them," Jonathan cried to Sara, "they're just animals. You've got to find some way out of this. And you'd better hurry, too."

"Oh, so now you're a pacifist, huh? Good timing. Really good." Sara took a moment as Jonathan dodged about to weigh all the alternatives. "Well, it's your lucky day. You don't need to hurt them all, just one. If you can nick it in the flank with your sword, you should be able to get it to bleed, and the blood in the water will cause the others to follow it."

"But then won't they hurt it?" Jonathan winced through their mental link.

"It's one of them or all of us," Sara snapped back, "hit the biggest one, she will be able to defend herself."

"Fine." Jonathan reached out as the largest of the sharks came in for another attack, and he grabbed it by the snout. Pushing up, he rolled over the top of the huge fish and grabbed a hold of the dorsal fin.

"Here," Sara sent, "I'll guide you to the right spot." Jonathan's arm reached out and slashed the shark just behind its fin. A spray of red clouded out of the wound, and the shark bucked and thrashed, tossing the chimera into the kelp. Behind them, the other sharks began circling their wounded cousin. Sensing the danger, the wounded shark sped off, leaving a trail of red behind and taking the others with her.

"She won't bleed long from that wound," Sara assured her chimera companion. "Besides, she is considerably stronger that the others; she should be able to outrun them and get them away from us."

"Well that's good at least," Jonathan returned, "where did Adam get to?"

"Oh oh," Sara sent, "we need to get to him fast." The chimera kicked off and began swimming forward, cutting through the kelp as it went. Soon they came into a clearing, and could make out the knight a ways off from them. A family of round-mouthed eels were busy circling him, looking for the right moment to strike. Adam was flailing all about with his hands and feet like a dervish, all the while using his wings to keep the eels at bay.

"What's he doing?" Jonathan sent. "He's going to run out of steam fast."

"He can't see," Sara relayed, "and if any of those eels bite him, I guarantee we'll have another problem on our hands. I don't think we can get to him in time."

"No," Jonathan sent back, "but we can help him." Sara suddenly saw an image flash into her mind. "You work on that," Jonathan continued, "I'll swim."

Adam could feel the long fish thrashing all around him. As long as he kept moving, they wouldn't attack him, but how long could he keep that up? The pressure was killing his lungs, and whatever oxygen remained in his telekinetic bubble was sparse at best. His head began to swim and his arms and legs grew heavy. He felt like going to sleep. But now what was this?

About eighty feet off, two bright lights suddenly kicked on, like the headlights to a submarine. Adam blinked twice and then realized he could now make out the lampreys circling him, their jaws dripping with venom. He held still, and the largest of them shot out towards his throat. Moving with speed only possible via select breeding and decades of intense training, Adam shot his hand out and grabbed the eel below the jaw, catching it fast. Using the larger lamprey as a whip, he spun about, propelling himself with his wings, and slapped away at the juveniles. Startled, the little fish fled, and Adam flung the big eel after them; but that was all he had left. With his focus broken, the bubble around his mouth popped, and the last bit of air came fizzing out of his mouth. His head lolled forward limply, just as he caught sight of the strange shape coming right for him, a vessel that looked unusually like the chimera... with big, bright, glowing eyes.

*****

"It's getting colder," Jonathan remarked as they rose. The knight was shaking as they approached the next kelp bulb.

"We're nearing the surface," Sara responded, "but I'm not sure that's entirely a good thing."

Moments later, two heads bobbed out of the water, one with a great gasp. Above them, a moonless night sky ran on forever, the stars shining brightly without the presence of any apparent civilization. A large mountain of white ice was about the only thing visible on the horizon, and small chunks of frozen water floated here and there.

"OK," Jonathan yelled, "blow the whistle!"

"Um... sorry," Sara answered, "I'm afraid that's not how it works, remember? Curiosity doesn't know the song for where we are now."

"Wait, what?" Jonathan stammered. "So how do we get back?"

"Same way we always do—the hard way. Now come on, dry out your wings, we need to get Adam out of the water." The knight was starting to turn pale. His lips had a sickly bluish tint to them, and his body was shaking rapidly. He was making quick chattering noises with his teeth.

The chimera stretched out his new wings and shook them, throwing off much of the water. He grabbed Adam with one arm and then kicked up, leaping out of the ocean. The pair shot upwards and then started coming down again, the chimera's thin wings catching only just before they hit the surface. The chimera hovered tenaciously for a second, and then lurched sideways and shot to the left before finally starting to slowly rise. The knight hung limply from his arms. "He's heavier when he's wet," Jonathan felt the need to explain.

"No," Sara's strangely altered voice came from the great beast's mouth, "it's just that he can't help us out with his own wings, they're still healing. Come on, there's the remains of a ship-wreck not far from here. Due north. We should be able to gather enough wood for a raft and scavenge some supplies.

We have to hurry though, there's some pretty nasty predators in the air here as well." Sara decided against telling Jonathan about the dragons.

The primal ocean churned menacingly beneath them as they flew. It was a strange landscape... one completely devoid of land. Above them, Sara could see the blurry swirls where the boundary region slowly turned into the realm of primal air. This was not the safest of places to have come. Before long though, the debris field came into view. This was not so much a shipwreck as simply a gyre, a place where the currents swirled and all of the various floating junk and garbage that ended up in this region of primal water accumulated. A red algae had formed across much of the flotsam, slowly decomposing it.

"Phew, this place smells," Jonathan complained.

"It'll have to do," Sara explained. "Now just over there where there's a break in the algae, there's some fresh logs, and...."

"I know," Jonathan replied, "your thoughts are starting to bleed into mine again."

The chimera flew down, set Adam's limp body upon what remained of the deck of a ship, and then turned to go gather more supplies.

"No," Sara relayed to her companion, "you need to let me out first."

"Ok," Jonathan nodded and moved across to a corner of the sinking deck where his weight balanced out Adam's. He arched his head back and spread out his arms. Nothing happened.

"It's not working," Jonathan cried through the link. "What's going on?"

"It doesn't want to let me go!" Sara wailed back. "It's burning me. It's got a taste of my blood and it doesn't want to stop! Without the water flask, I can't stay in this long. You have to get me out of here now."

"How?" Jonathan returned. "I'm trying!"

In lieu of a response, the chimera's hands lifted to its throat and its claws dug into its own mouth. As if fighting a stuck zipper, it tore slowly downward, parting one tooth at a time as it pulled open its own chest. The chimera moved its great pincers around and wedged them into the crack to hold it open, and then reached into the gap and pulled forcefully, tearing out the limp form of the young girl. He ripped at his own tendrils that still clung to the still body, and then threw it down onto the floor of the raft and then staggered backwards, splashing heavily into the water.

*****

"Sara? Lady Sara? Can you hear me?" The voice was steady and low, yet familiar, like something out of a dream. Sara opened her eyes. Above her, the face of the Neverknight loomed. "Are you ok?" he asked. "You are bleeding." His eyes pierced through hers, and his lips quivered with concern. Sara had actually had many daydreams in the last year or so that started like this, but unfortunately reality never quite worked out the same way. Sara rolled over and threw up.

A few moments later, the chimera had returned. He had lashed a collection of thin logs together and was now shoving the sinking planks of the ship deck up on top of them to make a makeshift raft. He took more rope and fastened the broken planks to the logs. Then, as an added precaution, he secreted glue from his palms onto the ropes. It was not the best looking of crafts, but it was sturdy. As he finished his labors, he made his way to Sara. "I'm sorry," he announced, looking worried.

"No," Sara responded between coughs, "it's not your fault. It's not you. It's the chimera. It's how it was built. I mean, it did the same thing to you once. You are just a passenger in there too. You have to feel it. I mean...." Sara broke off, looking concerned.

"What?" Jonathan hated when Sara held back, like he couldn't handle the truth. If there was something going on with his body, he wanted to know.

"Well," Sara sputtered, "I'm pretty sure my father is blocking the knowledge, but I think there's something else in there too besides you. Something deep and latent. I think it can only wake up under a specific condition."

"No," Jonathan replied, "I don't think so. I've gone pretty deep in this thing. I'm sure it was empty when it came to me. You look cold." Jonathan flew off again and returned a few seconds later with a great heap of mottled oilcloth. "It looks like this was once a sail," he mused, "but it should make a pretty decent blanket too." He rose up in the air and let the long cloth roll out, then he shook it once to free it of water and then lowered it down, letting it pile up on top of the raft. "You both need some sleep."

Sara and Adam crawled into the folds of the old sail. It was thin, but large enough to double up a few times. The weight of the thing was comforting, and even on the hard, rocking planks, the sensation of being in a bed felt good. Beside her, Adam shivered. He was still without proper clothes, and in the frigid polar air, he was losing body heat fast. Sara knew there was only one thing that could be done for him, and she gulped in fear as she thought of it. Of all the things they had faced, why did this scare her? Sara inched closer to the knight until she could hear his breath. She put a hand on his side and felt the cold, hard muscle of his flank. It was so firm. He shivered in response, and his teeth chattered. Sara inched closer again, slowly. Adam sensed her, and reached his arm out and over her, drawing her in. He was cold to the touch, and Sara began to shiver as her heat drew out and went into him, but she could sense a warmth growing somewhere beneath. Adam raised his metal wings, which were ice cold to the touch, slipping them out of the covers and folding the upper wing down around them. Slowly, between the heat of the two bodies and the envelope of the sailcloth and wing, the temperature began to rise. Exhausted, both companions drifted off to sleep, caught in each other's warming embrace.

*****

A gentle poke nudged Sara to consciousness. Two suns had risen above them, and the sky was now a deep, angry red. "Hey, Sara, wake up," Jonathan warned, "I think there's a storm coming."

23

INTO THE DRINK

"It's moving fast," Sara responded, "the edge of the storm should be on us in half an hour." Sara sat upright, the folds of the sailcloth falling open and revealing the still-sleeping Neverknight curled up beside her. Though clouds were moving in, the sun above was bright and hot, and the chill to the air had mostly gone. The makeshift blanket was now dry and warm.

Sara rubbed the sleep out of her eyes and stared out into the eastern sky. The clouds there looked big for an Earth storm, but Sara knew that they were considerably larger even then they looked. The curvature of the terrain was flatter here, so the clouds were farther off than one might have thought, but still, they were moving towards them very quickly. Ahead of the storm she could just make out (or maybe it was her mind's eye filling in the details for her) a few dark specks flying towards them at breakneck speed. Even the great predators of the air were fleeing for their lives.

"You think they will make it?" Jonathan asked. His eyes had no trouble spotting the fleeing shapes.

"It's possible," Sara tried to reassure. "They have a good head start. But...." Her voice trailed off.

"But what?" Jonathan snapped.

"Have you ever experienced a primal storm before?" Sara asked. She posed questions to Jonathan only out of convention and conversation—she already knew the answers.

"No," Jonathan answered, "but I take it you're not going to tell me any good news."

"We are on the boundary now between air and water," Sara explained. "These are some of the first worlds. The color palette, if you will, that was used to create the more sophisticated realms. Here the two primal realms blend together and the raw energy of creation constantly fights to form new elements. These are true storms. Every storm we've ever witnessed anywhere else has been simply an echo or a reflection of a primal storm. Kind of like every campfire is a reflection of primal flame, and every puddle on the sidewalk is a reflection of primal water."

"Like I said," Jonathan replied, "no good news."

"Well, we are unlikely to survive," Sara nodded, "but still, we can prepare."

"What about going back under the water," Jonathan suggested. "The storm can't hit us down there, can it?"

"No, not too badly," Sara agreed, "but still, Adam and I can't breathe under the surface, and this water's too cold to spend much more time in. I think our best bet is to stick with the raft. There's a number of items scattered about here that could prove useful to us. I can tell you where to gather them. Number one is rope. We'll need as much of it as you can get."

As the chimera's wings buzzed, lifting him into the air, Sara reached down and gently shook the shoulder of the sleeping knight. "Come on, wake up," she murmured, "it's time for breakfast."

Adam's golden eyes struggled open and hazily looked up at her. A pained sound escaped his lips. Sara could tell that he was still suffering greatly from the burns he had received at the hands of the fire queen—not to mention the starvation, the drowning, the pressure of the ocean water, the cold, and the fight with the lampreys. Well, Sara thought, at least one of these she had been able to see ahead of time. She pulled a slender tube out a hidden pocket in her organic suit.

"I have something for your wounds," Sara said. "We have to get you up and working again soon." She smeared some clear ointment out of the tube and began to rub it into the burns on Adam's arms. Curiosity had not had much in the way of fresh medical supplies, but this was better than nothing. "You should have some water too. You don't have to worry about drinking the ocean here, it's fresh and pure."

"Your hands are shaking," Adam commented.

"What?" Sara sounded surprised. "Sorry, I'm just cold." She knew that Adam knew that she was lying, but she was glad that he did not mention it.

"I can do that, thanks." Adam took the ointment tube from Sara and proceeded to apply it sparingly to the menagerie of burns scattered across his broken body. "Didn't you say there was something to eat?"

Sara gulped, nodded, and pulled a bucket towards them. Jonathan had caught a few fish while they had slept. "I hope you like sushi," Sara grimaced as she handed the knight the bucket.

"Who's Suzie?" Adam questioned as he peered into the wooden pail. "Oh, ugh, raw fish? Can't we build a fire? I mean, there's enough scrap wood around here."

"That was the plan, but there's no time now. Storm's a'comin'." Sara grinned and did her best to look cheerful, but it wasn't working. The worry showed through in her eyes.

"Oh…" Adam looked up at the sky. A great shadow that half-resembled an enormous dragon screamed by overhead, flapping briskly into the distance. "No offense," the knight explained, "but I'm glad I don't get rescued every day." The jest made Sara uncomfortable. Still, she joined him in a brief laugh so as to not show her true feelings.

Adam reached gingerly into the fish bucket and drew out a small, flat specimen. "Why did it have to be fish?" he sighed. At least the chimera had already cleaned them all. Adam pulled the flat fish open and bit into the soft, red flesh. "You aren't going to have any?" he commented as he came up for air.

Sara made a sour face and shook her head. "No, I'm good," she replied, "I ate yesterday."

Adam gnawed on the fish for a while in silence as the winds began to pick up around them. "You know," he spoke, "I've thought about you every day you've been away."

Sara's heart began to pound. "Yes… I know." She had all the answers to all of creation in here, but couldn't figure out how to respond to that sentence in a way that didn't make her sound like a fawning school girl.

"And I've thought about the Fish Man every day too."

Sara's heart stopped for a second. Adam had actually thought about the Fish Man a great deal more than he had thought about her. "He's still out there," Sara said. "If you want to come with us I think we can defeat him. We need you to help us find my father. It sounds crazy, but we've got a plan."

Adam took one more bite out of the cold fish and chewed slowly, thinking as he picked the thin bones out of his teeth. "I don't know, Sara," he finally spoke, "I've spent my whole life as a slave to someone else's plans. I just kind of want to be free for a while."

"Don't be ridiculous, you'll never be free with him out there, and you know it." Sara's voice shook with more emotion than she would have liked. "Besides, think of all the suffering he's going to cause. Even if you find a place outside of his reach, there will surely be millions thrown into misery, if not more."

"There will always be misery, Sara," the knight sighed. "I can't allow the Fish Man's transgressions to fall on to my shoulders, I only just discovered my true self again to find myself a prisoner of yet another evil being. I am tired, but all that I want right now is to be rid of all the pain and madness."

Sara could see that he was thinking of going off somewhere on his own, somewhere green and bright where he could fly free. She never imagined that he would not join her and Jonathan on their quest; she would do anything to keep him near. "Well, we rescued you with a purpose in mind."

"Oh?" the knight's voice sounded hurt.

Sara hated herself for having said it almost at once. "We were coming to rescue you anyway. It's just that there is more to it now."

Jonathan returned with more ropes and some supplies that Sara had guided him to via mental pictures sent through their link. Without interrupting, he began to quickly go about strengthening the raft.

"To be honest, I wish you had not come at all," the knight sighed. "After all, even with all your gifts, you're just a child. You should never have placed yourself in so much danger."

Sara's voice went cold. "That's what you think of me, isn't it? A child?" And Sara knew it was true.

"Well yeah... I mean, isn't that what you are?" Adam looked uncomfortable. Sara turned away from him and hid her anger. As if the very sky sensed her mood, the winds began to pick up.

"Hey, Sara, what do you want me to do with the rest of this rope?" the chimera asked. He looked about at the two silent companions. "Hey, cheer up. We're not dead yet," he offered. No response came back.

"I can help," Adam finally spoke. He stood up gingerly on the shaky raft and helped haul the massive coil of wet hemp onto the sailcloth. "Start tying it all around the raft," he continued. "The main goal is to keep the raft intact. The rest of it we can use to keep us tied to the raft."

"Got it," Jonathan nodded. "Sara, what are the best knots to use for this stuff?" He could tell he had interrupted something that had put Sara in a foul mood. Her silence in the wake of the oncoming danger worried him. Sara?"

Sara sat on the edge of the raft with her feet dangling over, toes skiffing through the top of the water. She stared blankly out at the ocean that bore them on its back. Then, without warning, she suddenly pushed forward, dropping off into the water. Seconds later, the first wave hit the raft.

"Sara!" Jonathan shouted. But the wave that hit them sent the raft spinning. There was no telling where she had gone.

"Tie me off!" Adam shouted through the spray. Jonathan looped the heavy rope around the knight's waist and held onto the end as Adam leapt off into the foam. The knight disappeared under the surface for a tense moment, and then returned, empty handed. Another wave crashed over them and Adam was swept out past the raft. Jonathan reeled him in, pincers and toes firmly gripped to the old planks of the flimsy boat. Another wave hit and the planks splintered, sending the chimera reeling forwards and grasping blindly for the wood of the raft.

"It's no good," Jonathan cried, desperation sinking in.

Then the chimera heard her in his head, "I will be fine. I know what I am doing. Keep Adam and yourself safe."

"We have to tie ourselves off!" Jonathan yelled above the now-roaring winds.

"By that time she could be miles away!" Adam hollered, leaping off again and flailing out in the foam with his hands. "Come on, monster, what good are you? Can't you see her with your magical eyes?"

"No," Jonathan replied coldly, "I cannot." The chimera gave another hard tug on the knight's rope and Adam came flying back, crashing heavily into the wood of the raft. The chimera wrapped one of his big hands around the dazed knight's shoulders and hefted him onto the raft. He pinned Adam down, easily overpowering the still weakened knight, and then began to tie him to the craft.

"Why would she do that?" Adam shook violently, his eyes filled with a frantic fear.

Jonathan didn't really know. He trusted Sara more than anyone, but for her to just jump into the water like that seemed mad to him. "Maybe it was something you said." He tried to reach her again through their link, but he could tell she was now out of range. At a loss, Jonathan began to tie himself to the raft.

As the red sky darkened, the chimera finished securing the ramshackle raft. He lay beside Adam and tied his own legs and waist down. He left his upper body free in case he needed to make any adjustments during the storm. Jonathan stared out into the blood-red clouds, keeping watch over the prone knight and the tiny boat as the storm moved in to swallow them.

24

ECHOES

Kili had the sharpest vision, and was the first to spot the bobbing object in the distance. "Hey, look ahead!" her chirping voice called. The others soon joined in.

"What's that?" Liv shouted.

"It's funny looking," Salal chirped back. "Must be some junk left over from the storm."

Kili was the first to reach the strange round object. She prodded it with her nose, and it rolled over in the water. "It's a girl!" she called.

"A girl," Salal chirped back, "what's one of those doing out here? Wow, she's a fat one, isn't she. She's lucky the sharks didn't eat her."

"She doesn't look too good," Liv butted in. "You sure she's not dead?"

"Give her a poke," Salal suggested. Kili kicked forward and struck the floating thing hard with her snout. It make a thump like a beach ball and popped up into the air, then fell back down again with a bounce. "Hey, fun!" Salal shouted. He swam forward and struck the ball again, sending it flying. Liv did a black flip and leapt over the ball, then she slapped it with her tail and sent it hurtling towards Kili.

"Stop!"

The three friends stared at the strange, round girl. No human could speak their language. This one was a mystery indeed. "Who are you?" Kili spoke, hesitatingly.

"My name is Sara," the stranger announced, still in the language of the sea. And as the three friends watched, the ball deflated, slowly transforming into a sleek, tight suit that covered the girl like a second skin. "But that's not important. You waste time in play that should be spent looking for your missing child."

The three friends chirped in surprise and wonderment, and their faces showed a hint of fear. "Time spent playing is never wasted," Kili finally spoke, "but what do you know of my son?"

"He is afraid," Sara chirped, "and in great danger. In the wake of the storm, he has fallen into the belly of a reaver. Come, I can take you to him."

Kili hesitated. Was this stranger some sort of messenger from the gods? Or something else. "It's a trap," whispered Salal. "They have sent her to draw us into their machine."

"How do we know you are who you say you are?" Liv called to the stranger.

"I have only said I was Sara," the stranger countered, treading water now in the calm ocean. "Is that so hard to believe?"

"Maybe," Liv answered. "Why do you have a dolphin name?"

"Why do you have a human name, Liv?" Sara replied. "And you Salal, why do you hide your feelings for Liv? Do you still think the pod does not see you as an adult after you fought off the sharks last month? You think your size is all that you are?" The little dolphin looked stunned. Liv gave him an awkward look.

"What about you Kili? How many of the others know of your songs? What is the point of being a composer if no one gets to hear your work?" Kili looked confused until Sara began to sing, in chirps and clicks. "Soft is the sun, and soft is the rain, but softest still is my calf's pain."

"I say we go with her," Liv announced. The other two nodded, dazedly.

Sara hung onto Kili's dorsal fin as she shot through the water. "Quickly," Sara chirped, "they will be coming in only a few moments, and then we will be too late. This ride was nothing like sitting on the chimera. The dolphin's skin was firm and smooth, and fantastically sleek. Sara began to laugh with the glee of the ride, but she had to hold herself back as the spray began to choke her. It was like riding a living torpedo.

Soon, land appeared ahead. Or at least it looked like land. Sara knew better though. A moment later, the thing that looked like a good-sized island coughed, sprayed up a geyser of water, and disappeared beneath the waves. A minute later it appeared again, a good mile from its original position.

"We'll never make it," Kili chirped, "it's moving too fast!"

"No, probably not. You are going to have to lure it over here," Sara shouted. "Kili, chirp as loud as you can. Salal, Liv, do what you do best. Start playing and flipping up into the air."

The dolphins started leaping and laughing. "Splash bigger," Sara directed, "it needs to notice us." Soon enough, the land mass in the distance began to turn and seemed to be moving towards them. "We got it!" Sara exclaimed. "Head right for it."

Kili kicked her tail and shot forward through the water. The massive, grey bulk was coming towards them fast. Just ahead, they could see the front of it beginning to rise up out of the water, liquid pouring down off of it in great rivulets, revealing a dark void beneath. "Ok, this is it," Kili chirped, "what's the plan?"

"Forward," Sara commanded. "We're going inside."

"What?" Kili screeched. The dolphin leapt up into the air and then came down nose first, flattening Sara against the surface of the water. As Sara recovered her senses, she saw the three dolphins speeding away to the left and right. Above her, the stadium-sized jaws of the reaver were starting to come down. This wasn't how the plan was supposed to work.

*****

The chamber at the center of the reaver was impossibly dark. There were some scattered glows from various trapped luminescent sea creatures, but no true light sources. The water vibrated with a low pulse, and a deep but constant rumbling could be heard not far off. Sara treaded the thick, sludgy water, trying to wrap her mind past the ungodly stench that filled the place. There was an access ladder in here, but it was over a mile away. There was just over five minutes before this place was going to be flushed. Where was her trusty bottle-nosed steed when she needed her? Oh yeah. There was an idea.

"Kona," Sara chirped as loud as she could, again speaking the language of the sea. "Kona, come to my voice."

A brief silence fell over the chamber, but then a moment later, a small, frail voice chirped back. "Who are you?"

"Your mother, Kili, sent me to help you," Sara whistled. "You must come with me fast. There is no time to argue."

A short echo of dolphin song burst out through the chamber, and Sara knew the little calf was scanning the area with its echolocation. Thank god dolphins can 'see' in the dark, Sara thought. A moment later, Sara heard a light splashing sound, and she knew the calf had swam up to study her. "You must take me to the far side of the chamber," Sara chattered. "I know you are a brave one. Your mother has told me much about you." That was only part true. Sara had really learned about the calf from the mother's thoughts. Same thing, Sara figured.

The little dolphin swam up and Sara grabbed a hold of its neck. It flapped its tail and they sped off through the dark, the calf chirping as it went so as to make out and avoid the other trapped creatures and any floating objects in their path. A few moments later, Sara reached out and felt the metal of the service ladder at the edge of the containment cell. "Thank you, little one," Sara called, "I will come back for you soon." She pulled herself up and began the high climb up the rusting ladder.

The top of the ladder ended at a small, unlit catwalk. Sara had played this game before—walking with her eyes closed. She kept her eyes shut and scanned the area around her. She moved along the wall to a small service door and reached up to feel the cold metal letters of the keypad. The runes were alien, but Sara knew the sequence and typed it in. The door bolts released with a hiss as the pressure seal broke. Sara reached out to pull the hatch open.

Beyond the door, the service corridor was long, narrow, and filled with a menagerie of tubes and pipes. Red lights had been mounted every twenty feet or so, giving the hallway an eerie, sinister glow. Sara stepped inside and closed the door behind her. Forty feet down the hallway, she opened a metal box in the wall and pulled out a handful of wires.

What was she doing here? She had no chimera to back her words up with muscle this time, no Neverknight to save her, no lucky cat to change her fortune, no mother to tuck her in and keep her safe. She was on her own now. One mistake, and it was all over. With a deep breath, she opened the next hatch to the engine room.

The chamber beyond was larger, and quite hot. Enormous, greasy engines pounded away here, creating a fantastic din that muffled any sound of her entry. Sara closed the hatch and slid behind a tall machine. A few moments later, a slim, insect-like man scurried up to the hatch she had just come out of and passed through it. Sara popped out from behind the machinery and slammed the door shut. She typed a few strokes into the keypad next to the hatch and the bolts slammed shut, sealing it fast.

Disabling a massive ship... hadn't she done this before? Sara approached a glass wall upon which glowing charts and runes moved about in a jumpy, but constant flow. She reached out and touched the wall. More runes appeared where she touched the glass, and after navigating a variety of charts and forms, Sara touched a final button, and the great engines ground slowly to a halt. She reached behind an instrument panel and pulled out a cord. The glass wall went dark. Time was now of the essence.

Sara slipped out of the engine room and scurried through the metal halls of the great ship, keeping constant track of all the workers on board at all times. After a few turns, she stopped at a small door and pulled it open, slipping inside amongst the mops and bottles of the janitor's closet. In her mind, she watched the officers scurry by on their way to inspect the engine. A second after they turned the corner, Sara slipped back out and headed towards the bridge. There was only one pilot left behind. This was going to be cake.

Sara typed in another code, and the door to the bridge slid open. Sara stepped inside. On the screen at the front of the bridge, she could see the spidery airship coming in to dock with the reaver. "Well, what did you find," the pilot croaked at her without even turning around.

"Zots," Sara croaked back, "vem bog tel shozz." Wait, that wasn't right. Sara realized she knew the insect men's language, but she lacked the secondary vocal chords they needed to speak it. There was her one mistake.

The pilot swiveled around in his chair. If it were even possible, one might have imagined that his bug eyes bugged out even more as they lay sight upon the small human that now stood before them. The pilot raised his pistol. "Freeze!" he shouted—in proper bug-speak.

Sara froze. And not just physically. Her mind went blank. All the knowledge in the universe at her disposal and none of it did her any good. All she could see was the gun pointed at her and those buggy eyes. The gun, she knew was a third-generation tech plasma thrower that would vaporize her in a moment, leaving only a hot flash and an acrid smell in the air. And those eyes—Sara just wished that they couldn't see her. Actually... now there was an idea. Sara couldn't speak to this bug thing, nor could she do anything else without moving, almost. Sara focused her will and, in response, her organic outfit turned a deep, solid violet. The material was damaged, but there was still enough of it to cover her if she left her feet and ankles bare. If she had questioned the Font right, the pilot's bug eyes registered different wavelengths of light than Sara's human eyes did—infra red to indigo only. Violet light was as good as darkness.

Like the Cheshire cat, Sara's body disappeared into the shadows of the doorway beyond. For a split-second, as the material moved up the back of her head and down over her face, only her smile remained, grinning nervously as she moved her focus directly into the creature's surface thoughts. And then she was gone.

Sara had seen enough soccer back on Earth to know how this next part worked. It was like a penalty kick. He could shoot straight, left, or right, and if Sara dodged the opposite way, she would live. If she moved too slow, or misjudged his intentions, she'd be vaporized. The bug fired straight ahead. Sara moved left.

A second later, she was running, dodging through the shadows
of the cramped bridge as the pilot desperately scanned the
room for a second shot. A chair vaporized just behind her. She
rolled under an instrument console and held still. To the bug,
she was no different than the shadows. She just needed more
of them. The bug spun around, confounded. He ran back to
his console and pushed a button, delivering a message to his
comrades to head back to the bridge. Sara was running out
of time, but this was all she needed. While he had his back
turned, Sara crawled forward and reached up and touched a
few buttons on the next panel over. The bridge lights went off.
Light still seeped in from portholes, but the bridge was now
plunged into shadow. Sara touched another set of buttons,
and the door to the bridge slammed shut. Sara overrode the
password, but that still left the pilot.

Another shot rang out, like a high, tubular bell. The panel
Sara was working at exploded. Some of the hot, melted metal
dripped on her bare feet, burning them. She bit her tongue.
A scream would give her position away. She still didn't have
the advantage she needed here. Didn't they have some sort of
defenses in place against this sort of thing? Oh yes, they did.
Brilliant thing about most intelligent species, they design their
defenses to work best on their own kind. Sara entered another
code on another panel. Pink gas started to hiss into the chamber and Sara slipped back into the shadows under the copilot's
console. She tucked her bare feet behind her to hide them.

Thirty seconds later, the pilot was fast asleep, slumped over
a railing. Sara could hear his companions on the other side
working at the blast door with their weapons. Sara turned the
main screen back on. The eight-legged airship had now docked
to the reaver, and was waiting for the airlock to open. Sara
opened it. This would prevent the docking clamps from being
released. The airship would not be picking up any cargo today.
Sara typed in the necessary code, and the great metal mouth of
the reaver began to open. She walked over to the pilot's chair
and turned the depth knob. The great ship shuddered and

began to sink.

Sara picked up the pistol that had fallen from the sleeping pilot's hand and finished off the rest of the functional consoles. This ship was going down, and everything in its belly was now returning to the ocean. With one nervous look back, Sara pulled open the small round hatch on the far left of the bridge. She climbed inside the little round room and closed the hatch behind her. Then she hit the only control in the entire pod—a big red button.

*****

As the red sun began to set behind the clear horizon, the little raft floated aimlessly on the empty sea, its two occupants not looking particularly happy about the spectacular show of color. "Hey, look on the bright side," Jonathan piped in, "at least if we're stuck on this raft for the rest of our lives then we'll never have to tell Tessa what happened." But the joke felt flat even to him. His faith in Sara was wavering, and he wondered if he would ever lay eyes on her again.

"I still can't believe she's gone," Adam replied. He sat cross-legged facing the sunset, wearing a spotty tunic crafted from moldy sail and rope. His limbs still showed many burns, and around his left eye, a blotchy, purple patch swelled.

"Neither can I," the chimera uttered back, "but hey, at least I didn't talk her into killing herself after she risked her life to rescue me from two years of solid torture."

"I told you to shut up about that. I'm sorry."

"Oh… you're sorry?" the chimera mocked, drawing out the penultimate syllable. "Well I don't think sorry is going to bring her back. Heck, it's not even going to get us off this raft anytime in the next, what, five years? It's not going to keep us from being eaten by dragons or sea monsters. What's your sorry good for?"

"Hey, now there's an idea," Adam muttered, "We could draw one of those dragon things down here and then jump on its back. It has to land somewhere, doesn't it? I think you'd make pretty good dragon bait."

"You know what, knight?" the chimera yelled, "I can breathe underwater. I can see fish in the dark. I don't really need you. But just how long do you think you are going to last without me."

"Is that what you want?" The Neverknight stood up suddenly, the raft tipping perilously. "You want to prove yourself against me? Go ahead, take your best shot." The knight stuck his chest out.

Jonathan stood up, his wings spreading open. "No," he called out as he stepped backwards off the raft and rose into the air, "but if that's how you feel you can keep your stupid raft. I don't need a soggy plank to come back to when my wings get tired, and at least mine are fully functional." He turned and started to rise into the air, moving away from the raft.

"Boys!" The voice startled the two companions. They turned slack-jawed to the horizon opposite the sun. Four low shapes were approaching in the water. Atop the smallest one sat a familiar young figure.

Sara pulled up to the raft. The little dolphin she rode splashed with excitement and poked its pointed face up out of the water to chirp a greeting. "Get on," Sara called out, pointing at two of the larger dolphins. "We have taken too much time here already."

*****

"I don't know what to say," Adam spoke as he pulled his speeding dolphin up beside Sara's. "I shouldn't have said those things to you. Or at least my timing was rotten. I owe you my life."

"No," Sara responded, "you were right; I needed to grow up. And you know what? I think I have."

"Still, you should know," Adam continued, "if there is anything I can do to aid you, I am at your service, Lady Sara."

Sara liked it when he called her that. "Well," she ordered, smiling at Adam, "for now, just try not to fall off." She steered Kona away from the knight and moved towards the chimera at the head of the pod. "We should be at the sacred grotto in seven minutes," she announced, "then it's just a quick dive down to a nexus point, but we need to time it right. How fast do you think you can learn dolphin music? My sister is in trouble."

25

~~~~~

HARMONY AND STRIFE

As the last notes of the gypsy song trailed off into the blur of sound, three robed figures slipped in through the slowly-fading, silver archway. The smallest of the companions came first, strolling swiftly and confidently, while the larger two moved in behind her with more trepidation and caution. The smell of incense wafted in on the air, and a pleasantly warm breeze stirred the sterile halls of the Heart of Music with a blast of fine, golden sand. The largest of the three creatures, a shaggy, hunchbacked figure, turned after entering and stood as if guarding the archway, watching the last little speck of light fade away into the odd, translucent, colored glass of the Heart.

"Is the coast clear?" Jonathan the chimera gasped as the portal was finally gone. He poked the hard surface of the wall with his fingers, as if testing it.

"Yes," Sara replied with confidence. "Besides, even if the watcher had seen us, he could not get back in here without Curiosity opening a door for him. We are safe for now."

"Is this where you have been saying we were going all this

time?" Adam asked, looking around a little askance along the maze of empty passageways. "It doesn't look like much."

"Oh, don't worry," Sara assured him, "this isn't a place in and of itself, it's just a passageway. But from here we can get literally anywhere you desire."

"That's pretty incredible," Adam grimaced, "but I don't think the place I desire to go even exists anymore."

"No," Sara murmured, remembering suddenly that Adam had no home to go back to, no family to reunite with, "but you'd be surprised what time can change. Someday remind me to show you something."

"Okay... and what would that be?" Adam asked, his interest piqued.

"I said someday," Sara frowned.

"What? Okay... fine. But what am I supposed to...." Adam trailed off. He was starting to understand what Jonathan meant about having a conversation with Sara often being like Sara having a conversation with herself while rummaging around in your head.

The chimera had discarded his robe and now, having decided the path behind them was safe, moved to the front of the group to defend them from any unseen dangers in that direction. "Whew, it's good to be back here," he exclaimed. "I didn't think we'd ever make it. That cat always made this look so easy."

"I've been wondering about that too," Sara replied. "I can't quite put my finger on it, but things always seem to go a little smoother when he is around. I say we make him our first priority."

"Fine with me," Jonathan answered. "What are the risks? Other than the cat box smell, that is."

"Not much," Sara replied, "as long as this time we don't take any chances. It seems El Gato has managed to wend his way back to the fair lands. I say we go in and out in one shot, keeping the portal open. Jonathan, you will need to stay at the organ with Curiosity and ensure no note is struck while Adam goes through and gets the cat. I'll stay in the doorway and relay any necessary information to whomever needs it."

"Sounds good," Jonathan nodded. "What do you think, knight?"

"Me? I wasn't aware I had any say in this little confederacy," Adam smirked. "But I'd say it's as good a plan as any, considering I don't really have any idea what's going on or who we are dealing with. But if you're talking about your cat, I thought you said you couldn't see him with your powers. How do you know where to find him?"

"He left me a sign," Sara smiled. "I'm pretty certain he is sitting around waiting for us to pick him up. This should be easy. Oh, it looks like we've arrived." Ahead of them, a round, red doorway loomed. Dozens of crab-like hermites scurried back and forth along the walls, piping their entrance. Fascinated, Adam reached out a hand to feel the back of one about two feet across.

"Don't touch them!" Sara scolded. Adam pulled his hand away.

Inside the treasure chamber, Sara was pleased to be reunited with her satchel, amused that it had been hidden there from the watchers safely in plain sight. Funny, all the amazing things in here, and this was all she really cared about. Of all the treasures from a thousand worlds, sometimes it was best to just have one's own simple belongings. Sara reached inside and felt the contents. It seemed a little silly to keep mementoes from all her travels when she could remember everything that ever happened anywhere, but it felt right. From the inner pocket of her robes, Sara pulled a small, speckled seashell and placed it in the satchel. Someday, she told herself, she would like to own more than just a bag.

Adam was not under any kind of spell, but he was entranced nonetheless by the treasures. "Wow," he whistled. "Do you think they have a...."

"Yes," Sara answered before the question had even been asked. She grabbed the edge of Adam's robe and led him into a side chamber. Here military wares were on full display, strange suits of armor, sleek death machines, and long spears and blades. On an ornate teak table at the center of the room lay a long ivory box, decorated with red gemstone inlays. "I don't think Curiosity would mind if you borrowed it for a while," Sara spoke solemnly. "It's supposed to be indestructible."

Inside the box, on a cushioned bed of red satin, lay a long, curved, two-handed blade, looking to have been carved from a single piece of ruby. Adam lifted it, and the light of the room shone through it, making it appear to glow in his hands. He hefted the sword, whistling at its feather lightness. "It's been so long," he spoke, "I don't know that I can...."

"You'll remember," Sara assured. She handed him a slim ivory sheath meant for the blade. "But best put that away now. We're all better off if you don't have to remember."

A shadow passed across the doorway. "Ah," a familiar voice spoke, "I see my uninvited guests have returned."

Adam whirled, sword still in hand. Curiosity stood tall in the doorway, eyes blazing. "I trust you have the wisdom not to use that against me here," he grinned. "But come now, that is beside the point; I hear you have a plan." Jonathan could be seen, skulking embarrassedly in the chamber behind.

"Yes," Sara stated unashamedly, "but first we must fetch our cat, and then my mother and her new friend."

"And I imagine you need my organ for all of this," the Elder intoned.

"If we may have your leave, of course." Sara curtseyed.

"Ah, now," Curiosity grinned, "but that all depends, doesn't it, on whether or not you pay the piper." He put his hand out as if collecting coin.

"I believe we are all paid up," Sara replied, staring back at him.

"Well now, are we?" Curiosity stroked his chin. "I believe we agreed to three trips. We never spoke of picking up your lost friends scattered around creation. That's another two questions."

"I count one," Sara spoke evenly. "Each question is a trip to and back. These side trips are only to, no back. So two for one question, that's only fair.

"Two more questions," Curiosity's eyes burned.

"I think you'd better stick with one," Adam snarled, pointing the ruby sword towards the Elder. "We don't really need you anyway. Sara said Jonathan can play the organ himself."

"I warned you, boy." The Elder snapped his fingers.

Instantly Adam whirled around and began menacing Sara with his weapon. "I don't know how you got behind me, friend," he growled, "but I'll bet you can't keep that little trick up." His eyes focused on a point in space about a foot above Sara's head.

Sara dodged backwards and grabbed at a small, ornate urn. Reaching inside, she pulled out a handful of a fine, pink dust and tossed it into the air in front of her. As Adam passed into the cloud, he froze, sword held high, like a statue. Sara walked over and picked up the ivory sheath and, standing on a chair, slid it over the knight's outstretched blade.

"One question," Sara again stated flatly. "The deal was for travel and return for each trip. You never picked us up, nor did you fetch my mother. Technically, you owe us two more trips anyway, but under the circumstances, I will consent to answer one more. Besides," Sara paused, "you were supposed to keep my sister safe. And you forgot about Jonathan."

Curiosity could feel the chimera's warm breath on the back of his head. "You drive a hard bargain," he sighed. "I supposed one question will have to do. Very well. I already have it picked out. When you are ready to go, answer me this." The Elder cleared his throat. "Why are all creatures given free will?"

Sara laughed. "Fair enough, that's no secret. To capture the first one's interest and imagination, and to appease his great loneliness." That was the oldest answer to the question, but it seemed a little too succinct. Sara scanned the Font for some expert mortal commentary. "Consider this, if all creatures followed his orders, he would never be surprised; nothing would ever be invented that he could not invent himself."

Curiosity scratched his head. "Interesting, most interesting," he nodded. "But I'm afraid you missed the real question. Why are ALL creatures given free will?"

Sara stopped and thought. She had a thousand answers to that question, but they all came from philosophers. Was this sort of thing even in the Font? This question predated the Font's creation. Of course, Curiosity wouldn't know if she was lying to him or not. Maybe she could just wing it.

"Sometime the biggest surprise of all is in who surprises you," Sara offered. Wait, was that even an answer?

Curiosity nodded and pursed his lips. "Yes, I suppose I can relate," he spoke, looking at Sara. He seemed a little pensive. "Well, when you are ready, meet me at the organ."

*****

Adam stood ready in the central chamber as the organ be-

gan to play. The translucent tubes of the great Heart could
be seen twisting and turning to the beat of the song. A high,
playful trill played, with just a touch of darkness—the sound
of Fairy. Soon, the branch with the opening portal could be
seen approaching. Adam crouched, ready to move, his new
sword strapped firm to his back between his wings. The branch
touched the wall of the rotunda and the wall melted away.
Adam stepped into the portal chamber and ran forward, nearly
tripping over the cat.

"Hey, watch it, lead feet," the little feline snapped, "a flat cat
never did anything for anyone."

Adam shook his head. That was easy. He poked his head out
through the portal anyway. The tail of a female tabby was just
passing into the foliage. Here, in a twilit forest clearing, eleven
miniature wooden treasure chests sat, arranged into a star pattern. All around the clearing, yarn of various colors was scattered, and the distinct smell of mouse hung in the air.

"I can't believe I lost them," El Gato rationalized to Sara back
in the organ chamber, throwing his paws up in the air, "but it's
not like I could stick around that place. I did what I could."

"Well, you'll get your chance to redeem yourself, my friend."
Sara replied, "I've got a job that fits the bill just about right."
Sara paused and turned to the Elder at the keys of the great
organ. "This next one is going to be tight. Curiosity, you have
to play the song perfectly. We need the portal as close to my
mother as we can get."

"Challenge accepted, my dear girl." The catlike Elder nodded
and grinned. "Name the tune."

*****

Suspended high in the treetops, El Gato paced nervously
along a strange, cage-like hall. This building by its very nature
seemed unsteady, and it swayed sickeningly in the wind—being
constructed of wood, bones, ribbons, and a strange variety of

other found objects all woven together into wicker-like grids that served as walls, floors, and ceilings. Even the accoutrements in the various chambers all seemed to be made from the same odd materials, though much more focused on the colorful add-ons. Through the many gaps in the floor, El Gato could see the forest below. He moved his feet hesitatingly as he went, careful to not step into a crack or hole. Periodically, the walls and floor gave way into large, gaping openings, wide archways leading to the outside air. This could prove difficult, he thought.

The cat turned a corner, and ahead of him, he spied his first target. Down the hall and away from him, a feathered soldier paced. From razor-sharp beak to taloned feet, the slender guard stood perhaps seven feet, with a pair of folded wings that could probably have spanned twice that distance. In his bony arms, the soldier carried a long spear balanced in front of him as he walked. Soon enough, the soldier passed by another guard going the opposite direction down the hall. They paused briefly, and exchanged some terse words. Just as they began to go on their way, they were disturbed by a loud, rasping, hacking sound. The guards whirled around. A cat?

El Gato arched his back and hissed loudly at the two guards as they pointed their spears at him and began cawing loudly. Yowling with all his might, the little feline took off down the hall with the guards in hot pursuit. As they ran, more of the bird-like creatures began to join in the chase, filing out of side chambers and halls. Both pursuer and pursued put up an infernal din.

Unseen in the commotion, another winged figure slipped silently out of the shadows and tiptoed back down the halls that the cat had just come tearing through. Meeting no further resistance, he made his way through the maze of flimsy passages and beaded doorways into a narrow block of small cells. Passing to the far end of the room, he approached a cage and lifted up the lock. It was primitive, but not ineffective. Not wanting to bother with the mechanics of picking it, the figure slid a long, red sword off of his back and, with one clean blow, sliced through the bone of the cage to which it was attached. With his other hand, he grasped the door and flung it open, peering inside.

On one end of the cramped cage, sat a handsome and well dressed, if rumpled, human man. At the other end, as far from him as possible, a woman of about the same age sat, red-faced and haggard looking. Both seemed surprised to be interrupted, and they looked up at the interloper with hope and relief.

"You the two needing rescuing?" Adam offered, rhetorically.

"Who the heck are you supposed to be?" Tessa asked, slowly getting to her feet and finding her legs somewhat cramped.

"Your daughter sent me, good lady," the knight answered with a slight bow. "But I can explain more later; time is of the essence."

Tessa and Michael stood wordlessly and hastened out to the cell block, where they gathered a number of their belongings that been left hanging on the wall. "Shouldn't we let the rest of the prisoners go too," Tessa asked, concernedly. A number of the tall bird men could be seen in other cells, and they stood now and cawed out at them, shaking the doors to their cages.

"No time," Adam replied, "besides, how do we know they don't deserve to be here? Come on, follow me."

Tessa hesitated momentarily and then turned to follow the fleeing knight. Michael paused and lifted a heavy key ring out of a wicker desk. "Captivity is the cruelest crime of all," he remarked, to no one in particular, before passing the key ring through the bars to one of the prisoners and then turning to flee himself.

As Michael and Tessa passed through the portal, Adam turned back and lifted a small, curved horn to his lips. He blew, though no sound was heard, at least not by his ears. He then stepped back through the portal and passed into the Heart of

Music.

A mere moment later, a commotion approached. A frantic El Gato turned the corner, almost tumbling end over end as he changed direction at breakneck speed. Behind him, a small troop of birdlike warriors hopped, some cawing, some hurling spears. The little black cat zigged and zagged as he avoided the missiles. A second later, he was to the portal, leaping as he came. "Ok, hit it, maestro!" he called as he flew through.

Instantly, the music stopped. Adam threw up a transparent shield to cover the doorway as it closed. A collection of spears and feathered talons bounced off in futility. As the portal closed, its chamber pulled away from the central dome. The snakelike vein curled away into the fog, taking Adam and Jonathan, crouched to provide backup if needed, with it.

"Sara!" Tessa shouted as she spied her daughter standing in the rotunda.

Sara smiled and ran towards her mother, catching her in a wide embrace. But it was cut short. Sara pulled away as she locked eyes on the newcomer, who was now crouched down and petting the cat, whispering in low tones.

"I think you will find that there is no point in secrets around here," Sara announced, "though I suppose you are used to that." She looked the inventor over, almost surprised at how striking the resemblance was that he bore to the father she never knew except in pictures. "I knew my mother was the right one to send for you," she finally exclaimed.

"She is a very persuasive woman." The newcomer stood and smirked over at Tessa.

"It is truly to your good fortune that you have come here," Sara remarked. "I know you have obligations, and I thank you for your attention to our cause. But if we do this right, this can be over quite soon, and from here we can quite literally take you anywhere you need to be, and you will be armed with

newfound allies. May I ask that you support us?" Sara curtseyed. "We would be honored to count someone with your...
um... gifts, on our side."

Michael smiled, the cold facade melting away. Here in front
of him stood a distinctly human version of the fairy girl he had
fostered and cared for at the request of the Seventh Star. However, this girl was more than a simple facsimile. Michael could
see a great deal of Tessa in her, and oddly enough, some of
himself as well. Yet even then, she was more than she seemed.
"Well, I have been brought this far," Michael explained, "I
expect at this point it would be simpler to acquiesce than to
fight fate. I do say that I am beginning to see the hand of my
mentor in this."

Sara laughed. Perhaps it was true. "Well, we do have a plan."

26

THE PALE HUNGER

"I don't like this plan," Tessa frowned, "it sounds like we are just walking into a trap. Are we really just going to walk right into the shadow's lair?"

"It's not a lair," Sara corrected, "it's just a place that the shadow prepared for us to meet him."

"Isn't that pretty much the definition of a trap?" Adam laughed.

"No, well…" Sara seemed flustered. "…to the cynical maybe. But you are forgetting something: us. We aren't just any old group of people walking into this; we are one of the most extraordinary teams ever assembled. And I know everything the Shadow has laid out in preparation. Somehow, his taking Aras has opened him to my vision. Besides, we need the Shadow; he is the final piece of this mystery."

"I get that," Tessa sighed, "but why can't we get this shadow to come to us, on our terms."

"Like he came for Aras?" Sara countered. "I feel more comfortable meeting him when all of us are together and alert, able to protect one another. If he comes to us, it won't be on our terms."

"We could set a trap for him," Michael offered.

"I thought you were the one who wanted this over with quickly," Sara sniped. "Besides, we don't have much time before the next watcher will need transport. It's now or never. Anyway, Jonathan and I have been working on something special to trick the Shadow. I said we had a plan, not just an idea."

"How about we put it to a vote?" Jonathan piped in. He raised both his hands as if to be counted.

"Is that two votes for or against?" El Gato squawked. "Anyway, I wasn't aware this was a popularity contest." Adam and Michael laughed.

Sara looked around at those present. This wasn't the most complex of calculations. "No, that's actually a good idea. Why don't we put it to a vote? All those for heading to the Shadow's realm now—well, right after we get some sleep anyway?" Sara put up her hand. El Gato and the chimera also raised their hands. "Adam?" Sara prompted.

The Neverknight sheepishly raised his hand as well. "I just want to get this over with," he declared.

"Thank you," Sara nodded. "Well, if the adults want to stay back here and cower until the watchers come for them, feel free, but the rest of us are headed out no matter what. Of course, you are more than welcome to come with us."

Tessa sighed again and looked away. "Fine," she finally griped, "as long as we can get some of that sleep you mentioned. I guess if you are going to go die off somewhere in some cave, then I may as well be there with you."

"There's the right attitude," Michael mocked, "no one ever needed hope or encouragement when they were about to go do battle with a creature of darkness."

"Oh, you shut up too. I've had enough with you today." Tessa stormed off.

*****

Five minutes later, Tessa's brooding walk was disturbed by something warm and soft rubbing up against the side of her calf. "What do you want?" she barked.

"Well, that's no way to greet an old friend," the cat yelped. "I merely wished to offer my ear. Something is obviously disturbing you here."

"I don't know," Tessa replied, "I guess it's just a mother's intuition."

"What is?"

"Well, all sorts of things. But on top of all that, it's that knight. Nothing against him... he seems honorable enough. But Sara just isn't the same when he is around. I can just see it on her face. He makes her nervous, reckless. She seems so willing to put herself in danger just to get attention from him. Not that it wouldn't be worse if she did get his attention."

"And you were different when you were her age?"

"Me? No, that's just it. But the stakes are so much higher now."

"Your daughter is going to grow up sooner or later," the cat offered, "you can't stop that. But you can be there for her. And don't think she can trust anyone else to do that job."

Tessa nodded. It was where she saw herself in her daughter that worried her the most. But the cat did have a point. She had a choice. She could be there for her, or not be there for her. Not being there hadn't helped much when her own mother had tried it.

*****

The final, bass note sounded, and the portal opened before them into a dim and dusty tunnel of earth. A warm mist filtered out and brought a stale taste to the air.

"This is the safe way in?" Adam scoffed as he ducked his head to enter the cave.

"It's beyond the reach of his sight," Sara offered. She had no problems walking upright in the low tunnels. After a tight turn, the tunnel widened and became a legitimate cavern. The air was wet and heavy, and the only light visible came as a dim glow from shaggy blue lichens that were scattered in patches around the walls and ceiling. No wind blew in the caves, and the space was unusually still. The smallest noises and footsteps made by the group cascaded through the caverns and echoed back as if amplified and distorted. Moisture gathered on the cold stone of the cavern roof and dripped down along stalactites into pale blue pools. Shadows lurked everywhere.

"I can see why he picked this place," Jonathan whispered.

"I still don't see why we didn't just open the portal right into wherever we are going to," Tessa complained. "What's the point of navigating all these caves?"

"Our goal is to make him underestimate us," Sara replied. "We need to play his game. A direct assault like that would undoubtedly put him on the defensive. I don't know that Jonathan or I would be able to stop him if he wanted to take you or one of the others right away. Besides, it is quite difficult to play the notes so exactly that you can open to precisely the desired place. Anyway, it's not far. A little hike is good for you."

"We should gather some of these lichens," Sara directed, "they are not so well entrenched farther down our path." Sara took out some glass jars that she had found in Curiosity's cupboards and had Adam and Michael fill them with lichens from the walls. She passed the jars around to the group.

Jonathan declined a light. "I can function fine without it," he declared. El Gato shrugged when offered, but Sara took a jar, as did Tessa, who decided to conserve the energy in her flashlight for a possible emergency.

"I guess I don't really need light to see either," Sara offered, "though it sure is a heck of a lot less complicated if I have it. But these lichens are our best bet here anyway. They mimic the natural light of the caverns. If we were to carry fire or some other outside light source, it would only invite predators. In particular, it could attract the inhabitants of this land."

"Wait," Jonathan said, "there are inhabitants here? What do they eat? Or do they just sleep here and go outside to hunt?"

Sara laughed. "There is no outside here," she returned. "This creation is just a few scattered pockets of air in an infinity of rock. There's no surface and no end here. And that's why we don't want to meet the inhabitants. There's very little to eat here—a few mushrooms maybe, so they are a pretty desperate bunch."

"Oh come on," Jonathan scoffed as Sara led the group through the tunnels, "that's impossible. There's got to be a surface somewhere."

"Really?" Sara responded, "Why's that?"

"Because everything has a beginning and an end. Besides, you can't have an infinite volume of rock... that's just too much rock."

"But you can have an infinity of space, like they have back on Earth?"

"Sure, why not," Jonathan offered, "that's just an infinity of nothing."

"But where did that nothing come from?"

Jonathan couldn't tell if Sara was serious or not anymore. "Huh? What do you mean? It didn't come from anywhere, because it was never there."

"But something had to create all that space there."

"No! Come on. What are you... wait, well did it? Why don't you just tell me, since you already know everything."

"Every world is a completely different concept of creation," Sara began. Jonathan could tell from her tone of voice that she was about to start seriously geeking out on this. She continued without pause. "Earth was conceived of as a small island of rock floating in an infinity of space. This place is the opposite—a small island of space floating in an infinity of rock. You could spend your whole life digging, and you would never reach an exit or a surface. Although I'm not saying you wouldn't end up right where you started from if you went far enough. Anyway, digging is frowned upon here anyway—see, digging produces dirt, which must be then put somewhere else, which only blocks up a different passage."

"Really?" Jonathan interrupted. "Well then what the heck else do people do for fun around here?"

"Fun?" Sara answered. "That's not really a thing around here. Mostly people just spend their time trying to find enough food to survive. They'll eat each other if they have to. The only food to be had here is mushrooms and sometimes meat. See, life didn't really evolve down here naturally. This realm is mostly used as a prison from other worlds, where the worst criminals are locked away in an impenetrable prison with no chance of escape and no need for guards. However, despite all this, a culture of sorts has formed, with various warring tribes battling over what little territory there is. Right now we are in the territory of the Bahak tribe, one of the largest...."

"Mrrrowwr!"

Sara, Jonathan, and Adam whirled to see El Gato struggling in a crude leather net. Small stones weighed the net down, and a long cord was briskly dragging it back roughly into the darkness of the tunnel behind them. Tessa and Michael were nowhere to be seen.

"Ambush!" Adam shouted.

Before Sara could even react and blame herself for getting distracted, the chimera leapt forward. A spike shot out of his mane and severed the cord that was dragging the cat away. Adam reached out with his mental powers and flung the net away. El Gato ran towards Sara as Adam and Jonathan ran past him down the tunnel. Jonathan could just see the heels of the first ambusher ahead of him.

"Stop!" Sara shouted. Jonathan stopped in his tracks, but Adam kept running, his sword in hand. "Adam, stop now!" The knight did not listen.

A clatter was heard up ahead, and then a low rumble. As Adam turned the next bend of the tunnel, a tumble of rocks and boulders came crashing down upon him.

*****

"He's definitely alive. I can hear him snoring," the cat remarked as he put his head to the rock pile.

"What," Sara responded, "now you suddenly don't believe me when I tell you something? Of course he's alive. He's had plenty of military training. He was able to cushion much of the blow of the fall with his telekinetics. We just need to get him out of there before he runs out of air. "

"How many more of these do I have to move?" Jonathan groaned as he hauled away another boulder.

"Nine," Sara replied, not bothering to ask herself if that had been a rhetorical question. "And you'd better move it. The whole village is astir. They are busily preparing for some kind of great feast.

"Let me guess," Jonathan groaned again as he rolled away another boulder, "it's not mushrooms."

"It's not mushrooms."

"Ooh, I've got a foot here!" Jonathan exclaimed.

"No, don't just pull," Sara chided. "That'll just hurt him worse. He's already broken an arm. Move this rock first, then that one. Now lift his leg."

A few minutes later, Jonathan had dragged the limp knight out of the rubble and Sara began to work on his broken body. Having all the medical knowledge in the world was especially handy when you knew exactly everything that was wrong with the patient. Sara popped the knight's shoulder back into place and then set his arm with a tug. She took a piece of the discarded leather net and tied it into the semblance of a sling. "Come on," she spoke, "I know you can stand now." Jonathan grabbed the knight around the middle and lifted him to his feet.

Adam grimaced. "Thank you," he finally managed.

"If you want us to survive this," Sara responded, "you are going to need to start listening to me. I'm not just some little girl, I'm your commander here, soldier."

Adam nodded, albeit painfully. "Understood," he murmured.

"Now come on, we've lost precious time. With this path blocked, we'll need to go the long way around. So much for our short hike."

Jonathan took the lead with Sara connected to his mind directing him telepathically. Sara scanned the area ahead for traps and defenders, sending El Gato forward to disable some of the more delicate snares. "I've picked the best path to avoid running into any of the Bahaks," she called out, "try not to hurt them. They aren't particularly malicious, just hungry."

"What's not malicious about a cannibal?" Adam argued.

"Who said they were cannibals?" Sara answered as they rounded a bend and came face to face with their first Bahak. Before them in the tunnel stood a pale, scaly creature, towering above them at a height of nearly seven feet. It carried a trident and a net in its clawed hands, and it roared at them through an elongated, toothy maw. From the back of the creature, a long, meaty tail sprouted above its oddly short legs.

Jonathan leapt forward.

"I said, don't hurt them," Sara cried.

"Don't worry, I got it," Adam answered. As the chimera leapt at the creature, it tossed its weighted net at him. Adam concentrated, and the net stopped in midair and flew back at the Bahak. The creature reached an arm out to block the net, and it wrapped itself around him. A second later, the chimera hit it and the creature was on the ground, entangled. The four companions ran on forward, leaving the Bahak to sort out his own mess.

"This path leads to the tribal village center," Sara called out. "There will be dozens more of those things. I hope you two can handle them all. They are a pretty superstitious bunch. I'm thinking if we can start some kind of fire, then we can scare the bulk of them away. Come on, they are untying my mom now, I think we only have a few minutes left!"

The friends ran breakneck down the tunnel. After several exhausting minutes, the path finally widened, and they soon came out at the top of a wide cavern. Below in the dim light, crude huts made of bone and hide could be seen, built all around the rim of the cave. At the center of the cavern, a circle had been cleared and the tribe was now gathered there. In the middle of the gathering, a small fire had been set, and a number of figures were visible standing around it. A large pile of something indeterminable was set in front of the fire. Most of the tribe was seated and appeared to be eating. The sounds of chewing and gnashing could be heard from below.

"Oh, we're too late," the chimera cried.

"Ha, not exactly," Sara laughed.

As the three friends descended the winding path, they could now make out Tessa and Michael standing at the head of the tribe. Michael was waving his arms dramatically, and Tessa was busily pulling loaf after loaf out of her fairy bread bag. The loaves were piling up in front of the fire, and the hungry tribesmen were busily gobbling them down. Many of the smaller tribe members looked uncomfortably thin, with loose skin and bony arms.

All of the Bahaks turned their heads in surprise when a strange, small voice from the darkness called to them in their own language, "Salutations, friends. We mean you no harm, but come only to rid you of your darkest enemy. I see you have already met my mother."

27

THE SHADOW CARNIVAL

The largest of the pale natives was the first to balk at the sound of the strange music drifting up from the tunnels far below. The large lizard man was soon joined in his apprehension by the two other warriors who the tribe had chosen to help shepherd Sara and her friends into the depths. The Bahaks all gathered near one another and whispered dire words back and forth. Finally, their leader pointed forward and, trembling noticeably, grunted out his decision against continuing.

"This is as far as they will go," Sara translated to her own small party. Then, in the growling language of the Bahaks, she dismissed them from any further service. Happy to be released, the natives scurried away. As they disappeared down the winding tunnel, the last warrior to go turned hesitantly to look back at the group, his expression half fear and half surprise to see them still alive.

"Lucky them," Jonathan hummed under his breath.

"Buck up, boy," El Gato chimed in from where he rode on the chimera's shoulder, "isn't this what you love, delving deep into the unknown to face danger and adventure?"

"I suppose," Jonathan shrugged, "I just don't know if I am quite up for what is expected of me this time."

"Yeah? And what would that be?" Tessa interjected as she watched their guides disappear back up the way they had come. "I am still not clear on what the plan is here."

Tessa still felt sour inside, perhaps now even more so. These new tunnels were far worse than those where the Bahaks dwelled. They were more confined, ribbed at the top, and rather than looking like natural caves, they gave off the feel of walking into the throat of a giant snake. The bottle filled with the glowing lichens that Tessa held above her head offered little comfort; its blue-green glow cast strange shadows that made the walls seem like they were flexing and constricting as she walked. Tessa's concern and fear were ever-present, which only served to drive up her anger—and Sara had warned them all to keep their baser emotions in check, as they could be used against them by the dark thing they now hunted. But just how Tessa was supposed to do that was beyond her; at the very least, someone needed to be concerned about the danger they were walking into... more than danger actually—an all too obvious trap. However, Tessa's questions went unacknowledged. Sara, with a gentle smile to her mother, simply turned and headed onward, followed in short order by Adam and the chimera, with El Gato along for the ride.

"Your daughter is keeping secrets," Michael said to break the silence, coming up from behind her. He held his arm out, palm up, and motioned her forward.

And then there was this one. He seemed to have taken all too well to being ordered around by Sara, and to make matters worse, Tessa had to keep reminding herself that Michael was not her husband. In moments of stress and fear she had always been able to turn to Ethan, and though Michael was not him, he looked, sounded, and even acted like him. It was so hard to resist the urge to seek comfort in his arms as they descended deeper into the cavern. Instead, Tessa folded her free arm tight across her chest, hugging her shoulder, and shot Michael a dirty look as she fell in behind the chimera. She knew it wasn't fair to be so hostile towards Michael—after all he was here helping when he had other pressing tasks that he clearly desired to be attending to—and truth be told, his presence did comfort Tessa. She could tell that there was more to him than met the eye, and not just because of what Sara had told her. She remembered clearly the weapon that she had shot him with, a weapon that should have vaporized him but instead only knocked him out, and then only briefly.

Tessa could not deny that it was also nice to have another adult along, even if he was passive and willing to follow her daughter's orders blindly. She supposed that Adam also likely considered himself an adult, but he seemed really more of a fresh-faced teenager than the fearsome knight she had imagined from Sara's original story. Of course, El Gato was technically an adult too—actually who knew how old he was—but Tessa discounted him because he was just as likely to sit off in a corner and clean himself as he was to be of any real use. So that left her and Michael, and because he was giving off the impression of being easygoing and unconcerned, Tessa found herself worrying even more for everyone. What a typical mom thing to do, she thought. Tessa did not like being predicable, but what else was she to do?

Lost in thought, Tessa almost walked right into the chimera's back as he halted his shaggy form. Hunched as he was due to the low cavern, he took up the whole of the passageway and blocked any view of what had brought them to a standstill.

"It is definitely getting louder," Adam said, quietly leaning in as Sara peered into the darkness beyond the light cast by his lichen torch. "What would be down here that could produce such music? I have never heard the likes of it before, so repetitive and so quick in tempo."

"Just sounds like circus music to me," Jonathan said, bringing his head in above Adam and Sara.

"It is," Sara confirmed. "Our host has prepared a little entertainment for us... or rather for itself."

"What are your thoughts, lady Sara?" Adam asked.

Sara's face took on the glazed look she got when she was looking elsewhere, but she still answered the question, her voice flat, as if somnambulant. "The music doesn't matter. In the end the creature will show itself to us. I could try and warn and brace you all, but it won't help. Just remember it's all a game until it's not, and trust me, you will both know when that is."

Adam stood tall and placed a hand on Sara's shoulder. He could tell that she was fighting back her own fear and trepidations. She had said that this thing would feed on them and exploit them. As far as he was concerned, there was little need for concern or fear; he had seen what Sara and the chimera were capable of, and if they had a secret plan in store for this creature, he trusted that it would work. He also doubted that anything could be as awful as Sara was making this thing out to be. He had seen monsters and fought many powerful creatures as the Neverknight. There was little in creation that he felt would give him pause.

"I hope you are right," Sara said. Adam realized she must have been looking inside his head. That was always unnerving, but what she was most likely looking for now was comfort.

"I am. You will see," he stated, and he believed it.

"What's wrong? What's happening?" Tessa called as she tried vainly to push past the chimera.

"Nothing," Sara said, "just that we are here."

"Where's here?" Tessa asked, but the only answer that came was another thin, sad smile from her daughter, almost like an apology.

Sara led the group forward and the cave grew wider and wider until they could no longer see its ceiling or sides. The six companions fanned out, walking side by side. The cavern floor gradually began slope downward, becoming loose and rocky. Tessa lost her footing for a moment, but was caught quickly on either side, by Michael on the left and the chimera on the right. In her current state of mind, she was simply too embarrassed to complain when Michael took her arm and said to her, "You provide the light; I will mind our path."

Tessa had the strange feeling that Michael did not need the light to see, but she put it out of her mind. That was just ridiculous speculation. However, she decided not to reject his offer this time; after all, he was simply being a gentleman. Where was the harm in taking the aid?

The vastness of the chamber they were now in became apparent when, far off in the distance and at a considerable depth below them, dim lights came into view. The faint, red lights formed a circle, and as the group grew nearer, it was clear that they framed several structures and even a large, vertical wheel that was rotating slowly. The odd music grew ever louder, and before long, Tessa realized she was looking at a carnival, made up of booths and attractions, complete with a Ferris wheel and a big top tent at the center. She could not make out any living patrons in this strange place, though shadowy figures appeared to be moving about through the whole of the grounds. Of these, she could make out nothing, as the area was too poorly lit by the dim lights. Before too long, a clear, paved path soon could be seen ahead of Sara's party, and following this, they soon came to a small, stone bridge that traversed a deep, black moat that skirted the entire fair. There, on the center of the bridge, stood a lanky, stilted figure dressed in the tattered clothing of a grand marshal. Though the outfit was genuine and complete with a high hat, where the marshal's face should have been, there was only blackness. Tessa could not stand to look at the face; she found herself instead staring at the marshal's brocade waistcoat with its rows of gold buttons.

At once the figure bowed without removing its hat, and then spoke in a dark voice that mocked kindness and hurt the ears at the start and finish. "Welcome, honored guests! No tickets required! No need to pay for any attractions! All is on the house for you and yours."

Sara ignored the greeting and the comically tall figure and walked past as if the marshal was not there at all. She was followed close behind by Adam, who could not seem to take his eyes off of the blank, dark face. The chimera was next, and he let out a low growl just as El Gato, still perched on his shoulder, gave the greeter a silent hiss, all of the hair on his back standing up. Tessa would never have been able to walk past had it not been for Michael's firm grip and support. Why this thing was so repulsive to her, she could not say. She held her gaze low to the ground and caught sight of the strange black water that filled the moat. She could not help but be reminded of the creature's face when she looked into that dark water. For his part, Michael, like Sara, seemed to pay the creature no mind.

They were almost through the outer row of tents and beyond view of the greeter when Sara stopped and turned suddenly. "Where is the main attraction to be held?" she asked the greeter.

"Where else?" chimed the grand marshal. The sound of his inhuman voice caused all the hair to rise on Tessa's neck.

Sara seemed satisfied and once more headed forward into the carnival. Once past the first ring of tents, the group was forced to switchback around, following the outer circle of booths. To Tessa's horror, the greeter was not the only occupant of the carnival. Everywhere there were people dressed in clothing from some forgone era... or rather a facsimile of people. For wherever their Victorian clothing left them exposed, instead of skin, there was only the same inky blackness. The patrons moved about, playing the various games and waiting in lines for rides, but they each in turn stopped to stare with barren faces as the group passed. Tessa could not stand their attention and she found herself looking down at her feet. She could hear the low growls of the chimera whenever one of these patrons came too close or failed to get out of the way quick enough. The animal rage that resonated from these rumbles was filled with a terrible warning that did nothing to quiet her nerves. Michael's arm went from holding her own to being wrapped around her shoulder, and she allowed it gladly.

"Pay them no mind." Michael murmured, his voice utterly at ease.

"But there are so many," Tessa replied, keeping her gaze low.

"They are all the same," Michael answered, "not a one worth your moxie."

Tessa felt warmer suddenly, though she had not even realized that she had been so cold. She forced herself to look up. Sara was focused on leading them forward through the maze of tents and was unwilling to even acknowledge or look at the patrons. Adam was just the opposite; he stared back at each one he passed with a wild look in his eyes, tears forming in the corners as if he could not believe that what he was seeing could really unhinge his courage so. The chimera looked as fearsome as ever, his teeth bared and his lips curled back, the low rumbles of his animal threats answering each shadow person. El Gato wasn't acting much differently; he was arched up on all fours, his hair standing on end and his tail held straight up. The low whine of the angered feline rose on occasion to a shrill yowl. Only Michael seemed at ease, able to watch the circus around them as if it was like any other normal gathering. He seemed to feel Tessa's gaze on him and looked down at her. Blast if his eyes were not the same as Sara's father... but the look he gave of reassurance and comfort was not an expression she had ever seen in Ethan. Not that Ethan had never comforted her, it was just that this was the look of a different being, one with his own idiosyncrasies. Tessa found herself drawing a warm courage from his eyes that seemed to wash away all her foreboding and angst.

"See, you are fine," Michael spoke as he squeezed Tessa a little tighter. And for the most part, she was. She was able to look around now without feeling sick. She still did not care to look directly at the patrons, but she found that she could stand it if she chanced on one of the vacant faces for a moment or two.

Their path led them around through ever-tighter circles towards the center of the carnival. Sara sighed under her breath in frustration at the tactic. They could have easily walked directly to the center of the circus if there had been a path, but instead it had all been conformed to make the journey as long and claustrophobic as possible. But the trick was not working on her. Sara refused to allow it to get to her—or at least she did her best not to. She had some idea of what it would be like when they finally saw it in its true form, and she could not suppress the quickening of her heart at the thought. Sara knew better than to imagine that she would be immune to it—seeing something in your mind's eye was not the same as facing it directly. Still, she had to steel herself against it. She had to be ready. If she was not, they were sure to fail.

The group finally rounded the last corner and came out into the center of the fair. The bulk of the space was taken up by a huge, multicolored tent. It seemed that all the faceless people they had passed had somehow beat them there and were now filtering into the tent. Sara did not let their numbers dissuade her. She made a beeline for the doors, and the throngs of void-faced patrons cleared a path for her. The rest of her companions followed close behind.

Sara reached the threshold of the big top and there was met by the same greeter from the bridge. He bowed briefly again and then spoke in his creaking, cracking voice, "Splendid. We have been awaiting your arrival. The best seats in the house have been made available for you, if you would allow me to guide you to them."

"If you must," Sara replied, looking past him.

The lanky grand marshal led Sara down to the front of the arena and there sat her and her friends in a raised box that provided the best view of the center of the three rings that made up the show floor. Sara sat in the middle with Michael and her mother to her left. Adam, Jonathan, and El Gato filled in the seats to her right. There they waited as all the other guests filtered into the big top, filling it to the limit. There was the palpable illusion that this was indeed a real event: the low chatter of all the patrons as they found their seats, ushers helping stragglers, and even vendors with balloons and refreshments going up and down the aisles. Michael was the only one who dared to take one of these bags, but when he looked inside, he found only black, squirming, worm-like things. He simply folded the bag's top and set it under his seat.

Tessa was at a loss. She could not help but feel they were in terrible danger, but for some reason everyone was going along with it, at least for the most part. This was madness. Sara seemed very impatient, as if she was ready to get on with the show, and Jonathan still snarled and growled at anyone who got too close, leaving the seats behind them thankfully empty.

At last, everyone seemed to settle down, and the lights dimmed. A dull red spotlight shone down on the center of the middle ring. Standing there was yet another faceless being, dressed this time in the garb of a ringmaster, with a top hat and a red waistcoat.

"Welcome, welcome one and all," the ringmaster proclaimed, and its voice sent chills down Tessa's back and caused the chimera to fold his ears tight against his head with a look of pure pain on his face, "Ladies and gentlemen, children and creatures, tonight we are honored to present for you a very special, very unique entertainment to please the eye and fill the senses. So, without further delay, I present to you... Aras, the fairy princess!"

Another beam of red lit the ring to the right of the master of ceremonies, and there, suspended by thorny, black tendrils, was Aras. The cruel, dark vines that held her began to pull up and down, forcing Aras to dance in a mockery of a ballerina. The look on Aras's face was one of pain and horror; silent tears streamed down her cheeks.

Tessa could not help herself. She pushed her face into Michael's chest and hid from the grotesque sight.

Adam started to rise, but his arm was caught by Sara, who pulled him back down. "We must do something for her," he protested. Sara somehow remained stone faced. She simply shook her head from side to side.

"But hold, this is not all we have for you today," the ringmaster declared, "we have with us the very clone of this fairy fair, locked in the flesh of a human girl." A spotlight found Sara. "Would you be so kind as to join us here in center ring? We simply could not continue without you."

"No!" Tessa and Adam echoed in unison from either side.

Sara placed a comforting arm on them both, and then with a quick look to Jonathan, she began to rise.

"You can't," Tessa commanded. She had had enough.

"Hold her," Sara said to Michael, and he firmly gripped Tessa with both hands, "and protect her."

"You have my word."

"You will let go of me," Tessa spat, turning to Michael. She could not believe how strong he was, yet still he managed to be gentle.

"Hush now," he said, "let your daughter to her work."

"Let my daughter what?" But it was no use; Sara was already descending the stairs to the floor, and struggle as she might, Tessa could not escape Michael's grip. Tessa looked to the others in desperation. Adam bore a tortured look on his face and was gripping the hilt of his sword, his knuckles white. His wings were held straight up behind his back, and he looked ready to explode. The chimera did not seem to be upset, though he had a tense look of concentration. Tessa saw that El Gato had moved off his shoulder and now sat in a seat on the far side. Just what where they up to?

Sara reached the center ring and joined the blank-faced ring-master, who raised his hands high above him. The whole of the crowd went wild with cheers. Many of the patrons were now standing and throwing whatever they had been holding high into the air. They all had the same voice like broken glass, and Tessa almost screamed at the horrible noise the chorus produced. Michael's restraint turned more into a hug.

"What is happening here?" Tessa cried.

"What must happen," Michael replied.

"If my daughter is harmed I will never forgive you," Tessa said, surrendering her struggle and leaning into him.

"Her fate is beyond us both now."

The cheers died and the ringmaster brought his gaze back down on Sara. "Now, our little star attraction. It was foretold by a fairy prophet that you would bring me my deepest desire, the one thing I have longed for, hunted for, though I have been thwarted at every turn and have come up empty with every search."

"And what would that be?" Sara asked, defiant.

"Do not mock me! You know full well what it is I seek!" the ringmaster roared. "Bring him forth; give me the Seventh Star of Twilight!"

The crowd roared.

28

~~~~

SELF DOUBT

"Sorry. I would bring forth my father if I could," Sara answered the shadow flatly, "but you have made that impossible."

The ringmaster cocked his faceless head to the side and stared down at Sara. In a low, growling voice he said, "You are going to upset the crowd. I have promised them the Seventh Star; work with me here."

"I would if I could," Sara returned.

Still in a low voice, and now leaning in, the shadow man hissed, "What sort of trick is this?" Then louder, to the crowd, he announced, "Fear not! We are only building the suspense!" Then he turned back to Sara, putting his empty face in front of hers. It struck Sara eerily that the creature gave off no scent whatsoever. The shadow's hollow voice came forth to her out of the blackness, "I know about the locket. Your sister has been kind enough to reveal that all seven of you must touch it at once to bring forth my prey, and all seven of you are here. So let's get on with it before this rabble gets restless." Indeed, many of the audience members had begun to catcall and boo.

"I am done with this game," Sara snapped. "This charade has gone on long enough." She raised her voice so all could hear. "I don't even begin to understand what you are getting out of this farce, but this ends here. If you want to treat with me, treat with me. I know you are all the same, all just pieces of the blacker whole. Show yourself."

"No, Sara," Aras called out from where she was still strung up.

The ringmaster stood tall, his body elongating to over nine feet in height. As he rose up, every member of the vast blank-faced audience did as well, all falling silent. Then the ringmaster spoke, and there was none of the flair or showmanship left in his voice. "Very well," he said plainly, "I thought we could enjoy all this, have a little fun along the way, draw out the moment of my revenge. Cutting it short only takes away from you and your friends that one last little moment of hope and companionship. I guess we will do it your way instead."

The audience members began to melt. As they did, their darkness ran down the bleachers and across the floor and began to pool around the ringmaster's feet. Tessa raised her feet off the floor so as to not be touched by the slow, dark flood. Jonathan stood up and was joined by Adam. El Gato jumped to the back of the seat in front of him, balancing on his hind legs with his foreclaws flexed out to his sides as if ready to attack. Michael was the only one who remained still, his hand firmly gripping Tessa's. The darkness flowed swiftly around and past his feet on its way down.

"You want me as I am?" the ringmaster crackled. His clothing was now melting into him as well, and his lower body was fading into the mass of darkness that now swirled and hummed around him. "Well then, you shall have me in all my bleakness."

The chimera braced a foot on the chair in front of him and prepared to leap. "Not yet, Jonathan," Sara sent through their link.

"When then?" he sent back.

The two of them had been in almost constant contact through their link the whole of the journey through the caverns. Sara had used the time to attempt to prepare Jonathan for what was coming and for the role he would play in it. Sara did not have Aras' gift for future sight, but that did not stop her from using everything she could to determine a way they might stand a chance against this creature. The shadow had made an error when it took Sara's sister. Somehow this act had lifted the veil that kept it hidden from her gift. Sara had wasted no time in trying to develop a strategy against it.

"We have to do this together if it is going to work," Sara thought back, but even as she did, she beheld the thing that was forming before her eyes and she was struck dumb. She realized that she may have underestimated this challenge.

The patterns of dark on dark wove together. Jet tendrils, slick and wet, convulsed into place. Ebony claws and dark teeth chattered and scratched. Shark-like eyes that betrayed no emotion blinked across the shadow's twisted form. The shapeless mass expanded and expanded, showing no end. And at the center, the infinite emptiness of the void lay waiting for them. Sara heard her mother scream, and the sound was soon joined by a deeper cry from Adam. The chimera roared and tried to leap forward, but stumbled and fell to the ground at the foot of the center ring. El Gato hid his eyes from the sight and let out a howl. Aras wailed. Michael stood, holding Sara's mother in his arms, pressing her face away from the creature and into his chest, his blue eyes ablaze.

Sara started to cry, tears rolling down her face. She of all of them should have been ready for this, but it was too much.

This thing that twisted and convulsed before her was madding. It was meant to drive one into despair and fear, it was made to devour hope and dreams. Its hate was so powerful it seared the whole of the tent in melancholy.

"Is this what you seek?" it bellowed, and Sara fell backwards. She could not think; she could not move. The thing was coming ever closer to her. It bubbled and writhed in twisted chaos, a wave of pure nothingness suspended above her, ready to crash down.

Adam's wings were extended to their fullest. His handsome face was twisted in pain. "You are horrible!" he cried.

"Look away from it," El Gato commanded, "it will make you mad with its hate."

Laughter like windows shattering filled the tent, and a tendril of black lashed out and struck El Gato, sending him flying across the room. He crashed to the ground, rolling over and over in the dust, "I must say, star cat, I did expect more of you. Come, look at me."

"No, don't, El Gato," Sara cried, but her eyes were soon drawn back to the shadow. "You are despicable," she managed. But she could not look away.

"I am despicable?" the shadow chuckled. "No, you of all should understand my nature; I am not anything more than a mirror. All the little things that pick at you—doubts, fears, the selfish acts of your selfish lives, they are all here for you to see reflected back upon you in my oily hide. In me you see yourself as you truly are, cruel, self-centered, greedy, worthless... filth."

It was true, Sara realized all at once; everything she did was for herself. She constantly placed everyone around her in danger and pain for her own self-indulgent desires. And for what? Sara could see her lifespan, just a tiny tick in the great wheel of time—a pointless waste of the ultimate power. What could she really change in that time? What did it matter what she accomplished? And really, what was she other than the Font... and that wasn't even her anyway. She'd never had any actual friends growing up, and everyone who paid her any mind only wanted her for her knowledge. But that at least wasn't so bad, because if it wasn't for that, then everyone would only notice how small and awkward she was, just like Adam did... how her feet were too big, and her ears too small. That shrill sound to her voice when she heard it played back on tape. Her frizzy hair, ugly kneecaps, and her smelly breath. What did she really have to offer anyone that was really hers? What made her think she of all people deserved to remake creation? She was nothing, just a hollow shell, and not at all deserving of those who stood beside her.

"Once more, you are alone," the voice continued. Sara looked at Jonathan, but he was on the floor, his mouth opened in a silent roar and his eyes rolled back into his head. "He is the same as you. He is using you just as you use him. You know he wants to simply consume you, but tell me, does he know that you intend to abandon him once you have no further use for him?"

Would she? Sara's tears flowed even faster.

"You call me despicable," the shadow hissed, "well, you are unlovable."

Sara collapsed. If she had a plan, it was forgotten in the up-welling of self-hatred that now swelled in her. The shadow rose up, gloating and proud. But then a small voice shattered the silence, causing a ripple across the shadow's body.

"I love you,"

The shadow whirled. Tessa was slowly pulling her face away from Michael's embrace. She turned her face to her daughter.

"Sara, you are loved!" This time Tessa's voice was louder and stronger. She could see the darkness undulating in the corner of her vision, but she did not look at it; she held her focus on her daughter. She did not know where the courage came from, but she could not stand to hear another cruel thing said to her child, her heart, her Sara.

The tendrils of the shadow lashed out towards Michael and Tessa, but they never made contact. Adam moved to block them. The ruby sword was in his hand. He held his face down and his dark hair covered his eyes as he erected a telekinetic shield around Tessa, Michael, and himself. The shadow rose up, growing larger, and began to move towards them, but it was again halted by another voice, gravelly and weak.

"You're my best friend, Sara." It was the chimera. "The most amazing friend I have ever had."

"How charming," the shadow hissed, "but Sara knows what she is. She knows because she sees it reflected in me, and she knows it is the truth."

"No," El Gato spat from off in the dirt where he lay, "it is the truth twisted, just like a carnival mirror warps one's image."

With the shadow distracted, Sara could feel herself able to think more clearly at last. Each word from each of her friends brought her back from the pit of wretched despair that the creature had been pulling her down into. "Yes, a twisted refection," she said, "perhaps you should see it for yourself." With that, she produced a small hand mirror from her tattered satchel, and she held it up in front of her. "Enchanted," she whispered, "so that even the Queen of the Dead could see her true reflection."

The shadow seemed to try and turn away, but it could not. It screamed from all of its many maws, and the cries soon fell backwards into a whimper. The tendrils that held Aras retracted, leaving her in a lump on the ground. The shadow retreated swiftly, moving from the dim red spotlight backwards into the dark at the rear of the tent. As it passed out of sight, the others could feel their normal selves slowly returning.

El Gato stood up and dusted himself off. He looked no worse
for having been tossed across the tent. "That was dramatic,"
he mused.

Michael reached forward and placed a hand on Adam's shoulder, "You can ease off now, lad." Adam shook as he lowered
his shield and folded his wings in behind his back. "You did
good," Michael assured him.

Tessa started to move to make her way towards Sara, but Michael held her arm firmly, "Wait," he instructed.

Sara found her feet, making sure to keep the mirror facing the
shadow at all times. The chimera came up behind her and
pressed the palm of his hand against her back for support.

"Well, you have me where you want me," the shadow wailed,
"all that remains is to bring forth the Seventh Star and let him
do away with me."

"I already told you that I can't," Sara repeated.

"Why not?" The shadow's voice betrayed its rage. "All seven
of you are here; just touch the locket!"

"There are seven of us, that is true," Sara confirmed, "but the
chimera is not one of the seven in which my father hid a piece
of himself."

"What?" the shadow boomed. For a moment, it passed briefly
along the edge of the light. "Where is the other?"

"She is here, after a fashion," Sara answered.

"Where then?" the shadow cursed. "It is I who grow tired of
games now."

"She is in you. She was Aras's mother, and you consumed her."

There was silence followed by a faint laughter. "I would think
you were trying to trick me, but then I know that you know

there is no way to free someone from my darkness once I have devoured them."

"Maybe one way," Sara said. Her voice held a threat in it.

"Oh... my destruction," the shadow snickered. "Well, forgive me if I do not choose that option."

"I don't remember offering you a choice."

There was a low snarl that seemed to emit from several sources scattered throughout the darkness at once, followed by a snort of disgust. "The mirror was a nice trick, but tell me, how will I see my refection when there is no light?" The dim red spotlight that lit the center ring blinked out. "You forget, this is my carnival."

Though she could no longer see it in the blackness, Sara knew that the shadow now moved forward. "Now!" Sara yelled, not bothering to use the psychic link.

Jonathan had already sprung into motion. He dived forward, slashing out and cutting the air with his claws and arm swords. Though he could see most things in the dark with his gem eyes, the shadow gave off no heat or aura; it was impossible to determine where the darkness stopped and the shadow started. Jonathan placed himself in front of Sara, and in the empty blackness he roared against the coming onslaught.

It was all for nothing. The shadow overwhelmed him in an instant, swirling around him at the speed of thought. Wherever the chimera struck the shadow, the darkness clung to him, coiling up his limbs and bubbling over him.

"Your best friend is mine," gloated the shadow as Jonathan struggled in vain.

Sara backed away from the conflict. El Gato joined her, and the two moved towards the bleachers into the dim light that filtered in from outside the tent. Tessa's hands were on her mouth. Even in the darkness, she could make out the chimera struggling and sinking away into nothingness. The memory of seeing that thing combined with the idea of it touching Jonathan terrified her. Adam started to move forward, but Sara raised a sharp hand to him and shook her head.

"We cannot allow him to face this horror alone," Adam yelled, but it was too late. The chimera had lost, and all that remained was the shadow. The darkness grew in the tent as the shadow moved forward towards the rest.

29

IN LIMBO

Jonathan found only himself remaining amid the unending darkness. The nothingness here was all-consuming—a trackless void. He tried rebelliously to lash out with one of his arm swords, but something was wrong. He opened his mouth to roar, but only a child's whimper came out. He flexed to jump, but his legs did not respond. He was cold now, very cold. What was this place?

Fortunately, even in this darkness, not all of the chimera's senses failed him. He was slowly becoming aware of himself, and was soon able to make out his own form. Wait, this was all wrong. Where were his claws? He could see only a frail, small human hand. He bent at the waist and the two dead, human legs that he had left behind long ago came into view. He was even dressed in the same old faded baby-blue PJs with baseballs on them. Oh, no. Not again.

"What have we here?" a voice from long ago echoed in his ears. "Not a monster at all, but a little burden of a boy."

Jonathan gasped; it was the voice of his old, cruel nurse. He tried to crawl away, but his hands stuck to the darkness and his legs would not work.

"Oh no, is the little lump going to wet himself again?" the voice taunted.

Jonathan thrashed his arms about.

"Fight all you want," the voice started out as old woman, but turned slowly into shadow, "with each passing moment you fall deeper into my core, into the heart of my hate."

Jonathan strained against the dark, clawing at it with his ragged, tiny nails.

He now heard his father's voice, "You were meant to follow in my footsteps, to play baseball, to be the athlete I was, to make me proud. Oh, how did we end up so cursed with this burden?" Jonathan slumped a little, his arms freezing up.

"Oh no!" This was his mother. "You're back! We thought you died in the fire at the hospital. Why did you have to come back? We were finally free, finally able to be a real family." Jonathan lowered his head and arms. The fight seemed to fade from him. His hair shook into his eyes and his shoulders convulsed as if he were about to cry.

"Oh there, there." The shadow's voice was back. "Fret not, little rat; here we are at my core at last. Here I will wrap you in your doubt, your self-hate, your fear. Here you will dwell forever and suffer endlessly as the little worthless boy you are."

Jonathan's shoulders shook again, but instead of tears, there came a giggle, a sound not heard in the core of the shadow in all of its existence. Jonathan slowly raised his face, and there was a wicked smile painted on it.

"What is this?" the shadow reverberated. "Why do you smile?"

"Because you don't know me at all," Jonathan replied. "You

think this is what I really am? You think we didn't know your plan? You think I haven't faced this fear before? You are wrong." Jonathan's body arched, and spikes ripped out of the back of his pajamas. The whole of the darkness around him seemed to vibrate with shock. His hand now grew claws and his arms stretched out, even as his legs swung into place under him. His ankles widened out, his feet rapidly growing pads and claws. The wicked smile grew larger, and long, sharp teeth replaced those of the boy. His eyes changed into gems, just as others popped up on his face and his ears extended up and out. "I am a chimera!" he roared, and he again was.

"Fine," the shadow rasped, sardonically, "so you are a chimera then, but you are still mine."

Jonathan could not help himself. He answered with another laugh that boomed forth with such joy that it echoed through the darkness. And the darkness now didn't feel quite so empty. For a moment, it almost seemed that there might be others nearby, others who, when Jonathan laughed, burned a ghostly image into his mind's eye.

"What are you laughing at?" The shadow's voice was completely enraged.

"You really have no idea who you're up against, do you?" Jonathan replied. "Look. I am a monster with the power to adapt any ability, and my best friend is a girl who knows everything. Do you really think that the moment we became aware of you that we didn't start working on a way to defeat you?"

"What?"

"And here I am, in your heart, your very core. And if there is one thing the heart of a shadow cannot stand, it's light."

The chimera's eyes lit up bright as headlights, just as they had done beneath the primal ocean, but he did not stop there. All the tips of the spikes on his back also began to shine.

"Whaaa...?" the shadow cried. "What are you doing? Stop this, you cannot defeat me, not alone."

"Oh, but I am not alone," Jonathan bellowed. "I bring light to all those that are trapped here." A moment later, he launched all the spikes on his back out in every direction. All around they could be seen, cutting away the black webs that held and separated the masses that were held here in the shadow's starless limbo. Like tiny comets, they tore through the bleakness.

The shadow cried out, "Stop! Enough."

Jonathan was not listening. He found the closest prisoner and took her hand, smiling, then he took another. Those squalid masses that so long had been without light were already gravitating towards him. They took up his queue and began to link hands, forming a chain.

"No, it's not enough," Jonathan returned to the shadow's plea. "You see, we are all leaving, and you are done for." He let out a roar that was then joined by the yells and calls of those around him. Like the chains they had formed, linking hands and paws and tentacles, the cry of freedom spread out through them—so happy to not be alone anymore, so tired of hating themselves.

The darkness now began to crack all around them, a pale yellow light seeping in through the gaps, like that from an old flashlight. Jonathan swore he could see a ghostly vision of Tessa's face in the distance, just beyond the light. The shadow's voice had now become as desperate and pathetic as the voices of those it preyed upon. "Nooooo!" it cried out, "No, master, I have failed you!" Then, all at once, the emptiness shattered. Pieces of the shadow creature hung briefly in the air, burned, and then fell away, like harmless grains of dusky sand.

In the center of the big top, the chimera stood, surrounded by all those who had been the shadow's victims. Their numbers stretched out and filled the whole of the arena.

Tessa lowered her flashlight, her hands still shaking. Sara's small group was gathered together behind her. To Sara and the others, it had only been a few passing moments since the chimera had disappeared, yet now he was there before them, the shadow destroyed and all those it had consumed set free.

"You did it!" Sara cried, rushing forward. "You saved them, Jonathan."

"Aww, no big deal," the chimera chuckled. But the crowd had other ideas, and within moments they were all chanting his name.

"Hail Jonathan! Hail the shadow slayer!"

Adam joined the cheer, one arm around Sara, the other lifting up El Gato. "I don't know how," he called out, "but good show!"

"That's the way, boy!" El Gato yowled.

Aras made her way to them. She was clapping and cheering, but did not tarry. She soon wandered into the crowd, searching intently for someone she thought lost long ago.

Sara just laughed. She was so relieved.

Tessa was cheering too, and still next to Michael. She looked up at him. He was quiet but smiling. "You knew," she stated.

"I hoped," he replied.

"No," she countered, pulling away and looking him over thoroughly, "somehow you knew."

In the center of the three-ring circus, Jonathan was being lifted into the air by two ogres and a large land octopus. They hoisted him above the crowd and cheered his name, "Jonathan, the slayer of shadows!"

30

~~~~~~

THE SEVENTH STAR OF TWILIGHT

"Mother!"

Tessa turned to look upon the source of the commotion. Aras had pulled a tall fairy from the crowd of refugees and was wholeheartedly embracing her. The scene was one of great warmth, but Tessa's heart turned to ice. This woman was disheveled and bent from years of torture, neglect, and self-hatred, but beneath she was still obviously very beautiful. And while humans wilted like wildflowers over the course of a few decades, the fair folk did not age. This fairy woman looked no older than Aras, and could have been easily mistaken for her sister. And now she was coming Tessa's way. Tessa felt very old.

Aras, beaming from ear to ear, took her mother around the cavern and introduced her to each of her new companions one by one. By the time they reached Tessa, Tessa was shaking and red-faced. However, under the circumstances, no one seemed to notice.

"Oh, Tessa, I have found my mother!" Aras seemed nearly out of breath from excitement.

"Why that's wonderful, dear!" Tessa exclaimed through clenched teeth, a forced smile set upon her face.

"Yes, yes it is! Mother, this is Tessa, Sara's mother. She's incredibly brave and resourceful. In fact, if it weren't for her, I believe the shadow would have consumed us all. Tessa, this is my mother, Hyperia."

"Thank you," the fairy woman extended her hand, "thank you for all you have done. You are indeed a blessing to us all."

"Yes," Tessa stammered. She looked at the hand extended before her. It was lily white and delicate as lace, and it bore upon it a plain silver band. Tessa grimaced. The woman attached to the hand was tall and very slender, with skin like ivory and hair like spun silver. Her almond eyes shone like white diamonds in the dim light, elegantly crowning her perfect features and regal cheekbones. Folded behind her, Tessa could make out a damaged but delicate set of butterfly-like wings. Tessa wanted so badly to hate this woman, but she couldn't. She knew that Hyperia had done her no wrong. No, it was someone entirely else she was angry with.

Tessa touched the hand extended to her and curtseyed. "Did Aras tell you why we are here?" Tessa asked.

"No, she..." the fairy woman replied, not catching the tone in Tessa's voice, before being interrupted by her daughter.

"In time," Aras murmured, gracefully changing the subject. "There are others here you must meet as well. This is Michael. He cared for me and educated me for many years in your absence."

Hyperia bowed, and Michael took her hand, kissing it. "It was my great honor to tutor your daughter," he announced. Tessa watched as Aras embraced Michael with a long hug and as wordless greetings passed between their eyes. These two knew each other well. Again a flare of jealousy spiked in Tessa, though this time she could not say why. Breaking away, Aras whisked her mother off in the direction of Adam.

"The baser emotions do not become you, lady." Michael had been left standing alone with Tessa. He touched her arm as if to offer his support.

"This is none of your business," Tessa snapped.

"I apologize if I offend, milady," Michael countered, "but there are still duties to be done this day. You are right to be angry, but yours is a personal anger, and not one that any of those gathered here deserve. And you do not even know the circumstances. I know this is difficult for you, but you must give him a chance. Don't hijack your own fate by making certain your fears come true."

Tessa looked sullen. There was truth to these words. Whatever fight she needed to have with her runaway husband could come later.

Michael leaned in and kissed her cheek, lightly. "Besides, you are selling yourself short. The fairy woman is beautiful, but unoriginal. I can see what he saw in you. You have nothing to be afraid of; let's bring him back."

"Mother," Sara called as she came racing up, "we need you."

*****

"Gather around," Sara called, "and try to spread yourselves evenly. We need everyone to be able to get in here."

Sara now wore the mystical pendant and had gathered together with her sister and Hyperia, Adam close at their side. Jonathan had escorted the rest of the refugees out of the big top to a more comfortable tent where Tessa had lent her food bag and where a makeshift medical clinic had been set up. Tessa and Michael were returning to the big top now. El Gato followed close behind on their heels.

"How does this work?" Tessa asked nervously, eyeing the necklace.

"Maybe Michael should explain it," Sara replied, "after all, it is his own invention." Tessa turned and raised an eyebrow to her companion.

"It's a simple thing really," Michael began, clearing his throat, "or at least the part that I imagine you have an interest in. It's a device that can contain a living being of pure energy. It can then separate that energy into its component parts, much like a distillation. And then that distilled energy can be transferred into other containers, in this case, living bodies. To reverse the process, we all must join with the necklace at the same time and then activate the device with the proper voice command. Since the pendant originally separated the energies, it still knows the right pattern to put it back together again."

"Wait," Tessa interrupted, "you mean to say that this necklace was used to get Ethan into us in the first place? I've never seen it before? Did Ethan use it on me in my sleep?"

"Well, yes and then no," Michael replied, "once the Seventh Star entered the necklace, he would have been completely incapacitated. It would have been his agent that distributed the energy to the chosen targets."

"Agent?" Tessa snarled, "So we have met before! I knew you've been lying to me all this time."

"Milady," Michael patiently explained, "no. I did not see the Seventh Star again after making the jewel for him. In fact, I was surprised as anyone to find that he had used it upon himself. I had assumed it was intended for his enemies. The Star would have had to have had some other agent distribute his life force for him, someone probably quite slippery and, given the intended targets, able to move from one reality to another at will—and certainly someone very trusted with such a precious cargo."

"What? Well, who would possibly have had the...." Tessa glanced confusedly around the group and caught the cat nonchalantly licking his paws and avoiding her gaze. "Oh," she finally sighed.

"What would have happened," Hyperia spoke for the first time in an eerie, lacy voice, "should anything have happened to the necklace, or to any of us in the meantime."

"That's unclear," Michael replied, "it's possible that the energy could have congealed and survived on its own in some form, or merged with the remaining pieces. Beings as old as the Seventh Star are not as fragile as mortal souls. Quite likely though, part or all of the Seventh Star would have died."

"But why would he have taken such a risk?" Aras interjected. "I don't understand the point of it all."

"You will have to ask him," Michel answered. "The process won't take long; simply link with the pendant and say the command word."

"And what is that?" Adam asked.

"I have no idea," Michael shrugged. "The Star would have set it himself before engaging the gems, so only he would have known it. Although it undoubtedly is recorded in the Font of All Knowledge."

"It is not," Sara stated flatly. "I have studied the pendant thoroughly. Although if my suspicions are correct, I suspect the answer might come now were I to ask the question again." Sara paused for a brief moment and then smiled. "Yes, he is ready to show himself. OK, everyone, join hands. But we need to stand in a particular order."

The companions rearranged themselves, and fourteen hands reached out and joined together. As each contact was made, a different gem on the pendant at Sara's neck began to glow, until all of the colors were lit and the gems all turned white, giving off a bright light that filled the small arena and blinding those who looked upon it. Sara noticed that her feet no longer touched the ground.

"We each have a different word to speak," Sara continued, shouting, as if somehow the brightness made it hard for those around to hear her. Sara gave each person their line and began the chain of words. "Speak in counter-clockwise order from me," Sara instructed. "And the last part must be spoken in unison." Sara cleared her throat and started the chain, "Sahasrara!"

"Ajña," Aras continued.

"Vishuddhi," shouted Adam.

"Anahata," Tessa spurted out.

"Manipura," croaked the cat.

"Svadhisthana," Michael offered.

"Muladhara," Hyperia murmured.

And then in unison, seven voices rang out, "May the circle be unbroken!"

Sara felt a slight queasy feeling in her stomach as she began to spin to her right. The glowing gems of the pendant had split off from the necklace now and were floating in the air in front of her. She could make out the faces of the others as they twirled about the light, their eyes rolled back and their mouths open. From each of them, a white mist or smoke seemed to flow, billowing out of their throats and streaming into the gems, which only seemed now to grow larger and brighter. Soon, Sara felt a weight in her own lungs, and she could contain it no longer. She opened her mouth and the steam poured out. And then her brain began to buzz. Another queasy feeling hit her and she could tell she was falling. Sara blacked out.

The Seventh Star of Twilight hovered in the air and looked down upon the seven figures gathered together in the big top with him. Six had fallen and lay sprawled and snoring on the cold dirt floor. One remained standing, and looked up at him with blazing eyes. The look was not one of complete trust. The Star dimmed his lights and hovered downward, caressing the faces of the fallen. The cold bodies stirred to life, and began slowly to stagger to their feet. Sara sat with her head in her hands, curled up and staring at the ground.

No one said a word, but all gazed up at the seven small points of light that buzzed around them. The jumbled stars moved together and then began to orbit about one another, forming a perfect circle of light in the air. From the light, a voice came, deep, but clear as a bell, and soothing. "My friends and loved ones," it uttered, "I have placed my life and my faith in each one of you, and as I had foreseen, each one of you has fulfilled that trust. The first stage in your journey is over, and together, we can now begin to forge the second chapter in the history of all living things."

Tessa swatted her hand out at the floating lights. "You idiot!" she hollered. Her hand passed through the lights as if through an illusion. "You put us all in so much danger! And for what? So you could act like the hero and come in and save us all once we'd risked everything to get you back?"

The circling lights moved together into a single point, and then expanded, taking on the shape of a man. As the bright light receded, a figure could be seen standing there in its place. It was like Michael in shape and size, with perhaps a few more age lines on the face. It wore the work clothes of a painter, heavy smock and white pants covered in colors. The man took Tessa's hands in his and held them still. Looking into his face, Tessa began to weep, but whether the tears were of joy or sadness, it was impossible to tell.

"My dear Tessa, it brings me joy to see that you have not lost your passion, nor your sense of right and wrong. You are, and have always been, my moral compass, my judge. I am sorry if you feel that what I have done was wrong; it was what was needed. We have a long and difficult journey still ahead of us. If we are to survive it, there will be many difficult choices, and many grey areas, but we will all need you to tell us when we have strayed too far and to bring us back to our centers."

"Necessary?" Tessa sputtered. "You left our daughter but a year old fatherless and alone, not able to comprehend or understand what was growing inside of her. And you left me without warning, without explanation. You call that necessary?"

"But she was not alone," the man called Ethan answered, "I have been there with her since the beginning. Not enough of me for my enemies to detect, but my consciousness remained, enough to act as filter for that gift that is the greatest ever given to mortal flesh. And I was there to guide her and train her; at each step of the way I released a little bit more access to the Font to her, teaching her what she needed to know as she needed to know it. Look, even now that she has grown tuned to it and practiced with it over so much time, its full force keeps her curled up into a ball, completely oblivious to her body or to the world outside. Can you imagine what that kind of knowledge would do to an infant brain?" As Ethan turned to look at his ailing daughter, Tessa pulled her hands free and recoiled from her husband, folding her arms over her chest.

"Yes, Sara," Ethan continued unfazed as he stooped down to help her to her feet, "I have been with you through all of it. And I will continue to guide you through your next trials. But do not think that you did not succeed on your own power. All of your actions and decisions were your own. I only served to act as a filter to keep you focused and present. And even I have been astounded at times at both the nimbleness of your mind and the courage of your heart. You have taken gifts from both of your parents, and you have made us both very proud. And while yours is the mind that all of creation will be depending on for survival, it is your heart that will get us through in the end." He embraced his daughter, who nodded sleepily and smiled warmly. It was so incredible to have her father back again. This was the moment Sara had dreamed about for years. She wrapped her arms around him and squeezed as tight as she could, making a mental note to go back in the Font later on and find out what exactly he had just been saying to her. She had forgotten to listen.

As the two embraced, a slender cat mewed and rubbed itself against its master's leg.

"Well well," the Seventh Star laughed as he picked up the cat in his hands, "if it isn't my coconspirator." As he spoke to the cat, his form changed, his body growing taller and his clothes turning to white robes, much in style like those worn by Curiosity. His skin turned a dusky grey color, and his eyes became three blazing stars, his hair forming into a wild shock of white flame. "I know you of old, cat, and of all my race, only I know your secrets and your true gift. You have not misplaced your trust in me, and I will repay what I owe you. Watch out though; Sara no longer has someone to filter you out of her mind's eye— you may find you will have to change your tune. You will no longer be able to run things from the shadows."

The Seventh Star caught sight of Adam. "Ah, you must be the boy. Well, you were the greatest risk of all. I imagine you are wondering why you are here."

"The thought did cross my mind," Adam stated flatly.

Again, the Star subtly changed form, becoming shorter and stouter, aging and balding, his weathered skin turning to a deep shade of bronze. His eyes flickered out and became grey. His robes changed to the armor of a warrior, and at his side rested a wicked sword. Two iron wings sprouted from his back, reaching high up into the air. Adam gasped.

"You are my soldier," the Star spoke, "you know everything I know about combat and warfare. And we will have many conflicts in the days ahead. The Mongrel thought I made you for him, but he was deceived, and in his own arrogance, he wiped out his own memory of what I really trained you to do. I know betrayal does not suit you well, but how could I trust one for whom it did? But do not fear, all of this was planned long ago."

"Which brings us to Aras," the Seventh Star smiled, turning to look upon his older daughter. "Ah, beautiful as ever." The armor faded from his form, but the wings remained, becoming smaller and more delicate. His body thinned and his skin smoothened and grew milky. His eyes widened to almonds, and his ears grew points, and long, white hair streamed from his head. His clothing turned to natural leaves and vines. "Your gifts are more powerful than you know, and you have already performed your main role in all of this." Aras seemed confused at this, but the Star continued. "Like most mortals, your true potential is only reached when your consciousness steps out of the way. But thanks to our sixth friend here, we have had the equipment to interact with you in your dreams." The fairy man looked over at Michael.

"Ah, Michael, my oldest of acquaintances," the Seventh Star mused. The Star's fairy body thinned more and slowly became transparent, revealing only seven points of white light positioned in line along his spine. Soon the body faded altogether, and only the lights remained. Now freed of their physical form, they swirled upward, becoming again a circle. The Star's voice came forth disembodied, floating out from the air. Actually, Sara could tell that the voice was in their minds; it was not a sound at all. "It is an honor to have you with us. You don't know how long it took me to search for something that would catch your interest in this frail form you wear. And I see you have taken the bait. But do not worry, our cause is your cause. The moment you have sacrificed everything for is at hand, and there is at least one way to best your adversary in this. The darkness shall give way to light. Jonathan, step forward."

A beam of light shot from the Star and lit upon the chimera, who had crept back into the big tent to watch the events. Startled, the chimera froze, looking embarrassed for a moment, and then unable to think of anything better to do, stepped forward into the ring of companions. The Star appeared to examine him for a moment.

"You have proved an unlikely gamble," the Star finally spoke. "Your body was foreseen in our plans, but not your spirit. You have the largest part of all to play. You were meant to be the empty vessel through which our change took place, but providence dealt us a more masterful hand. Your innocence is your strength, let it guide you to your true destiny. Lose that, and the power you wield will consume you, much like it did your original body."

"And finally," the Seventh Star again turned back to his wild, fairy form, "Hyperia, my muse. It is in you that I see the future of all living things, a harmony and peace that comes from self-lessness and a cooperation and balance with all other aspects of the living spirit. I know you long to return to your home, but I pray you will consent to stay with us. I know the good that will come from the others having a chance to see your heart. But come now, enough talk, we have been apart too long."

The Seventh Star stepped forward and embraced the fairy woman, taking in his arms her daughter as well. Then smiling, he turned and embraced Sara, and finally Tessa, who did not hug him back. "Ah, that's the Tessa I knew," the Star laughed, "willful as always. But then again, that is why you are here." The Seventh Star had now taken on a new form, something between the fairy aspect and that of a man.

"You still haven't explained all this," Tessa snapped.

"Do I need to?" the Star replied. "This is my strike force. The team to change the history of all things. The necessary lineup that was determined long ago. Aras foresaw all of this, it is the last best path to a better future for all creations."

"Yes, I got that," Tessa returned, "but why all the games, why risk yourself, why risk all of us? Why not simply assemble your 'team' and tell us what you want us to do? Why widow your wife?" Tessa glanced over at the fairy woman. "Wives." Tessa cleared her throat.

"Ah," the Star answered, "well, unfortunately I'm afraid it

would risk undoing the good all my plans have wrought to explain it. But trust that there is a reason, and a good one at that."

"Explain it." Tessa's tone left no room for arguments.

The Star sighed. "Sorry," he stated, firmly.

"I can tell you," Sara interrupted. "See father, now that you have left me, even you are no stranger to the Font. For a task as dire and difficult as we have before us, a team cannot simply be assembled. You cannot force the necessary bonds between people. We had to come together on our own, to imprint upon each other so that we can trust one another. A team this small cannot survive any betrayal. And secondarily, this was a test of sorts. We had to prove we were ready before we could face true danger. And besides, if father had been alive, his masters surely would have hunted him down. As it is, he has thrown them off his trail and given us some time. And there is still time yet before his return is discovered."

The Seventh Star smiled in pride at his daughter.

"Well, I'm afraid your plan didn't work," Tessa huffed, "I'm not on your team, and for your information, we're not married either."

"That is indeed your decision to make," the Seventh Star sighed. "I have had to sacrifice much for what I believe I have to do. And there are more sacrifices to come, but I do know you will join us. You would never let your daughter face this challenge without your protection."

"My daughter?" Tessa cried, "She's not going with you on this fool's errand. She's only a child. And I will not allow it."

"No," the Star answered, "she's not only a child. She is far more, and she is in this whether we want it or not. Even if we do nothing, they will still come after her. Our only choice is to stand up and fight. And do not think that I don't love you."

Tessa seemed visibly shaken. She looked to Michael, and was surprised to see a dark look across his face. "He has a point," Michael conceded.

"And what exactly is this plan of yours," Tessa asked. It couldn't hurt to ask.

"Look now," the Star replied, taking a softer tone with Tessa, "we have many battles before us, and our goals are far from completed. We are worn thin, and we have many refugees yet to return to their homes. Know that there are greater powers at play here than the Mongrel and his shadow. But this is not the time to dwell on such things; all will be illuminated when it is needed. We are safe, and we have a moment to breathe. We are a family again, perhaps even for the first time. Let us celebrate."

EPILOGUE

A pure, blazing light danced amongst the ancient crystal pillars of the Lost Sepulcher of Tears, offering up a grand illusion of perpetual melting and reforming. For a time, the spectacle blazed soothingly, but then the light appeared to tire of its dance and wandered out of its empty cage. As the shimmering shafts of white passed out of the central dome of the unholy barrow, they cut deep into the stale darkness that lay beyond, laying stark and exposed the tomb's long-unseen walls and massive low-relief sculptures. Swift as an arrow, the light moved with a certain purpose, with no hesitation nor need to consider all the many paths that lay in this forest of pillars. In the wake of the light, the halls again fell back into the grip of shadow that had held this place haunted for eons.

Within minutes, the blinding glow found its way to the center of the massive underground maze, and there it came to a rest. Its streaming branches began gradually to dim and weave back in closer to their source.

As the light retreated from it, the first fish soon became visible, just floating there in the air. Almost immediately, it was joined by another, and then another. Soon enough, the thin strands that tethered the toothy fish to their grotesque cargo came into focus as well. Like a sick puppet, the skin of the empty arms and eyeless face hung stretched across the rusted wires. As the light slowly concentrated into a single point just behind the puppet, the Mongrel smiled. On the weathered wall beyond, his twisted form cast no shadow—and never would again.

"It is an odd thing to think that a shadow could stand between me and domination of light, but it is pointless to argue with the truth," the Mongrel hissed, several of the fish above him parroting various parts of the statement as he spoke. The Elder continued, still grinning, seeming to be talking to no one in particular. "Such wonderful things have come to me of late—freed from my worldship and fealty to the masters of the first realm, gifted with light and all of its powers, and now... this new gift." His laughter cut the air and echoed rattlingly through the pillars.

"Light is now mine to wield as I see fit!" the Mongrel now roared. He clasped his empty hands together like a happy child. "My own shadow has been a grave detriment to the use of its full force, ever blocking its rays and dividing its power into pieces, like the very pillars of this hall. I shed my shadow long ago and placed it on a fool's errand. I would have done away with it myself, but I lacked the love necessary to truly snuff it out. I always hoped that without my shadow, my light would function as it was meant to, spreading out from me in all directions and burning away my enemies and former masters—no chance of a blind spot through which to catch me unguarded. And now, thanks to the girl and her monster, I am free of it for all time; I need never again concern myself with its return. I am light now, and there will be no shadow to warn them all of my approach."

As if to prove his point, a dark watcher, shrouded in its powdery wings, passed forth into the burial chamber from out of an ornate carven archway. Seemingly upset by the intruding presence of the Fish Man, it slowly unfolded its wings and let the full effect of its burning red glare fall upon the form of the Mongrel. "No, no," it hissed, "head unbowed, not allowed! The masters bid you break. You cannot walk in this wake!"

"Oh," mocked the Mongrel, "I think I can walk where I want from now on." White light cascaded forward out of him and began to slowly and cruelly burn away the feathers and form of the stunned watcher, leaving only a small amount of a fine, silvery dust in its place.

"Now," the Fish Man cackled, "this is going to be fun."

SARA AND THE CHIMERA

BOOK 1: A PRISON OF LIGHT (AVAILABLE)

Sara Starbright has been born with an unusual gift—the ability to immediately know the answer to any question—and all manner of creatures want it for themselves. Kidnapped by the sinister Mongrel and taken prisoner aboard his dimension-hopping Worldship, Sara makes a daring and unlikely escape with the help of a fellow prisoner—the Chimera. Jonathan Wheeler is a boy trapped in the body of a constantly-evolving monster that can adapt to nearly any physical situation. Under the guidance of a mysterious cat, the two fast friends flee the Mongrel's forces and race across a madcap variety of realities before finally realizing the only way they will ever know peace is to turn the tables on their pursuers and go on the attack themselves.

BOOK 2: SEVEN STARS (AVAILABLE)

Free for now from the foul attentions of the Mongrel, Sara and the Chimera are still unable to find a place for themselves. An ill-fated attempt at going home again sends them again on the run, with Sara's mom in tow. With their options quickly running out, Sara decides to gamble everything on locating her reclusive father, the mysterious Seventh Star of Twilight.

BOOK 3: STAR SAILOR (2013)

The machinations of the Seventh Star have come to fruition, and creation is plunged into full-scale rebellion against the forces of control and power. The legendary Starsailor finally reveals himself and takes his place at the vanguard of the forces of freedom. Yet no matter the outcome, no one will escape unscathed. Families are torn, relationships broken, and nothing will ever be the same again.

BOOK 4: A VESSEL OF DARKNESS (2014)

Civil war has now erupted amongst the Elders of the prime reality, and Sara is forced to make some unpleasant alliances in a desperate hope to survive. The fight for creation finally leads to its ultimate conclusion, and the girl who knows everything and the boy capable of anything must learn the hard truth of what it means to grow up.

12821030R00187

Made in the USA
Charleston, SC
30 May 2012